FULL BREACH

A Suspense Novel

BY

N. Lawrence Mann

Timeline

FOR MY MOTHER

(1942-2015)

PROLOGUE

The bliss was dangerous.

Never before had Brennen's world been so rife with possibilities. From the follicles of his hair to the nerves in his toes, he felt, for the first time, content. As he sat contemplating her question just moments earlier, he studied the rays of morning light pouring through the window of his apartment and onto her golden hair.

This was the world he had heard so much about from his older sister who, until now, seemed like an endless well of useless knowledge and archaic anecdotes told by someone who was trying too hard to be wise beyond her years. *It will all work out someday, Brennen. You will see. I promise you.* As it happened, his sister was right.

*****

"I prefer dogs," he answered her through a mouth full of breakfast cereal. Freshly showered and dressed in a towel wrapped around his waist, he propped one of his legs on the kitchen chair opposite his. He finished the last bite and set the bowl beside her handbag.

"Oh? And why is that?" she asked.

Her back was to him, but she kept eye contact via the mirror in her make-up kit. He could tell she was smiling. She was always smiling. It was an electrolyte smile that provided much needed substance to an attention-starved room. And in her bra and panties, she exhilarated his kitchen.

Brennen smiled and crossed his arms defiantly. "Well, I will tell you why. Dogs are loyal. They actually care when you come home after a long day. They are genuinely interested in your well-being. Cats just want their food and they are done with you. Total dicks, the lot of them."

She gazed at him adoringly through the mirror while finishing her mascara, her eyes sparkling blue in the sun.

She had his full attention, as always.

"Yes, but cats are independent," she said. "They don't need to be taken outside; they use litterboxes. They can hold down the house for a couple of days without getting post-traumatic stress disorder, and they are much cleaner. *You* just want something to be completely dependent on you. You want something to rescue, kind of like Scott and red-headed rescues."

He surrendered a guffaw, despite his current stance. Scott Barrett had been his band mate in high school and a true friend ever since. He was, first and foremost, a good person with good intent. He cared about his friends and family and was dependable, for the most part. He was also a die-hard Philadelphia Eagles fan with a talent for sarcasm. Whether they loved him or were incensed by him, everyone in Scott's small circle of friends did agree that he possessed quite a weakness for girls with red hair. He had gone through two in as many years.

She had him there. "Hey, Scott is a good guy. Go easy. And say what you will about dogs, at least they truly try to help people and contribute to society. Tell me this, when was the last time you saw a seeing-eye cat?"

At this she giggled. She clamped her make-up mirror shut, swung her legs around the chair, and hoisted herself to her feet. As she circled the table toward him, his world froze. This was not his average reaction to people of the opposite sex, but this was no ordinary girl. This was Draya Harris.

Though she'd lived down the street from him his entire boyhood, she'd only scarcely known of his existence. Try as he might, he was never able to gain her attention, let alone her affections. Her code was difficult to crack and he'd spent a good amount of his teenage existence trying to figure out why: Was it him? He'd thought it might be because he was ugly, though he bore no facial irregularities, acne scars, or other features often associated with teen ugliness. At one point he'd attributed her lack of interest to his Asian heritage. Though he never experienced any sense of otherness, unless, of course, one of his classmates felt compelled to point it out . . . but perhaps he'd simply not been Draya's ethnic cup of tea.

As it turned out, he'd been unsuccessful in his attempts at her because he was awkward, and awkwardness in high school was a girl deterrent, rendering invisible any guy unfortunate enough to be stricken with it. Individuality wasn't applauded in the teen echelons of Tempe, Arizona. Not as much as say, emulating the latest movie stars and fashion magazines—a talent Draya had perfected by the age of six. Furthermore, playing tenor saxophone in the school band was not usually considered an aphrodisiac, nor did it promise of any sexual experience at all worthy of homeroom bragging.

Ironically, it was music that brought them together some years later. He was a local singer/songwriter enjoying moderate success. He had traded his saxophone for a guitar, and his awkwardness for a lyrical voice that wasn't half bad. She'd approached him in a chance meeting at a local hangout between sets. He was sitting at the bar discussing his pay with the owner when she bought him a beer and introduced herself. Had it not been for the mood lighting, she might have seen how pale he became at the sight of her. She looked the *same.* Better than the same. How was that possible? He played along with the introduction and realized, after some time, she had no idea who he was.

It wasn't until three nights later and after a flawless set that he confessed his identity. To his surprise, she was unfazed. In fact, she seemed to like him all the more for it. She was a fan of his angry alternative music. To her, it was fitting that she never met him in high school. *We obviously weren't supposed to meet until it mattered*, she told him as she kissed him for the first time just three nights after their re-introduction. She had pursued him.

Draya Harris pursued Brennen Reynolds. Sometimes he could not wrap his mind around it. Yet it was true.

Now, three months later, he knew her inside and out. She was the life of the party and adored by his tightly knit and carefully selected circle of friends. Scott remembered her well from school and was a shoo-in for her charms. Where she found her constant energy to dazzle and amaze them, he did not know. He only knew he felt lucky for the first time in his life. She was a dream, yet she was part of his life and he felt as though he was the center of hers.

Droopy-eyed, he pondered her question as she approached. Perhaps he did crave dependency.

"You look tired," she said while slowly straddling him.

He wasn't so much tired as he was dazed, once again, by her mere presence. He smiled and gave a fake stretch. "I guess I am a bit tired," he fibbed. "I have that blues guitarist

I have to record this afternoon, and my brain is scrambled from not enough sleep." He clasped his hands behind his head and gave her a smirk. "Thanks to you."

She flashed a close-mouthed smile and cupped his face with her hand. "This will be your third session this week. We are definitely moving forward, baby."

That was the plan. He would write music. That was his passion. To supplement income, he would record other artists and musicians at his studio, which he co-rented with Scott, in downtown Tempe. Draya, on the other hand, was to start a personal fashion shopping business; she already had many potential clients in Scottsdale—one of the more fashion-conscious cities in the United States—and was well known for her sense of style. Their future was intensely lit.

Her facial expression changed from adulation to concern. "No man of mine is going to be too tired to do what he was born to do. I've got something to help."

He watched her in fascination as she moved his cereal bowl aside and began rummaging through her handbag. Her legs held her securely to him.

"What are you looking for?"

"You'll see," she said through a repressed grin.

She produced a lipstick case, a straight razor, and a tiny Ziploc baggie with a chalky substance in it. His heart began to both sink and accelerate. He was no stranger to such sights. He had seen several such baggies in his profession. It wasn't a question of if there were drugs in the baggie, it was only a matter of which type.

His palms began to sweat as he felt his life begin to shift. It was a subtle movement, but the significance was far-reaching. "Okay, wow," he said, "what exactly am I looking at here?"

By then, she had moved an old CD of Pink Floyd's *The Wall* out of the way, poured a small rock of the substance on the glass table, and begun crushing it with her make-up case. With obvious skill, she used the razor blade to scrape the powder into a tight, neat line. She sensed his nerves and looked at him. "It's okay. It's just something I like to call The Glow. Just to take the edge off a bit. Not a big deal."

He crossed his arms, snuggly fitting his fingers into his armpits. He felt a shiver at the base of his spine. The puzzle to her energy source was being solved before his eyes, but he didn't want to see it. He would have been just fine having never known this information. He wondered how the rest of his friends would react to this knowledge. Maybe betrayed that Draya was less than what she claimed to be, that her energy was drawn from synthetic sources? Were they victims of false advertising? Would they care? He watched as she produced a twenty-dollar bill from her handbag and began to roll it tightly into a snorting straw.

"I don't know about this," he said.

He and Scott dabbled only in hallucinogens—Ecstasy, shrooms, or the occasional acid tab—and surrounded themselves with like-minded, moderation-oriented people who held down jobs and avoided the addictive things. If the bunch had to be classified, they were more akin to hippies than to junkies.

Draya listened but had a way of negating millions of years of evolution with a variety of simple gestures. In this case, she used her most effective: She laughed.

7

The face has forty-three muscles. He was always amazed at the ways she could arrange hers to change his world, and change it she would. This was more than just a giggle. This was a gesture that soothed his fears. *Trust me*, it said.

How bad could it be if she used it? She obviously knew what she was doing and made him feel unafraid to follow her. At that moment, he could see himself following her to the end of the world. Besides, what if this was a deal-breaker for her? What if his refusal to partake of this would cause her to think less of him, or even leave him? The thought sent an uneasy feeling bouncing around his gut, as though he'd swallowed a lit sparkler.

He realized two things at that moment: First, though they had only been together for a short time, he could not remember life before her and was terrified of life without her; second, she had already placed the rolled twenty-dollar bill in his hand. He looked at the bill and back at her, still looking at him, promising forever.

Using the razor, she pushed the line nearer to him. The high-pitched squeal emitted from the table traversed his nerves but never truly reached his ears. He couldn't hear it. How *could* he hear it? His heart was too loud, and he was too much in the habit of obeying it.

He then made a decision for which he would find himself apologizing, to himself and others, for years to come. Ordinarily, he would have refused. Ordinarily, he wouldn't let anyone talk him into anything or dictate his future. But this was no ordinary girl. This was Draya Harris and this was True Love. He bent over The Glow, plugging one nostril with the rolled bill up the other.

He did the line.

Part 1: Defense

Three Years Later

1
In A Dark Space

The false prophet woke from a dreamless sleep with a gasp. He had questions that would need some answers soon. He was weak from whatever substance had knocked him out as he lay on his back, slack-jawed and bleary-eyed. As he scanned the cramped space in which he was confined, he could see only the multi-colored lights of various computers poorly illuminating the gurney from which he figured he needed to lift himself.

No. He was strapped to it. Both his arms and his legs were immobile due to rubber fastenings that resembled stethoscope cords. He moved his mouth to speak and realized he was gagged. Saliva poured from the corner of his mouth as turned his head and gasped again. His eyes had never been as wide with fear as they were now. He swallowed hard and realized how loud he was breathing.

"Ah, the prophet awakens," a muffled voice said.

It was coming back to him. He was a man with a name. His real name was John Provancher, but his followers knew him only as the Prophet John. He'd surrendered his last name twelve years earlier when he fled his home town of Evansville, Indiana when his neighbors had reported suspicious activity to the local police, thinking him guilty of publishing pictures of naked children to a national child pornography website, but the cops had not found enough evidence to convict him (he was guilty of course, and had demagnetized and burned his collection of incriminating digital photos before his house had been raided).

John Provancher decided, with all the unwanted attention surrounding him, it would be best to cut his losses and leave. Without the ties of friends or family, it was easy for him to disappear. Armed with only his wits and a Bible, he floated wherever the highway tides took him. As it happened, an unsuspecting community south of Las Cruces, New Mexico was a perfect place for him to work his charms. By befriending a local DJ working at a small radio station run by a religious cooperative, he was able to reach and influence a small group of susceptible individuals. Though he didn't exactly believe in what he preached, he enjoyed the power religion awarded him over people. He loved it as much as he abused it. To them, he was the Prophet John and his word was as good as God's.

There were only small portions of time in which the Prophet John allowed himself to worry that his actions might elicit consequences. There were moments after imposing God's will on the wives of his devotees where he'd feel something close to guilt or fear, but it soon passed. Another applauded sermon, perhaps a neck massage from his secretary, and he was a cleansed man.

This was not the case now.

There was something eerie about the muffled voice. He sensed this voice could not be reasoned with or talked into (or out of) anything. The Prophet John's mental Rolodex flapped a windstorm. He searched the lies and the lies of the lies to find the perfect rebuttal. He failed. He knew this man was here to confront the prophet with the boldest lie of all. He did not speak to God, nor did God speak through him. This was a fact somehow known by this voice. And yet it referred to him as "prophet." It mocked him with his own lie. Somewhere in the back of John's mind, he knew this voice had been a long time coming.

He tried to speak through his gag, but it was futile. The fear in his eyes stretched his eyelids as he scanned the room. The ceilings were low. They couldn't be more than four feet high. His confines looked like a large white coffin with lab equipment placed throughout. He could feel it vibrating. Where the hell was he?

Suddenly, the man with the muffled voice appeared in front of him, breathing heavily. In one motion, he pulled the gag from Prophet John's mouth and crouched down, meeting him face to face. He was wearing a mask, but it was still too dark to see the details of it. There was only enough light for John to see the whites of the other man's eyes, which were enormous with wide pupils, well-adjusted to the dark. His breathing was short and faltered often with hard swallows and gasps.

The action was familiar—too familiar. He realized the man was imitating *his own* breathing. He was matching every heavy breath like a demented mirror.

"Where, uh," whispered John, "where am I?"

The man continued to mock the breathing, drawing out the terror within his guest. He finally spoke, imitating John's nervous whisper while frantically shaking his head. "Well, John. It doesn't matter where you are. It only matters that you have something I need."

John's eyebrows went up his forehead.

Again, the other mocked him perfectly.

"Yes, of *course*," John erupted, "anything I have is yours. Name it!" A look of hopefulness spread across his face.

The muffled voice dropped a chilly octave. "I need proof, John."

The glimmer of hope in Prophet John's face disappeared. Proof? The man couldn't be asking what he thought he was asking. Could he?

"You claim you are a prophet and that God speaks through you," the other continued. "I am a doubter. I doubt very seriously that any of it is true. However, John, I am willing to believe you, but I require proof. That shouldn't be a problem for you, should it?"

The man reached around the side of the cot, produced a 100cc hypodermic syringe, and filled it with air. He spoke as he leaned over to swab the underside of the John's forearm with rubbing alcohol. "You have twenty seconds," he explained as he pushed the needle into a vein on the inside of John's elbow, "until I inject you with this."

Prophet John, known to his followers as a man of many words, now had none to say. Though his eyes suggested his brain was trying desperately to think of the right combination that would remove him from this predicament, his mouth remained without speech. His tear ducts had no problem functioning and his cheeks were wet with their labors.

Ten seconds now.

He felt a small pillow being placed over his face. This, no doubt, would muffle his screams. And scream he did.

"*Pleeaassee!*" He was much too weak to free the needle from his arm, which was nestled tightly in his vein.

"Time is up, John."

The air slammed hard into the vein.

Oh, my God, John thought, as the air bubble traveled through his arteries for thirteen seconds before fatally reaching his heart.

2
October 28: Evening

A

Through the eyes of Beth Perkins, the world had recently turned grim. She sat in an uncomfortable plastic chair, trying to conceal from others the horrible news from her face. Her husband had demanded she attend this present event as a matter of courtesy, but was not, as far as she could see, in attendance himself.

The dance was going on around her. Jacob's warehouse had been converted into a dance hall complete with tables topped with red-and-white checkered tablecloths and limitless punch and pie. Floating balloons coated the ceilings and joyful music played over the PA system, but she was anything but joyful. Ever since her sister-wife, Betty, had uttered that awful word earlier that afternoon, Beth had been terrified. She couldn't bring herself to say the word. She could only replay Betty's words in her head.

Beth, dear child, listen carefully. The news I have just told you is grievous, I know. And I must be honest and say that this means you must do your duty for God.

Beth remembered the soulful look in Betty's eyes as the two of them sat facing each other in the nurses' section of her northern Arizona community. She could still feel the warmth of Betty's hands around hers, giving occasional empathetic squeezes.

But, God forgive me, I don't want to see you die.

Betty's eyes had had turned icy and wet as they stared deep into Beth's.

Do you hear me? I won't see you die! You are my sister and you have kept me sane at times I thought Jacob would surely send me over the edge. So I am going to tell you something even though God will hear. I can only pray he understands and will not tell Jacob. God help me, Lou Ellen already read the tests today. It's only a matter of time before she spreads the word.

Beth had begun to shake her head in protest, but Betty's gaze was formidable.

Jacob has given me the spare key to the mail truck. I have been his obedient wife for seven years and he finally trusts me with this key. Only me and Ben Millard have one. Listen, Beth. There is a compartment in the back of the truck that holds the mail. Hide in it. It leaves for town at seven-thirty this evening. You can leave during the dance and go hide in the truck. When Ben stops that truck on the way to town to use the bathroom, you get out and run. You have to get out of here!

When given the news, Beth had bowed her head and begun to cry. Jacob and the community were all she had ever known and the thought of leaving scared her.

Betty was unmoved. She grabbed the key off the nearby desk and thrust it into her weeping sister-wife's hand. She continued as if she knew Beth's thoughts.

I know you don't know any different than right here. This is all we have, and it's all I'm going to ever have. But there is more out there, and you can find it. Go to the authorities if you have to, but just go . . . and God forgive us both.

She was distracted by a woman with three little girls, all waving to her from across the dance floor, as though on a parade float. Her mind was made clear again, if only briefly. It was her sister-wife, Jane, and her three daughters. Though not always close with the families of most sister-wives, the bonds with Jane were strong as they were with Betty. Beth had not only known these girls since they were born, but had been actively involved in their upbringing. She was present when two of them spoke their first words and taught the third to ride a bike on the gravel road just outside the warehouse. She had never imagined, nor wanted to imagine, a life where she would not see these girls blossom into contributing women of the community with families of their own, but Betty's words were changing everything.

She did her best to hide her inner turmoil and waved back at them with a moist smile.

"Excuse me, Beth," a man said, "would you like to dance?"

It was a young man in his early twenties, close to her age. He stood with his hand extended to hers, wearing a white, short-sleeved button-down shirt with brown polyester pants—tailored too high for her taste—and polished black dress shoes. His build was slim, and he had chiseled features with heavily greased hair parted to the side. Aside from this, he was an attractive young man, though she could never acknowledge or admit it. She had made a covenant to God that she would not fall in love with any man who was not chosen by her husband, the Prophet Jacob Perkins. She could not violate the promise. This was forbidden.

How bold, she thought.

It was looked down upon in the community for younger boys to ask the ladies to engage in any kind of activities, especially something as intimate as dancing. This was reserved for the older men in their late forties to eighties. These were the men allowed to take wives. It was the prophet Jacob, an old man himself, who would arrange marriages through what he called "divine inspiration." God would reveal the names of suitable husbands directly to the prophet via revelation. This excluded young men. Young men were potential competition to the older ones, and God rarely allowed their presence.

Embarrassed by her absent-mindedness, she looked at the young man and smiled. She remembered his name was Henry Locke. Henry was the son of the bishop Locke, who managed the daily life of the community. This dance between them was no doubt planned and pre-approved between the prophet and the bishop. She was, after all, married to the prophet.

She felt the stares of the partygoers as they noticed the interaction. She scanned the crowd, through dozens of older men dancing cheek-to-cheek with their younger counterparts, until she found the bishop, clad in prayer clothes, smiling at her from across the room, motioning her to join his son.

Perhaps a dance with a young man might take her mind of things. Besides, rudeness was frowned upon.

"Of course, of course," she said, collecting herself. "How very thoughtful of you to ask."

She received his hand with as much grace as she could muster, straightening her dress as she stood. Aside from her exposed neckline, her mint green temple dress covered her from her wrists to her ankle, as did all her dresses. Only the husbands were allowed to see more.

She let Henry lead both dance and conversation, nodding and smiling while his nerves got the better of him. Her mind returned to the key Betty had given her. As her dress was not equipped with pockets, she'd hid the key in her shoe and it was now jabbing into the ball of her foot when she leaned on it.

Was Betty losing her mind? Was she really suggesting Beth leave the community? Tell authorities? Did she not remember what they had always been told? The government is *evil.* They will surely design the destruction of the community's way of life. Without question, they will cause darkness to consume the world.

She could not have been serious. She knew that the Othersiders, as they were called, were infected with ungodly education. That is why the community banned the college books and burnt the literature years ago. Othersiders were devil-agents and wanted only to kidnap the community children and take them away. They wanted to destroy the work of *God.*

She had pledged herself to God and swore she would never undermine him. If she were to do as Betty suggested, she would be turning her back on him and the prophet. She would become an *apostate.* There was nothing lower. The punishment for being an apostate was condemnation in the afterlife to the lowest realm of hell. It was so terrifying that her teachers in her youth had once described the brutality of that realm as "beyond human comprehension."

And what about *second* death? To be cast out in the afterlife and killed off for a second and final time was an unbearable thought. Nonexistence was a concept she was terrified to grapple with. She searched her mind for any other thought that might give her comfort.

The key jabbed the underside of her foot again.

Barren.

There it was. In her lack of concentration, she'd allowed Betty's word to resurface in her thoughts. She was barren. She was an insult to God, and the news came as an utter shock. In Jacob's community, it was also a death sentence.

"May I step in?" asked an elderly man dressed the same as Henry.

Her stomach turned at the sight of him. He was ancient. The wrinkles by his mouth suggested a mean streak worsened over time. Except for a few wisps of white hair, his head was sprinkled with age spots. His teeth were sparse and yellowed by bad habits. His breathing was labored. His cloudy brown eyes beneath thick prescription glasses appeared twice the size of hers. His waist, bound by an over-sized belt, lacked the significance to properly hold his pants to his hips.

He limped closer to her.

She did not recognize the old man. He must have been with a visiting community from Canada. She remembered Jacob informing her and her sister-wives of their visit. He had told them that some of the men might be looking for new wives, and to humbly notify hungry suitors of their marital status. It was of great importance, however, not to come off as rude. These were guests in their home with interests in expanding Jacob's construction business. With any luck, there would soon be a Perkins Construction Company in Lethbridge, a town in Alberta, Canada, south of Calgary.

In an instant, Henry was away from her and wandering off the dance floor with his head down. He brushed some balloons aside as he exited.

Beth could have refused Henry's invitation. In fact, it was encouraged that the women refuse the younger men. Should they accept, the time spent was limited to one dance. This elderly man, however, was another story on a different level, and he knew it. A girl was never, under any circumstances, allowed to refuse the attention of an older man. This would be considered an insult on the same level as slapping his face or laughing at his manhood. There were consequences to be had, and there were many black eyes among the women in the community to prove it.

It was, however, a sin to speak about such things.

"Of *course* you can step in," Beth said.

"Well, thanks, woman. Thanks for *allowing* me to get on in here." His voice was as pompous as his actions were presumptuous. He smiled a quick wide smile that deepened every wrinkle on his face.

He clasped his hands in hers. They were shaky, as was the case with most men his age, and somewhat moist. She tried not to wince as he put his cheek to hers and began to sway to the music.

His breath was sour.

Beth slipped through the marital crack when she was married to Jacob. Traditionally, it was of high importance that a new wife establish herself carnally in able to compete with the other wives. However, Beth was part of a double marriage, one in which Jacob married both her and Jane simultaneously. Jane was much older and the more aggressive of the two and garnered the most attention from Jacob. This suited Beth fine. She had been added to the marriage at the last minute anyway, having been reassigned to Jacob after her first husband, Darryl, died of old age at 85. Darryl had never lain with Beth as man and wife. In fact, Jacob accused him of being "true monogamous" to his first wife, usurping the convenience of celestial marriage.

It was not until recently, soon after Jacob acquired her, that Beth had been with a man at all. Unfortunately, it was with fifty-seven-year-old Jacob Perkins. An impatient man, he'd become frustrated by the end of the third month when Beth was unable to produce life. He took her to the nurses' station, run by Betty and Lou Ellen, to have some tests done. She now faced the results.

As the community's social hierarchy went, a woman with two children stood on thin ice for not producing enough children. A woman with just one child had very little value and a bleak afterlife. But a woman *unable* to have children at all stood on deadly ground. Not being able to replant the seed of God, she had to sacrifice herself back to him.

Once the news reached Jacob, a ritual would be performed and she would be dead in a matter of days.

"I come all the way from Alberta," the man said, "lookin' for a friend." With their cheeks pressed together, his voice sounded feeble.

Beth struggled for something nice to say. She then remembered Jacob's orders to identify herself to the

Canadians.

"Wow. Alberta," Beth responded. "That *is* very far. Hey, I'm sorry. I haven't introduced myself. My name is—"

Before she could finish, he turned her so they stood mouth to mouth. He breathed out as he spoke. "So what do you say? Let's be friends." He put a hand around her waist and pulled her pelvis into his. His face was stone cold as he looked between her legs and back up into her eyes.

There was no question he was aroused.

Her hands reflexively let go of his. She showed both hands as if in surrender, unable to look at him. "My name is Beth Perkins, wife of the Prophet Jacob," she exhaled, "and I have to go to the bathroom. Please excuse me."

Without giving any chance for a response, she pushed herself through a set of double doors and ran for the outside.

B

Brennen Reynolds lived as he had for over four years, in the Nantucket Apartments, unit one twenty-eight, in Tempe, Arizona. His apartment was nestled against the Nantucket sign written in bold, blue Helvetica font. To the owner's dismay, Brennen looked like an advertisement for the entire apartment complex when he smoked his hand-rolled cigarettes in front of the sign, as he was doing now. Being a small building, it would be difficult for a prospective tenant to miss the black-clad young man taking heavy drags off his cigarette under the sign.

The feeling was within him now. The Glow, as Draya once referred to it. Having become increasingly more potent over the last several decades, law enforcement had other names for it, but Brennen preferred The Glow. It was a total and absolute sensory boost. To his retinas, it was comparable to a dreamlike neon haze that allowed for quicker focus and ability to detect color and contrast. To his ears, it was as close to echolocation as a human being could achieve. It was accompanied always with a high-pitched drone throughout his ears, ringing as though from a blow to the head. To his mind, it was a thought machine allowing him to form perfect, coherent sentences with diamond precision. It allowed him to exist this day, as it did the day before and every day preceding it for the last three years.

He scanned the landscape. There were work trucks pulling into an industrial plaza, some annoying cats pawing at each other in the parking lot and Minnesota Viking's fans cheering across the street at a popular neighborhood bar. His eyes scanned all three with the precision of an auto factory robot.

Zing.

Zang.

Zoom.

There was no sign of Dante.

It was a typical late October dusk in Tempe. The weather was still warm from the late afternoon sun, about seventy degrees, with a light breeze. For most, this was the weather for which vacations were planned around. Brennen's mind was far from vacations. His mind was in pain. The headache was back. It started with a tickle in the back of one eye and moved to the center of his head with increasing pressure. Only The Glow provided him with any amount of relief. He was running critically low and the delivery guy was late.

Where the hell was *Dante*?

Brennen smoothly ran his fingers through his hair and did an about-face into his apartment. He scanned the living room as the door shut behind him. Microphones were placed with care onto their stands. He had installed a floating ceiling, suspended by wires, for more precise recordings. In the corner was a folded-up bed, allowing for a larger recording area. He had long ago given up a traditional living space for one that would accommodate his passion for songwriting and music recording. He could not afford the rent compiled by leasing an apartment in addition to a recording studio, so he combined the two. His living room was now a recording room and his bedroom was now a mixing room. Where his dining room had once existed was now a soundproofed vocal booth which allowed him to get a professional sound while recording in a one-bedroom environment. Built of plywood wrapped in black cloth, it stood seven feet tall. It was makeshift, but it worked.

There were some tidiness challenges to combining a living space with a recording studio, but he felt he addressed them well. There were a few scattered items about the place, but nothing that a thirty-second power clean wouldn't remedy. He took no notice of them as he made his way across the recording room on the way to the bathroom. His movements were smooth and exact.

As he passed the mixing room he noticed that Allen, having been snooping around again in his personal items, had found some old pictures and was riffling through them with fervor. Allen was a fair-weather friend, but a lovable guy. He always listened to Brennen with interest, but had a tendency to make appearances in accordance with Brennen's supply of Glow, or "shit" as Allen referred to it.

Brennen stopped short of the mirror. He rested his arms on each side of the sink and exhaled. He avoided gazing at it most times. The headaches, however, forced him to examine his eyes, as if he might better see the cause of the pain through his widened pupils. There were no headaches to be seen, only rivers of swelled blood vessels meandering through the whites of his eyes.

"Are these the group of friends you've talked about?" Allen asked from the control room. "Why don't you hang out with them anymore?"

Shame.

There were other reasons for his infrequent communication, but shame was at the top of his list now. It used to be that he had no phone. The life of recording had left him with little money at times and no money at others. Many months would go by when he was unable to pay his mobile phone bill, rendering him unreachable to the outside world. Only Scott and Dante knew the secret knock that prompted him to answer his door. This drove a wedge between him and his larger group of friends. *Well, if I had a phone, I* would *contact them more often*, he'd tell himself, because it was easier than confronting the real reason for his absence. The shame.

The truth, which he would seldom engage, was that he could not bear revealing to them how far his addiction had taken him. He had always promised them success in his ventures and anything less than that now would be considered failure. Emotionally, he could not afford to let them see he had not only failed to deliver on his promises, but had become a drug statistic in the meantime—a junkie.

All but Scott had remained, but only for a year into their excursions with Glow. Or was it two? He had trouble piecing time together. He could remember conversations from years ago as if they were yesterday, but timeframes eluded him. He knew Scott had since straightened out and, from what Brennen could calculate, was two years into law school.

After a painful falling out, even Scott became a distant memory.

These thoughts were fire to Brennen and he felt engulfed within it now. He had burrowed inside his work to protect himself from the flames and used The Glow to float far enough above them to avoid being burnt. He was adept at avoiding situations such as these, but was nevertheless annoyed at Allen for igniting the fire.

He was defenseless now, standing in front of his worst nemesis: the mirror. He stood helpless as the reflection of his pupils locked with his own. No traffic court judge could ever match the disappointment seen in these eyes. He was the harshest critic he had ever known.

He raised his index finger to his cheek and traced a one-inch scar that lined his cheekbone just under his right eye. He watched as his mirror image began to dissolve into Draya, face-to-face with him, frozen in a memorable scream of rage with bloodshot eyes and coagulated spittle foaming from the corners of her mouth. His mind would conjure the image from time to time. Of her many faces she once presented to him, this was the most frequent. It was a silent scream of scream from a damaged past.

Flames . . .

"I need a hit," he said to Allen in a monotone voice. He pushed himself away from the memory and, in one smooth motion, moved into the control room that was once his bedroom.

He was always impressed by the room: He was able to put together a state-of-the-art recording studio in this small space. The windows and walls had been covered with sound-deadening material that minimized unwanted echo. There were cubes in the corners of the ceiling made out of specialized foam, or bass traps as they were called, which kept the low-end sound from becoming too prevalent.

He surveyed the room. His desk was a giant triangle nestled in the corner. Instead of drawers it holstered racks garnished with various brands of recording gear speckled with different-colored lights. Two video monitors sat on its surface side-by-side, with studio-grade speakers at both ends. The center of the desk boasted a large mixing board into which all his hardware/software was connected. With its eyes as the monitors, its ears the speakers and the faders on the mixing board as its teeth, the desk collectively resembled a droid from *Star Wars*, communicating with its blinking lights and awaiting the next task. He could imagine it speaking to him. *Let's write some music, Brennen, shall we?*

Allen, aware that the subject had been closed, set the pictures aside and went to work loading the pipe. He dropped two small, quartz-like pebbles into a glass bowl about the size of a ping-pong ball. Rocking it back and forth with his fingers, he put his lips on the stem and heated the bottom of the bowl with a pocket torch. The blue flame targeted the glass with precision, causing the pebbles within it to boil at once. Allen observed the process with cross-eyed enthusiasm as he inhaled in accordance with the resulting smoke. When his lungs had had their fill, he stamped the bowl in a wet sponge to avoid unnecessary smoke loss, and blew out an opaque, white cloud of The Glow. Allen tapped his feet and squeaked out a sentence in the middle of the exhale.

"We are almost out of shit."

Brennen sat down on his plush office chair. There were some scratches on it, but its functionality was not affected. He picked up his beer bottle and brushed tobacco from the condensation. He rolled his own cigarettes, causing occasional tobacco flakes to land on the desk. It was a minor nuisance and nothing that a quick run of the Dustbuster wouldn't fix.

Taking a swig, he set the beer down and swiveled the chair around to Allen, who already had the pipe, lighter, and sponge extended toward him. Brennen grabbed all of them with grace and control. He began repeating the same ritual as Allen.

"Dante is on his way," he said as he began to exhale his own cloud of smoke. "I don't know what is taking him so long. He said he'd be here in forty minutes. That was forty-five minutes ago."

As he spoke he could feel The Glow hoist him comfortably above the flames. Calmness claimed him, keeping Draya, his friends, his past, and any other pressing issues at bay. Until, of course, the headache worsened. As he snuffed out the pipe into the sponge and handed it back to Allen, he bowed his head in pain.

"Are you okay, man?" Allen asked, but not before he had

set himself up with another healthy rip. "Is it your head again?"

Brennen reclined back in his chair, pressed his thumb to the middle of his forehead and winced. "Yeah, it's acting up again a little bit." He ran his fingers through his hair in a smooth manner. "Not a big deal. It will pass. It always does."

Allen squeaked out another sentence during an exhale. His face was twitching with repressed laughter. "What you need is a big old hit of shit."

The room erupted in laughter which sent Allen into a fit of coughing. Both were doubled over and tearing up. Allen had a perverse logic. Any advice or solutions to problems commonly revolved around taking a hit of shit. The degree of accuracy of his wisdom was surprising at times. Although he never paid for The Glow, Allen did provide much needed daily comic relief to Outcast Studios, also known as Brennen's apartment.

"Okay, twist my arm," Brennen retorted with a smile that stretched from jawbone to jawbone. This reignited the laughter. Laughter kept misery and company occupied.

BAM. BAM. BAM-BAM. BAM.

As it often did, the first *bam* widened both their eyes, brought panic in their faces and silenced the laughter. Cops? Was it the cops? Were they being too loud? But by the last *bam* they rejoiced. At long last it was the secret knock.

"*Dante!*" Brennen shouted, leaping to his feet with controlled, smooth abandon.

Allen raised his hands above his head like an over-happy football referee signaling a touchdown. He blew a cloud puff out of the side of his mouth.

Every visit from Dante was a new lease on life and Brennen was every bit as excited for Dante's arrivals as he was for the first twelve Christmas mornings of his life. He began to hum big-band era music to himself as he crossed the living room once again. The Glow was roaring through him like white water rapids. His movements reflected this. Smooth. Genuine. Exact. He felt in his pocket to make sure Dante's money had not magically disappeared. It hadn't. He was good to go. More Glow. More life. It could not be more perfect. Well, it was almost perfect.

"Allen!" Brennen shouted as he approached the front door. "Put those pictures away, please."

Now it was perfect.

C

Dan Tenner never thought of his name as intimidating, or even original. When he changed his profession, from Circle K employee to Glow dealer, he decided he would also change his name. He kept the Dan part and added the first two letters of his last name, omitting the space in between. He would forever after be referred to as Dante. It was simple and easy to remember. And with his sizable frame and tattoo-laden skin, he eventually became intimidating.

The name Dante was not only a play on his birth name, but it was also the name of his favorite character from his most cherished piece of literature, *Dante's Inferno.* He read the poem two additional times after it was required reading in his senior year of high school. He tried to finish the other parts of *The Divine Comedy,* but neither *Purgatorio* nor *Paradiso* resonated with as much brute force. He identified with Inferno and often thought himself as Dante Alighierilike, observing people and their behavior.

During his college years, his English professors were impressed with his knowledge of the poem and would often tell him he was headed for a successful career in whatever field he chose. As fate would have it, Dante never found a field that held his interest for long. It also happened that he was much better at writing term papers than he was at interviewing for a job. Time after time, his nerves would get the best of him, leaving would-be employers with the impression he possessed a combative personality and was prone to fold under pressure. Soon, with student loans compounding and the wages offered by Circle K insufficient to pay down his obligations, he found himself a nice niche in the illegitimate world. He was a dealer that made house calls, and he was damn good at it. The profession allowed him to pay his loans ahead of the interest. It brought him respect with his peers and offered a certain degree of adventure unobtainable with boring desk jobs. It also allowed him to meet interesting and beloved characters such as Brennen Reynolds.

Dante had just ended a phone conversation with his fiancée, Stephanie, who helped manage his schedule. When he told her his next stop was Brennen's he could hear her sigh.

Oh, boy, she said, *Good old Brennen. I hope he's doing better. Tell him I said hello. And call me right when you leave so I know you didn't get lost in that place.*

Dante pulled up to Brennen's apartment laughing to himself while the conversation replayed in his head. Stephanie had great insight. He loved that about her.

He double-checked Brennen's text message: HOWDY!!

One exclamation point meant a sixteenth of an ounce was requested. Two exclamations was code for eighth of an ounce, or an eight-ball—one hundred twenty dollars' worth. Brennen must have done well in tips the previous night to be requesting this much. This was always good for both of them.

Dante opened a jar of peanut butter, which reportedly threw off the scent of dangerous substances from police dog noses. Embedded in the peanut butter was a small metal tin, which Dante opened with latex gloves. Within it were pre-weighed sacks of pure Glow. He grabbed an eight ball sack and placed the tin back into the jar and closed the lid to the peanut butter. He discarded the gloves into a trash bag located in the back seat, stepped out of his weathered red Dodge Neon, and walked to Brennen's door—number one twenty-eight, just next to the Nantucket apartment sign, and wrapped on it with the secret knock while admiring the evening sky.

BAM. BAM. BAM-BAM. BAM.

At first glance it appeared as though no one was home, but Dante wasn't fooled. Brennen had taken calculated steps to give that illusion. He had fitted heavy Styrofoam in all the windows, behind the shades. The purpose of this was twofold. First, any outsider could not tell if lights were on at night. Secondly, according to Brennen, it helped with the soundproofing on the inside. Sound couldn't bounce around, providing for a better recording. In short, it was hard to tell if Brennen was awake or asleep, home or at work, or being loud or quiet at any time of the day. Only a handful of people knew the secret knock and Dante felt a strange pride to be one of the few.

As if on cue, Brennen opened the door and greeted Dante with a wide smile and a complex handshake the two of them had developed over the years. His jet-black hair was oily and his face was gaunt. His eyes were sheathed in dark circles and looked as if his brain were sucking them back into it. Seeing the effects of his product on his customers was a pitfall of his profession and always caused an internal moral debate. He had known Brennen for a few years now and could see beyond doubt that he was headed toward a wall which most addicts had a tendency to hit pretty hard. Some never recovered.

Dante was skilled in hiding his emotions and did his best to conceal his concern as he returned the handshake. Brennen was shaky to the touch.

"Dante, my friend. I thought you skipped me today, man."

Dante laughed. The entertainment value of seeing Brennen's apartment was never lost on Dante. None of his other customers had apartments with quite this amount of unique charm. What used to be his living room now held only small remnants of any past living accommodations. Otherwise, it was the most trashed apartment Dante had ever seen, and he had seen his share.

The couch was only recognizable as a shape in the corner of the room. From Dante's vantage point it was just piles of random knickknacks suggesting a couch may lie somewhere beneath. Random items grew like moss above and around it: piles of old clothes, fishing poles, a bullhorn, dirty half-burned candles, cobwebs, a headless Winnie the Pooh doll, a broken skateboard, scattered tarot cards, a crumpled

Godfather II poster poking through a broken frame. It looked as if Goodwill had dumped a warehouse of unusable items on Brennen's apartment and blown them about with a leaf blower. This was the only condition in which Dante had ever seen the apartment during the years he had known Brennen.

To his left was the kitchen, or what he assumed could function as a kitchen if need presented itself. Otherwise it was a storage room for empty boxes, plastic bags from Safeway, and various computer components and cables. Dante knew that Brennen didn't eat a lot of food, but he wondered how he could even reach the food he *did* have should he ever be hungry. This was not the first time Dante worried about Brennen.

Just past the kitchen was Dante's favorite attraction. The vocal booth. It was ugly, but it was cool. Dante had tested it himself many times and never tired of the results. He'd stood inside it and had screamed as loud as he could and was told by Brennen that he sounded as if he were three apartments down. Dante laughed to himself as he noticed Brennen had stapled a picture of Carl Sagan onto the front door of the booth. Something about Mr. Sagan's grin among the disorder of this place was fitting. It was almost as if he were saying "Curiouser and curiouser, science continues to explain Brennen Reynolds."

"What's up, Dante?" a voice asked just as Dante rounded the corner into the control room. He took a moment to put a face to the voice. It was Allen, of course.

"What's going on, Allen?" Dante replied. "I see you've put yourself in the right place at the right time, as usual."

The insult being lost on him, Allen laughed and prepared

the Glow pipe for use. Dante stood between the only two seats in the room. Allen was busy in one seat while Brennen plopped down into his dedicated chair in front of the mixing board. There was tobacco everywhere. Since Brennen started rolling his own cigarettes, the room had since been coated with it.

"Did you get a new tattoo?" Allen asked Dante.

"No, Allen." Dante sighed. "These are the same tats I've had since you've known me." He pointed to his tat-covered forearm and right calf. "Had them for years, man."

Dante noticed that Allen had set his beer on a stack of pizza boxes. In fact, there were pizza boxes stacked everywhere. In the corner of the room, there were two stacks, each of them at least five feet tall. He remembered something about how Brennen would sometimes wait in the back of Papa John's pizza until they threw out their missed orders of the day. He would seize them the moment the employees turned their backs and take them home. No harm, no foul, he imagined. Papa John's was going to throw them out anyway. However, it made Dante wonder if Brennen just enjoyed saving a buck or if he was making enough money to feed himself. And if he was making money, was he spending it all on the eight ball he was purchasing today?

He shook his head to dislodge the thought. He was a dealer. If he spent time worrying about the health and well-being of his clients, he would be out of a job very quickly. He grabbed the eight ball package from his baggy jean-shorts and tossed it to Brennen, who fumbled the treasure before securing it.

He flashed Dante with the smile of a twelve-year-old.

"One-twenty to you, Brennen." Dante said.

Brennen put down the eight ball and reached for the bills in his pocket. His movements were jerky and unsure of themselves. His jaw jabbed outward as if he suffered from a massive under bite.

Dante frowned to himself. Brennen was high as hell. The last thing this man needed was more product. When Brennen ran his fingers through his hair, his eyes looked like they'd burst from his skull. The overall effect was both grotesque and comical, which made Dante uneasy.

Brennen produced the cash and started counting it out. "One, two, three, four, five . . . six twenty-dollar bills to you, sir," he said in his best bank-teller voice. He wadded the bills up and handed them to Dante. "I even exchanged my tips for all twenties to make it easier for you."

Dante shoved the wad into his pocket and announced he was in a hurry to his next drop-off and made for the door. Brennen offered to walk him out. Outside, evening was just setting in and the low-hanging sun only accentuated Brennen's withered look.

"Dude, drink some water," Dante said, "You look dehydrated as hell."

Brennen looked confused. "What? I'm totally fine, man. I've been writing that song I let you hear and have been indoors for a while."

"Isn't that the same song you were working on last year?"

"I'm *refining* it." Brennen laughed. "I am almost done this time. I swear."

"What about the headaches?"

"They are better. Haven't had one for a while." Brennen

fished out one of his self-rolled cigarettes from a weathered Marlborough pack. When he lit his cigarette he bounced onto his toes a couple times as if he were exercising his calves.

"Okay, cool," Dante said. "Take it easy." He walked to his car. When he opened the door to get in, he paused and looked to Brennen. "And if you need anything—food, water, whatever—give me a text. I'll meet you wherever."

"I'm good," Brennen said, holding up a thumb with the lit cigarette between his fingers.

"I'm serious, dude. Don't go all weird on me. And lose Allen, man. He's taking advantage of you again." Dante disappeared into his car and drove away.

D

Though the sun had yet to set, the moon was visible and nearing its most spherical phase in the northern Arizona sky. The air was crisp in October and Beth could feel it in her lungs as she ran from God and the warehouse. Something about the way the old pervert looked at her made her feet move without thinking. She distanced herself by twenty yards through a gravel field before the pain in her foot caused her to finally stop. Here, the desert breeze overpowered the now faint music coming from the warehouse.

Judging from the fading skyline, she guessed it was around seven-thirty. If she hurried, she still might be able to hide in the truck before Ben Millard took it to town, then make her escape at the midway stop at the Shell station when he grabbed a coffee and used the restroom. It was her only chance.

She could not move fast enough as she crouched to remove her shoe, letting the key drop in her hand.

She'd always been taught that celestial marriage, or plural marriage as Jacob referred to it, was the key to the celestial kingdom. Man, wives and children—that was how it worked. Man and wives to make the children, and children to seed the work of God, the same God she loved and served. How, then, could she turn her back on him? By not allowing her to bear children, he was calling her home. What torment was she facing in the afterlife by refusing him?

Perhaps she was making a mistake. Would she see Betty again? Jane and her daughters?

"Beth Perkins?" a male voice asked. "Is that you?"

She recognized the voice as Tom Riggins, a second cousin of Jacob's. He was now in his thirties, which meant he was getting old enough to assert power and attempted to wield it at any chance he could get. He was twenty feet from her, laboring with a heavy backpack over his shoulder.

"What are you doing out here all by your lonesome?" His voice was condescending. "Don't you know the party's over there?" He motioned to the warehouse.

Beth swallowed with unease, hoping it did not telegraph her nerves. She tried to conceal that she had been running. "Hi, Tom. How are you? I was just . . . catching some fresh air. It was getting warm at the dance."

Tom stared at her for several seconds. "Are you out of breath? Looks like you've been running a bit."

Beth smiled despite the increasing rate of alarm. "You know, Tom, I was feeling a bit faint in there. That's why I came outside. I needed to catch my breath."

"I thought you said you were warm?"

"I was both, Tom. Faint and warm. But I'm feeling better.

I will be back in there in a minute. Don't you worry."

He remained, taking a step toward her. His voice had begun to develop an accusing tone. "What you got in your hand, Beth?"

Beth's nerves became gelid. She would need to think of something fast. If Tom were to discover the key, he'd hand it over to Jacob in no time. In turn, Jacob would know in an instant how she came to be in possession of it. Betty would be punished, and all she had done to ensure a happy afterlife would be jeopardized. The Prophet Jacob would speak to God, and through God he would punish Betty.

From her crouched position, she let the key drop from her hand as she stood up, being sure to drown out the clicking of metal on gravel while she scuffled. She could only pray he was too far away to notice it. "I had a rock in my shoe." She pointed at the shoe in her hand and smiled. "Darn thing was poking away at my foot."

An angry man's voice shouted from the warehouse. It was Tom's father. The party was in desperate need of the punch Tom was carrying and he wanted it immediately.

"On my way now, Pop!" Tom returned his attention to Beth and began to survey the ground by her feet. "You get back to the dance within five minutes. It could be that you're dizzy because you are with *child.* I'll be sure to let Jacob know what's going on. Maybe we'll join you in a prayer circle later on." Tom took to a jog and disappeared into the warehouse.

Beth watched him, frozen in time. It wasn't until he was at least fifty feet away that could she breathe. The breath came in short, uncontrolled bursts as she reached down, reclaimed the key, and ran away.

She could have heeded Tom's warning. She could have answered God's call. On any other day of any other year, she might have chosen differently. But today was today. There was something about Tom's tone that irked her beyond explanation, something in the presumptuous manner in which the old man had made his advances that made her want to challenge the Prophet Jacob, if only to see if she could. She was tired of having her will bent on an hourly basis. Perhaps God would understand this.

Beth looked down at a scar in the fleshy area of her right hand, where she had been kissed by God. She kissed it back, as she often did, and apologized to the sky. "I'm so sorry. I hope you will understand."

She was aware of how crazy her behavior was, but come tomorrow, she could be sacrificed, or at least well on her way to being. She wanted to see more sun rises in *this* life—the one life she had ever known—not the promise of one she *heard* about in prayer. Plural marriage and children may hold the biblical key to the celestial kingdom, but she, Beth Perkins, held an actual key to a mail truck and she was reinvigorated to find it.

She was able to traverse the compound within a few minutes. The streets and corridors were empty, as most of the community was at the dance. When she did see somebody, she was able to keep out of sight with little issue.

She passed the gated playground where the children would scream with laughter while the wives would watch from the side benches, talk among themselves. Those yet without children would be left at home to do the other wives' housework. The more children, the more power.

On the right was Home Base. It was a barricade of sorts, built with high concrete walls, used for reconditioning both adults and children to the community rules, should they disobey them. She remembered being sent there once as a child when she became angry with God for killing her goldfish. There was no food and very little water available when serving punishment. This was necessary for the members of the community to take time and think about their wrong-doings until the prophet felt God was appeased.

The memories sped past her as she ran, until she came to an abrupt halt when saw that the carport, which contained the mail truck, was empty. She looked with frantic pupils to the nearside of the office building for any trace of it.

Nothing.

She was heartbroken. Slow-witted Ben had chosen tonight of all possible nights to leave early with the mail truck. She had come all this way and put herself in very real danger. Even if she wasn't spotted on the way back to the dance, her absence was felt by now. Tom Riggins would no doubt have alerted Jacob or the apostles. Punishment was imminent.

Before she could finish picturing in her mind a small platoon of men with flashlights searching for her, she thought she saw something at the far end of the building. Was it white? Was it a bumper?

It was indeed—and not just any bumper. It was the bumper to the mail truck. Ben had parked the truck on the wrong side of the building. Thank the Lord for Ben! She mused for a moment how absent-minded people could inadvertently cause more happiness than a clown hired at a birthday party.

She rattled the key in the lock on the back panel of the truck.

It wouldn't budge.

"*Are you serious*?" she rasped.

She heard the unmistakable sound of Ben's whistling, which was well known throughout the community. Not a very bright guy, but a hell of tunes man.

"Come on, Mr. Lock!" She turned the key hard to the right, causing an indent in her thumb.

Clack

From there, the door opened without issue. She was inside in an instant.

Just as Betty had described, there was a compartment used for the mail in the right side of the back compartment and it was half full of letters. She closed the door behind her with as little racket as possible and squeezed into it. There was a metal gate between the front seats and the back section where she lay. If she strained her neck enough, she could see the driver's seat.

She breathed through her nose and tried to be as silent as possible.

Several moments passed before Ben appeared at the driver's-side door. The door exploded open and Ben came crashing down on the seat, all two hundred-odd pounds of him; he smelled of moldy towels. He set a cup of coffee in the cup holder. She was relieved when his odor was replaced by the aroma of the brew.

He turned his head and looked in her direction. Lord, did

he see her? He seemed to be looking right at her, yet he went about his business as though nothing strange was happening. She was having trouble keeping her breathing under control and was quite sure he could hear her. She wanted to either run or surrender—she would explain the situation to Ben with a level head, or make up another story, and beg that he didn't report her to Jacob.

When the dash lights illuminated Ben's face as the engine turned, Beth noticed a curious glossy sheen near his ear. As he began to fidget with the seatbelt it became clear that headphones were tucked in the folds of his ears. Ben was listening to music—against community doctrine! She could breathe easy knowing she was not the only rebel this evening. As long as Ben continued to listen, she was out of both sight and earshot of the mammoth driver.

An intruding voice broke through the community loudspeaker. Wired for transmissions to be heard across the entire community, each distorted syllable cut through the night air like a live telephone line into a swimming pool.

BETH PERKINS, REPORT TO THE DANCE HALL AT ONCE. BETH PERKINS, TO THE DANCE HALL.

She kept her wide eyes on Ben the entire time, but he heard nothing. Ben, thank the Lord, liked his music loud. Nothing short of a thunderbolt would catch his attention at this point. For this, she was grateful. For the moment, he was deaf. For the moment, she was safe as Ben, whistling a familiar tune, pulled out of the parking space headed to a place Beth could only describe as Unknown

3
In A Dark Space

“I just need some proof,” the muffled voice said.

Randall Willis, a self-proclaimed faith healer, tried several times to see the man’s face, but it was always clouded in shadow or too far behind him. The straps holding his head to the gurney made it difficult to see anywhere but straight ahead. The room was tiny, if indeed it was a room at all. It could be a closet for all he knew, but that didn’t explain why the room seemed to vibrate at times.

He was disoriented, having just awoken and could not remember how he got here. Randall Willis, otherwise known as the Prophet RW, was also nervous about the sizable syringe sticking out of the underside of his forearm.

He looked as far down his body as the restraints would allow. His Armani suit was ruined. It had tiny rips by the pockets, made by the mysterious man, no doubt. The restraints over the rest of his body had caused large wrinkles that would require a trip to the cleaners. His Hugo Boss Brossio Italian leather, double-monk-strap dress shoes were nowhere to be seen. Only his Ralph Lauren socks protected his wiggling toes.

The prophet RW cleared his throat and tried to remain calm.

“Good day to you, dear sir,” the prophet said. His tone sounded low and well-rehearsed. “I think we . . . we may have a misunderstanding, you and I."

The muffled voice sighed. "There is no misunderstanding, Randall." He approached the prophet, but remained out of view. "I just need proof that you're a prophet, and you can be on your way."

The prophet RW closed his eyes and swallowed hard. This voice had called him by his birth name, Randall. This man had done some serious homework to find his identity. Randall knew what this was about. He would continue to try to maneuver his way out of the situation, but he knew the truth had caught up to him. This man was the karma landlord, come to collect a *big* check.

He was no more a prophet than he was Abraham Lincoln. He knew it. He didn't have any self-delusions about the matter. He was a highly skilled interpreter of the Bible. Always was. Even at a young age in Harlem he'd been able to fit the Bible into any given point he was trying to make. He was a persuasive speaker, and oh, did the people listen to him! He was a self-ordained minister in no time. In Memphis, around his mid-thirties, he grew into his own with a fervor unknown to him. The older he got, the wiser he seemed. He was confident and respected. It should have been enough, but with each level of respect he gained from the people, new ways of taking advantage of people arose. Now a respected prophet in New Mexico, he had reached his summit.

"Listen," the muffled voice said, "I want proof because I bought *this* for twenty-four ninety-nine on your YouTube site." He extended an item close to Randall's face.

Randall took a moment to focus.

It was a DVD titled *The Prophet RW's Holy Ghost Power.*

On the cover was a photoshopped picture of Randall that looked to be created by a first-week graphic design student. He was dressed in the same suit as he was now, with his arm around a ghost, a transparent version of Randall, both with teethy, ostentatious grins. They looked like Don King twins, promoting each other.

Randall turned away as far as he could. “I know what you are saying, sir.”

“That’s a nice suit, Randall,” the voice said. “Armani?” He threw the DVD aside and squatted down next to his guest. His face was just out of Randall’s sight.

Randall tensed as he began to sense the gravity of the situation. The needle protested deep within his arm. He began to mutter to himself. “No. No. No. Please, you don’t understand.”

“Is that what you buy with the money your followers give to you?”

Randall was silent.

“I’m just wondering,” the voice said, “what prophets do with their money after they take it from a person, that’s all.” He adjusted his seat for better comfort. “Because, according to your DVD, we are to trust that you are a descendent of Jesus Christ and that you can perform miracles. And in exchange for your word, they give you money. Correct?”

The voice met Randall face-to-face at last. Though it was dark, Randall guessed that the man was wearing some kind of clear plastic mask with the dead-pan expression of a mannequin. The result was eerie and caused Randall to look away in terror.

The man watched for some time as the Prophet RW

morphed into regular old Randall Willis.

"Look, man," Randall said, "if you want your money back, I can do that for you." His lack of courage allowed him to meet his captor's eyes only a few times. "I-I understand you being upset and all. I made the sermon available on YouTube because my website guy said I could get a lot of—what do they call them? Clicks? No. Hits. He said I could get a lot of hits for my Holy Ghost channel. So, I—"

"Listen to me, Randall. I don't want your social media strategy, I want my miracle." He crouched over him, being careful not to bump his head on the low ceiling, and placed his thumb on the syringe. "You have five seconds to prove you are a prophet before I shove a sizable air bubble into your heart."

Tears streamed down Randall's face. His heart was racing on the inside, but the needle and the force of the restraints kept him still. He had this coming. He had known this for a while.

To the mannequin, Randall said, "I am not a prophet."

"I'm sorry, what did you say?" the man asked. He put his hand to his ear. "I didn't catch the last part."

Randall's chin was quivering. His eyes were down. Fear and sadness battled for Randal Willis' prominent emotion. At long last, he met his tormentor's eyes. "I said you know that I am not a prophet."

The eyes beneath the mannequin mask stared at him without emotion. "Well, I certainly do now."

He injected the air bubble.

In the thirteen seconds before the bubble stopped his heart for good, many thoughts raced through Randall Willis's mind. The Holy Ghost was not among them.

4
October 28: Night

A

Brennen dreamt in color.

In the dream she was wearing a blue-and-white knit sweater, tight blue jeans and flat, faux leather shoes, each topped with a silver buckle. She was screaming at him from a distance among a steady stream of people. Her expression was enigmatic. She seemed excited to see him in some moments while stifling tears at others.

It was only after noticing the train behind her that he realized he was at a train station. At first it was unclear whether the girl was boarding or exiting, but assumed the latter as she moved toward him. In an instant, she was embracing him. His accepted the fragmented movement as natural and within the laws of physics. Questioning it seemed somehow unnecessary.

He hugged her back, and smiled. “Hey, Triana!” Brennen said. “Wow, how long has it been?”

This was Triana Zigler, his flirting partner in the eighth grade. She sat in front of him in history class and would pass suggestive notes behind the teacher’s back. Brennen would respond in turn. Nothing ever came of it. The two never engaged in perverse acts or shared an afternoon of under-age passion. There was never so much as a peck on the check, but it had been thrilling just the same.

Her squeeze on him tightened and he could sense she was speaking by the vibration of her voice box against his chest. He could not, however, hear what she was saying. Instead, his ears were focused on a repetitive grinding sound seeming to come from omnipresent source like the eerie soundtrack of a motion picture. To his mind, it was most similar to the sound of wiper blades scraping across a dry windshield. His mind again assured him the sound was of no consequence.

Triana released her grip and brought her hands to Brennen's face, cupping his cheeks to ensure his attention. She spoke, her emotions oscillating from elatedness to tearful. Her eyes scanned his face as she spoke. "Tell them—" she said.

The last part of the sentence was drowned out by the scraping noise. Brennen smiled and shook his head. He gestured around him and pointed to his ears, implying he could not hear. He focused on her face. She had aged as much as he had in their time apart. In eighth grade, she was cute and playful. In her twenties, she was quite striking. Her dark, curly hair drooped over her soft brown eyes and fell around her neck. Her teeth, once veiled in metallic braces, were straight and white.

He admired her, but he wasn't sure why. Was it because she had blossomed into such a beautiful woman or was it because of the journey she had just taken?

Where had she been?

She spoke again. This time she spoke in the moments between the scraping. To Brennen's dismay, he still could not hear her. He watched as her vocal chords strained, but no sound emerged.

For a second time, Brennen gestured to his ears. This time, he was more emphatic and put his hands around her waist, eager to hear what Triana needed to say. The scraping noise grew louder at an increasing rate as Triana's attempts at communication failed her again, raising her anxiety level. Her eyes locked into his as if to conjure her thoughts and clearly speak through them, but he was again deaf to them.

Triana turned and looked panic-stricken at the train. With renewed intent she forced Brennen to look at her once again. She screamed her message. Her brown eyes were glossy with tears, but her face signified that she was happy.

At long last, the voice arrived, but only after the lips had moved. It was as though he were watching a video with a bad audio sync. Beneath the scraping, he heard the sentence from her shouting voice. "Tell them I'm okay!"

The sentence rang out in his mind and he tried to ingest it. Of whom was she speaking?

He opened his mouth to ask this question when he realized she was no longer in front of him, leaving him holding only the empty space where her torso had been. He looked up in time to see Triana wiping tears from her face and waving at him from the train, which had now started moving away to his left. As he attempted to wave back, the mechanical scraping became too much to bear. He put his hands to his ears as the sound rattled him from the world of dreams into the one which was real.

He was on the floor of his mixing room piecing together where he was, *who* he was, and the source of the sound. The answers were arriving, but they were lackadaisical about it.

After Dante left, he had been working on a song when he must have passed out. He had programmed the recording software to repeat a section of the song indefinitely. Called a "loop" in recording terms, this allowed for more precise editing of small sections of waveforms. In this case it was a one-second, grinding section of the song heavy with guitar and bass, all in the same note. The sound was passing from a high-pass filter into a low-pass filter, giving the loop the sense of going from sounding as if it were coming through a speaker phone to sounding as though underwater, and back again. He loved using filters. Taking away sound frequencies and adding others became something of an art form to him. There was a time and place for it, however, and during sleep was not one of them. During a dream, it was madness.

He tried to reach for the space bar on his keyboard sitting on top of the desk, but found he could not move his arm. He couldn't move at all. All he had was the sense his body was twitching involuntarily. This happened sometimes. He didn't know the medical reason for it, but he knew it would pass.

It came back to him. He was Brennen Reynolds.

He was a self-proclaimed songwriter and he was working on his future. He was going to write songs that helped change the world. He was going to do something that mattered. He had the will to write, the will to succeed, and now, the will to move his arm.

Taking a deep breath, he opened his eyes. The ceiling tiles stared back at him as they came into focus. They seemed to be looking at him with both amusement and disappointment. *Really, Brennen,* he imagined them saying, *you passed out again?*

He finished scanning the room and found nothing out of the ordinary—nothing except for the scruffy, orange cat sitting on his chest.

"Reer!" said the cat. Its yellow eyes locked into Brennen's. It looked annoyed, as though it thought Brennen to be trespassing.

"Whoa!" Brennen said. He scrambled to his feet, brushing the cat off as he did.

The cat remained unafraid of him as it repositioned her stance on the carpet beside him, glaring at him. "Reer!"

"No way. *No* way are you supposed to be in here!" Brennen stomped out of the control room and glanced at the front door. It was wide open. Allen must have forgotten to shut it on his way out.

"You are out of here, cat," Brennen continued. He rummaged through some items in the hall closet. Several knickknacks spilled into the hallway.

"Reer!" answered the cat from the control room.

Brennen had no better liking for cats than he had in the days of Draya. Assholes, the lot of them. They scratched for no reason, peed on everything, and knew nothing of loyalty.

"Ah ha!" Brennen grabbed a broom from the back of the closet and yanked it out. He stumbled as the cat watched him approach with broom in hand.

The cat grew more annoyed with him.

Brennen ran up to the cat and raised the broom in a threatening manner. But the cat remained, daring him to do it, and after Brennen shook the broom and jumped up and down like a Maui tribesman in a war dance, it dared him still.

Brennen stopped in his tracks and stood motionless. It occurred to him after a moment that he had just had a battle of wills with a cat, and lost. The cat knew just as well as Brennen that he wasn't going to hit it with the broom. He was a pacifist and that was all there was to it. The cat had called his bluff and it made him laugh out loud.

He made the surrender sign with the broom still in one hand. "Fine," he said. He tossed the broom back into the closet causing more items to fall into the hallway. "But I'm not feeding you."

B

Beth sat with her head in her hands as she used the toilet at the Shell station. The adrenaline in her system had passed the tipping point, causing her to tremble against her will. The bathroom floor went in and out of focus as she fought to control her breathing.

Ben had been brilliant. The coffee had filled his bladder, just as Betty had predicted, forcing him to stop here. When she saw him collect the restroom key from the station attendant and disappear around the corner, she had seized the moment to wriggle her way free from the back of the truck. The latch had opened easily and she darted around the back of the building and hid until she heard Ben emerge from the bathroom and drive off into the night.

She said good-bye to Ben Millard, to perverted old men, to Jacob Perkins, and even to Betty and Jane. She could not, however, say her good-bye to God. The mere thought of voicing those words terrified her.

The woman attendant looked at her mint-green temple dress with curiosity when Beth had asked for the restroom key. Beth imagined few customers arrived wearing such garments and wondered if the attendant knew about, or was affiliated in any way, with the community in which Beth lived. If so, she could report her to Jacob's apostles, making this a very short trip.

Beth looked at the bathroom key now, which she had placed on the edge of the sink.

What now?

With her head made clearer by an empty bladder, she fumbled her thoughts around as to her next move. Only one word made it out into the world.

"Godtastic." That was her response to the little challenges in life, though this one was, by far, the most imposing yet.

After drying her hands, she raised her head to face herself in the mirror. Her flawless skin seemed extra pale under the harsh fluorescent light, and her eyes appeared more chestnut in color than the greenish hue the emerald specks in her retinas would emit in daylight. She turned her head to further examine her face. The ugly mole above her upper lip glared at her, as usual, causing her to frown. Her long auburn hair, in tradition with the community, was pulled up and back, leaving one large wave up and over her scalp. There were several hairs out of place, which she rectified before gathering the key to return to the attendant.

A sleigh bell attached to the door of the station announced her return. To her surprise, there was another customer engaged in a conversation with the attendant—a chubby man in his thirties wearing an un-tucked flannel shirt, loose jeans, and work boots. They both looked at her as she walked in. The man's gaze lingered a moment to look her up and down. His five o'clock shadow gave him a disheveled look. He raised an eyebrow at Beth and turned back to the attendant, placing his elbows on the counter.

Stricken with shyness, Beth opted to peruse the snack aisle rather than approach the two of them with the key. She realized she was quite hungry. Even the Oreos, though forbidden in the community, looked as good as any steak and corn dinner she had ever had.

"Phoenix, huh?" the attendant said to the man.

"Yeah," he said, "I've got to deliver some parts downtown. Then I'm headed to Tucson and then down and around Interstate 10 all the way to Florida."

"Wow, you sure do get around," the girl said, unamused.

"I certainly do," the main said. "What about you? Do you get around?"

They were interrupted by a noise around the pastry aisle. Beth had dropped a packaged apple pie causing the others to once again look her way. She bent down without haste and picked it up, apologizing several times.

Ignoring her, the attendant finished the sale. "Well, Mr. Traveler, that will be sixty-five fifty-six for the gas, the sandwich, and the Oreos." She was successful in averting his innuendos and wasted no time ringing up his order and returning his change.

Beth's ears perked at the idea of Phoenix and her mouth watered at the sound of "Oreos." She began to see an opportunity presenting itself that might never arise again. She imagined hitchhiking her way to Phoenix, standing on the side of the road with her thumb out. This man, however, could save her a step. This way, she had pre-screened the driver to a certain extent. She knew what he looked like, she knew where he was going and she knew he had food. Perhaps, out of kindness, he might allow her to tag along and have a couple bites in the meantime. Heck, she could ride in the back of his truck. She would be so silent he wouldn't even know she was there.

The man accepted his change, stuffed it into his wallet, and bid the attendant farewell.

Beth watched him as he made for the door. Perhaps this was a bad idea. For all she knew, this man could be a Godless lunatic. She battled with the thought of going to the authorities as Betty had suggested, but the thought of the evil government imposing their will on her community made her feel queasy.

Had Lou Ellen told Jacob by now?

Lou Ellen. The mere thought of her domineering sister-wife made her cringe.

She did not know the answer to these questions, but she did know that staying at the Shell station another moment would be very unwise. She shook off her doubts and tried to keep her hands steady. She needed to be calm, but she needed to act fast.

The splashing of the sleigh bell smacked through the air and the man disappeared out the door.

There was no time for Beth to make a rational, informed decision. At this point any distance she could place between herself and the Prophet Jacob was a good thing. In an instant, she was at the counter returning the key to the attendant. With an awkward exchange, she thanked the attendant with as much politeness as she could muster and was out the door soon after.

"Excuse me!" Beth shouted after the man. "Sir?"

The incident did not go unnoticed by the attendant.

C

The prophet Jacob Perkins sat listening at his desk, leaning back on his office chair while catching his reflection in the office window. He was nearing fifty-seven years of age but looked older. His face was beginning to sag over his skull like a wax museum figure suffering from heat exposure. His eyes were vacant and brown, canopied by bushy black-and-gray eyebrows. He was thin but for his gut, which always made his short-sleeved button-down shirts and the waist of his brown pants snug in the midsection.

To his left was his enforcer, Mr. Bratch, a former member of the Philadelphia Police Department. His security guard uniform was form-fitting over his solid frame. Though the prophet had never inquired about Mr. Bratch's age, he guessed it to be between fifty and fifty-five.

In a dark corner of the room was the prophet's first and favorite wife, Lou Ellen. Her features were barely visible, but her presence was felt.

Jacob turned to look at Betty Perkins, one of his problematic wives, sitting on a backless chair in the middle of the room. She was slouching forward and looking dejected. She was well beyond bothering to remove the disheveled hair from her tear-stained cheeks. She rubbed tears from her hands on her blue temple dress.

To avert her husband's menacing face, her eyes were cast to the floor, which had been covered in thin sheets of plastic. Jacob told her it was because they were fixing to paint the office, though she saw no signs of paint buckets, rollers, or any other tools associated with painting. This did not surprise Betty. She had, after all, committed a weighty sin against God. She had not only encouraged a barren woman to flee the compound, but helped her escape. Her afterlife was in question for sure, and the only road to redemption was through God, through Jacob.

Jacob put his hand to his face and nibbled on his knuckle. "Are you telling me the truth, Betty?"

She sniffled and wiped her face with the palm of her hand before she forced herself to meet his eyes and lie to him, for better or for worse. "I've told you everything I know, Jacob."

"And how long ago was this?" Jacob asked.

"About forty-five minutes ago." Betty said. She dropped her eyes back to the plastic on the floor. She could not endure his stare any longer.

Jacob leaned forward to rest his hands on his knees. He interlocked his fingers and rubbed them together while he addressed the corner of the room.

"Lou Ellen," Jacob said, "you mind steppin' outside for a bit? And send Larry on in here as well."

Lou Ellen shot Jacob a look of protest and rose like a dark wraith from the corner, glaring at him the entire time. Angry flashes of hate burned from her eyes as she rose from her seat and crept across the room toward the door. Her large frame seemed to float in slow motion as her temple dress hid the movement of her ankles. The protest was, until now, silent, but it caught Jacob's attention nonetheless.

"Are you blocking me out now, Jacob Perkins?" she asked. Her stare exploded through the room and detonated into Jacob's eyes. "I swear to God above I should make you a letter box." With this, she slammed the door behind her, breaking their gaze and sending a loud booming throughout the room.

Larry Hitchcock entered the room, replacing Lou Ellen's space in the corner. He did his best to pretend nothing had happened.

Jacob rubbed his face in his hand and spoke to no one in particular. "Sometimes I think that woman is absolutely possessed by the devil himself. Talking nonsense again."

No one in the room commented.

To Betty, the prophet said, "You know you put me in quite a pickle here, Betty. You come in here and tell me that my wife, your sister-wife, is barren, and that you can't find her anywhere and that you think she's ran off somewhere on foot." He glanced over at Mr. Bratch, who was now consulting data on a mobile device.

Mr. Bratch nodded.

"But," he continued, "I've got this feeling, a *divine* feeling that she is much farther away than anywhere she may have gone on foot. Now *I'm* thinking there's only one truck that runs out of here at night, and that's the mail truck."

Betty shifted her weight at the mention of the truck, but kept her eyes peeled to the floor. She was aware of the shadow that was Larry, lingering silent in the corner.

The prophet rose and rested his hands on his hips, letting out a long sigh. "How do you suppose she got in that mail truck, Betty? If I were to ask you the whereabouts of that mail truck key, what are you gonna tell me?" The prophet stared her down. "Betty? Now remember that I speak for God when I ask you: Where is that mail truck key?"

Betty's voice quivered when she spoke. "Jacob, please—"

His voice grew deeper by an octave. "I am the Prophet Jacob, child. And you will address me as such."

"Prophet Jacob," Betty corrected herself. "I gave her the key. Please forgive me." She fell to her knees and sobbed.

The prophet walked around the desk to approach her. He put his hand under her chin and lifted it until their eyes met his. "I know you did, Betty. I have already spoken to God about it. Would you like to know what he said?"

He wasn't interested in her answer. It didn't matter if she was telling the truth now; she'd betrayed him. Betrayal had consequences. Without further conversation, he gave a nod to the shadow in the corner. "He said you shall be cast out of the afterlife forever."

Just as he said the words, she began to scream in protest, and just as that scream began, her head was struck from behind. She dropped lifeless to the plastic.

Larry Hitchcock, the shadow, stood over her with a heavy, bloodstained pipe wrench.

The prophet stood over his wife's body and checked for vital signs. There were none. He let out another sigh. "Well, Mr. Bratch, it looks like we've got ourselves a homicide. I can't believe Beth would do such a thing."

"It's a shame," Mr. Batch replied. "She always seemed like such a nice girl."

Jacob thought for a moment. "But let's not go to the police just yet. We have some time yet before we play that card. Let's see if we can't fish her out ourselves. Do you think we can catch up to her?"

"I do," Mr. Bratch said.

"That's just splendid. Now get your guys on it." The prophet pointed and accusing finger at Mr. Bratch. "Now maybe in the future you can monitor your toys a little closer, too."

"I will, sir," the ex-cop said. He looked disappointed with himself. The last thing he wanted to do was piss off the prophet.

Motioning to the body, the prophet said, "Good. Now roll her up and freeze her."

"Yes, sir."

5
October 28: Night

A

The cat was eating Purina cat food, the wet variety, purchased with Brennen's last dollar bill. From a quick Google search, he had deduced he was the proud owner of a female, long-haired red Tabby. She had long, orange fur from the top of her head to her bushy tail. In contrast, from her chin to the underside of her back legs was cotton-white. Her legs were orange all the way down to her white feet that made her look as though she was sashaying about in ankle socks. She was pretty cute for a cat, but not as well-groomed as her Google counterparts.

He remembered the Triana Zigler dream.

How the hell had she found her way into his subconscious? He had not thought about her in at least seven years. They had never hung out, nor did they speak to each other outside the history class they shared. However, in the dream, she was so . . . likable. So pure. What was she up to these days?

"Reer!" said the cat. Her pink nose crinkled.

The Glow was all over him as time sputtered away like an outboard motor to lake water. The dream had distracted him from checking his phone for texts or voicemails. Out of job necessity, he had just recently joined the twenty-first century and charged a phone to his credit card and was not used to using it.

It was dead.

Frustrated at himself for letting this happen again, he dug through some items in his desk to find the phone charger. He plugged it in and waited for it with the patience of a four-year-old as it went through its boot sequence. He was relieved to see there were no work-related calls. There was, however, a missed call from his older sister, Jen. His nerves received a small spark. This was the third call from her in as many days. She didn't leave a message. Brennen imagined this was due to his lack of returning her calls.

The shame oozed within him as he sat with his head bowed, staring at the phone's screen. He would love to talk to his sister, just not now, or last month or the month before that. If he talked to her, she would want to talk about how things were going. To avoid breaking down, he would have to lie and explain that everything was great and that he *wasn't* facing compounding credit card debt, he *didn't* have a probable eviction happening, and no, he *hadn't* failed miserably at life. Besides, if he spoke to her right now, she would without a doubt sense that he was high, and *knowing* he was high, would inevitably center the conversation around that. Whatever it was that she wanted to speak about would be overshadowed by the disappointment in her voice. She was ashamed of him, and should be.

Flames

Brennen inhaled through his teeth as though his mind had just experienced a blast of extreme heat. He set the charging phone down and reached for his pipe. As he looked up, he was surprised to see the cat had taken a seat in front of him. She sat with defiance, licking her chops with fervor, placated by the cat food.

"Eer," said the cat. She looked annoyed with Brennen.

A realization flashed through Brennen's mind. "Oh my God, I gave you food and totally forgot the water, didn't I? Do you need some water?"

Did the cat bob her head up and down?

He trotted to the kitchen, moving small boxes of knickknacks out of the way to reach the bowls. The clutter was an annoyance, but nothing that he couldn't clean up in two seconds. Perhaps tomorrow would be a good time to clean, just not now. The bowls were scattered about in several places, but he found the one suitable in the empty spice rack. Someone must have misplaced it there at some point. It didn't matter. Laughing at himself, he twisted his body over another box to use the sink. The cat, who he'd been ready to broom out of the apartment earlier that evening, had him literally bending over backward, and telling him to be snappy about it. By the time he crouched in front of the cat with a full water bowl, he was out of breath.

"Here ya go. So sorry about the slow service today. Am I out of the doghouse? Or cathouse, in your case?" He put his right hand up to receive a high-five. "Either way, gimme a high-five."

She stared at him

"Okay, maybe not," he said. Just as he put his hand down, he noticed she started to move her paw. He did another double-take. His legs were cramping from squatting and he was considering getting up, but the way the cat looked at him, in a way that could be only described as enthusiastic, kept him still. Did she want him to put his hand back up? He raised his hand again. “High-five?”

She lifted her right paw and tapped his hand. “Eer!”

B

Beth awoke sitting shotgun in the semi with her head against the window. The vibration of the wheels against the road sounded like a low note of a men’s choir gashing through an oscillating fan. She kept her left eye shut to give her driver the illusion of sleep. She prayed she had not stirred so much as to draw his attention.

She had been dreaming of playing Doomsday with her childhood friends at the construction company’s gravel yard. It was a game of faith. It was their version of King of the Hill. A group of five or six children, mainly girls, would sneak through the perimeter fence and find a giant mound of dirt that had been set aside for future projects. The goal was to separate the chosen ones from the Othersiders. Othersiders, of course, were people who lived outside the compound and, according to Jacob, would all be eradicated when the Judgment came.

Beth and her friends would run up the mound and shove each other around until only one remained: The chosen one. The chosen one would then pretend to ascend to the celestial kingdom while the rest of them would writhe at the base of the mound and pretend to be burning in hell.

She’d had no love for Othersiders since those days. Yet here she was, defenseless and sharing a truck with one of them, and a creepy one at that.

Several times before she fell asleep he had glanced over and flashed a smile at her. She smiled back out of politeness before looking away and assuming her position against the window. He had not asked her name and she didn't want to know his.

Beth didn't know long she'd been sleeping or how far away from home she had traveled. She did know, however, that she was beyond forgiveness of the community by now. As the desert raced by the truck's headlights, she knew she would be hated and hunted. She remembered her cousin had tried to escape years ago. God found her with a speed only reserved for a being such as her and she was shunned for years until she birthed enough children to be accepted again into the community. It was doubtful the group would be so forgiving for a barren exile such as her. The denial of sacrifice was an unforgivable sin.

He would find her soon, she knew. He always did.

Had she not run, she was certain she would have been taken to The Trees. The Trees, a sacred group of pines in the middle of the desert, was a place for sacrifice. They would tie her to an altar and send her off to God. Jacob would tell her she was part of God's elite, and that although plural marriage and children are a sanction for which many strive, being called back to God is the ultimate blessing. At that point, she would be sent away to God and her physical body would disappear.

She forced her mind from the thought. There was nothing she could do about it now. She had passed the point of no return miles ago. All she could do was stare out the window, keeping her left eye closed, as road signs went by. She was on Arizona state route 89 south.

She kissed the scar on her hand, forgetting for a moment

that she was supposed to be sleeping, and rolled farther to her right. She could only hope the sudden movement would not spark conversation from the Other-sider.

As far as she could tell, he did not take notice.

She fell asleep for real.

C

Triana Zigler.

He researched her with the image of her face beveled into his memory. There was little doubt the omniscient powers of Google would be able to track her down. To his surprise, this was not the case. In fact, every search effort, LinkedIn, Twitter, public records, Classmates.com, peoplefinders.com, and other similar services had frustrated him with their ineptitude. He had such an unexplainable urge to contact her that it was almost worth reactivating his Facebook account, which he had cancelled long ago.

Tell them I'm okay.

The scene played in his mind in vivid Technicolor.

"Tell *who* you are okay?" Brennen asked out loud. A lit cigarette dangled from the corner of his mouth and his eyes squinted from the rising smoke. "And why am I doing this?"

He worked from a cramped desk, adjacent to the vocal booth, hunched over his laptop which he used on occasion when he wasn't working on his music. The spacebar was stubborn, which was a hindrance, but the mobility of the computer allowed him a much needed break from the mixing room every once in a while.

He exhaled the last drag of his cigarette and snubbed out the butt in an ashtray that was nearing capacity. Although difficult to shake the feeling of being a stalker, he continued his relentless Google searching. Perhaps this was how stalkers began: They start out at as normal, law-abiding citizens. They get a little curious about somebody and the next thing you know, they're a leading story on "Good Evening, Arizona."

He tried other searches.

TRIANA ZIGLER PHONE NUMBER-*click*

There were pictures of people with similar last names, but none with an exact match. It was obvious by the photographs that none of them were Triana.

TRIANA ZIGLER ADDRESS-*click*

This only attempted to connect him to a paid service guaranteeing, for a fee, the person of interest would be found. He was tempted, as he was aching to speak to the girl. He imagined walking up to her with arms open. She, in return, would receive the embrace without question or reserve. The feeling was not so much sexual as it was spiritual. He wanted to help her, but he wasn't sure how. Just the thought of it made Brennen vibrate with anticipation.

He specified his search by adding additional key words.

TRIANA ZIGLER ARIZONA PHONE NUMBER-*click*

Nothing. The thought had occurred to him that Triana could be married. In which case, the odds of finding her by any conventional means were not favorable. He again considered paying for the service. When bathed in The Glow, Brennen had the persistence of fire ant rebuilding the ant hill after being crushed by the shoe of a restless boy.

TRIANA ZIGLER ARIZONA HOME

"Reer!" said the cat.

Before clicking on the link, Brennen looked around the

side of the vocal booth to find the cat glaring at him from the kitchen counter. She had opened the kitchen cupboards with her front paws while she supported herself with her back paws, her legs wobbling as they fought to keep balance.

"Hey! Get out of the cupboards!" Brennen demanded.

"Eer," said the cat. She closed the cabinet door with her paw. Using one of the boxes on the countertop, she hoisted herself atop the refrigerator and began scenting items with her whiskers. When she approached his trophy, Brennen jumped.

"Whoa, whoa, whoa! Not the trophy!"

She protested with an impressive amount of volume as he took care to lift the cat from the refrigerator and placed her on one of the boxes below without harm.

"You can't be knocking this down," Brennen said. "And stop being so snippety."

Brennen looked around the room for a safe place to put the trophy. In his ears was the familiar humming of The Glow, like a streetlight in the dead of night. "As a matter of fact, let's just put this somewhere else." He held the keepsake as though it were made of eggshells and took a moment to look at it. It was a bronzed musical clef attached to a mahogany base, on which there was an engraved brass plate. He wiped a thick layer of dust across the words.

Never give up. Love, Dad.

Brennen's father was a hard-working Michigan man of few words. Instead of using heart-felt talks and face-to-face encouragement, Hank Reynolds expressed his love by presenting gifts which spoke the words he could not. When Hank wanted Brennen's mother to leave her career overseas and be his bride in Arizona, he did so, not with words, but with a ring and a poem. It worked like a charm. When Brennen and his sister were born, Hank opted not to express his joy with words to his wife, but rather with the hiring of a string duet to play their favorite songs while they held their newborns and each other. And though Hank had been against Brennen's decision to write songs for a living, he expressed his encouragement with this trophy.

Hank had always wanted more for Brennen than he had himself. To Hank, songwriting was a risky venture that would guarantee a struggle for his son. Regardless, he scraped together enough cash to buy some of Brennen's recording gear before dropping lifeless from a heart attack. The funeral was not only brutal, but when both Brennen's sister and mother deduced he was high during the service, it was detrimental to their relationship and continued to be to this day. To Brennen, it was a necessary move. It was either be high at his father's funeral or fall asleep at it. Brennen had no other choice than to assume that his father would have preferred him to be at least awake. Either way, the situation was glum.

"Mrow?" asked the cat. She had an inquisitive and empathetic look about her, as though she were asking what was wrong.

Brennen frowned, and said, "Nothing. I'm fine. I just need to find a place for this." He found a space near the television next to some trivial items that he would clear out tomorrow. "You know, you're freaking me out a little. It's like you can—"

He watched as she examined her right paw, top and bottom, as though it were newly assembled. She gave a quick look around her, a bit dazed, before repeating the examination process of her left paw. She splayed her toes, moved them away from her face and back again. She blinked, as if she were testing her focus. She shook as if water were in her ears before taking notice that she was being watched.

"Eer!" said the cat.

"Nothing," Brennen said. "You're a crazy cat." He moved to walk away when she meowed at him again.

The cat put her paw up for a high five.

Brennen approached her with caution. Perhaps this was just an odd idiosyncrasy of hers, something she'd done since kitten-hood. He left her sitting on the box for a moment with one paw suspended in the air.

"Eer!" the cat insisted.

Brennen bumped her paw with his hand and they both lowered their arms. Brennen sat astonished for a moment. Who was he kidding? This was more than just a little weird. The cat had deliberately waited for him to give her paw a tap. He had seen other cats do similar things, when prompted, but never did they initiate the process. He had never seen a cat, or even a dog for that matter, run up to him and *ask* for a handshake. They are trained to respond to commands in exchange for rewards. Now, it appeared, she was training him.

She looked at him with expectant yellow eyes.

He scratched her head and she pushed harder into his hand, to maximize the affect. "Fine, I'll pet your head, Snippety."

The name was fitting.

The exchanges with the cat had left Brennen forgetful of

Triana Zigler. He left the cat on the box and returned to his laptop. In front of him was his last search effort staring back at him, cursor blinking in anticipation.

TRIANA ZIGLER ARIZONA HOME-*click*

The first search result was intriguing. It was the only result that hadn't been inundated with ads for people-finding services. He read the link as if it were out of focus, his body alive and excited.

TRIANA LINDEN HAS COME HOME-TEMPE, AZ

Linden could be her married name.

Click

There she was, beaming into the camera, just as she had smiled at him in the dream. She was so pretty—not just pretty but elegant. She was adorned with dark hair and a soft complexion, complimented by the warmest eyes he could remember seeing. He was overjoyed for her.

Until he read further.

With every line, his jaw dropped more. Some sentences he had to read more than once to unite his comprehension with their meaning. He felt the silence burrow deep within his ear and lungs, making breathing problematic. The Glow was screaming for his body to move, but his eyes demanded stillness. He learned much about her in the brief paragraphs. She had a brother, a dog, and a loving mother. She had been an animal shelter worker, a student, and she, Triana Linden, formerly Triana Zigler, had been murdered.

D

Every sense her body had told Beth that something was wrong when the truck jolted her awake from a deep sleep. The man was pulling over in a secluded area in the desert, just off the I17 freeway. He maneuvered through a narrow clearing with skill, as though he had pulled over here before. He whistled through his teeth as he straightened the wheel. She recognized the look in his eye. She had seen it many times in Jacob when they were first married—the sidewise glance that traversed up and down her body, the thin smile, the hard swallow—this was the look of desire.

She let out a fake yawn and played innocent. "Are we at a rest stop?"

"No, ma'am," said the driver, "we are definitely not at a rest stop." He brought the truck to a stop and turned to look at her. He smiled at her again.

The cabin boasted semi-bench seating, making it easy for the man to inch his way closer to Beth. She could smell his peppermint gum as he smacked it with enough sound to cause her to flinch. In the poor light, his wool hunting jacket made him appear bigger than he was. He had looked to possess an above average build at the Shell station. In here, he was grizzly-like.

Beth tried to cover her fear. It was a tactic she used against the men of her community. She had grown quite skilled at defusing a situation by becoming a connoisseur of body language. If she could infuse humor in the situation, he would be less likely to sense her fear. Further, if she said something vulgar or unattractive, it might help to quash his desire.

"Well," Beth said, "I was hoping you were getting us to a toilet." She lowered her tone. "I have to go number two if you know what I mean."

The man, ever leaning in Beth's direction, stopped his

advances. He swiveled his eyes away from her to collect a thought. "Well, maybe you can hold that for a few minutes. I've got a surprise for you." He moved closer to Beth, reinvigorated.

"What surprise are you talking about?"

"This," the man said. He moved in on her and began kissing her neck. Forbidden passion burned from his lips as he moved his hands up and down her arms.

Beth started to squirm. She put her fingers near her mouth to block his affections. His lips kept puckering and un-puckering like some parasite alien using instinctive feelers to attach to a host.

"*What?*" the lips cried.

"What the heck are you *doing?*" Beth screamed. "I needed a ride, not your hands all over me." She had shifted her body to cut off his angles.

The man looked shocked. "Well, what the hell did you expect, woman? You been smiling at me all night, I saw you kissing your *hand,* and I thought you was *signaling* me!" A Southern drawl became noticeable in his anger. "Now you're shovin' me in the face? Do you think I'm some kind of *rapist* or something? What the hell is *wrong* with you?" He wiped his mouth where her fingers had been. There was genuine hurt in his eyes.

"Those weren't signals, sir. I was just trying to be polite. It didn't mean for you to stop the truck and start kissing on me!"

The shock remained on the man's face for several moments as he stared at Beth. His breathing was weighted. "So, you don't want to make it with me?"

"*No*!" Beth screamed. She had lost her patience. "I don't want to make it with you!" She became livid. "First, it's the perverted old man at the dance who tries to have his way with me. Now *you* pull over here in the middle of the desert?" Beth could feel her throat tighten and her tear ducts begin to fill. "This is *God's* work, isn't it? I could not do his work and he is punishing me. I will have no afterlife! I am running away from God, and he is punishing—"

"Oh, *hell* no," the man said, unwilling to listen further. "You're one of them religious girls, right?" He shook his head. "Unbe-freakin'-lievable. I should have known from that dress." He scooted himself out the driver's-side door, muttering to himself. "You are one of them cult girls."

He slammed the door behind him. She heard him yelling to himself as he walked around the front of the truck. In the headlights, she could see he was agitated and felt helpless as she watched him approach her door.

". . . eating *my* food . . . religious crazy kook girl *teases* me, playing with my emotions, in my *own* truck." The door opened with force. "Get out," he said.

Now it was she who looked shocked. Her voice returned to mousy. She made a pleading gesture. "But it's the middle of the night. In the middle of nowhere."

"Lady," the man said, "this is Arizona in October. It's not exactly Alaska. It's a great night for a walk." He pointed at zooming cars through the Palo Verde trees. "There's the seventeen freeway south. Follow it to Phoenix. Best of luck to ya."

She got out of the vehicle and saw no reason to continue the conversation. All she could do was look at him as he got in his truck and slammed his door.

An instant later, the passenger window rolled down and he yelled to Beth, “Maybe God can teach you not to hurt people’s *feelings*.” And with two honks of the semi, he pulled out, kicking up dust in Beth’s direction.

She watched as the man pulled onto the freeway and disappeared. She wasn’t sure which one was worse: being in the truck with another pervert or walking in the middle of the desert at night, alone.

Beth let out a sigh. “Godtastic.”

She thought of Jane and her three daughters. Would she ever see her nieces again? Could they ever forgive her for leaving them, if she did? Perhaps Betty or Jane could explain to them one day why their Aunt Beth had to leave.

She prayed that all of them were safe.

E

Brennen stared at the email, finding it quite hard to think of what to say. Not since his corporate job, over three years ago now, did he need to conjure the talent of sounding like a sane, competent person. With The Glow pushing his fingertips deep into the keypads, he had managed a few paragraphs, but was struggling with the introduction. Each draft sounded crazier than the last.

DEAR MRS. ZIGLER,

YOU DON’T KNOW ME, BUT I WENT TO MIDDLE SCHOOL WITH YOUR DAUGHTER, TRIANA.

Now that just sounded plain stupid. It sounded like every spam email he had ever received. *Hi, Brennen, you may not know me, but I have left a great sum of money in your name. If you are a sucker, you will respond to the email.*

He selected the text, deleted it, and started over.

DEAR MRS. ZIGLER,

PLEASE EXCEPT MY CONDOLENCES REGARDING YOUR DAUGHTER. TRIANA WAS, FROM WHAT I REMEMBER, A GOOD PERSON.

Feeling more satisfied with this version, he ran his fingers through his hair and rose off the chair with grace. He moved to the kitchen counter, where he rolled a cigarette and stepped outside.

The night air felt perfect on his freshly showered skin. He was dressed in a white dress shirt, jeans, and black dress shoes, ready for clients to start phoning him for rides.

He had several thoughts pin-balling around his head. For one, he'd recently acquired a very odd cat that seemed able to communicate with him. Secondly, a dead girl had given him a cryptic message in one of his dreams. And lastly, he needed to remember his car charger tonight. He had forgotten it on two separate occasions now, causing him to miss several potential rides. It was simple logic. If his phone dies, the GPS dies. If the GPS dies, he can't locate the rides. Without the rides, there is no cash, and no cash equaled no Dante. No Dante equated to no Glow, and that was just unacceptable. The priority was the charger.

He thought of Triana. The article was published by the church Triana's mother belonged to. According to it, Triana had been missing for some time. Feeling discretion was best, the Tempe police department, as well as Triana's mother, decided it best to keep disclosure of the case to a minimum.

From what was reported, it was the worst-case scenario. To the horror of her friends and family, Triana's body was discovered by a neighborhood dog-walker in an empty lot in the southern outskirts of Tempe. She had been buried there and remained undiscovered for just shy of two years until the curious canine discovered her. There were no details on the nature of the homicide, only that she had been found and was now at peace.

Tell them I'm okay

At first, Brennen was not going to get involved, but it wasn't long before an immense sense of obligation to the girl to deliver her message began to overtake him. He wasn't comfortable with it. In fact, he didn't like the thought of it at all. But the fact was that Triana had asked a favor of him. She was either speaking to him, somehow, through some means he wasn't willing to accept at the moment, or it was the most coincidental dream of the century, if not the millennium. Brennen wagered the latter. Either way, her mother seemed religious. She might appreciate the story. As it happened, her email address had been at the bottom of the article. What could it hurt?

It was the right thing to do.

After snuffing out the cigarette, Brennen checked his phone and returned to his chair to finish the email. Snippety followed, continuing her meowing.

After it was finished, Brennen began to proofread.

. . . FOR WHAT IT'S WORTH, SHE WAS WEARING A BLUE-AND-WHITE KNIT SWEATER, BLUE JEANS, AND BLACK SHOES WITH SILVER BUCKLES. SHE WAS SMILING. SHE SAID "TELL THEM I'M OKAY."

"Blah, blah, blah," Brennen said while scrolling further down the page.

. . . AGAIN, I'M SORRY FOR THE STRANGE (AND POSSIBLY INAPPROPRIATE) EMAIL. AFTER MUCH DEBATE, I CONCLUDED IT WAS THE RIGHT THING TO DO AND SOMETHING YOU MIGHT APPRECIATE KNOWING.

"Looks good."

In an instant, Snippety was at his lap again trying to burrow her way onto the keyboard. She added several *K*'s to Brennen's closing remarks. She was more agitated than Brennen had yet witnessed.

"What are you doing, ya Freakazoid?" Brennen asked. His hands buried in the fluff of her belly as he hoisted her up and away. Protesting all the while, she tried to bat the keyboard with her hind legs as she went.

Brennen deleted Snippety's handiwork and felt his phone vibrate. It was a text from his first ride of the night. Someone at Ra Sushi Bar in Old Town Scottsdale needed a ride and was in a hurry.

"That's my cue," Brennen said to the cat. "Gotta go, Snippety."

Snippety scurried around the back of the vocal booth and leaped on the back of Brennen's desk. Brennen managed to send off the email just as she pounced on the screen of the laptop, closing it shut with a good amount of authority.

"Reer!"

"Damn, cat!" Brennen scolded. "We will talk about this when I get back tonight." He put on his sports coat, nearly forgetting to un-pop the lapel before rushing out the door. He gave Snippety a high five and whooped out loud, causing the cat's ears to flatten.

And with a slamming of the door and the clicking of the

lock, he was gone.

In the mixing room, on his desk, next to the blinking lights of the big droid, lay Brennen's phone charger.

F

The Scottsdale nightlife was moving in superfluidity. Old Town Scottsdale, by day a historic, high-brow shopping mecca where Arizona's elite gather to window shop at small boutiques and peruse trendy contemporary art, transformed into a vespiary for party-prone twenty- and thirty-something's at night. Within a square mile, there were as many watering holes as could be found in any major metropolitan city.

Unlike New York or Chicago, walking in Scottsdale was not practiced and being seen in a cab was equally unfashionable. This was where Brennen's Cadillac Escalade came into play. It was their bar-hopper. It boasted a thirty-two-inch LED screen in the back window, which ran advertisements for the various clubs in town. Brennen was paid on the advertisements, so he didn't charge for the ride itself; he relied on tips. Brennen's partner, Johnny, owned the vehicle's lease and handled the advertising money. Because Johnny was not a late-nighter, Brennen handled the driving. In exchange for the service, Brennen pocketed one hundred percent of the tips. For him, it was the perfect gig. He could drive all night and work on his music all day. Sleep was not an option these days if he was going to write something important—something that mattered.

The system had worked for several months, allowing Brennen to keep his landlord, Dante, and himself happy. But the tips had been thinning as of late due to a failing economy, fading generosity, and competitive online driving services and apps. Because of this, Brennen was forced to make changes in his budget: All money was allocated to Dante.

Many of his clientele were what Brennen referred to as thirty-thousand-dollar millionaires. They spent their medial paychecks on trendy fashion, bar tabs, and fancy transportation, all to create the illusion of wealth. But at the end of the night, they were broke. The irony was never lost on him: The money always flowed to the bartender, responsible for countless crippling hangovers and bad break-ups, and ran dry for the person who returned them to the safety of their homes where they would vomit away the remainder of their nights. Like any job, there were highs and lows.

Tonight was no different. It was an average night. There was an incident with a drunken couple who, after having engaged in a fist fight in the back seat, were asked by Brennen to kindly take the fight elsewhere. As they rolled out of the vehicle and chased each other around a fountain, neither seemed too concerned with providing any type of gratuity. There was also the guy, who, after being taken ten miles from the bar, jumped out of the Escalade at a stoplight, ripped his shirt off in the middle of a neighborhood and waved it in the air, screaming that he had forgotten where he lived. As the man scaled a wall and disappeared, Brennen doubted he'd be back with a tip.

But it was not all bad news. Brennen had a few legit high-rollers who understood the concept of gratuity. All in all, he was up about two hundred forty dollars. He'd still have enough for Dante even after gas. If, and only if, he had some to spare, he decided he might get a cheeseburger at the Circle K.

He sat parked at his favorite spot outside the Blitzkrieg Club on Stetson Drive where he counted his cash. Its central location made it an ideal place to wait on a call. There was always a chance someone coming out of the club might need a ride as well.

He felt smooth and in control. He cranked the mp3 player which pounded out custom re-mixes of top hip-hop songs combined with underground thrash metal. Brennen's mash-ups, as he called them, gave him more energy at night. They were not popular with the clients, but in these moments alone, they were therapeutic.

He was startled by a knock on the driver's side window. It was a thin girl, around his age. Her hair was pulled back, her face done up with makeup and dressed in the shortest dress she could legally wear.

He turned down the music and rolled down the window with the auto button. It made a mechanical whine as it lowered.

"Hi, Brennen!" the girl said.

*****

The drive seemed to be taking decades. The girls smelled like a mix of Chanel No. 5, peppermint gum, booze, and a hint of body odor. It was as familiar to Brennen as the smell of desert rain. The girl had called him by his name, but he had never seen her in his life. His name had most likely been dropped by the owner of the club and she used it to give the illusion of familiarity. It was common social practice.

The three girls didn't need a ride within the one-square-mile hot spot as he had hoped. Instead, their destination was Anthem, an up-and-coming affordable housing community, forty-five minutes north of Old Town. Monetarily, this was a bad scenario for him: It was the end of the night and instead of scoring several short jaunts, he was dependent on one, gas-heavy journey. If these girls didn't tip well, he would eat through the cash he had by having to dump more gas in the Escalade. In his experience, the club girls of Scottsdale were unaccustomed to paying tips. In fact, most left the house with no cash at all. It was also common knowledge within his profession that intoxicated people, as these girls were beyond reasonable doubt, seemed to struggle when confronted with tasks such as calculating gratuity.

If the situation wasn't enough to sour Brennen's mood, the return of his headache was. It was grinding his brain, exacerbated by the girls' shrill voices. Two in the back seat were consoling a girl in the second row. It was not his custom to eavesdrop, but the alcohol had loosened their vocal chords and the sound was difficult to block out. The girl was crying while the other two consoled her.

"I've been meaning to tell you this for a while," consoling girl number one said. She was also the one who'd flagged the ride. "He's, like, kind of not worth it. I mean, look at his clothes. He's a total loser." She was proud to be defending the crying girl in her time of need.

"I'm, like, freaking out a bit?" consoling girl number two said. Her speech was slurred. Every sentence, regardless of context, sounded as though she were asking a question. "Who did he get the drugs from?"

Brennen ran his hand through his hair and adjusted his

eyes. For reasons unknown, this seemed to catch all three girls' attention. He was somewhat taken aback when he looked in the rearview mirror and met all six of their eyes. Several awkward seconds rolled by and Brennen found it difficult to concentrate on the road.

To Brennen, consoling girl number one said, "Are you okay?"

"Yeah. I'm fine," Brennen said. His tight lips pinched out a smile. "Why do you ask?"

"You look, like, gaunt or something?" consoling girl number two added. "Do you need some water or something?"

"No, I'm all good. Thanks." He was caught off guard by this line of questioning. To his fortune, the GPS voice on his phone let him off the hook by rattling off driving directions.

"She goes by the name Stevie," the crying girl said while her hands buried her tears, "but the owner of the club told me her real name was Draya."

*****

Brennen kept his eyes on the road and his teeth clenched the rest of the trip. If there had been any further conversation, he hadn't heard it. He was heavy-hearted and found it almost impossible to keep up a friendly façade with his passengers. He had dropped them off at the destination house and sat idle in the driveway while the girls huddled outside the front door discussing his tip. He was out of earshot, but their body language spoke volumes. Heads were shaking, one pair of hands were crossed while the other pair were raised in surrender. After what seemed to be several minutes, it appeared that consoling girl number two was to be the elected negotiator. She was having trouble keeping her ankles from turning in her heels as she approached the driver's side window of the truck.

"I am *so* sorry," she said, "but we have like, *barely any* cash? We kind of spent more than we thought at the *bar*? And stuff? And we were kind of like wondering if *this* would do?" She held up two disheveled dollar bills.

Brennen looked at the girl and glanced at the others, now absconding into the house.

"Again, I'm like, *so* sorry. We will *totally* get you back next time?"

He wondered how much cash was lying around that house, and how, had the situation been reversed, he would be, like, trying to be scraping together as much as he could.

"Sure," Brennen said. "Thanks. You all have a good night."

She smiled without looking at him and began to scurry into the safety of the home. Without giving him courtesy look, she said, "You should drink some water or something?"

"Whatever," Brennen said to himself.

Out of respect to Johnny, he never carried a supply of Glow in the vehicle. That was the rule and Brennen respected it. But man, did he need some. Tonight was difficult, and the supply in his veins was running low. He needed to run by his apartment to refuel before sleep and nausea overtook him. But his apartment seemed a million miles away now. The long ride had taken up the entire golden hour of closing time and then some. It was now around two in the morning and he was fading fast.

The girl's conversation had made his hands shaky. He counted the money he had made for the evening, deducting the amount needed for gas on the way home. One hundred twenty dollars. It wasn't a killing, but it was enough for a Dante-visit.

He put the Escalade in reverse and checked the GPS.

His phone was dead.

"No, no, no," Brennen pleaded, "not now." For just an instant his problem was solved as he remembered the phone charger, for which he began tearing through the center console to find. The truth soon ram-rodded him. He had left it at home. He could see in his mind where it was, sitting just to the right of his mixing desk. Only now did he remember his intent earlier to bring it with him. Preoccupied by the email to the dead girl's mother, he once again failed to take it with him.

The thoughts began pelting him in concession: Triana, the strangeness of the cat, and now the mention of Draya.

Draya.

The name crushed him. Whether or not the girl was speaking of Draya Harris, he didn't know, but the memories of her started pouring out into the real world regardless. Over two and a half years had passed since they'd last spoken and he could still hear her screaming at him with a piercing voice and glaring at him with icy, poisonous eyes.

Without realizing it, he rubbed the scar on his cheek under his eye as he started the engine and pulled out of the driveway.

His efforts to navigate without the aid of GPS were fruitless. He had made all left-hand turns before finding his way back to the freeway. From there, his travels became more compromised. His mind was so entrenched in unproductive thought that he missed the many freeway signs indicating he was headed in the wrong direction. He screamed when he made the connection.

"*U-turn, you idiot*!" Brennen belted. He screeched across both lanes to make the exit he was passing. "You have to go south!"

6
October 29: After Midnight

A

Beth talked to God as she walked down the side of the pitch-black I17 freeway. She wanted to know if He was angry at her for running away from Him. She supposed she was a little angry at Him as well. In truth, He infuriated her at times. He was enigmatic, brash, and always made it so difficult to make the right decisions. He must know that He was catching her at a moment of physical and mental weakness, and walking down the endless stretch of road only exacerbated her emotions. She at once became shameful of being angry with God. She decided it would be safer to curse Jacob for caging her like a stray animal, or her father for bringing her into the community to begin with all those years ago.

Her father had sold alarm service contracts door to door, before he joined the community. Because of his charm, she supposed, he was one of the few Othersiders ever accepted into their way of life. Beth had been in public school through the third grade and had only imprecise memories of that time period. Great efforts went into her "re-education" provided by Bishop Locke, which her father oversaw personally. It was then she began her relationship with God and His many laws. The first of which was the Law of Following. Just as the community follows God, so does God follow the community. Jacob warned that God would always know where she was and would report this information to him. The thought of this made her look up and scan the cloudless night sky as she walked. He was up there somewhere, peeking through the stars and contacting Jacob this very minute.

She picked up her pace.

Her mind again turned to the Doomsday game. She remembered tumbling down the dirt mound, exhilarated by the feeling of falling, yet scared of the idea of becoming an Other-sider—so scared she would brace her fall at all cost. Beth, try as she did, never won the game. She always lost to a more determined girl.

Her self-esteem began to sink as she began to equate her failures of Doomsday with her failures at flagging down a ride. She had tried eleven times, five by waving her hand back and forth at incoming vehicles and six by sticking out her thumb to grab the attention of a nighttime driver. She was denied every time. Her body's requirement for water was driving her actions. Her faux leather shoes offered little in the way of support as the pads of her feet were ground raw against the ridged material with every step.

A twig broke under her weight with a crisp snap and her ears were at once filled with an alarming sound that might as well have been an air raid siren.

She froze.

It was the unmistakable din of a rattlesnake.

Her father made certain she was able to identify the poisonous wildlife of the desert. The compound was remotely located and it was required by the prophet that these animals were to be avoided at all costs. Doctor's visits were forbidden. Healing was done with prayer and fasting, and anyone who required more was considered not in harmony with God. Whether or not they lived was left to fate. In fact, snakebites were often used as a way to test one's faith. If one survived a bite without issue, they could be comforted in the knowledge that God considered them to be on the right path to the celestial kingdom.

It could be that God had found her after all.

It was either an Arizona Black or a Diamondback. She guessed the former, as Arizona Blacks were known for their higher altitude habitats. However, she did not know how far south the pervert truck driver had taken her before leaving her at the side of the freeway.

The light of the moon and stars were not enough to illuminate the position of the snake. It sounded as if it were coming from all directions. She whipped her head behind her, anticipating the feeling of venomous fangs piercing deep into her Achilles tendon.

There were headlights coming toward her a few hundred yards away. The sound of the engine was faint as it hummed beneath the rattle of the snake as it dared her to move.

Beth tried once again to judge the snake's location, but snakes were often difficult to spot in broad daylight, let alone in the dead of night. As it was, the only direction she assumed the snake was *not* was behind her, but she was too scared to move. What if the snake had since slid behind her, anticipating her move?

The vehicle was one hundred yards away now.

She closed her eyes to collect her thoughts. She felt herself tumbling down the doomsday mound, failing once again to reach the top. Maybe this was her punishment for attempting to run from the Prophet Jacob. The snake's rattle was another form of scolding, just like Jacob, just like her father, and she was to obey without question.

No.

The thought of succumbing again to snake or man moved her feet to action, and before she had any time to direct herself otherwise, she was sprinting toward the vehicle. The rattlesnake noise echoed in her head as she waved her arms in the air as though attacked by bees, flagging the vehicle down in a battle of will. If it was her fate to be mashed by a truck on the I17, so be it. At least she, alone, was in charge of the decision.

The SUV was engulfed in a cloud of dust as it came to a stop on the side of the highway. The light from the headlights formed two distinct white cones of moving sediment. It illuminated a dirt path that led into the desert vegetation.

The engine remained running.

She approached the passenger door before the driver had a chance to pull away. Fortunately, the door was unlocked.

Inside was a thin, wide-eyed young man, no less than eighteen, no more than twenty-five, with an oversized sport coat and an expression of disbelief and disgust.

"What the hell are you *doing*?" he screamed. His voice cracked, pushing his voice to a higher octave. "I almost ran you over!"

Beth looked behind her, sure that the rattlesnake was within striking range, and jumped in the cab, giving the door a good slam.

"I am so sorry!" Beth explained. She spoke through shortened breath. "I was walking on the side of the highway.

There was a rattlesnake too dark to see."

"Did you get bit or something?" he asked. His movements were jerky. "Are you hurt?"

At least he was a younger man, but he was a man just the same. He made her nervous and she wasn't comfortable explaining the entire situation to him. He could be a crazy person, or worse, another pervert who would mistake her niceness for flirtatiousness. On the other hand, she was alone and thirsty with a rattlesnake on her tail.

"No. . . not hurt . . . just— Can you please just take me to Phoenix?"

He looked indecisive. He ran his fingers through his hair, looking as though his eyes were going to drop from their sockets.

Without warning, both their heads were jolted back into the headrests. Another vehicle, a pickup truck of some sort, had smashed into them from behind. It must have approached with the headlights off because they seemed to have come out of nowhere.

"Beth," a man's voice said, "Jacob needs you home, honey. Now get on out of the truck and come with us."

Beth could hear boots crunching on gravel approaching her window. She kissed the scar on her hand and hoped her driver did not take notice. "Lord in Heaven, they have found me," Beth said, "I should have known."

"Who the hell is this?" the driver asked.

"You had better drive," Beth said as she fumbled to lock the door.

The driver locked all the doors from his side. He looked into the driver-side mirror to examine the pickup truck. His eyes squinted and burst open again to their original size. His jaw moved back and forth as he assessed the situation.

The man on the outside worked the door handle, his efforts lit dimly by the SUV's headlights. They could hear the hulking figure's labored grunts.

Beth caught only a gleam of the tire iron before it exploded into the passenger-side's seat, spreading glass shrapnel across the front of the SUV.

The driver sprang from his seat in anger. He leaned over Beth for a better look at the assailant. "Are you *serious?"* he screamed. "What the *hell*, man! This vehicle isn't even *mine!"*

With machine-like relentlessness, the assailant reached for the door handle while Beth began to scream, thwarting his efforts.

"Get out of here!" Beth yelled to the driver.

The driver, beginning to understand the gravity of the situation, whipped his head around to look out the driver's side mirror once again, where he saw another figure taking something out of the extended cab of the pickup.

"*He's got a shotgun!*" Beth shrieked, fumbling for her seatbelt. "*Drive!*"

In an instant they were moving. The driver moved the vehicle skillfully down the dirt path leading away from the highway. The ground was unsteady, making it difficult to gain headway. When Beth turned around, she was surprised by how fast the men were able to jump back into the pickup truck and give chase. They were only about twenty feet away and picking up speed. A sharp curve allowed them to catch up all together.

The desert wind tunneled into Beth's eardrums through

the broken window. Holding the security handle on the upper part of the door, Beth tried, and failed, to avoid the shards of glass. Her shoulder had a minor cut.

The pickup was able to gain the inside track on the curve and was now almost beside the SUV. A shout from an angry man was the volume of a mere whisper when heard under the combined volume of the two engines. Beth heard her name called and something about the Prophet Jacob.

Beth's driving companion snapped his head over his right shoulder to see the approaching pickup. As if his eyes were spring loaded, they returned to the road and back to the pickup truck again. "He's got the shotgun out! Get down and hold on!"

Before he finished giving the command, he swerved to the right, cutting off the pickup's lane and forcing it to slow down. The effect was short-lived and the pickup was again gaining speed. It answered by a swerve of its own, crashing into the right rear fender of the SUV.

The impact jostled Beth's head around with uncomfortable force. Her hand flew from the security handle, leaving her at the mercy of the seatbelt. She turned toward the pickup truck; its windows were too dark to make out any figures within. She imagined the shotgun pointed right between her eyes, its gaping muzzle eager to expel its shell into her brain. *This is it. This is as far as I will go in this life, or any life. Snake bite or gun-shot, it's all the same. This is the first and second death. I'm going to die.*

In another life, she may have. In this life, however, her driver swerved to the left.

The shotgun went off.

Both Beth and her driver yelled out in terror, but no one seemed to be hit and the car was still running. Perhaps it was a warning shot meant to scare them into submission. They wanted her alive, after all. They couldn't very well offer her to God with a hole in her head. They could, however, shoot out the tires.

"I think they are trying to shoot your tires!" Beth yelled.

In a stroke of good fortune, the dirt path became smoother and straightened out. The driver grimaced and moved the gear shift into another position. "They aren't going to get a chance!" he said.

"Why not?"

"This is a supercharged Cadillac Escalade!" He pushed the accelerator to the floor.

The engine howled with the maliciousness of a Bengal tiger as it tore away gravel and propelled the passengers forward. Beth's head pressed against the headrest as she saw the landscape, through the eyes of the headlights move closer to her at a speed she had never experienced.

They heard another shotgun blast. This time, it was fired out of desperation, like a spoiled child punting a soccer ball away after losing a big game. Beth saw the pickup in the side mirror getting smaller with each passing second.

She was happy to be breaking free of their attackers, but was becoming very aware of the speed they were traveling. Jacob had allowed her to watch television on rare occasions, mainly race-car driving. Her driver reminded her of a NASCAR driver, though more insane. His eyes shifted from the rearview mirror to the road ahead.

Beth could see an obstruction in the road. In the ever-shortening distance, it looked as though a long black line was cutting across the path at a slight angle; Beth thought of the snake. She could see it was a straight line stretching across the desert as far as she could see. It was some sort of pipe.

No. It was water.

It was a ravine, an irrigation ravine with a ridge on both sides, and they were moving close enough to crash into it at any moment.

"Hold on!" the driver warned.

The world was moving by in turbulent flashes within tunnel vision. The *Do Not Enter* sign, warning unsuspecting drivers of the ravine ahead, was hardly legible as it came and went. Her heart was hammering as the world rushed toward her like a criminal escaped from the darkest section of an asylum.

"Hold on!"

Beth closed her eyes and braced herself the best she could.

The Escalade hit the ridge.

For an instant, the vibration from the friction of the tires disappeared. They seemed to float in the air for eternity. Though the engine must have been humming, Beth could hear only silence while she moved over the ravine in slow motion. Flashes of Betty, Jane, her nieces, Lou Ellen, the old man at the dance, and the Prophet Jacob raced through her mind like digital distortions. Even though she was terrified of the speed, she hoped they had gained enough to clear the ravine.

The answer came with a jolt as the front end of the Escalade collided with the ground, bringing Beth from her silent wondering and back into the Arizona night. The vehicle rocked back and forth twice, each time threatening to flip, but was able to recover thanks to a life-saving maneuver her driver managed to execute. Having lost speed during the landing, he hit the brakes to assess any damage. Both of them turned their attention to the pickup truck attempting the same jump.

The F150's flight did not last as long. It started strong, enough to cause Beth significant anxiety as its headlights rose above the ridge. But no sooner did the nose of the truck rise, it fell again. Having failed to gain enough momentum, the back tires caught the ridge, causing it to nosedive into the near bank and become straddled over the water. The truck stalled, its nose buried in the dirt, snuffing the headlights out altogether. The occupants were helpless for the moment. The only evidence of the truck in the darkness was the angered whine of the engine as it tried to free itself.

"Are you okay?" the driver asked.

"I think so," Beth said, rubbing her injured arm. "I think I may have cut my shoulder, but I don't feel like anything is broken."

He seemed lost in thought for a moment before turning on the cabin light and examining the wound. He produced some Wet Naps from the glove compartment and handed it to her.

A moment later, one of the F150's headlights winked at them, indicating progress was being made escaping the embankment. Not taking any chances, the driver crammed the Escalade in gear and put as much distance between the two trucks as possible.

B

The parking lot of the gas station at the Desert Ridge Marketplace was empty, save for the few late-nighters who kept the city alive in the small hours. At this hour, cabbies and cops patrolled the North Phoenix streets. Anything out of the ordinary, such as an SUV caked in dust with a smashed passenger-side window, was a sitting duck to a police officer's curious eye.

Brennen stood smoking outside the SUV, playing the current conversation over in his head while contemplating the wisdom of calling the cops. He had considered it previously while being pursued by shotgun-wielding psycho-billies, but had since thought better of it. Chances were a conversation with a police officer could very well land him in jail for driving while high. For this reason, he *avoided* cops at all costs.

He put his cigarette out on the curb and disposed of it in a nearby trash can. "So what do you mean they just *knew* you were in the truck?"

The girl sighed. "The prophet always knows where I am. Chances are, he knows where I am now."

"I don't know about all *that*," Brennen said while opening a carton of chocolate milk. "They'd obviously been looking for you, I'll give you that. They obviously saw you standing on the side of the road. I mean, they snuck up on us." He lowered his head into his hand and began rubbing his temple. It was late and his headache was worse now that the adrenaline had subsided. He was running low on Glow. He didn't know whether he and Allen had smoked all of it; perhaps Allen had made off with some while he slept. It didn't matter. He needed more.

"I never thought I'd hear myself say this," Brennen said, "but I really think you need to go to the cops."

"No!" the girl snapped at him. "Cops are evil. They are set out to destroy us." She waved off the subject. "Can you just get me to a women's shelter in Phoenix?"

The girl was bat-shit crazy, that's all there was to it. He understood she had her own beliefs, but he didn't know, for the life of him, what he was supposed to do about it. He needed to get off the streets. The last thing he needed was to drive around in the city in the dead of night, tracking down a women's shelter that was likely to be closed at this hour. He had no working phone to research their locations, anyway. On the other hand, he couldn't just leave the girl here. After the night she'd had, she deserved some time to regroup. There was also a good chance she was more whacked out on drugs than he was.

Just then, his eyes caught the distinct outline of a Phoenix Police Department cruiser skulking its way into the gas station.

Adrenaline flushed through his spine.

He could hand the girl over right here and now and be done with it. He glanced at the broken window and the condition of the vehicle. How would he explain that?

He caught his reflection in the driver's side window. His eyes looked as if they had been dowsed with pepper spray. He had no Visine to diffuse the effect. There would be no avoiding a blood test if he went anywhere within twenty feet of that cop. Blood test equals arrest, arrest equals license revocation and loss of driving job, jail equals no writing music, no redemption, no fulfilling of his goals, and worse of all, no Dante tomorrow.

No cops. Absolutely not.

Brennen jumped in the driver's seat, jammed the keys in the ignition and started the Escalade. The cop parked the car and began walking up to the station, oblivious of Brennen's presence. Brennen took the opportunity to keep it that way.

"I don't have a way to look for a shelter right now," Brennen said. "Just crash at my pad and I'll get you hooked up tomorrow. No worries."

The girl gave him an untrusting look.

"Hey, it's me or *him*," he said, gesturing to the cop, "Or your buddies out there in the desert."

She lowered her head and nodded.

"Excellent choice," Brennen said, "I'm Brennen by the way."

"Beth."

"Nice to meet you, Beth." Brennen fired up the engine and headed toward his apartment.

C

Mr. Bratch approached the prophet's office with reluctance.

It was near dawn. The birds were singing and the cool October air promised a good day. It was probable that his day would have been fine as well if Beth Perkins not given the community the slip during the annual dance the night before. Now, however, the prophet had a problem, which meant *he* had a problem, and problems were something he'd dealt little with since fleeing the Philadelphia police department a decade ago.

He had grown to love the responsibility of keeping order among the members in his time in the community. They were kept in line by the intimidation techniques he'd used since he was a young cadet on the force. As a kid in his neighborhood, he had always been just that much quicker and tougher than the other guy. Within the compound there were few men to contend with and none could be considered threatening. The children were the easiest to deal with; it was a simple matter to keep them in line, as violence toward children was common. In fact, Jacob forbade anyone from questioning the black eyes that would appear on children's faces from time to time. In the eyes of the prophet such as he, no man had the right to question another man's parenting, especially his tactics with regards to disciplinary action.

The women were almost as easy to control (until last night). If physical intimidation didn't work, the threat of a tormented afterlife would. It was how the system self-corrected. As far as Mr. Bratch knew, it had always been like that. To him, threatening one's afterlife was one of the most effective techniques of all. It kept things running smooth and hassle-free.

There were times when things did not run with such fluidity. One of the Prophet Jacob's cousins had expressed interest in keeping only one wife and offered to divorce the others and dole them out to other suitors. The prophet accused him of being a "true monogamous" and excommunicated him. A heated argument turned to a bloody battle, ending with the prophet bashing his opponent's brains in with a paperweight in the very office he now approached.

"Divine inspiration," the prophet labeled the murder. Divine inspiration was the reason behind many unplanned actions carried out by the prophet. Mr. Bratch didn't question it. It was his job to carry out orders, nothing more. And when the Prophet Jacob ordered him to take the bloodied body of his cousin to The Trees for burial, that's what he did.

These stories, and many others, were not the healthiest thoughts to be had as he came to the prophet bearing bad news. The truth was that the prophet scared Mr. Bratch. Not because of his intimidation tactics or his temper—Mr. Bratch was confident he would destroy Jacob in hand-to-hand combat—but because of the prophet's power to excommunicate him. In a single word, the man could throw him out into the streets of the real world, where his past lay, coiling like a snake, awaiting his return. A low profile would be difficult to maintain without the cover of the community. It would only be a matter of time before someone would ask the wrong question in a job interview or take a cue from his Philadelphia accent or probe him about his origins. This would not do at all. As it stood, it was in his best interest to keep the prophet happy, and Beth Perkins was not making it easy for him.

He straightened his security uniform and switched his clipboard into his opposite hand before reaching for the door. The windows to the office were reflective, giving an observer from within the advantage of being able to see who was approaching without himself being seen. He could already hear the incessant metal clicking of the prophet's knife.

He rehearsed his thoughts for the last time, clenched his jaw, and entered the prophet's office.

Before the door had time to close, Mr. Bratch was confronted by the prophet's voice. Jacob was sitting in his chair behind the desk, swiveled away from him. As usual, the office was without clutter or pictures on the wall. It was as if the office had just been rented and only the computer equipment, chair, mahogany bookcase, and desk had arrived thus far. The bookcase was full of dusty books, and manuals of outdated computer software. Its outside was scourged with tiny slits, as if an attempt to hang a picture had gone awry.

"Mr. Bratch," the prophet said, "I see you had to collect yourself briefly before coming in here." The clanking continued in groups of three, sounding like a set of keys being fumbled with.

Mr. Bratch said nothing.

The prophet guffawed. "Now why would a big son of a gun like you be afraid to come in here and talk to little old me?" His tone became lighter. "You're supposed to be the big Philly cop, remember?"

Even after ten years, Mr. Bratch had not become accustomed to being patronized. He pretended to ignore the comment. He brushed his pant leg and straightened his back to regain some of his dignity.

"The pickup truck is in a shop in Anthem, sir," Mr. Batch said. "It's not functional at this time."

The prophet swiveled around to meet his guest. His white, short-sleeved, button-down shirt was stained with coffee at the gut. His high-fitting brown trousers exposed his boney ankles and over-sized shoes. His eyes were hidden beneath his bushy-gray eyebrows from that angle, but the stare was unmistakably Jacob Perkins'. The noisemaker, a six-inch butterfly knife with stainless-steel handles, was in his hand. He continued to flip it open and shut while he stared at Mr. Bratch. Glints of silver flashed as the blade lay exposed one second, and concealed in another.

Click.

Clack.

Click.

The clicking stopped and, with some labor, the prophet hoisted himself from his chair. Mr. Bratch made no notice of the knife, though the sight of it was not a good sign. The knife was often unsheathed and waved about at times of agitation, keeping those around him on edge. Mr. Bratch, though not frightened of a superficial knife wound, was eager to stay clear of the blade just the same.

Jacob latched the handles of the knife together in a smooth movement, and made a motion to stab the desk. At the last moment, he stopped and flashed a smile to Mr. Bratch, followed by a gaping frown. He began flipping the knife again and wandered to the window to peer out at the parking lot.

"So let me get this straight," the prophet said. "They tracked down my wife, but she escaped in a magic SUV that was able to jump a river that your boys could not. In fact, they got stuck in the river and had to get towed out of there, probably attracting all sorts of attention."

"No police were notified about the incident."

"Ah, but they *could* have been, Mr. Bratch. They could have been."

"Yes, sir."

"And *had* they been, your boys would have probably had

a heck of a time explaining the recently fired shotgun they had with them. You do know the plates on the car would lead to the construction company, right?"

"Yes, sir."

"This is some sloppy horseshit, Mr. Bratch." The prophet traversed the space between the two men with knife in hand. "You need to get two trucks out. One of them gets those knuckleheads back here and the second one gets my wife. Get Larry and Chris on it. We don't have any time to waste." The prophet looked up, standing eyeball-to-chin with Mr. Bratch. "Do you understand me, Mr. Bratch?"

Bratch nodded. "It will be done, sir. I can have them down there by mid-morning."

"Where is Beth right now?"

Bratch consulted the GPS screen embedded into his clipboard. The digital light illuminated his time-chiseled face. His eyes were cold and focused as he tapped the screen with his free hand. "She's in Tempe, sir. It's five-thirty a.m. now, and I can have Larry and Chris there in five and a half hours, maybe less."

"Make it happen. If we don't return that girl to God, we could all be in a world of shit."

Taking the cue as a dismissal, Bratch nodded and turned to leave.

"And Mr. Bratch," the prophet said, leaning in close, "those men had better do their job or I will hold you personally accountable. Don't think for a second that you are immune to excommunication."

Without warning, the Prophet Jacob wound up like minor league pitcher and hurled the butterfly knife into the bookcase. It wobbled for a moment as the blade took its place among the other puncture holes.

Mr. Bratch did not flinch.

D

As a precaution, Brennen parked the embattled Escalade down the street in an adjacent apartment complex lot. Just in case their assailants found the truck, which was doubtful, at least it wouldn't lead them to his apartment. If they had the wherewithal to run license plates, a DMV search would lead them to Johnny, not Brennen. He was quite sure Johnny was not going to kill him.

And what about this girl? Who the hell was she and what kind of company did she keep? All the talk about God was off-putting, but she was in obvious need of help and wasn't bound to have found any on the side of the highway. From what little she divulged about her home life, he could ascertain her situation was serious. He would Google-search a shelter for her soon.

His headache was so severe at this point that he'd started to humor the idea of a nap. Dante only operated between the hours of 10:00 AM to 10:00 PM, and wouldn't be up for another four hours.

He began to scramble for his keys as they approached his apartment. They weren't in their usual pocket. Perhaps the girl made him nervous. As odd as she was, she was the first girl to set foot in his apartment for a very long time. With his wits running low, he made poor attempts to conceal it. He winced as he dug in each pocket for the missing keys.

He noticed that she had noticed.

"Are you okay?" she asked.

"Damn," Brennen said, "everybody is *asking* me that tonight. Yes, I'm fine. I have a little bit of a headache, but it's no big deal." He ran his hand through his hair. "I also seem to have misplaced my keys." He moved Beth aside to give himself more effective leverage on front of the door. "Excuse me real quick. Let's give this a try." With a good amount of weight, he threw his shoulder into the door, forcing it open.

Beth made a startled noise at the sudden movement and was surprised to see the door open.

"The door sticks. If it's locked, sometimes you can just give it a good shove." Brennen shrugged his shoulders and gave an innocent smile. "Don't tell anybody." He put his finger to his lips to give the universal *quiet* sign. As he did so, flashes of metal dangled from his fingers.

"Are those the keys?" Beth asked.

Brennen removed his finger from his lips and noticed his keys were bunched up in his hand. He must have had them in his hand the whole time. Fatigue had overpowered The Glow. If he didn't take affirmative action, he would be passed out cold within a few minutes.

"Oh, my God," Brennen said, "I am an idiot. Don't pay any attention to me. I'm really tired and need to get some rest." He motioned her inside.

"What are all these wires and stuff?" Beth asked.

"This is a recording studio and a one-bedroom apartment built into one." Brennen gestured about the room. He noticed she remained silent, not seeming bothered by his awkwardness. "People record out here, vocals, guitars or whatever, and I record them in there." He pointed to the control room. As he said this, he realized there might be incriminating paraphernalia by the mixing board and made a beeline for it. Within a few seconds he had it stashed away before she came around the corner.

As he was leaving the room, he saw the phone charger sitting in the very place he imagined it would be.

He put his dead phone on a separate wall charger on the desk by the vocal booth and found a clean bath towel for Beth should she want to shower.

"Reeer!" said the cat. She had appeared from somewhere around the couch and planted herself in front of Beth where she was now demanding attention.

"Oh, that's Snippety. I just found her little while ago. She's a freakazoid."

"Mrowr!" Snippety protested. She shot him a dirty look.

"I'm *joking.*"

Beth let out short laugh. Brennen imagined it was the first laugh she'd managed in quite some time.

Brennen addressed his feline friend, "Snippety, give Beth a high five."

At once, Snippety raised her paw and stared at Beth, expecting a response.

Startled, Beth looked at Brennen and again to Snippety.

"Well," Brennen said, "don't keep her waiting all day." He was doing his best to stay engaged, but he was fading fast.

Beth knelt down and held her hand to the cat, which tapped it and returned her paw to the ground. "That is Godtastic," Beth said. "That is the cutest thing I've ever seen."

Brennen had no polite way to change the subject. "Hey, Beth, not to be rude, but I'm going to pass out for a while.

There is some water in the fridge. Just move those boxes to get into it." His gestures were sloppy and his voice was failing him. "There is a fresh towel in the bathroom if you need to shower. Have fun with Snippety, and I'll be up in a few hours and will get you to a women's shelter when they open. Feel free to clear some space and get some sleep, too. You must be exhausted."

Beth didn't answer right away. She remained kneeling by Snippety, petting her from head to tail. "Okay."

Basking in the attention, Snippety seemed to snicker at Brennen as he disappeared into the mixing room.

7
October 29: Morning

A

When he awoke, he ritualistically scanned the ceiling while getting his bearings. He was groggy and disoriented. The pieces of the previous night began to coagulate in his mind and ooze back into his memory. That horrible drive to Anthem with the club girls, getting lost, almost running over the girl, the car chase, the damaged Escalade—it all seemed to be a dream. He was almost willing to surrender to the notion, until he heard Beth giggling from the other room, no doubt playing with the cat.

He managed to get showered and ready for the day without drawing attention to himself. He had some clean clothes placed in various parts of the control room. He was ready to roll. Somehow, it was already well passed 10:00 AM and he needed to refuel. Dante was already operational.

To his surprise, Beth had taken him up on his offer to get showered. Aside from her dress, which was still quite dusty, she looked squeaky clean. Her auburn hair had crimson highlights that were not visible in the layer of last night's dust.

Brennen closed the door, turned on the water to drown out any suspicious noises, and sat on the toilet with the lid down. He went to work with vigor, inhaling and exhaling monster hit after monster hit. Unlike other smoke-ables,

Glow had no distinct smell and would not be detected by a novice such as Beth. It was an embarrassing vice, but at least it didn't reek.

He stamped the pipe into a wet sponge and put everything away in the lower bathroom cabinet. He ran his fingers through his hair with a smooth motion, closed his eyes, and breathed deep for a few moments.

He was back.

And he was losing track of time. He wasn't sure if he had been in the bathroom for longer than a normal bowel movement. Or had it been less? The thought of her fretting that he had died having a bowel movement was embarrassing. He turned off the water and cleared his throat, thinking that would be sufficient evidence that he was alive and well. He sprayed some potpourri air freshener to add to the illusion of defecation. He felt like an ass, not only for putting on this whole charade, but for exposing her to dangerous substances. Either way, he would make up for his foolishness by taking her to a shelter after Dante had made a delivery.

"Hey, Beth?" Brennen yelled from the toilet.

He heard a muffled reply.

"My friend has to drop something off here. Do you mind if we wait for him real quick before we go?" It was awkward having a conversation with a stranger while on the toilet, but it was what it was.

He produced his phone from his back pocket with fluid movements. There were two missed calls from a Tempe number he didn't recognize and another call from his sister. She did not leave a message. He put a mental pin in it, and moved on. There was no way he could talk to his sister now. She was too far down in the flames now that he had just risen himself above them. It just wouldn't make any sense to go there. He swiped her missed call aside and set up a text to Dante.

HOWDY!!

Every day was a new day when Dante delivered, and this one was going to be a good one. He began to hum classical music as he flushed the imaginary bowl movement down the toilet and exited the bathroom.

Snippety was waiting for him in front of the kitchen counter, tapping her food plate. Brennen traversed the boxes with waiter-like reflexes to prepare her food.

Beth had found a fold-up chair somewhere among the scattered items and taken a seat. She was examining the boarded-up windows. "How are you supposed to look out the window? Don't you ever want to see who's at the door?" She looked uneasy.

"I installed an extra-large peephole," Brennen replied. "It usually gives me a good idea who's out front." He noticed Beth's timid demeanor and changed his tone accordingly. "Do you need to see outside or something?"

Beth shook her head and looked down. "I feel like those men will find me here. We should probably go soon."

"We will be out of here the minute my friend shows up. It shouldn't be too long." Brennen checked his phone to see that Dante had already replied.

ON MY WAY

Just as he read it, there was a knock at the door. It was not the secret knock so Brennen knew it was neither Dante nor Allen. This person was a either a stranger or somebody he hadn't spoken to in many years. Same difference.

Beth turned to Brennen, her eyes wide in terror. "*It's them!*"

Brennen was having none of it. Though he was distraught by the idea a stranger invading his private space, The Glow would not toy with the notion that the men in the pickup truck had tracked them here. He kept his voice low so the intruder could not hear. "Don't worry, I will figure it out." He motioned for her to stand out of the way.

He put his eye to the peephole. The scene was distorted through a fish-eye lens, but he could see there was only one guy standing out front. He wore a blue polo-style shirt and khaki cargo shorts. The figure looked from side-to-side before knocking again.

"No way," Brennen said. If he didn't know better, this was his old friend, Carl. "Carl-freakin'-McShirley."

Without further consideration, Brennen yanked the door open.

The mid-morning sun blasted into the apartment like a cosmic storm, stinging the backs of his retinas. Brennen took a laser-quick survey of the world outside: people talking in the parking lot, a man walking a sizable pit-bull terrier across the street, and a teenage boy in front of him with a clipboard.

Zing

Zang

Zing

This was not Carl McShirley.

Bothered by the sun and that he had been tricked by the

fish-eye lens, Brennen raised his hands to his face. His movements were liquid again as the Glow was reaching maximum effectiveness.

"Can I help you, man?" Brennen asked.

The teenager stammered. "Um, hello, sir."

Just as the words were spoken, Brennen felt a sharp pain in the middle of his skull, as though a railroad spike had been hammered into it. The chirping of the birds in the trees sounded like a car alarm at close range. He cupped his forehead with his hand and squeezed his temples to try to quell the pain.

The teenager continued, "My name is Brad *(Don),* and I am with the Youth Starter Group, which is a company dedicated to getting kids like me off the street *(this guy looks like a fool).*"

Brennen was disoriented. The teen's sentences were fragmented, with parts seeming to arrive in his ears without first passing through the boy's vocal cords.

"I'm sorry," Brennen said. "Did you say your name was Brad or Don?"

The teen looked stunned, but soon recovered by attempting his pitch again. "Hello, sir, my name is Brad *(how did he know my real name?)* and my company helps less fortunate kids better their public relation skills *(what the hell is wrong with this guy?)* All I need is one thousand more points to reach twenty-thousand, and I will win a trip to Washington DC *(I just want your cash, dude).*"

Brennen waved his hand to stop the spiel. He rested one hand on the ledge outside his front door and tried to concentrate. The boy's mouth had not moved on the last sentence. In fact, it overlapped with sentence he was speaking.

"Wait, did you just say you wanted my *cash?* And what do you mean what is *wrong* with me?" He looked at Beth, who was watching with disbelief from inside the apartment as the conversation unfolded.

She kissed the scar on her hand again.

"Slow down, man," Brennen urged. "Speak slowly. What do you want?"

As he was giving these orders to Don, a sparrow landed on Brennen's shoulder. He looked at it with a slack jaw and a loss of words. He brushed it away, only to have it return to the same place.

"Um . . . *(buy my overpriced magazines, sucker)* my company helps less privileged kids like me *(I could swear this guy is reading my mind)* improve their public relation skills *(birds don't just land on people)* and . . . uh . . . *(holy shit I have to record this on my phone)*."

With Brennen busy brushing off another bird, the youth put down his clipboard, pulled his iPhone out of his cargo pocket, and began filming the entire episode. He zoomed and panned with skill, pointing the phone at Brennen's confused face as yet another sparrow joined the others in their attempt to land on him.

"Oh my God, dude *(this is priceless)*," Don said to his video. "This is Don, here. I'm in Tempe, Arizona, and this guy here is totally reading my mind . . . no lie."

"Please stop filming, my friend," Brennen protested. He reached through the birds at the iPhone to grab it, but Don was too quick. Brennen's mind was consumed with questions as to what was happening.

Another railroad spike hammered his head.

From across the street the owner of the pit bull was shouting after his dog. It had just broken away and was now charging into the scene at full speed toward Brennen, dragging the leash with it. Its lips were curled back against its teeth and its eyes were black with madness. When, at last, the dog reached Brennen, instead of tearing into his ankles, it lay down over his feet. Damned if the dog wasn't submissive, even playful.

Don backed up to get a wide shot.

Brennen had had enough at the sight of the dog at his feet. He waved as many birds away as he could, taking care not to swat any out of the air, while scooting the dog away from his feet. He made a final effort to step back into his apartment to grab the door, waving at birds as he did.

He slammed the door shut.

B

"What was *that* about?" Beth asked, terrified. "What was with the birds . . . and that dog?"

Brennen rested with his head on the door, his hand still on the doorknob. She was right. What *was* that? How any of that could be explained with rational thought was a mystery. His mind was racing at a rate he was unaccustomed and his body was shaking in spite of his best effort to hold still.

"I don't know," he said. It was all he *could* say. "I don't know. I really don't know."

She looked in his eyes. "Are you feeling well *(Why were you answering questions that weren't asked?)*?"

It was as if the questions were blended together—two

separate sentences spoken by the same voice, but only one was spoken from her mouth.

Brennen looked at her as if her eyes and nose were trading places. “What did you ask?” He tried repeating the question back to Beth as he heard it. “Was I feeling well, like answering questions that weren’t asked?”

Beth’s mouth went slack.

“Please speak slower, Beth.”

She spoke at a slow tempo. “I asked if you were feeling well *(and why were you answering questions that were not asked?).*”

Clear as day, he had heard the second sentence, though her lips remained motionless. He was frozen in time with an answer that he didn’t care to speak out loud, yet it hovered between them as real as a steel rail.

He had read her thoughts. “To answer your first question, I am not feeling great,” Brennen said. “And as far as your second question goes, I answered the questions that I heard.”

They could do nothing but stare at each other for a few moments.

Bam, bam, bam.

The door shook as it was struck. It must be the boy again. Brennen’s bewilderment gave into frustration at the young man’s inappropriate persistence. He motioned for Beth to stay out of sight as he turned the door knob. He would let Don have it this time.

Beth gasped. “*(It’s them).*”

Brennen dismissed the comment and made to pull the door open.

“Reeer!” Snippety protested from the floor. It was the

same behavior she'd demonstrated when Brennen was trying to send the previous night's email.

He yanked the door open and was again hit with the sun and another surprise.

Four men dressed in tactical SWAT gear stood facing him with raised assault rifles, all pointed at his head.

"Brennen Reynolds?" a stressed male voice asked. "We are from the Tempe Police Department, Criminal Apprehension Unit. You're wanted downtown for questioning in the murder of Triana Linden."

C

Beth watched helplessly through the peephole as Brennen was ushered to a police car. There had been no time for the two of them to discuss when he would be back or what the plan was regarding the women's shelter. Nothing. He had simply pulled the door shut behind him as they took him without another word. Just as the Prophet Jacob preached, the evil government police cometh and taketh away.

Did Brennen kill somebody?

The thought made her even more uneasy. When he had first found her on the freeway, she wondered if Brennen was another tainted soul like the ones before him. But she reasoned that he, though strange, had saved her from both the snake and the men from the community. He had been respectful of her space and had made no unwanted advances. This was more than she could say for most men she had ever encountered, especially Jacob.

And what about the birds? The image of the sparrows trying to land on Brennen's head, shoulders, and hands was still fresh in her memory. The angry dog turning from aggressive to submissive added to the bizarreness. This was not normal behavior for animals. None of this was normal. Mind-reading was not normal. *How in Goodness's name had he done that?* He had answered questions that had been solely in her mind. Not even Jacob had ever exhibited such ability. Perhaps God could speak through Brennen as well. Perhaps her savior last night was, in fact, *the* savior. A savior *and* a murderer?

Who or what was Brennen Reynolds?

She looked down at Snippety, who had been staring at her since the door shut. The cat flashed her eyes to the peephole and back at Beth.

"Do you want me to look through the peephole, Snippety?"

"Mroow!"

"I'm taking that as a yes. And I can see why your name is Snippety."

The cat was extraordinary in its own right. Small wonder she belonged to Brennen.

Beth placed her fingertips on the door and leaned into the peephole. She could see the police officers place Brennen into one of two squad cars and drive off. Keeping her eyes to the peephole, she surveyed the distorted landscape. There were no signs of the dog, its owner, or the magazine-selling teenager. The sight of the police must have prompted them to leave.

Movement in the parking lot caught her eye as an old Ford F150 crept across the parking lot and pulled up in the space that had recently been occupied by the squad car.

It was one of Jacob's trucks.

D

Bam. Bam. Bam. Bam. Bam.

She saw Larry Hitchcock and Chris Hanner standing at the front of the front door through the peephole. One carried a tire iron while the other held some type of device in his hand. She could hear their voices through the door.

"It says she's right here," one of the men said, "not five feet away."

Bam. Bam. Bam. Bam. Bam.

"Come on out, Beth," Larry said, "Jacob knows where you are."

"To whoever has got her in there," Chris said, "you should know that Beth has done some bad things at home and needs to get home to deal with them. It's best if you send her with us."

Bad things? Beth thought. Her mind scrolled through the possibilities of what they might be referring to. They could be considering her escape a brutal act toward God, but she wasn't sure. It wouldn't be beyond them to frame her for something just to get her back home. She was at once overcome by an uneasy feeling. Something bad had happened.

"Did you try the door?" Chris asked.

"Do you think I should?"

"She ain't coming out on her own, that's for sure."

Beth's eyes widened as she realized she had not locked the door after Brennen had shut it. She cursed herself as she locked it and looked around trying to form a plan. She saw the cat by the vocal booth.

"Errow!" Snippety said, pointing her paw in the direction of the booth door.

Without second-guessing, Beth crawled across the floor and dove into the booth and crouched down, making herself as small as she could. Just as she shut the door behind her, she heard the front door burst open. Her loud breathing was deadened by the soundproofed interior.

"Holy goddamn," Larry said. "What kind of a place is this?"

"This is some kind of pigsty, Larry," Chris confirmed.

Beth heard Snippety protesting the intrusion.

Larry sighed and said, "Doesn't look like anybody is home, except, of course, for Beth. She's in this booth here."

In an instant, the booth door was flung wide. Standing over her was Larry Hitchcock wearing a messy, navy-blue work shirt, matching double-knee work pants, boots, and an evil grin, visible through a scraggly beard.

"Well, well," Chris said, "look who it is." He stepped into view behind Larry. "You're in a lot of trouble, Beth."

Larry grabbed Beth with one arm while threatening with the tire iron in the other. He hoisted her to her feet. "Let's go, girl."

"Reer!" said the cat.

"Chris, take care of that cat."

On cue, Chris, dressed in similar garb, took a swing at Snippety, which she dodged with some ease. The second attempt was more successful, as Chris was able to grab the scruff of the feline's neck and put his hands around her throat. He held her up to his face as if to antagonize her.

Small choking sounds emitted from the cat.

From the doorway, a voice said "You had best put the cat down."

Both men froze in their respective positions to witness a hulking, six-foot-six-inch figure standing in the doorway with high-top sneakers, long shorts, a sleeveless tee and a backward hat—a tuft of blond hair poking through the fitting band. The man was covered in tattoos and carrying a box full of groceries.

Taking advantage of the distraction, Snippety used her back claws to put a gash in Chris's cheek and squirm free.

He cried out, checking his cheek for blood. By the time he could focus on the situation, the giant man had set down the box and was nearing Larry. There was an unpredictable spring to this man's step, as though he had done this sort of thing before. He moved with purpose, yet he remained as stealthy as a jaguar preparing to pounce on its prey.

"Who in God's name are *you?*" Larry asked.

"My name is Dante. Who the hell are *you?*"

Larry and Chris exchanged glances.

"Don't even answer that," Dante continued. "You only need to know the answer to one question. Who lives here?"

Chris looked confused. "Don't you?"

Dante gave a relieved look, as though he had been awarded a prize. "So both of you admit you are not friends of Brennen, and that you are, in fact, breaking and entering."

Another exchange of looks passed between the intruders.

"Now I don't need the cops here anymore than you do," Dante said, "but if you think I can let you walk out of here unscathed, you are dumber than you look. Especially you."

He pointed at Larry.

Larry rushed his opponent when the insult soaked in, letting go of Beth in the process. He was quick with the tire iron and slashed it toward Dante's face, but Dante was quicker. Much quicker.

He used the follow-through of Larry's swing to his advantage, catching his wrist as it went by. In one motion, he pulled Larry farther off balance and broke his arm at the elbow. The tire iron went flying into the television set and disappeared among the many knickknacks in the apartment. Larry, disarmed and neutralized, began to scream and writhe on the floor.

Before Chris could figure out a way to help his friend, Dante had grabbed him and knuckled his side, snapping a rib instantly.

With a man in each hand, Dante ushered them out the door. "I told you I couldn't let you leave unscathed."

Both men ran for the parking lot, nursing their respective injuries while Dante followed them, making sure they left for good. Dante made it a point to take a Glock handgun out of his glove compartment and shove it between the belt of his shorts and his naval.

The men jumped in their F150 and backed out of the parking lot. Larry poked his head out of the passenger window. "The Lord has got your number." He was wincing in pain. "There will be no afterlife for you."

"And I'm all teary-eyed about it, too," Dante replied. He lifted his shirt to expose the gun to them. "The next time will not end so well for you, and you won't even be alive for *this* life."

Without further exchange, the intruders pulled out of the parking lot and away. Dante, feeling rather spry, went back to Brennen's apartment to find the whereabouts of Brennen and why there was a girl hiding out in his vocal booth.

8
October 29: Around Noon

A

Sergeant Pederson stared Brennen down again as he sharpened a pencil with a pocketknife. Pederson looked to be between forty-five and fifty years of age with graying temples and laugh lines, to boot. It was obvious he kept himself fit. His gut was still well within the standard acceptable waist size and he, despite his age, had powerful-looking guns for biceps.

During most of the interrogation, Brennen focused on everything about Sergeant Pederson except his eyes. He avoided them at all cost. Not that the man was intimidating, which he was, but his *thoughts* kept leaping into Brennen's head every time their pupils engaged. Looking downward was much more comfortable, as was looking sideways or up.

Brennen shifted in his seat, uncomfortable with the situation. His wrists were still sore from the handcuffs placed on him earlier.

The Tempe Police Department looked different from what he'd expected. He'd often walked by it on his way to downtown Tempe where he and Draya would spend their leisure time. He remembered being intrigued by a statue of Judge Charles Trumbull Hayden, founder of Tempe, just outside the station. His hat in hand, garbed in early twentieth century business attire, he stood with a proud expression on a pedestal looking onward toward the university. As Brennen was hauled into the station via squad car, however, the statue took on a different life force. Instead of pride, the man seemed to be looking away in shame, as if to say, "Oh boy, look what the cat dragged in."

The two squad cars had pulled into the station through a sally port which weaved through the back of the building into a covered parking garage. From there, he was ushered into the back door of the building, pushed up a flight of stairs, and into the cramped, windowless room. On the wall was a large corkboard caked with flyers of local wanted criminals.

It was just him and Sergeant Pederson sitting across from each other, divided by a small table with a pile of papers and a telephone to one side and a video camera at its center (no doubt recording his every word and movement).

Brennen rubbed his face and looked away from the camera. "I told you all I know. I had a dream; Triana was in it. I knew her way back in eighth grade. I woke up, I googled her and found out she'd been killed." He paused to sigh. "I don't see what the big deal is."

Sergeant Pederson scratched his scalp with the eraser side of the pencil and produced a sigh of his own. Wincing, he said, "The big deal, Mr. Reynolds, is that you emailed the victim's mother about classified details of the case." He lifted a piece of paper and began to read. "I will quote, 'For what it's worth, she was wearing a blue-and-white knit sweater, blue jeans, and black shoes with silver buckles,' end quote."

"Okay, so?" Brennen said.

"We never released Triana Linden's wardrobe to the public. She was a reclusive girl and no one at the time knew *what* she was last wearing because she never talked to anybody except her dog."

"Officer Pederson, I have no idea what has happened here. Yes, it sounds . . . it looks bad for me, but you have to believe me, I have no idea what's going on."

The sergeant locked eyes with him. "Oh, I can see that you have *no* idea what's going on, but maybe you can see why we would take this sort of thing very seriously."

Even though the sergeant glared in his eyes, Brennen couldn't hear his thoughts anymore. Whatever mind-reading abilities he had previously experienced were wearing off. He thought he heard laughter through the walls, but he trusted nothing auditory at this point.

"So," Sergeant Pederson continued, "sooner or later, you're going to let us know how it is that you know facts about this case that we didn't even know."

Brennen didn't answer. He thought of any lawyers he might know. The closest he could come up with was his estranged friend, Scott Barrett, who was in all likelihood finishing his second year of law school by now, and whose father also happened to be a judge.

He looked away from the man, scanning the room for distractions. He found one in the corkboard on the wall. His adrenaline level shot straight up when he saw, printed on fresh flyer, a picture of Beth Perkins. She was wanted for the murder of one Betty Perkins.

Sergeant Pederson put the pencil down and crossed his fingers, leaning closer to Brennen. "Now, since this conversation is going nowhere, and we happen to have what we call 'due process' in this country, I can't book you on the spot. But I will say that I wouldn't go anywhere for a while, if I were you. And it wouldn't hurt to lawyer up. Don't be surprised if you end up back here real soon."

Brennen looked at the sergeant. No thoughts entered his mind. "So, I can go?"

"You may go."

Brennen ran his fingers through his hair and stood up.

He thought he heard more laughter.

B

Rookie officer Mark Davis and Detective Janette Oakley of the surveillance unit watched the interrogation with amusement. Officer Davis laughed out loud, a gesture frowned upon in the monitor room, but he was given a pass by his superior, Detective Oakley. Even she, not known for her light-heartedness, couldn't help but crack a smile and shake her head at some points.

"This guy is high as shit," Officer Davis said. Resting his elbows on his knees, he leaned with excitement toward the video monitor causing the pant legs on his uniform to ride high up his leg. "Can't we just book him right now for coming in here wasted?"

Detective Oakley had returned to "all business" mode. "Nah, that gets a bit tricky. We didn't bring him in here on suspicion of being under the influence of drugs, so we can't just charge him for it." She gave him a condescending look.

They were polar opposites: he a male, she a female, he white, she black, he a rookie, she a veteran, he in uniform, she in plain clothes, he overweight, she slender, he with twenty-twenty sight, she blind without glasses.

Aside from Officer Oakley's lack of humor, Officer Davis

enjoyed working with her. She knew her stuff. He was not sure, however, if the feeling was mutual.

"Damn," Officer Davis retorted, "we can't book him for murder, we can't get him for being on drugs, what do we have to do?"

Detective Oakley answered without looking at him, keeping her eyes glued to the interrogation. "We have to be patient."

He gave a quick nod and looked at the screen. "Oh, he's going to do it again, just watch." He leaned even closer to the monitor. "Wait for it . . . wait for it. . . ."

On the video monitor, the Reynolds suspect widened his eyes the size of Mars and ran his fingers through his hair.

Officer Davis burst again into laughter. "There it is! What the hell is *that* about? He has *no* idea how funny that looks."

Detective Oakley was not amused. She gave him a look of disapproval. "Be quiet, Davis. He's only in the next room. He can probably hear you."

Officer Davis apologized as they both watched the Reynolds suspect stand up and leave the room, bumping into the doorway as he passed it.

Soon after, the telephone rang. It was Sergeant Pederson.

Detective Oakley answered the phone in speaker mode. "Hi, Sarge. What do you make of him?"

"It's hard to say at this point. It seems like a slam dunk, but you just never know. I think we should get a tail on him as soon as we can. Davis will have to join you because my other surveillance guy is out sick."

Officer Davis chimed in, "Copy that, Sarge."

"Do you have the Tahoe ready to go?" Sergeant Pederson

asked.

"Uh," Officer Davis said, "I sent the interns out to wash it. It should be back in twenty minutes. Half hour at the most . . . and I need to gas it up. Shouldn't be long."

The sergeant's voice growled through the intercom. "You've got to be shitting me!"

Detective Oakley shook her head.

C

The city of Tempe provided the Orbit bus system as free transportation. There were five Orbit routes: Mercury, Venus, Earth, Mars, and Jupiter. The Mercury provided stops at the police department as well as Eighth Street, near the Nantucket Apartments. It would not take him long to return home.

He sat in the very back of the bus, avoiding any communication. Brennen could think of nothing else but the very serious legal troubles he was now facing. The look on Sergeant Pederson's face was impactful enough to keep his throat tight. The cops weren't messing around. On a case with few leads, he was a lead suspect. Of *course* he was. He'd written the victim's mother a cryptic email, for Christ's sake. He'd jumped head first into the shallow waters of a homicide investigation.

He cursed himself, *What the hell were you thinking, Brennen?* Though the cops were still in the dark and without proof, Brennen was still without an alibi. Thanks to his stupid dream, he knew details of the case. This would prove very difficult to explain in a court of law. Though he was down to his last couple hundred bucks, he needed some legal advice from anybody.

For the second time in as many days, Brennen thought of his old friend Scott, and wondered how long it had been since they'd spoken. He ran the months through his head while The Glow battled against his calculations. To his best recollection, it had been just over two years since Scott, at the expense of his family, checked into rehab, pulled his life together, and gotten accepted to the Sandra Day O'Connor School of Law at Arizona State University. His original goal had been achieving an MBA at the business school. His grades were good enough and his future—until Brennen started using with Draya—had been bright.

Unlike Brennen, however, Scott was able to overcome The Glow's pull after a year of abuse. To Brennen's understanding, Scott changed his ambitions from business to law during his stay in rehab, citing that his talents would better be suited for that field. For that, Brennen was proud beyond measure, but could only observe from afar. Scott's father, a second dad to Brennen in many respects, had contacted Brennen only once after Scott's overdose to inform him that he was not welcome in Scott's life again. The conversation was hazy in Brennen's mind, but he thought he heard the word "junkie" once or twice.

Disappointing his own family was a level of lowness to which Brennen was uncomfortable with as it was, but disappointing someone else's was lower still.

Brennen had thought about contacting Scott many times over the past years, if only to attempt an apology or to at least open a dialogue. He even went as far as to find Scott's address, but never could muster the nerve to execute a visit. Scott, of all people, would pick out the signs of Glow in a heartbeat. How would Brennen explain bringing his friend within reach of the very substance from which he worked so hard to break free? It was a very real possibility Scott would reject him on the spot.

On the other hand, he might be receptive to such a visit and would be willing to try to repair the friendship that had lasted close to a decade. Regardless, each go-round with the thought ended the same way. He would do it later, when he was done with The Glow, or at least when he was much less high.

The Mercury's breaks whined as it came to a halt at Brennen's stop. He walked down Eighth Street with his head low to avoid any eye contact. He scanned the trees in front of him, weary of any curious birds. There were some, but none seemed interested in landing on him.

He saw a group of girls walking into the Brewery across from his apartment, one of whom had auburn hair. It reminded him of Beth. He wondered why her face had been posted in the police station. Who was Betty Perkins? He wondered how she was holding up at his apartment, if she had decided to stay there at all. What was going through her mind right now? She had been followed by some crazies from her home town, subjected to a car chase, and now the person whom she appeared to entrust with her safety was hauled off for questioning in a murder case. If he'd been her, he would have skipped out.

His mood lifted when he saw Dante's beat-up Neon sitting in the parking lot. But as excited as he was, he was just as curious as to how he got in his apartment and why he'd be here instead of out making his rounds. He was surprised to find Dante leaning on the kitchen counter, humoring a much gigglier version of Beth Perkins than he'd witnessed before.

They both looked at Brennen as he came through the door.

"What the hell *happened*, bro?" Dante asked. He approached and gave Brennen a handshake and a pat on the back. "Beth said the cops came?"

Brennen examined each of their eyes, but as far as he could tell, was not receiving any extrasensory information. He responded, "I think I'm in a lot of trouble, man."

Without thinking about the logic behind any of it, Brennen explained to the both of them about his dream. They listened as he explained everything: the girl, the train, her expression, her message, the stupid email he wrote the mom, and the subsequent visit from the Tempe police.

"So," Brennen continued, "because I thought it might help the family, I wrote the email." Brennen threw his hands up, shaking his head. "And now, because of the details on Triana's clothes, I'm a suspect."

Dante leaned back on the counter, rubbing his chin. His frown smacked of disbelief, as though he were near suggesting Brennen was not so much reading thoughts, but just high as a kite. However, if he thought it, he didn't mention it, at least not in front of Beth. Brennen was confident Dante had not disclosed to Beth the nature of their business transactions.

"What about that magazine kid?" Beth asked. "It was like you were reading his thoughts, *both* of our thoughts." She glanced to Dante and hesitated, as if embarrassed. "Are you some kind of prophet?"

"What?" Brennen screeched. "That is total bullshit. Let's not go down that road. I understand your community is God-heavy, but let's not jump to any conclusions. I have no idea what that was about. I can't explain any of it." He fumbled for his tobacco pouch in his pocket, grabbed the cigarette maker from the kitchen counter and rolled a smoke.

Neither Beth nor Dante were able to breach the silence until Brennen spoke again.

"I also can't explain how you guys know each other's names like you're old friends. Dante, I know you're a busy guy with other places to be. How long have you been here?"

Dante checked his phone. "About two hours. We haven't had a chance to tell you because of your busy afternoon, but we had a little run-in with Beth's buddies."

Brennen inhaled his cigarette, blowing each drag out of the side of his mouth. It was his turn to listen in shock as Dante explained the encounter with Larry Hitchcock and Chris Hanner.

Brennen's face contorted with lingering questions. "Well, how the hell did they know she was here? I parked the Escalade up the street. They couldn't trace it back to me if they tried. How is that possible?" To Beth, Brennen asked, "Do you have any jewelry or anything on you they could track?"

"No. We don't believe in jewelry. It's against God's work. All I have is this plastic hairclip to keep my hair up." She pointed to her head.

Dante scratched a tribal-style tattoo on his neck. "I don't know, man, but it's obvious they know she's here and they'll probably be back. I never thought I'd say this, but she might be better off with the cops."

"No good. I saw her picture up at the station."

Beth looked at Brennen with dread.

"Yeah," Brennen continued, "there was a picture of Beth wearing a similar dress. It said you were wanted by the Paiute Rock City Police. Something about the murder of Betty somebody?"

Beth's dread morphed into terror as she repeated the name. "Oh, my God. Betty." She looked at Dante and Brennen. "They killed Betty."

"Who's Betty?" Dante asked.

"Jacob's wife," Beth said.

"I thought *you* were Jacob's wife?"

Beth put her head down.

Dante and Brennen looked at each other, both picking up on the implication. Dante made a wincing face and clenched his jaw while Brennen scratched his head and stood on his tiptoes for a moment before snuffing his cigarette butt in the ashtray. Their demeanor softened somewhat.

"It doesn't matter," Brennen said.

"*Who* killed Betty?" Dante asked.

"Jacob and his men. They found out she gave me the key to the mail truck and they killed her." She put her hands in her face and began repeating, "Oh God, oh God, oh God."

"Your husband would kill her," Dante asked, "for *that?*"

"You have no idea what Jacob is capable of," she said. "He sent guys all the way here to break into Brennen's apartment, didn't he?"

Dante nodded.

"Besides," Beth said, "if he blames it on me, he'll get the

whole community against me. And once they all give the same story, they'll call the cops. The state will come after me and I'll *have* to go home."

"What about the cops up there?" Brennen asked. "Do they know what an animal Jacob is?"

"They all know The Prophet Jacob. The cops will take his word for it. Not to mention Jacob can ask anyone in the community to say they were a witness . . . and they will." Beth shifted in her seat, uncomfortable with the subject. "Jacob killed his own cousin, for God's sake. It was in front of five people. The Paiute Rock City police called it a suicide because none of them would tell on the prophet."

Brennen believed her story. Perhaps he was a sucker, but he had seen, first-hand, the lengths this man would go to capture this girl. He was powerful enough to talk grown men into committing crimes such as kidnapping and now breaking and entering.

He stared for a while, looking at Beth and Dante. "Okay, Beth. Let's assume Jacob is the Charles Manson-type. Why does he want you back so bad? He's got other wives, obviously."

Beth shot him a scowl, still uncomfortable with the talk of plural marriage. "Because I can't have *children!*" she shouted. "There. I said it. I just got tested and I am barren, and women who cannot do the work of God must be sacrificed back *to* him! If Jacob doesn't get his sacrifice, God will send the Othersiders, destroying our way of life!" She returned her head to her hands for a moment, after which time she continued in a quivering voice. "I shouldn't have left."

"Jesus Christ," Brennen said. He corrected himself after

Dante shot him a look of disapproval. "I mean, holy shit. Dante, can I see you outside for just a second?"

Taking the cue, the two men went outside around the corner of the Nantucket sign, out of Beth's ear-shot.

"I'm thinking of taking her to Scott's pad," Brennen said.

"That's *right.* He's a big shot law student guy now. Good for him." He shifted his weight. "You haven't heard from him forever, huh?"

"No, not at all. As far as I know, he and his family think I'm a scumbag." He breathed in, not wanting to offend Dante's profession. "And that makes me pretty nervous. But Scott was always a smart guy. He's been in law school for at least two years. Even if he doesn't know what to do, maybe he knows somebody who does."

"That's true."

"It's not like I have any cash to pay a lawyer for legal advice anyway, and God knows, I need legal advice. Apparently, so does Beth." Brennen ran his fingers through his hair. The flames were getting nearer. "I just don't see any other options."

"Yeah," Dante agreed.

"Oh! And speaking of cash." Brennen dug through his pockets to a pack of cigarettes. He opened it and produced two empty cigarette tubes. One contained a carefully rolled one hundred dollar bill, while the other contained a twenty. It was a perfect guise for public money exchange.

In return, Dante produced a deflated tennis ball from the cargo pocket of his shorts and handed it to Brennen. From within a small slit, Brennen could see the eight ball peering back at him.

“And bro, I don’t know how those guys found her. They must have tailed you all the way home from the desert and waited for six hours before showing up.”

“That just doesn’t make any sense.”

“Either way, they found your pad. I would suggest getting her out of here. Just let me know whatever address you’re at next time you need something and I’ll meet you there. Let’s let this place cool down,”

Brennen nodded.

“And what the hell are Othersiders?”

Brennen motioned everywhere around him. “We are.”

9
October 29: Afternoon

A

For the most part, Mr. Bratch loved being a Philadelphia cop, until the urges forced him to leave.

He even loved some of the training necessary to become a cop. He didn't appreciate the drill sergeants' yelling when he was a young police academy cadet back in the early 80s, all that obsessive-compulsive focusing on the length of his hair or the exact time he was to report to this or that, but he did love the field trips to the county morgue where he was allowed to take notes during the autopsies. He remembered doing everything he could to keep from laughing at the dead bodies. There was one instance when he let a laugh slip. When he saw his fellow cadets looking at him, he had to pretend that he was gagging, that the sight was just too much for him. It was better than being psychoanalyzed and kicked out of the academy for laughing at a corpse.

From then on, he got a reputation for being somewhat weak-stomached. He wasn't a pushover by any means, but the guys would tease him every once in a while. Mr. Bratch was fine with that. He used it to his advantage. Being deemed a weakling was the perfect cover for his off-duty behavior. In fact, if it hadn't been for his best friend and partner, no one would have ever suspected him capable of the things he did.

He remembered the moment he was sworn into the force.

I do solemnly swear to uphold the Constitution of the United States of America, the laws of the Commonwealth of Pennsylvania, and the laws and all directions of the city of Philadelphia so help me, God.

Ha!

He didn't uphold the Constitution, but he did end up working for a prophet, so the God part, at least, was accurate.

His first assignment was the Fishtown neighborhood of Philadelphia, in the famous Twenty-Sixth District. Encompassing East Kensington, parts of West Kensington, and North Philly, the district could turn into a multi-cultural war zone at times. With no one willing to trust another, it was great exposure for Mr. Bratch to explore the extent of the power his badge held. A shakedown here, some intimidation there, it was a perfect playground for him, the weakling cop, to be a bully. It was all straight under the noses of his do-gooder fellow officers on the streets. He much preferred those curvy, unpredictable streets to the straight desert highway he now raced down.

Mr. Bratch had not been to Phoenix or the surrounding cities for ten years. Now, on direct orders from the prophet himself, he found himself speeding toward Tempe to fix the botched retrieval job. Twice he had sent trusted men to apprehend Beth Perkins and twice they'd failed. The first men assigned to Beth's capture damaged their truck in a ravine. Now, Larry and Chris, reliable men, were nursing broken bones inflicted upon them by one man.

Chris sounded hysterical on his mobile phone, describing the assailant as "a crazy giant with blond hair." He had pulled a gun from his car to intimidate them. It worked, as did smashing their bones. At least Larry had the good sense to write down the thug's license plate number. If he wasn't able to track Beth down with the GPS, the license plate might be useful when run through the Arizona Department of Transportation system.

According to the tracker, Beth was still in Tempe.

Mr. Bratch was going to handle this on his own, this time. He should have gone earlier, but he had become overconfident in the ability of his men to get the job done. Now, with excommunication looming, he would have to go near Phoenix, the biggest cesspool of Othersiders Arizona had to offer. He could see the warning in the dead-eyed stare of the prophet as he threatened to send Mr. Bratch away. This could not happen. This would not happen. His past was out there waiting for him to resurface, just waiting for those damned FBI files to pop up. He must succeed this time, or there would be no reason to return.

He pressed the accelerator down, closing the gap between himself and Tempe with every second.

B

Not long after Dante left, Brennen hurried around his apartment, gathering a change of clothes (and against his better judgment, The Glow), and drove Beth and Snippety to the Sun Devil Auto Wash on McClintock Drive in Tempe. It was a do-it-yourself car wash with several large working bays, allowing serious car owners an inexpensive way to keep their vehicles in showcase-condition without the inevitable paint scratching caused by the sloppy automatic machines. A little tender loving care and a clean microfiber rag could go a long way. The Escalade seemed to enjoy it. Aside from a missing window, the SUV emerged from its bath in acceptable condition. Even the impact scratch on the back bumper was more superficial than Brennen assumed and was buffed out after some effort.

Brennen labored with one eye over his back. Having no idea what a tracking device would look like, he checked the underside of the vehicle for anything out of the ordinary. There was nothing. Besides, the men never bothered with the Escalade. They went straight to his apartment. Dante was right. He and Beth had to have been followed. That was all there was to it. If they had, they could be following him now. He would have to be extra cautious while driving today and take back roads.

While buffing the hood, Brennen looked at Beth in the passenger seat, baby-talking to Snippety. She was cradling her, exposing the cat's white belly. Though he was concerned the cat might make a bathroom of the back seat, he was glad they brought her along. After Beth had explained the aggressive behavior the men demonstrated toward the cat, Brennen wasn't going to take any chances by leaving her behind. Twice Snippety had tried to prevent him from making poor decisions and both times he hadn't listened In the excitement, he had not had time to consider just how extraordinary she was or how she became that way.

At the thought, his mind flashed to the pit bull rushing at him, only to lie at his feet while the birds fought for space on his head and shoulders. Animals seemed to like him when he was high. People, not so much.

He would soon need to refuel on Glow.

Snippety escaped from Beth's clutches and began exploring the back seat of the vehicle. Brennen watched as Beth smiled. It was clear the cat made the circumstances easier for Beth to handle. There she was, lost in a world of Othersiders, and smiling. Without Snippety to take her mind off things, Brennen might have been dealing with a different girl. The sensible thing, Brennen knew, was to drop her off at a shelter like they'd planned, but with her name posted all over the Tempe Police Department, the shelters would be the first place the law would look. She'd stand out with that dress like a campfire in the middle of the woods, landing her straight back to her crazy husband up north. In good conscience, he couldn't send her to the wolves like that, unless she wanted to go. After several chances to change her mind, she chose to stay.

"All right, then," Brennen said, "it's settled. But we are going to have to do a little shopping first."

"For what?"

"Some clothes for you. We need to ditch that dress." He fired up the engine and caught Snippety's glare in the rearview mirror. "And *you* need a toilet."

Snippety gave him a look of interest.

"No pooping on the leather."

10
In A Dark Space

The man in the mannequin mask stared at the screen. It was the only light by which the small space was lit. The mask was pushed up onto his forehead, making it difficult to tell where the mask started and the man ended. The LED screen revealed a stubble-laden goatee as he lifted his head to scratch it. As he lowered his head to type, the mask again regained his personality, dead-panned with an expressionless mouth.

His knee bounced as he typed search queries into YouTube, looking for potential false prophets and faith healers residing in the Southwest area. He'd need a new face to visit soon, as the one strapped in the gurney behind him would, in all likelihood, soon be gone.

From behind him, there was an impactful thud and the sound of a man's voice moaning through a gag.

Someone had just awoken.

"Shut up," the mannequin said. His voice sounded flat and annoyed. "If you want out of here, then go ahead and miracle your ass out the door."

The man in the mask searched a few more titles on YouTube before addressing his victim again. "Oh, you're still here. No miracle, eh? Now that is interesting, isn't it?"

11
October 29: Afternoon

A

Before shopping, Brennen took a precautionary drive to the Salt River Native American reservation, about fifteen miles north of Tempe. Here, from the side of Highway 87, he could see several miles in each direction. From this vantage point, it would be easy to tell if they were being followed. With no building or housing developments to be seen, or cars to use as cover, someone intent on tailing him would have to stop at some point. Any such move would be obvious.

After a while, feeling satisfied that they were not being tailed, they drove to the Tempe Marketplace, a million-square-foot interactive dining and shopping center. Located on Loop 101 and 202, it was within reasonable distance of Phoenix, Scottsdale, Chandler, Gilbert, and Mesa, making it a busy shopping destination, day and night.

This day, the credit card gods were on Brennen's side, as the PetSmart employee rang up a kitty litter box, litter, Science Diet cat kibble, a poop scoop, plastic disposable bags, a cat brush and three catnip-enhanced cloth mice.

He had similar luck at Ross, where he let Beth pick out a bra and underwear, and then onto Buffalo Exchange on University Drive in downtown Tempe. It was a popular used clothing store that Arizona State students used as often as Facebook. Every semester, students would sell their seldom-worn designer clothing in order to make their student loans last longer, only to turn around and buy more clothes at their next loan distribution. Brennen had no doubt he could find a chameleonic outfit here that would blend Beth deep into pop culture, leaving no trace of the community from which she was escaping.

It worked.

By the time she was done, there was no difference between Beth and the forty-thousand other girls infusing the campus with the next generation of clothing trends.

As far as Brennen knew, a form-fitting V-neck tee-shirt, snug-fitting jeans, and Chuck Taylor Converse shoes would be perfect for any foreseeable occasion.

She emerged from the dressing room with a sulky demeanor, like a dog returning to its master after having an accident on the bedroom floor. "Oh, my God," she said, "I can't wear this. It's too tight and I look ridiculous."

Brennen laughed. He couldn't believe his eyes. The dress she had been wearing covered everything but her face, neck and hands. Now, in modern clothes, she looked stunning.

"Are you laughing at me?" she asked.

"No, no," he said. "I just can't . . . I just can't *believe* it. You look *great.*"

Beth was unconvinced. Her face had an expression that said she'd just been thrown in a pool.

"Beth, I'm serious. You look—and don't take this the wrong way—you look like an Othersider." He put his hands up before she could a form a rebuttal. "And that's what we *want*, right? You need to blend in." He looked around to make sure no one was picking up on their conversation. He ran his fingers through his hair. "You totally blend in."

She pressed her lips together and frowned. "Okay. If you say so."

"Yes, I say so!" he almost shouted. "Just wear it out of the store. I'll pay for it at the front of the store."

On the way up to the register, Brennen grabbed a package of black nylon hair ties.

Beth pointed at them. "What are those for?"

"Oh, they're for, uh"—he made the motion of pulling his hair back, then he pointed at the large, red wave in her hair—"you know, we just gotta, uh, clean that up."

Beth patted her head in defense.

Brennen handed the girl at the counter the price tags for all the clothes Beth was wearing and explained that she would be wearing them out of the store. The girl agreed with the purchase and reassured Beth of her decision.

The cash register beeped.

APPROVED

Brennen gave thanks that the card wasn't declined as it sometimes was. He'd pay the minimum soon.

They were glad, but not surprised, to see that Snippety had stayed in the vehicle during their absence, and was peering at them through the open window when they returned.

During his shopping spree, Brennen had been so wrapped up in the good feeling of helping the girl, a joy previously obtained only by songwriting, he lost track of how tired he had become and how close to the flames he was being lowered. He could feel the sickness of sleep threatening to overtake his senses. What if he passed out here? Should

The Glow run too low, there was very little he could do to stop it. He was at twenty percent, fading fast and in desperate need of a hit. Using in public restrooms was unwise. Someone would call the cops the moment the spark hit the bowl. He was ten minutes from seeing Scott again for the first time in two years and couldn't imagine the humiliation he would suffer if he passed out at his apartment.

With the car doors shut, Brennen deduced in seconds that Snippety had indeed used her toilet to defecate. The stench soon wafted to Beth, who was busy battling her hair back into one of the hair ties. Her nose crinkled in disgust as she looked over at Brennen.

This was Brennen's chance. If he excused himself to scoop the poop, there would be no suspicion on her part. As it happened, Buffalo Exchange backed up into a secluded area covered by dense ground cover and queen palms. If he was quick about it, he might be able to catch a few moments of privacy while he scooped the litter and lit up.

"Damn, Snippy," Brennen said. "Excuse me real quick. I'm just going to go behind this building and scoop the poop. When you gotta go, you gotta go, I guess."

Snippety looked at him with something akin to pride.

With that, Brennen absconded around the corner with the soiled kitty box. For the first time in his life, and at the risk of everything, he stepped back into the Glow behind a public building.

B

Scott Barrett kept himself busy while waiting for his package to arrive. The squeaking sound of microfiber buffing Windex into the mirror reverberated throughout the bathroom.

The towels had been hung with meticulous care on the shower rack, each the exact shape as the other. The toilet had been buffed clean enough to see his reflection in the porcelain and the linoleum was as spotless as any rental unit could be. All chores in the bathroom were nearing completion, except for the damn purple paint stain on the mirror which had become an indescribable annoyance in the year Scott Barrett had occupied his apartment. There was little that could be done, he knew, about the negligence of previous tenants, but the lack of control over the circumstances was frustrating and he had to try once again to fix it.

Unsatisfied with the progress, he reapplied the Windex and commenced scraping the spot with a straight razor. The mere handling of the precision blade made his nerves resonate at a higher frequency. It wasn't the ease by which razors sliced into flesh, it was the year he spent cutting lines of Glow to blow his mind and disassociate from the world. Even now, the scraping noise of the paper-thin blade conjured images of Draya Harris, his former high school acquaintance—and girlfriend of Brennen Reynolds—cutting his first line and presenting it on a mirrored plate.

Brennen Reynolds.

The mere thought of his name made Scott cringe, but he thought of it often and against his will. The two of them shared a decade of life; inseparable friends since their early days in high school. They bore witness to each other's self-discovery, laughed at each other's awkward encounters with the opposite sex, obtained their driver's license at the same time and learned to drive in Mrs. Reynolds' minivan they referred to as "The Party Bus." The term soon transformed from a form of transportation to a state of mind. If everything was good, it was described as "all party bus."

Their language contained many such inside jokes, so much that others either had to join their world to follow the punch lines or be left outside scratching their heads.

To Scott, the friendship itself was on par with a supernatural event, for he had never been close to anyone until he ended up in Arizona. His family had moved around quite a bit when he was young and making acquaintances was awkward. He was a shy kid and did not possess the social skills to bond with any kind of consistency with others. It took great effort. With Brennen, however, there was no effort at all. The minute Brennen sat down next to Scott on the first congregation of the high school band, they hit it off. Within weeks neither could seem to remember life without the other. They collaborated with their guidance counselors to assure they were in the same classes and helped each other with their homework. The pressure of high school life would have been much harder had their friendship not been there to pad the pitfalls.

It was a good friendship, until, of course, it ended.

Scott's father, Remy Barrett, was an accomplished and distinguished man. One of the first African American quarterbacks at the University of Wisconsin, he later graduated summa cum laude from Stanford Law School and sat as a judge in the Scottsdale City Court. He was intimidating, even at fifty-nine, and demanded much of Scott. It was no surprise, then, when he demanded answers after

Remy Barrett kicked in Scott's apartment door after three days of non-communication and found Scott unconscious in the bathtub with a Glow pipe wedged between his fingers. Horrified by his son's account of Brennen and Scott's year of debauchery, he called Brennen on the phone only two more times: once to explain that Scott was in the hospital and once to extricate Brennen from Scott's life. The exact details of the conversation were never fully disclosed to Scott.

Now, even after successful rehabbing, after being accepted to Arizona State Law School and well into his second year, his father's trust was still obliterated. No matter what path to redemption Scott attempted, be it taking out his own loans to pay for tuition or volunteering his spare time to help troubled teens, he was still being watched, doubted, and judged by his father . . . always *judged.*

Scott would remind his father of his more redeeming qualities with the excitement of a puppy, only to be met with patronizing reminders of the past with a patent brand of pooh-poohing only Remy Barrett could administer. The conversations were always cued up in his mind.

Hey, Dad, I got a three-point-eight GPA this semester.

That's two points shy of a four-point-zero, Scott.

Hey, Dad, I got a four-point-zero this semester.

Mine was higher, Scott.

Hey, Dad, I've been in school for two years.

Two years is the easy part, Scott. Now you need to pick a concentration.

It was true. He did need to choose which area of law in which to specialize, and sooner than later. Because of his love for music, at least when music, in his opinion, was *good,* he had been considering the field of Intellectual Property. Copyright laws and music publishing rights fascinated him. He had witnessed Brennen attempting, and failing, to write songs and had always wondered what would happen were he to catch the eye of music publishers. Yet, with his disappointment with the current state of music styles, he was cautious to enter "the music biz" at this point. Alternative music had become stale, metal was obsolete, and pop music was the most creative force music had to offer. There was a time when he was young when homogenized, sanitized, put-in-a-digital-box and upload it at 120 beats/minute was fun. After all, he'd loved acts like Rappin' Duke and The Fat Boys at one point. But after years of developing his musical taste, he no longer fell for gimmicky production tricks applied to faceless music with zero reliability.

He realized he had stopped scraping the razor on the mirror and was now staring into space. His Philadelphia Eagles tee-shirt was beginning to develop sweat pools at his chest. Though he had several Eagles shirt, this one, gray with green block lettering, did the best job at hiding his small gut that had been an unfortunate byproduct of sobriety. Instead of blowing cloud puffs of Glow, he now pounded chocolate-covered almonds like they were going out of style. Instead of spinning his mind out and listening to music, he studied law. When he wasn't studying, he was eating . . . and cleaning.

His love life had been on hold since his hospital stay, not that it was wonderful beforehand. He had a history of short-term, passionate relationships with girls afflicted by jaded pasts and tortured souls, inappropriately deemed "red-headed rescues" by Draya.

His ex-girlfriend Rachel, a drug addict in her own right, left him after the bathtub incident. There was little he missed about her, except her red hair. His latest girlfriend, also with red hair, had accused him of cheating on her time after time. It was a daily event, like rolling surf onto a beach, that exhausted him to the point of madness and he had to let her go. The break-up hadn't been as epic as Brennen and Draya's, but it was enough to keep him indoors.

That was it and there he was: He was a boring, study-and-clean kind of guy. When he would admit to himself he was lonely, he would hit the books harder and clean longer, just as he was now.

He buffed the mirror again, but the purple paint remained. Frustrated, he placed the straight razor on the side of the sink and decided to seek out his Philadelphia Eagles Nerf football. In times of frustration or intense exam preparation, Scott squeezed the football for relief, throwing it a few feet in the air, each time attempting a better spiral than the last. He found it in the kitchen, by the refrigerator, and began squeezing it while checking in the pantry for almonds.

It was almost four o'clock and FedEx had promised his package by three-thirty. He'd ordered a copy of Carl Sagan's book, *The Demon Haunted World,* for some leisure reading. While browsing Netflix, he had re-discovered Sagan's 1980s series, *Cosmos*. It was ironic; the very series that fascinated him as a child now reignited his curiosity of the universe. While Sagan's astute mix of stoicism and nerdiness was a source of ridicule back then, he now hung on the scientist's every word with the deepest respect and adoration. He was saddened by Sagan's early passing and became somewhat of a groupie, collecting Sagan memorabilia when he could. He came across a signed copy of the book on Craigslist. Even on the very limited funds allowed by his loans, he splurged for it. To him, it was a pleasant break in law studies to hear Sagan's historical account of the battle between science and religion. It was a guilty pleasure.

The almonds were running low. He debated whether to save them for later or eat them all now.

"Why not?" he asked himself. "It's all party bus here."

He poured several almonds into his mouth.

He heard kids laughing outside and turned his head in that direction. He always turned his head. He could never get used to his apartment's position to the pool area. He was on the second floor, overlooking it. The noises didn't bother him, there was nothing wrong with some kids having some fun, but sometimes the sudden shrill of children would catch his nerves off guard. In those moments, Scott imagined an infant being kidnapped or an accidental drowning happening. He would always creep to the window just in case he was right, which he never was. To this day, he had never witnessed anything alarming happen, except perhaps a poolside game of duck-duck-goose gone awry.

As he peeked out of the curtains now it was the same: children playing in the pool area set against a dirt field with sparse patches of desert brush.

Bam bam bam bam.

At first, Scott was startled. A knock on the door was a rare occurrence in his tiny one-bedroom apartment. Aside from a local auto shop representative or annoying magazine salesmen, his doorway was a desolate place. It was, in all likelihood, FedEx come to deliver the book at last.

He set the almonds on a table by the window and hustled to the door, wiping his hands and doing his best to speed up chewing his food. He looked through the peephole, a habit formed since hanging out at Brennen's, and was puzzled by what he saw. Instead of a FedEx employee waiting patiently at the door, it was a girl with red hair carrying some sort of case and a nervous-acting guy to her right brushing from his shoulder what appeared to be . . . birds.

Scott opened the door.

Words escaped him. Memories rushed him. Curiosity froze him. He stood, zombie-blank, in the doorway with his head tilted. There were several issues happening and he was not prepared for any of them. There were sparrows sitting on this guy's shoulders, going about their day in a casual manner.

They all stared cockeyed back at him as if to say, "*What? We're birds. We're birds and we're sitting on this guy's shoulders. What* of *it, asshole?*"

Scott looked at the girl. She was the best-looking girl he'd seen in a long time. Straight out of a magazine and complete with a beauty mark on her upper lip, she kept his voice from formulating words. She looked at him shyly, as if she were uncomfortable in her clothes, and turned her gaze to the crate. It was a pet-carrying case which harbored a pet—a cat, in fact.

"Reer!" said the cat.

Though in reality this information took no more than a few moments to process, he felt like a contestant on the game show *Jeopardy*, slack-jawed and well into the famous musical jingle played when a contestant is clueless. The object of *Jeopardy* was to deduce the question from the answer. He imagined the conversation with the show's host, Alex Trebek, as he struggled with the answers.

They are small little wonders, Mr. Trebek said, *with feathers and beaks.*

What are birds, Alex.

Very good, Mr. Trebek said, *Next question: She is amazing. Never seen a smile like that in your life.*

Who is the girl in front of me, Alex.

Great. Now for the daily-double. He screwed you over. He didn't care that you overdosed and hasn't made an effort to talk to you since.

What is Brennen Reynolds, Alex.

Ding. Ding. Ding.

It was simple. He was an asshole, and had a lot of nerve showing up here.

Scott only managed a squeaking noise from his throat. He was never good at Jeopardy.

"Hey, Scott," Brennen said, "is it cool if we come in for a second?"

Scott was disturbed at how sickly Brennen looked. He was pale-green and at least twenty pounds underweight. He wanted to send him on his way, but his mouth betrayed him. "Um, I guess *(of course it isn't cool. It's absolutely un-cool to even suggest it).*"

Brennen waved the birds away from the front door and stepped inside. His actions were jerky and unpredictable. He ushered the girl through the door and shut it behind both of them. It slammed louder than expected.

"What am I saying?" Brennen said. "Of *course* it's not cool. It's probably un-cool even to suggest it. I have a lot of nerve."

Scott scowled at Brennen and said, "Dude. You can't just— *(come into my apartment and act like nothing is wrong; I haven't seen you in over two years and you just show up with a girl and a cat.)"*

"Listen, man," Brennen said, "I am not just coming into your apartment and acting like nothing is wrong. There is a *lot* wrong. Please, just try to listen. I know it's been over two years and I *know* it's weird that I have a girl and a cat with me. This will sound crazy, but we need your help, and haven't got anywhere else to go."

Scott watched as Brennen's enlarged pupil's moved with erratic cadence from side to side. *How dare you show up here, high on Glow, asking for help?* he thought. The gaunt look of Brennen reminded Scott of how he, himself, had looked in the hospital mirror the night of his overdose. He could still hear the buzz of the fluorescent lights as the staff worked on him. *Where were you, then?*

To Scott's surprise, Brennen seemed to comprehend. "Scott. You are right. I am high right now, and this won't work any other way than to just have this out right now. I owe you an apology." Brennen's voice tightened. "For everything. It was me, my stupid ego, and fear." He ran his fingers through his hair. "Two things should have happened when Draya cut my first line. Either I should have broken it off with her, or stopped hanging out with you so we wouldn't influence you. I did neither because I was disrespectful and weak. I was in love with her, you were my best friend, and I wanted both and I was just too *weak* to do what I needed to do."

Scott's scowl turned to a frown and his eyes turned mean. His chin began to quiver. "Hey, man. I think you had better *leave*."

"And the hospital thing," Brennen continued. "I couldn't face you or your dad, man. I felt responsible. I thought you were going to die and I felt *responsible*." Now it was Brennen's chin that began to spasm. "I know you still hear the buzzing of those hospital lights. I've thought of you in that hospital every day. Scott, I am so sorry, man."

Scott was off-kilter and somewhat neutralized as Brennen seemed to be plucking every angry thought out of his mind and addressing it before he could voice it. He shook his head, keeping eye contact with his nemesis. *And when I finally visited you, straight out of rehab, you offered me a bowl of Glow.*

Brennen broke from Scott's eyes and grabbed his temples as if hit by a blunt object. "I know! I offered the bowl. You'd just worked your ass off to get better, and the first thing I did is offer you Glow. You see, in my mind, I thought I was being *polite*. I assumed you would want it and I didn't want to get high in front of you. *Total* dipshit move." Shaking, he locked eyes with Scott. "I am so sorry, Scott. I've been waiting two years to say that, and if you kick us straight out now, it will have been worth it."

Scott stared at Brennen, now very aware that he had somehow entered his head and was mining his thoughts at the same rate he was thinking them. Looking at Brennen, in poor health and on the ropes, part of him wanted to shove his ass out the door, but another part wanted to switch the subject to something they could laugh at. Like the old days, maybe he could just blurt out one of their inside jokes just to see what would happen. Brennen had apologized and there was no questioning his sincerity. This was, after all, his best friend of almost a decade. Regardless, this guy was a bad influence and an addict. Dangerous. From what Scott could tell, he had gotten much worse. So much that he actually *looked* like a later-stage drug user.

"*Do* I?" Brennen asked.

Scott had had enough. "Okay, what the hell, man? What is this reading my mind shit?"

"Please," Brennen said. He looked disoriented. "You have to speak slower. The words get jumbled up in my head." He raised his index finger to pause any response. "To answer your question, I don't know what is going on. That's part of what I have to talk to you about. Please, just give us five minutes to explain. If you don't think you can help, you can kick our asses out the door."

Wiping away any unwanted tearlets, Scott said, "I can kick you out anyway." In his showdown with Brennen, Scott had forgotten about the girl and the cat. He looked at them both now. *Who the hell is this girl? A model? And what's with the cat?*

"That's Beth," Brennen said, "and that there is Snippety."

Beth waved with a gentle hand and Snippety made the high-five motion from within her case.

To Brennen, Scott said, "You've got four minutes."

At once, there was a pounding on the door.

C

I know what you did, Luigi said.

It was unexpected. His partner, Officer Luigi Ortiz, had spoken it in such a matter-of-fact tone that it was almost eerie. To what might he be referring? Mr. Bratch had done a lot of things, many of which were not one hundred percent legal. He'd withheld some information from his superiors regarding a group of squatters in 1985, just a few years on the force. They had occupied an abandoned house and chose to defend it with shotguns when officers attempted to reclaim the property. After a mass-scale shootout lasting an hour, the mayor, along with the police commissioner, employed an explosive device to remove the roof. Mr. Bratch, having previously dealt with the squatters earlier that month, had knowledge of several barrels of gasoline stored in the basement, but kept the information to himself. He wanted an explosion the likes of which Philadelphia had never seen, and he got one. When all was said and done, the resulting fire destroyed over sixty homes, leaving hundreds homeless. All told, there were eleven dead, including five children.

It was doubtful Luigi had come into possession of this knowledge, but Mr. Bratch's conscience was far from clear. He pursued other after-hours activities to which Luigi may have, despite great concealment efforts, become aware. Soon after the fire, Mr. Bratch had begun a habit of sneaking into the detective's office to study the un-cleared homicide cases in the city. He paid close attention, not to how the cases *could* be solved, but to why they were *not* solved. Between the lacking DNA evidence, mismatched fingerprinting and the uncertainty of forensics regarding the location and timing of certain murders, it was enough information to keep a succinct journal of how to kill someone without being caught, should someone be inclined.

Had Luigi seen him in the detective's office? Was this what he was referring to?

It must have been the prostitutes.

Luigi had shared Mr. Bratch's dark sense of humor. He had also shared his hatred of prostitutes. In fact, he had often joked about how much cleaner the world would be without them. When reports surfaced that a prostitute had been found in a lake or in a dumpster, he would howl like a wolf and smile like a child. By all logic, Luigi shouldn't have given two shits about Mr. Bratch's extracurricular activities concerning the prostitutes. In fact, Mr. Bratch had, on several occasions, considered bringing Luigi on board. Now, from the sound in his voice, he already knew something, if not everything.

I love you like a brother, Bratch, but I swear to Christ I will turn you in if I turn out to be right.

Mr. Bratch set the memory aside and looked at the GPS tracker. Beth had moved north on Highway 87 for a brief time and was now headed back to Tempe.

"Just stay right there, Beth. I'll be there soon."

D

Scott waited for Beth to emerge from the bathroom. She, fearing the knock on the door had been Jacob's men, had locked herself away for a few minutes. With a calming voice, Scott explained to her from the hallway that the intruder had been nothing more than a FedEx employee delivering a package.

After a few moments, his soothing demeanor had won her

over. She emerged with the timidity of a stray dog as she joined Scott and Brennen in the living room.

Scott listened as Brennen explained his situation with the police, ending with his new talent for reading minds. He sat across from him on a La-Z-Boy chair, leaning forward with his forearms resting on his knees. His hands were pressed together, prayer-like, with his fingers touching his chin intermittently. He had listened with care to each part, asking few questions. Only a few times did his face glaze over in disbelief.

He exhaled through expanded cheeks. “Do you know how crazy that sounds?”

“I do now, yes.”

“And you don’t have an alibi at all.”

“The murder was two years ago. How the hell would I remember what I was doing on that day?”

To Beth, Scott said, “And what about you, Beth? How did you get involved with this? Did Brennen dream about you as well?”

“She is a different story entirely,” Brennen said.

Scott rubbed his face in his hands. “There’s *more?*” He checked the clock on his phone: Twelve minutes had passed; he set it down with a surrendering look. “Go on, then.”

Scott listened as she explained how she was being pursued by her husband who she was certain meant her great harm. She rushed through it, using small words, although what she lacked in vocabulary she made up in her smile. She moved with grace, despite her shyness, and caught his eye with every gesture. Her eyes were emerald-green and penetrated him like spring sunshine when she found the courage to look his way—so much that he found it difficult to focus on her story. He was frazzled by her and could only hope she didn't notice.

"So Brennen said you may know about this kind of stuff," she said. "What do you think I should do?"

Scott gazed at her a moment longer. She was asking him a question and he needed to give her an answer.

He looked away and rubbed his hands together. If what she was saying was true, she would have the right to explain her side of the story in a court of law. On the other hand, she could be insane, a very hypnotizing insane person, who happened upon Brennen, the Glow-head, and was manipulating him to corroborate her story. Somehow, he doubted this was the case, just as much as he doubted she was telling him the whole truth.

The law was the best option.

"Well," Scott said, "I really think you should go to the police on this."

"No way," Beth said. "I'm not going to trust the government with my life."

Scott raised his eyebrows. She had a fire within her, that much was certain. Had another person said that at another time, it may have been concerning, but through Beth's lips, at that moment, it was somehow an acceptable part of her charm. It was obvious she was brought up not to trust the government. Hell, from what Scott had learned at law school, a little governmental distrust was sometimes *advisable*.

"She can't go the police," Brennen interjected. He explained the flyer at the police department.

Scott's jaw dropped. "So you are *both* murder suspects?"

He looked at Brennen. His old friend was sitting with an almost comical rigidness on the couch with his eyes threatening to pop out of his head. It was ridiculous. "I have some ideas for your situation, Brennen, but I will get into *that* later. Right now, the most intriguing part I find about Beth's story is how these guys keep finding her. First, they get pretty lucky by finding her on the side of the freeway to begin with, and at night no less." He rubbed his chin. "Now, after the chase, you say you parked the SUV up the street from your apartment when you two got home."

Beth and Brennen nodded.

"Yet they showed up to your apartment the next day. There was nothing leading the SUV back to your name. All they had to go on was your face."

Brennen leaned forward. "But Dante said the men who broke into my apartment thought Dante was the owner. They had no idea what I looked like. They only knew Beth was there."

"It's Jacob," Beth said. She began to tear up. "He talks to God, and God will always know where I am. He's going to show up here. I'm so sorry I involved both of you. I am so, so sorry."

"Stop apologizing," Brennen said. "No one forced us to help you."

Scott leaned over and put a hand on Beth's arm as a form of consolation. Her skin was smooth and flawless, angelic, or at least Scott's version of what an angel might feel like. If he wasn't so into science, he might have believed she *was* heaven sent.

12

October 29: Later that Afternoon. Closer.

A

The air was much warmer in the Valley of the Sun than the crisper temperatures of northern Arizona to which Mr. Bratch was accustomed. The added heat caused his polyester security guard uniform to itch at his inner thighs, forcing him to adjust his pant leg. The familiar feel of the garb reminded him that he was a cop, or at least was at one time. He loved being a cop. He was proud to be a cop, not so much for the power to protect people, but for the power he held *over* the people. The fear he could instill into them; *that* was the true reward. Now, with Beth within range, he couldn't wait for the opportunity to instill fear into her.

He loved the chase.

He'd watch late night nature programs when he'd lived in Philadelphia to pass the small hours of night. He was always amazed at how the different species of animals developed individual styles of hunting. He was thrilled to see the cheetah, the lone hunter, pursuing a gazelle across the Serengeti before shredding it to pieces, or the wolf pack, the collaborative killers, spending their precious energy giving chase to their evening's meal. His favorite, however, was the method employed by the Komodo dragon when hunting water buffalo. With their saliva acting as a slow-release poison, one bite was all that was needed. From then on, it was only a matter of following the water buffalo with disciplined patience, sometimes for days, before the victim would lie down in surrender. Resistance was minimal as it was eaten alive during the course of a lazy afternoon, half paralyzed and exhausted by the bite wound.

He thought of Beth Perkins, *his* water buffalo. Now threatened with ex-communication, he wanted nothing more than to see her squirm, and with Jacob's foolish APB out for her arrest, he was sure she was doing just that. By now, her picture had been plastered over every police station in the greater Phoenix area. Her resources, no doubt, had grown thin. In all likelihood, the only person helping her was the tattooed giant responsible for injuring Larry and Chris. He was also the man who would lead Mr. Bratch straight to Beth before the cops did. He would be dealt with soon enough. And Beth, kicking and screaming, would be headed home.

He glanced at the GPS. According to it, she had taken refuge near the Papago Park Apartments on Taylor Street in Phoenix, just north of Tempe.

Five minutes.

B

"All I am saying is that something is wrong here, Beth," Scott continued. "I know you believe that Jacob is using God to track you down, but there has to be something else at play here for those of us who—how should I put this?—don't have the relationship with God that you do."

"Well, I don't know how else they keep finding me. You said it yourself, they had no way of knowing, yet they knew exactly where I was."

"It sounds like you're being tracked," Scott said. "Do you

have any rings or jewelry that may have tracking capabilities?"

"No," Brennen answered. "I asked that earlier. All she had was a plastic hair clip and we ditched that at Buffalo Exchange."

Beth's fear began to spread throughout her face as she searched Scott's face for answers.

"You know," Scott said. "I read a case last semester where a hospital was sued for the use of under-the-skin identification chips, like surgical implants, but they were short-range. Not like GPS or anything."

"Well, what are you saying, then?" Brennen asked.

"Do you have any scars of any kind, Beth?" Scott scanned up and down her arms.

"None," she said.

Brennen sprang forward like a jack-in-the-box. "Wait! Yes she does!" He looked at Beth, then pointed to her hand. "I've seen you kiss that scar on your right hand."

As if to protect it, Beth rubbed her hand and began to step away. Her face was enveloped with worry. "This isn't a scar. This is where I was kissed by God."

Scott grabbed her hand and examined the scar. "This looks surgical to me."

"What do you mean?" Brennen asked. "Beth, when did this happen?"

Beth was reluctant to answer. "This is my kiss from God. About five years ago, we were all kissed by God. One by one, we woke up one day and there it was."

"Who is 'we'?"

"My sisters." Beth was shaking now. "The Prophet said

that it meant we were assured a place in the celestial kingdom . . . that God would always be here . . . and could always find us."

Brennen and Scott looked at each other. For the first time in two years, they were on the same wavelength. Scott ran to the window and peered with wide eyes out the Venetian blinds.

"What?" Beth asked. She continued to step backward, clutching her hand. "What *is* it?"

Scott rushed Beth and placed his hands on her shoulders. "Beth, we may have a serious problem." He was very persuasive.

"You're scaring me," Beth said. Her face was contorted and her eyes began leaking tears.

"There is more than a good chance that Jacob inserted some type of tracking device in your hand. Now I'm not even sure if they *make* shit like that, but it's the only thing that makes logical sense to me right now."

"But."

"Listen, Beth," Scott interrupted. "I know you think that God kissed you, and I know that you don't trust me at all, but if you have some device in your hand—"

"Then what?" Beth demanded.

"Then that means that whoever is out there looking for you knows exactly where you are right *now*!" Brennen shouted.

Beth's face was encased in veritable emotion, shifting her mood in different directions. There were multiple facets, compounding within her a terror too great to endure. There were the old fears, the fear of Larry Hitchcock breaking the door down, the fear of being banished in the afterlife, but there was a *new* fear growing within her, as though it had been encased in ice all of these years. It was doubt.

Where these Othersiders telling her that she had *not* been kissed by God? Were they telling the truth?

No.

She would show them, once and for all. She shook her hand free from Scott and ran to the bathroom.

Scott and Brennen looked at each other. The fear had spread its way across the room.

"Well," Scott said, "you obviously know what I'm thinking, so I'm not going to say it."

Brennen looked around the room with concern. "Actually, I *don't* know. The mind-reading effect seems to wear off after a while."

Both men whipped around in unison as they heard Beth scream from the bathroom. The hallway seemed to lengthen as they ran to the source of the scream. Scott was first to arrive at entrance to the bathroom followed soon after by Brennen. Both were at a loss for words when they saw what lay before them.

Beth was crouched between the toilet and the shower, gushing a good amount of blood from her right hand. Her left hand was closed into a fist.

Scott saw at once what happened. She had used the razor blade previously used for cleaning to dig into her scar, looking for God (or lack thereof).

Thick drops of blood ran down the clean porcelain as he asked her if she was all right. She could only answer with sobbing.

She lifted her head to meet them, holding out her fist. “What is *this*?” She opened her hand wide, revealing a small metal capsule the size of a Tylenol gel cap. Her face was smeared with blood. “Is this from God?”

“Holy shit!” Scott said.

Brennen ran his fingers through his hair. “I don’t believe it.”

“Hand her a towel!” Scott yelled. In an instant, he was down the hall.

Brennen handed her a nearby towel and with reassuring words began rummaging through the medicine cabinet for disinfectant. To Scott, he yelled “What are you *doing,* man?”

From the living room, Scott said, “We gotta get rid of it!” A moment later he had returned to the bathroom with his Eagles Nerf football. “Beth, give me that thing.”

She complied.

Brennen watched as Scott tore a tiny hole in the spongy material and shoved the capsule inside. In another moment, Scott opened the balcony door, and let it fly like a pro-style quarterback. Over the pool area it went, in a perfect spiral, before bouncing into the adjacent dirt field and coming to rest at last among a group of creosote bushes.

Three minutes later, the three of them watched from behind the blinds as a shady figure in a security guard uniform approached the ball and picked it up.

C

“What the hell is this?” Mr. Bratch asked himself as he held the football. It was a Philadelphia Eagles Nerf, green on one side, white on the other, with the screaming eagle logo stamped in the middle.

He double consulted his GPS device attached to his clipboard to double-check its accuracy. According to it, he was standing directly on top of where Beth was hiding. He surveyed the surrounding area. Behind him, there was a multi-building apartment community with a gated swimming pool area, alive with screaming children. Ahead of him was an open desert field wedged against a golf course. To each side was Taylor Street leading, for the most part, to the 202 Freeway from which he'd exited just a few minutes before.

As he examined the football, a gust of mocking wind blew dust in his face, adding insult to injury. For the most part, it was a new ball. The green side looked as though the rubber paint had been newly sprayed. It was a commemorative souvenir of the 2004 conference championship game. It was puzzling why somebody would choose now to leave it outside in the dirt after all these years. Further scrutiny revealed a smudge of blood on the white side of the ball. More times than not, blood led to a clue, and this was no different. Next to the blood was a tiny tear in the football's fiber, inside of which was Beth's tracker.

"I'll be damned," he said.

The water buffalo had gotten away.

He squeezed the device in his hand, cursing Beth Perkins in his mind.

Despite this setback, Mr. Bratch vowed that this was not over. He would not wait for the police to fish her out. He would do it himself and he knew the exact means of how to go about it. Larry had mentioned that the arm-breaking giant had mentioned someone named Brennen as being the owner of the apartment Beth had been using as a hideout. The giant and Brennen were connected, that much was certain. Chances were that finding either of them would lead him straight to Beth.

Now that his technological advantage lay stuffed in a football, it was time to administer some good old-fashioned police work, just as he did in Philadelphia. The hate was coming back to him and the urges were creeping into his fingertips. If he never did anything else on this Earth, he would find Beth Perkins and salvage his place in the community. If he could just hurt her a little bit before returning her, perhaps take her eyes away, he would be a happy man.

He returned to his truck and drove off toward the freeway.

D

A few hours later, Brennen and Beth sat on the couch while Scott sat across from them on his La-Z-Boy. Long bouts of silence dictated the conversation. For just having jumped in the mess headfirst, Scott was on good behavior, all things considered. He had listened intently to the both of their accounts of the last twenty-four hours and accepted it to a reasonable degree. He had seen and heard enough that afternoon to challenge his idea of what was possible.

With Beth, he tried to dig a little deeper as to her affiliation with Jacob. He understood that Jacob was her husband—her criminally abusive husband—but he didn't understand about the sisters, Betty and Jane. When asked about them, however, Beth would dance around the subject, if not change it all together. She kept the focus on the man in the security guard uniform, Mr. Bratch.

He was considered by many in the community as the Eye of God. He was not an apostle, he had no direct contact with God, but being the prophet's right hand man, he might as well have. Mr. Bratch was responsible for keeping order in the community. If the community had a cop, he was it. He also had the only communication with the Paiute Rock City police, should an emergency arise in the community that would require their assistance. This happened only on rare occasions, to Beth's knowledge.

"For the most part, the Paiute Rock City police leave us be," Beth said, "but they know who Jacob is, and they respect him, so they usually don't question him."

Scott took a drink out of a water bottle, and said, "And that's why you think they were able to label you a murderer. They are working with Jacob?"

"Yes," Beth said. She had spent a good amount of time washing blood out of her new white shirt and was glad when the stain had been removed entirely. The little Band-Aid that Scott offered was no match for the wound and it was soaked in blood. "I know that's what has happened."

To Brennen, Scott said, "I bet that picture of Beth was sent out to all the cities in the greater Phoenix area."

Beth turned to Brennen when he did not respond. She gasped. "What's wrong with him?"

Brennen had slumped over on the couch, unconscious. His eyes were fluttering intermittently as his body emitted small convulsions.

Scott maintained a calm demeanor. Having been able to ease her nerves thus far, he did not want to put her in a state of panic. He had seen Brennen in this state many times before.

“Oh, he does that sometimes,” Scott said, not wanting to rat out Brennen on his drug use. He laid Brennen flat on the couch, taking care not to let his head dangle as it blindly obeyed gravity. The quivering stopped. Scott looked at his old friend, still incapacitated with drugs, and thought of how furious his father would be if he knew Scott was harboring him. Scott couldn’t blame him. He was angry at himself for permitting any of this. Yet there was something inescapable about it. “He’s . . . a little sick.” He rose from his chair. “Not much we can do except let him rest.” He extended his hand to Beth. “Let’s give him some time to rest and get you some better bandages and Neosporin at the store. We don’t want your hand getting infected.”

On their way out, they ran into Scott’s nosy neighbor, Mrs. Elhenicky. She was always at the pool and eager to socialize. It was easy for her to see Scott exiting on the second floor and had plenty of time to ambush him with a loaded conversation by the time he had descended the two flights of stairs to the ground level. She was in her fifties, overweight, and from some northeastern state, which explained why she was at the pool in late October. Her sun visor covered her thin, dyed hair, and her one-piece bathing suit looked to be from several seasons earlier. Still, Scott remained polite.

She asked the usual questions, how he was, how were his studies going, and isn’t the weather fantastic? Though he did not request it, she caught him up to speed on many details of her life since last speaking with him. She inevitably noticed Beth.

Beth flashed a bashful smile as she brushed away stray hairs loosened from her pony tail, bringing her bandaged hand to the woman's attention at once. Before it became a topic of discussion, Scott created an excuse for departure and broke away clean, tugging Beth as he went.

Unfazed by the sudden departure, Mrs. Elhenicky waved a happy goodbye and wished them both a wonderful afternoon, reminding them that hydrogen peroxide was the best remedy to clean out wounds.

At the Walgreens on East Washington Avenue, near his apartment, Scott once again tried to breach the subject of the community with Beth. She acted like she didn't hear him and went in search for large bandages and disinfectant. He was getting accustomed to her coyness and took less offense than he had earlier. In fact, he was rather enjoying being around her, with or without conversation. His doubts about her had been subsiding in steady increments as he spent more time with her. He found her fascinating. He even caught himself wondering if he would have helped Brennen at all had she not been at his side. He was, after all, disgusted with Brennen. The clown had let himself go so far down the rabbit-hole that he was damn near unrecognizable. He had always imagined Brennen sober by now. Instead, he was worse for the wear. Still, if the situation were reversed, and he was crashed out on Brennen's couch, he would have liked to think that his old friend would at least try to sympathize, if not empathize.

"Sorry to keep bugging you about this," Scott said, "it's just that I really believe you have a serious case against your husband here. I mean, it's unfortunate that I had to stuff a key piece of evidence in a football, but human GPS micro-trackers, or whatever that was, are a big deal. As far as I know, they haven't been approved for use."

Beth stopped at the bandages section of the aisle. "What do you mean?"

"I mean to go as far as implanting a tracking device in somebody's flesh just to instill the fear of God and perpetuate a lie is *illegal*, and highly immoral."

She looked at him with what he could only describe as hurt. Of *course* she was hurt. Her entire life had been constructed of lies built on lies built on lies. The only salvation she had was that she was approved of by God in the form of a kiss. Now, even *that* was untrue.

"What about Brennen?" she asked, changing the subject. "Do you think he's a prophet?" She looked for some disinfectant only to see that Scott had already picked some out and was holding it up, smiling. She laughed as much as her bashfulness would allow.

Scott guffawed. "No. I think he's an idiot, but that's another story." He motioned for her to follow him up the aisle. He thought of Carl Sagan and how he might respond to assessing the validity of a faith healer. He treaded with care on the subject. "I've been giving that a lot of thought. I know it seems all crazy supernatural, but there has to be some explanation to all of it. There was a rational explanation for you being followed by Mr. Bratch, and there's a rational explanation for Brennen as well."

Beth looked at him, her green eyes requesting more information.

"Okay, here is what I've come up with," Scott said. "I'm

what you call a science guy. I believe in science and I follow all the science programs at Arizona State. There is a professor that teaches there, Professor Navarro. She is an astrophysicist, kind of famous actually, who believes there's a way to reconcile spirituality without breaking any rules of physics. She wrote some book on how things that seem supernatural maybe, as of yet, are just unexplained science. Do you follow me so far?"

Beth looked vacant. "Not exactly. It sounds kind of crazy."

"Yes, it does." Scott laughed at the irony of a girl, having just discovered a GPS tracker in her hand, calling anything crazy. "Anyway, she holds office hours tomorrow morning. Obviously, since I'm a student, I can get us on campus, and we can all go down there and hear what she has to say."

"I *guess* so."

"Perfect," Scott said. "And what better way to hide out than to be among fifty thousand students?"

"Fifty thousand?"

Scott laughed again. "Oh, you will love it."

It may have taken a while for Beth to smile, but when she did, she lit up the store. She appeared to be warming to him and he could only hope there was something akin to trust beginning to develop between them.

Later that night, after several attempts to wake Brennen failed, Scott had offered the couch for the night so they didn't have to worry about going back to Brennen's, should Larry Hitchcock still be prowling around it. His one condition to the arrangement was that she *not* sneak into his room at night to attempt any funny business.

This made her laugh again.

13
In A Dark Space

The man in the mannequin mask studied the YouTube video from the vibrating room. There had been other false prophet potentials, but this was by far the most intriguing. He sat, rubbing his goatee.

The amateur sound quality spilled out into the room. The voices were thin and the microphone rattled as an unpleasing breeze blew into it. Still, the man watched and listened with the same intensity as a farmer monitoring weather reports. He had watched it three times in its entirety and was in the final seconds of the fourth now.

"Get that dog away from me, dude!" the creator of the video said. He sounded to be in his teens. The shaky camera revealed he was avoiding a pit bull terrier while its owner struggled to pull it back with a leash.

Through further tremulous camera work, the dog owner said, "Jesus Christ! Is that a SWAT team?"

The video ended on what appeared to be a team of officers, dressed in tactical garb, approaching an apartment. One of the men demanded he stop filming.

The man in the mask read the title of the video once again.

JESUS: ALIVE AND WELL AND LIVING IN TEMPE, AZ!!!

To quintuple-check what he'd just viewed, he clicked on the refresh button to watch the video from the outset. There was a young man, with short black hair, wearing a long-sleeved dark tee-shirt and jeans, and waving his arms trying to keep birds from landing on his head and shoulders. How he was able to accomplish such a feat was a mystery to the mannequin.

"Oh, my God, dude," the cameraman said, addressing the YouTube public, "This is Don, here. I'm in Tempe, Arizona, and this guy here is totally reading my mind! No lie."

"Please stop filming, my friend," the subject said. He was looking up as birds continued their attempts at landing on his head.

A voice shouted a command from a distance. The cameraman panned to see a pit bull running at the subject, full speed, while the owner chased helplessly after it. Gasps of disbeliefs from the cameraman could be heard as the dog, instead of tearing the birdman to shreds, lay at the subject's feet and emitted a playful whimper.

It was another cheap animal trick. The subject was without doubt a charlatan.

As the cameraman backed up into a wide shot, the subject waved his arm at the camera—one motion down and another across. The mannequin was certain it was the sign of the cross. He had long been acquainted with men waving the sign of the cross at him. To him, it was hard to mistake.

Just moments after the subject managed to shut the door, the animal's behavior changed in an instant. The birds flew away, as though they'd all snapped out of hypnosis, and the dog's demeanor changed from placid to vicious as it channeled its aggression at the cameraman.

The man in the mask paused the video on the wide shot. This was not a typical subject for him. So far, his travels had exposed him to false prophets of a different breed. Traditionally, they were men who used expensive gadgetry and impressive sermons to lure the gullible into their narrative. He had encountered a few such men on his trip and the mannequin had been able to tease the truth out of these men by his own means. These men were not prophets. They were not even men. They were a virus with their sermons, spreading distortion to language and stunting the potential of human evolution by injecting fear and self-loathing into their subjects. They were not in the business of healing, but rather in the business of self-preservation and iconography. This animal trainer was no doubt of the same moral fiber as the other men. Instead of sermons, he persuaded the weak with cheap animal stunts and pre-conjured videos depicting him as in possession of power. It was the same game repackaged in the guise of social media and distributed as something new.

It wasn't new.

After staring at the frozen scene on the computer monitor, he decided this subject, among all others, was worth visiting. He was just screaming to be visited. Not only would he be easy to recognize in public, but the address was glaring at him on the monitor. The subject had shut the door, inviting the world to see his apartment number, while the name of the apartment complex was printed in bold letters on a nearby sign.

The Nantucket Apartments, apartment 128.

"Hello, Jesus of Tempe," the man said. "Nice to meet you."

14
October 30: Morning

A

Brennen's eyes popped open when Scott attempted, for the fourth time, to wake him from the dreamless sleep to which he had been submerged since early the previous evening. His eyes could not focus on any one thing and his brain could not deduce where he was. For several seconds he lay staring at the surroundings of Scott's apartment before the events of the previous day began shyly identifying themselves.

"We have to go, man," Scott said. He disappeared into his bedroom with jeans and a gray tee-shirt, only to emerge a moment later wearing a Philadelphia Eagles hoodie.

When Brennen propped himself to a sitting position, he noticed Beth staring at him with concern.

She waved at him. Her hand had been bandaged with care. "You okay?"

Brennen rubbed his eyes and practiced his focus on various household items. "Yeah, I'm good." To Scott, he asked, "Where are we going?"

As Scott spoke cryptic sentences about visiting a certain professor at the university, Brennen thought more about Beth's question. Was he, in fact, okay? Something deep within him told him that he was not. He had "Sniper Syndrome" as he and Scott used to refer to it. It was the uneasy feeling that a sniper was spending his hours waiting somewhere outside the front door, to avenge something stupid they did while black-out drunk. It was conscience incarnate, and it was hitting him hard now. The flames were approaching.

I didn't go to work last night.

He dug through his back pocket and pulled out his phone. There were seventeen missed calls, none of which contained messages. Not only did he miss the short-term opportunity for customer rides, but he could have lost their *long*-term business to whatever competitors picked up the ride in his stead. His stomach flipped once at the notion of losing income and again when he noticed one of the calls was from his sister. From there, the thoughts cascaded, lowering him downward at a steady, but relentless pace.

Why does she keep calling?

I'm getting evicted.

The cops think I'm a suspect.

Triana Linden.

Beth had a tracker inserted into her hand.

Mind reading.

I am a Glow head.

Shame.

As the flames consumed him, he rose from the couch. His auditory functionality was disoriented, as if he were passing through one of the filter effects of his music. As he turned his head, his hearing sensitivity fluctuated between being insignificant to overbearing. He was in desperate need of Glow.

"Excuse me just a sec," Brennen said, and slipped into the bathroom.

The hit of Glow was not what he was used to, but it was better than nothing. He sat on the toilet cover with his eyes closed as The Glow went to work improving his mood. The effect was almost immediate. Not as intense as other times, but enough to get him through the next few hours.

When he emerged, Scott and Beth were showered and waiting for him. They were serious about having to leave. In the interest of time, Brennen forewent the shower he had imagined himself taking and followed them out the door.

His mood had elevated somewhat and he was ready for the day. He was glad to have Scott in his life again, even if the time was temporary and the reason circumstantial. He wanted to crack some old jokes and reminisce about old times, but felt inhibited to do so in case his efforts were rejected on any level. What he needed, more than words could allow, was a chance to start over.

"Hey, Scott," Brennen said as they walked to the car, "there's something I've been meaning to give you." Brennen handed him one of his business cards. "It's my number." He extended a hand to Scott. "I'm Brennen. Nice to meet you, my friend. Give me a call if you need a ride."

Scott accepted with hesitation the number and handshake. "You're an idiot, dude," Scott said while shaking his head, but he was smiling. Scott changed the subject to Snippety. He was floored by her abilities. He imitated her movements with his hands while he explained how she opened the refrigerator and chose her own food. She was particularly fond of the rotisserie chicken.

"Do you think she's smart because you're smart?" Beth asked.

"I have no idea," Brennen said, "It's a great question to ask this . . . professor person."

B

The astronomy department at Arizona State University was situated near an older section of the school, boasting a classic-college feel compared to its ultra-modern counterparts at the edge of campus. The architectural aesthetic of the time revolved around red brick and right angles harboring cold hallways lit by fluorescent bulbs, with little in the way of natural light. To Dr. Diana Navarro, the place reminded her more of a hospital than a learning institution. Her office, despite her attempts to de-sterilize it, was just as devoid of personality. She had a large, multi-positional halogen light to better illuminate her desk, but the depression she felt here wasn't so easily thwarted. The only object in the room that gave her any comfort was the picture of her with her late husband, Manny.

Manny had been the bright star in her life, her most cherished friend, and the would-be father to their planned children had his life not been taken by a drunk driver high on cocaine. Until that moment, he had changed her in the deepest of ways. His ever-dependable kindness turned her from an embittered daughter of tough love, to a trusting and attentive partner. Manny's tenacity for life was rivaled only by her mother, a devoted, yet fiercely judgmental woman. His love, however, transposed Diana from a part-time defeatist to a fully committed optimist with a biting will to succeed. His faith changed her from a reductionist scientist to someone who believed that there could something more to consciousness that just randomly evolved chemicals in the brain. It was Manny who influenced her to publish her book.

Though Manny did not hold her academic merits, nor understand the mathematics behind some of the more complicated scientific theories she had studied, she considered him her intellectual equal. Pushed hard by her mother since youth, she became the poster-girl for the scientific mind. She was the president of the physics club in high school, and always at the top of her class in any subject involving mathematics. She turned down a graduate scholarship at Cornell for one at Harvard, setting into motion a mildly successful career in astrophysics. Before long, she found herself writing multitudes of peer-reviewed papers for such publications as *Science* and *Nature*, serving as a scientific editor for the *Astrophysics Journal*, and participating in several NASA projects. Being a member of the American, European, and International Astronomical Societies, her reputation—until her book was published—was respected enough to grant her observation time on large-scale NASA research satellites such as Exosat, ROSAT, ASCA, and the Einstein X-ray Observatory.

Tenured as the head of Arizona State's budding astronomy department, Diana had managed to make use of her time. Still, with every ounce of knowledge she had acquired, she could ever gain only a slight advantage when engaged in existential conversations with Manny. He would always hit science where it was most vulnerable.

So you are telling me to accept this theory that can't be observed, he would say in their many conversations, *yet you flat-out reject the existence of God.*

As much as she protested at the time, she knew in her

heart he had a point. There were some scientific theories surfacing as of late that relied just as much on faith as Manny's beloved Catholicism.

Kitty Cat, as he referred to her, *listen to yourself. If relativity and quantum mechanics do not agree with each other, this can only mean that either someone is wrong or there is something going on that we just don't understand yet. What if that something is God?"*

As if by a wave, Diana let the memories overtake her as she touched the picture frame with affection.

For the most part, Manny was very respectful of her profession, but he was not without his judgments regarding the scientific community, or her colleagues who surround it. One night at a dinner function, after being scoffed at by her peers regarding his faith, he later compared Diana's dinner gatherings to religious revival meetings.

There is no difference, Di, he would say. *If they reject any kind of spirituality, they are just another religion—a religion called fundamentalist scientism.*

She was blessed to have known him.

Diana shifted her eyes to another picture, one that featured a much younger and slimmer Diana surrounded by three equally youthful girls. Holding a high school diploma in her hand, Diana's Latino facial features shone brilliantly among her blonde counterparts. Garbed in cap and gown, they posed with their backs straightened by confidence and eyes glinted by hope. They were best friends then, and promised they forever would be. Although the inevitability of life padded the years between them, slowing communication to the occasional social media post, she was looking forward to their rapidly approaching twenty-year reunion. As much as she was excited by it, the thought of seeing them again after all these years terrified her. She wondered what on Earth she would say to them. Chances were good they had heard of her controversial book that had shaken up the scientific community as of late, putting her career in jeopardy. The prospect was dreadful. She always imagined seeing them again under much lighter conditions—and twenty pounds lighter and with Manny on her arm. Here she was, her future now coming to pass and she was ill-prepared and shorthanded.

The intent behind the book was pure. It was an ideological truce between Manny's beliefs and her own, an attempt to reconcile human spirituality with science, but it soon grew to something much bigger than either of them expected. To them, the book was a triumph that elevated their understanding of one another on a profound level. It was Manny's wish that the book be released, and, at great risk to her professional career, she published it as a memorial to him several months after his death.

To her peers, it was pure rubbish. Review after scathing review emerged from within the scientific community, some written by the very people she considered friends.

"Paranormal shenanigans," Dr. Orthon Medina wrote in a review in the *Astrological Journal.* Likewise, her mentor, Dr. Robert Crawford described it as "Fringy with a capital 'F.'"

It went on and on.

Initially, the negative press caused the board at the university to consider suspending her, but reconsidered on the account of Manny's recent passing. It was now three months since the release of the book and just seven since he'd died. She was at a crossroads, not knowing if she'd get fired or downgraded to a less ostentatious position.

There came a squeaking sound from the opposite side of her desk.

Diana smiled as her pet chinchilla, Dave, appeared from underneath his house in the corner of his cage. He was just over twenty years old, ancient in chinchilla years, and walked with a hobble attributed to a bad hip. He stood upright, grabbed an oblong piece of food with one hand, and began to devour it with speed. He looked as though he were an auctioneer, microphone in hand, bidding up a new item.

Dave, named after the sometimes guitar player of one of her favorite 90s band, The Red Hot Chili Peppers, was a joy to look at, but could be an ornery little fellow when handled by people. He disliked people, except for Diana, and much preferred his cage to the outside world. She had several times attempted to let him roam in the living room, but instead of exploring the human realm, he would stare into space on wobbly legs until he fell onto his side. The vet described the behavior as a "freeze-and-flop," a condition normally associated with dogs or cats experiencing a negative reaction to leashing. As long as Dave was happy, Diana didn't care where he preferred to spend his time.

She spoke to Dave with affection while tapping on his cage. "Hang in there, Dave. Remember, you have to live forever."

There was a knock on the door.

The clock on her desk read 9:58 PM. The students were two minutes early. They were always early. As much as she was thrilled by the idea of taking part in the molding of fresh young minds, holding office hours was not her favorite perk, especially as of late. With her mind preoccupied by her current troubles, it was difficult to engage the students. Whether it was about debating a grade a student received or an elaboration on the concept of magnetic resonance imaging, it was exhausting.

She shook off the resistance and rose to open the door. Had the students *waited* two more minutes, they would have found the door wide open. Whoever it was, they were knocking on the door again as she opened it.

There were three students standing at the door. One stunning girl with red hair dressed in typical student attire, a young man in an Eagles hoodie, and another much shadier character dressed in a dark, long-sleeve tee-shirt and jeans. His bloodshot eyes were sunken in and his hair was oily. He looked as though sleep had evaded him for several days. She distrusted him without question, but treated him with courtesy regardless. The two young men took a seat in the chairs opposite her desk. The girl preferred to stand, looking curiously around the office.

She greeted them all with a smile.

"Hello, Professor Navarro," the young man in the hoodie said. "My name is Scott Barrett. I'm actually a student of the law school across campus, but I've recently run into a situation that you may or may not be able to shed some light on."

Diana looked at him with an awkward regard. "So none of you are actually in my classes?"

"No, Professor," Scott confessed. "But we weren't sure

who else we could address. It's unique situation, to say the least."

Diana turned to see that the girl had turned her attention to Dave and was admiring him through the metal bars of the cage.

"His name is Dave," Diana said.

"That is Godtastic. What is it?"

"He's a chinchilla." Though confused about the visit in general, Diana always had time to accept compliments about Dave. She couldn't help but smile. To Scott, she said, "Well, then, how can I help, Scott?"

"I know this is going to sound a bit crazy, but it's regarding your book."

Diana's smile faded.

"I haven't read the book personally as of yet, but I understand it had something to do with a way to fit science into the existence of spirituality, psychic phenomena . . . and even God." He scratched his head. "For lack of a better word."

Diana shifted her eyes from Scott back to the girl, who was now staring back at her, awaiting her answer. "That's a pretty broad way of stating it, but—"

"Because I think my friend here is psychic."

Diana looked at the disheveled young man. She was certain he was under the influence of something. He shifted uncomfortably in his seat. His movements were jerky and his jaw was moving back and forth.

"Hello," he said. He gave an awkward wave. "I'm Brennen . . . I, uh, started getting these headaches a few days ago and . . . as weird as it sounds, I've since been able to, from what I can tell, uh, read people's thoughts."

Diana fixed her gaze on Brennen's eyes. How dare they bring this person into her office? Her memory of the phone call with the police the night Manny was killed flooded into her mind. They explained that the blood test for the driver came back positive for alcohol and cocaine.

"It's true," the girl said. "I've seen him do it."

"And what is your name?" Diana asked.

"Beth, ma'am. Very nice to meet you."

Diana gave an infuriated look to all her guests. She would have never guessed that dealing with crazy students would be a consequence of writing her book. Yet here they were making light of her and Manny's years of work. She was annoyed.

"Brennen," Diana said. "Can you look me in the eye and say, with any degree of certainty, that you are sober right now?"

Brennen looked into Diana's eyes and over to Scott's, only to look down. "I . . . I can't."

"You can't perform any psychic abilities or you can't tell me you are sober?" Diana said.

Brennen continued to look down.

"I see," Diana said as she collected herself. Her hands shook as she used them to hoist herself from her seat. She straightened her blouse and skirt as she addressed her guests. Nervous energy encompassed her face. "Scott, Beth, Brennen, it was very nice to meet you, but I think you had better leave the premises immediately or I *will* call the campus police and have you checked for suspicion of intoxication." She motioned to the door. "Please do not approach me again."

15
October 30: Mid-morning

A

Mr. Bratch was headed to his next destination when he ended his call with the angered prophet. Jacob wanted to know how it was that Mr. Bratch was still in Tempe without Beth. Mr. Bratch fibbed that he had his eyes on her, but needed to wait until she was in a less conspicuous area. He dare not tell him that Beth had somehow realized she was bugged and removed it from her hand.

From the conversation, it was difficult to assess whether the prophet believed the story. All he could do was hope for the best and complete the task at hand: to find the girl no matter what it took. His life, or at least his prison-free life, depended on it.

The truth was that he had spent part of the previous day brooding over Beth, listening to heavy industrial music as loud as the speakers in his F150 would allow. He had taken an instant liking to the music genre when he was on the force. The distorted screams accompanied by grinding guitar tones and sonic drums gave him both the adrenaline and clear thought he needed to work on homicides, either investigated or committed. It had been almost twenty years since the music style disappeared from the scene, but he still listened to it religiously, as if it were brand new.

He also managed a quick visit to the apartment belonging

to Brennen, where Larry and Chris were assaulted by the tattooed giant. Not knowing if Larry's intrusion had been reported to the police, he kept his visit short, taking a quick survey of the grounds.

Judging from the boarded-up windows, he deduced that Brennen was an addict of some sort. Somehow, Beth had teamed up with either a heroin or amphetamine user (he suspected amphetamine, as heroin bangers rarely left the house). The tattooed giant must have been a friend, in all likelihood a fellow user or dealer who happened to be around at the right time. It was only a matter of time before the two were in communication with each other again. A friend in need is a friend indeed.

Today was Friday, mid-morning, and after running the license plate of the Dodge Neon, Mr. Bratch was ready to visit the home of its registered owner. As he drove, he was disappointed to see that the outside world hadn't changed. It was still filled with self-serving people stepping over one another for a piece of the American dream. That morning, after watching the tragic headlines of the day, he felt no compassion, not that he possessed a great amount to begin with. Even as a child, he lacked sympathy. The world, to him, was a disaster waiting to happen. Nothing he did, or didn't do, was going to make a difference.

When was all said and done, he was a nihilist. He would, of course, never admit this to the prophet, but it was nonetheless true. In the name of self-preservation, he would go along with whatever the prophet was selling, but as it were, he believed human beings were a collective pile of eventual worm dirt with no hidden or higher meaning of existence. It was a pointless universe doomed to freeze. Logically, what did it matter if a few Philadelphia prostitutes died? Prostitutes, male or female, white or black, had given up on life anyway. He helped them find their way into the ground at a quickened pace. One way or another, be it a train wreck, natural disaster or nuclear war, they were all going into the ground.

Luigi eventually notified the Philadelphia police force as well as the FBI as to Mr. Bratch's secret. It was evident he *did* care about dead prostitutes.

Merely thinking these thoughts loosened inside of him the urge to kill again, an instinct that had long lain dormant at the prophet's compound. It would be difficult to kill with anonymity in his close-knit community. There were so many opportunities for random acts of violence among the Othersiders, however. He didn't know any prostitutes in Mesa, Arizona, but he *did* know a potential drug dealer. His name was Dan Tenner, the giant, owner of the Dodge Neon, and the rescuer of Beth Perkins.

He smiled at the prospect of Breaking Mr. Tenner's face should he become uncooperative. He would have no problem killing him and taking him back to the compound for burial. The police would never find him there, nor would they ever think to look. Who would miss another dealer anyway?

According to the Bratch School of Thought, nobody.

B

Back in the parking lot of Arizona State, Scott unlocked the passenger-side door of his old Nissan Altima and opened the door for Beth. Brennen assumed his position in the back seat where he sulked for a few moments.

The walk back from Professor Navarro's office had been spent in awkward silence. Brennen had failed, on all levels, to make his case or sound at all like a rational human being. He looked the professor in the eye, but could not hear her thoughts as he was previously able to with Beth, Scott, and the magazine salesman. It was simple. He had not been able to infuse himself with enough Glow. It was The Glow that was somehow the key to all of it. No Glow, no show. It was as simple as that.

But how could he return to the professor now? He was mortified. Never in his life had he been sized up, judged, and rejected by anybody with such speed. On the other hand, Professor Navarro was the one person who might shed some light, if only theoretically, on what was happening to him. All he could do was prove it to her, and he might not have another chance.

The slamming of the driver's side door freed Brennen from his thoughts.

"Well, that sucked," Scott said, inserting his keys into the ignition.

To Brennen, Beth said, "So why didn't you . . . or why couldn't you . . . you know, do your thing?"

Brennen struggled with words while Scott answered for him. "I told you, Beth, he's an idiot." He looked back at Brennen with a look of disgust. "And you do look pretty high. Did I hear you light up in the bathroom before we left?"

"Light up?" Beth asked.

Brennen felt as though he were being lowered into a fire, the flames tickling his toes. Being interrogated by the cops was one thing, but for Scott to put him on the spot was another sensation altogether. His palms were sweating and his heart was panging hard in his chest. At the risk of both re-injuring his friendship with Scott and breaking his trust with Beth, Brennen found only one exit from the fire pit. As it happened, it was the same solution that might influence Professor Navarro to listen.

"Turn off the car, Scott," Brennen said while digging deep into his front pockets. "Turn off the car and get out, both of you. I don't want you around this stuff."

Scott turned again to the back seat to find that Brennen had produced a Glow pipe and a torch lighter from his pockets.

Taking notice of the paraphernalia, Beth asked, "What is *that*?"

Brennen locked eyes with Scott. "I'm serious. Get out of the car. I know you can't be around this. You've worked too hard to straighten yourself out. You're a stronger person than I, man."

Scott moved to protest when Beth interrupted.

"What are you doing, Brennen?"

"This is what Othersiders call drugs. It's what *I* call The Glow. And I can only read thoughts when I am using it. There, I said it. So just get out of the car for one minute so you don't have to be around it—and tell me if anyone is coming." Making himself as small as possible, he hunkered down in the back seat. "Trust me; she will listen to us this time."

He lit up.

C

The red Dodge Neon was parked on the street outside the

house. The house itself was small and nestled against adjacent houses. Lucky for Mr. Bratch, the side fence nearest the carport entrance was covered in bright pink-red bougainvillea plants, supplying all the privacy needed for an interrogation. Daylight hours were not optimal for such activity, but the sooner he could get the information he needed from the giant, the sooner he could recover the girl and return to the safety of the compound.

He crept the truck into the carport and began to gather surveillance gear from the back seat. Unlocking a combination lock, he removed a long-range shotgun microphone, high-powered amplifier, a wireless headset, and brass knuckles from a toolbox. When pointed at a specific target, the microphone could pick up noises as far as ten feet away. The amplifier boosted the signal even more, doubling the microphones' range. In the case of a small house such as this, the odds of picking up on conversations were good. With any luck, he'd be able to tell how many people were in the house before he invaded it.

He scanned the outside of the house, listening for murmurings within. He could hear footsteps causing hardwood floors to groan in protest, suggesting the owner of the feet was of substantial weight. As he followed the steps, the sound of a refrigerator door opened and closed, followed by cupboards doing the same.

Without warning, something related to a parrot squawked so loud Mr. Bratch's eardrums rattled. Cursing the bird, he shot a quick look down the street to check for any nosy dog-walkers or joggers. There were none. He was clear for the time being, but was aware his window of time was narrow.

He looked in the extended cab of the truck. The painting tarp was laid out, covering the upholstery.

It was all prepared.

He wiggled his fingers through the brass knuckles.

"Who brought you the snack?" a male voice asked. There were several seconds of room noise picked up by the microphone before the voice repeated, "*Who* brought you the snack?"

"*Daddy* did!" shouted a toddler, followed by a high-pitched giggle.

The male voice laughed. "You're darn *tootin'* your daddy did!"

"*Tootin'*." The toddler laughed. "You said *tootin'*."

"I *did* say tootin', didn't I?"

As though from a tickling attack, the child exploded into loud fits of laughter.

The man repeated, "Toot! Toot! Toot!"

"Mom! Daddy said toot!"

Mr. Bratch rubbed his eyes while the two carried on for a few moments, until a female voice broke it up.

"Baby," the woman said. She sounded worried. "There is someone in a truck in the carport. I think it's one of your friends. Deal with it. I'm jumping in the shower."

Mr. Bratch knew his opportunity was coming very soon. If Larry's reports were accurate, he was no match for the giant physically. This would have to be a sneaky job with cheap shots.

He popped off the earphones, set the microphone aside and turned up his music at full volume through the truck speakers. The song playing had a tribal drum beat, a repetitive guitar hook and angry vocals, sounding as though underwater, screaming about being burned internally.

In the anticipation, he caught his own smile in the rearview mirror. It had been years since he last saw it. He got out of the truck with a gallon of distilled water and popped the hood, pouring the water on the radiator, causing it to steam with vehemence.

The giant came out of the house visibly annoyed by the loud music. He was clad in a sleeveless tee-shirt, cargo shorts, and bare feet. It was true. The man was enormous. Well over six feet, he moved without fear or apprehension. This was a mistake.

It was clear that Mr. Bratch's security uniform confused the giant as he scanned it, looking for a badge number or a company name. He batted waves of radiator steam from his face as he motioned to his ears, signifying that the loud music was not appreciated.

Mr. Bratch, posing as a man in need of mechanical assistance, waved the giant over to the source of the steam. The giant tried to yell something, but Mr. Bratch just nodded his head and continued to wave him over. When the giant was near, Mr. Bratch poured the rest of the water over the radiator, engulfing the area in a cloud of hot mist.

The giant yelled, "*What do you want, dude?* You need to take your truck and get the hell out of my driveway! Now!"

Mr. Bratch yelled back over the music. He was pointing at the radiator "Every man ha— idge— eh nose!"

"*What?*" the giant belted out, leaning in and cupping his ears.

"I said, *Every man has a bridge of the nose!*"

Before the giant could respond, Mr. Bratch, with blunt force, slammed his brass knuckles between the giant's eyes. The crack of bone was drowned out with ease by the din of the grinding music. The truck's popped hood shielded Brass from the neighbors across the street from witnessing any foul play while the bougainvillea provided perfect cover from any homeowners flanking the giant's house. Within moments, Mr. Bratch had hoisted Dan Tenner over his shoulder and onto the plastic tarp in the back seat of the truck. Once he was finished, he closed the hood, hopped back in his car and turned the music down. Through the bougainvillea a burley voice shouted at him.

"Dan! Keep that music down, kid! I'm hard of hearing, but I can still hear that shit from my living room!"

"Sorry," Mr. Bratch said in the giant's stead. "It won't ever happen again, trust me." He rolled up the tinted window and drove away.

Down the street, Mr. Bratch pulled into an empty parking lot at a public park. He searched the unconscious giant for his mobile phone. It was, after all, what he had come for. If the giant was indeed Brennen's dealer, Mr. Bratch was sure Brennen would be contacting him soon. If all went as planned, the phone would be a direct link to Beth.

Mr. Bratch watched as the giant murmured inaudible words. His nose was swelled with rich blood running from the nostrils.

He was too much of a liability alive. As soon as he regained consciousness, he would not only be seeking answers, but revenge, and Mr. Bratch couldn't allow that to happen. Why not just satisfy the urge now? It would be best for everyone involved. The sooner he got it over with, the sooner he could concentrate on tracking Beth and getting back to the compound. Besides, it was only one little dealer.

He climbed in the back seat and grabbed his guest's head between both hands. The blood had stopped dripping on the plastic, but had soaked giant's tee-shirt.

"You look like hell, Dan," Mr. Bratch said. He reached in the giant's pocket and retrieved his mobile phone.

The giant murmured again.

Mr. Bratch grabbed his face between his hands. This was not the undefeatable hulk that Larry described. This was just a big kid who had survived the fights in his life by intimidating with size and throwing the first punch. This time, however, he'd missed that chance. He was now just a pathetic drug dealer with a swollen face taking up space. He was no different than the prostitutes in Philadelphia—useless and going to die anyway.

"Sorry, kid," Mr. Bratch said. "I can't hear what you're saying." He put his knee on the bloody chest and wrapped his hand under the giant's head until his fingers were firmly grabbing his battered nose. With his free hand, he grabbed the back of the giant's head. "This one is for Larry."

He snapped Dan's neck with surprising ease.

D

Brennen led Beth and Scott back through campus like a man possessed. He had taken a few steps' lead and could hear Scott, in his best words, explain to Beth about his and Scott's history with the Glow.

It sounded almost too simple the way he described it and Brennen was tempted to correct him, claiming it was more complicated. But it wasn't. It *was* that simple. He chose to stay behind and de-evolve, which drove a wedge in their friendship. End of story.

He continued to walk ahead, not wanting to talk to Scott and say something that would offend him or make him change his mind about helping. After the stunt in the parking lot, Brennen was surprised that Scott bothered to continue at all. Brennen would have held no ill will toward Scott should he have yanked him out of his car and driven off. Yet Scott had held his tongue. His eyes burned with anger and disappointment, but he agreed to come and Brennen was grateful. Perhaps his concern for Brennen was genuine. On the other hand, Scott seemed to be taking an immediate liking to Beth as well. She did, after all, have a full head of red hair and was in serious need of rescue. Perhaps he remained for her sake.

Perhaps he was staying for both of them.

Soon he was a few feet ahead, avoiding head-on collisions with the many students on the campus sidewalks. His eyes, wide and wild, scanned the campus: Girl walking dog on the right, Native American group protest to Christopher Columbus on the left.

Zing.

Zang.

A few times, he made incidental eye contact with several students, during which time his mind attracted their thoughts like grains of metal to a high-powered magnet.

Why is he looking at me? one girl thought, referring to Brennen as she passed him by. *Get some sleep, dude,* another thought while collecting his bags near a bike rack.

Some thoughts were much more personal in nature. Masochistic sexual perversion, detailed suicidal planning, and other disturbing secrets were inadvertently disclosed to him, so much that Brennen kept his eyes to the ground to relieve himself of the burden of hearing it. At first intriguing, his new abilities now seemed debilitating. On the other hand, he was overjoyed to be back in the cradle of the Glow, free from his *own* negativity and the flames of his life.

Professor Navarro's door was open, allowing Brennen to enter without issue. As though in a daze, her eyes were fixed on one of the many pictures on her desk. It took her a moment to acknowledge a visitor and another before she realized who the visitor was. The shock had delayed her response somewhat and she was slow to rise from her desk. The look in her eyes was enough to let Brennen know he was still unwelcome.

She reached for the phone.

Scott and Beth appeared in the office just as the drama began to unfold.

"Professor Navarro," Brennen said, "please put the phone down and just hear me out."

Diana drenched him with an untrusting look. "And why should I do that? *(This guy is higher than last time)*."

"Yes," Brennen said, ignoring her words and answering the thought. "You got me. I am higher than last time. To be completely honest, I am amped up on amphetamines. I just smoked some in the parking lot before coming here . . . and I apologize for that."

To Beth, Diana asked, "Is he serious?"

Beth nodded. "Yes, ma'am."

"Professor Navarro," Brennen continued, "you asked me earlier to provide proof of my abilities. Well, I don't know how else to put this, but I can only read thoughts when I am high, and I wasn't high enough earlier." As he completed the sentence, a wave of pain washed though his head, forcing him to grab his temples.

Diana put the receiver down and glanced at Scott. "Is he okay?"

"Just hear him out," Scott said. He closed the door behind him. "He may be under the influence of a dangerous substance, but he is telling the truth." His inner lawyer was surfacing.

"And you have to look him in the eyes for it to work," Beth added.

To Diana, Brennen said, "Just tell me a number you are thinking about, any number, and please speak slowly."

Diana looked at Brennen as though a carnival worker had just hit on her. "What? *(07509)*"

"You heard me," Brennen said. "And the number is 07509."

"I'm sorry," Diana lied, "but that is not the number I was thinking about *(That was impossible. 180,361)*."

"Up until a couple days ago, I would have agreed with you. It does seem impossible. But it's not. And it *was* the correct number, Professor Navarro. And now you've changed it to 180,361."

Diana looked around the room as though the source of his trickery were written somewhere on the wall. She refused to believe that this young man was capable of these very strange coincidences. "Again, that was *not* the number I was thinking of *(180,361.086. . . .* 6,475,888)."

"These are not coincidences, Professor Navarro. And you changed it to *180,361.086*, and again to 6,475,888." He shrugged his shoulders. "I can't guess the number if you keep changing it."

Diana looked back to Beth, who nodded her head with a hopeful smile. This was indeed difficult to grasp. The evidence was compounding at a convincing rate, but her mind refused to secede. "Ah . . . look. . . ." *(Clear your mind. Think of nothing. Shit. I can't think of nothing. Even if I try, nothing is still something. Think of Disneyland, then.)* "I'm not sure how exactly you think you can extrapolate my thoughts."

"Disneyland was a nice touch, Professor Navarro. What better way to clear your mind than with Goofy!" Brennen released a quick smile. "I understand. It's hard to clear your mind. It's like . . . trying to dig a hole in dry beach sand. No matter how fast you dig, it just seems to fill right back up."

Diana looked to her pictures on the desk and back to Brennen. *Okay, Mr. psychic, what can you tell me about my family?*

"What can *you* tell me about your family?"

Diana stared at Brennen while trying to repress any thoughts about her mother.

"Well," Brennen said, "from what I understand, she was a walking contradiction. She was charming one minute, withdrawn the next. She had a deficient education. She was ignored by *her* parents, which made her overzealous in *your* upbringing. Because she grew up in feeling abandoned, she had a mean streak. She would find your weaknesses and exploit them. She told you her secret that she never told anyone else—that she was a self-proclaimed witch. You almost ran away at one point"—Brennen counted each event with his fingers. "But, she *did* introduce you to the brain-teaser books and forced you to study harder than any of your friends. And because *she* was so irrational, *you* became rational. Like it or not, you, according to what you're thinking right now, are a product of your mother. You would not be here without her. And yet, at the funeral—"

Diana broke eye contact and looked down at her desk. The succinct account of her mother appeared to have a wavering effect on her. She raised a finger to Brennen and looked into his eyes again. "That's quite enough, Brennen *(There must be a rational explanation . . . and my final number is 3).*"

"Your final number is three." Brennen gave her a reassuring nod. "And I do agree with you, Professor Navarro, there must be a rational explanation. And according to Scott, you wrote a book about it."

Diana looked away at last. As though being urged in several directions at once, split between the scientific method and gut feelings, the result was motionless uncertainty.

There was an uncomfortable silence for several moments, before it was lifted by several chirping sounds.

"Professor Navarro," Beth asked while pointing at the aquarium, "what is Dave doing?"

At some part during the conversation, Dave had emerged from his home and was standing on his hind legs, gripping the bars of the cage with his fingers. He focused on Brennen as he chirped. His large round ears stuck straight out on both sides as the determined rodent jumped up and down.

"This type of thing happened before with animals," Beth said. "A mad dog lay down at his feet."

"Dave hates everybody," Diana said. "He always has."

"Well, see what he does with Brennen," Scott suggested. "If you remember, Dave wasn't doing this when we were here earlier." He motioned to Brennen. "Why don't you have a seat by Dave's house?"

Brennen approached the cage. "Professor Navarro, if you don't mind, why don't you take Dave out and set him on the desk."

Both Dave and Diana did as Scott proposed, though with some reluctance on Diana's part. Brennen sat himself in the nearby desk, rolled down his sleeve and placed his hand, palm down, on the desk while Diana removed Dave's roof, picked him up placed him near her guest.

The result was immediate.

The geriatric rodent hobbled to Brennen without hesitation, and with the determination of a chinchilla possessed. Nowhere to be found was the rumored ill temper or dislike of people. Instead, Dave not only crawled on Brennen's hand, but up his forearm. Using the cotton material of Brennen's shirt as leverage, Dave hoisted himself over and over until he had made the climb all the way to Brennen's shoulder, where he spun around, looked at Diana and lay down.

"Way to go, Dave!" Beth said. Her smile was uncontrollable as she looked at Scott. "That is Godtastic! You are such a good chinchilla!"

Scott returned the smile and attempted to transfer it to

Diana.

Diana could neither smile nor frown. She sat dumbfounded. After Brennen's demonstration, she refused to scoff as her colleagues had once done to Manny. There was nothing to scoff *at*. Any scientist, given the same test, would agree. There was no way for a person to guess numbers to that degree of accuracy. Further, she had never divulged to anyone her mother's claims to be a witch. This was not simple dupery or con-artist circumvention. This was her life's work staring at her. It was her and Manny's book incarnate.

Scott cleared his throat. "Ah, Professor Navarro, maybe now it's a little easier to understand why we thought the best thing, or the *only* thing we felt we *could* do, was come to you." His voice was sincere and persuasive. "Obviously, we're worried about Brennen, in more ways than one, and I thought it would be best to first look at this phenomenon from a scientific standpoint while we seek some answers. I happen to be a big science guy. I love Carl Sagan and spent a bigger part of my life than I care to admit watching old DVDs of *Cosmos*." He brushed some lint off his hoodie and continued. "Now I haven't had a chance to read your book, my apologies, but the students are going crazy over it, and the minute Brennen pulled this surprise psychic shit on me, naturally, you were the first person I thought of. I guess my question is: Can any of this be explained?"

Diana relented. She let out a big sigh and retreated to the corner of her office, where she produced two fold-out chairs and brought them to the front of her desk where she gestured Beth and Scott to have a seat next to Brennen. She then walked to the front door and switched the plaque to read

Office Hours Closed. She waved off Scott's protest. "Don't worry, Scott. They will understand." From her desk, she pulled out a pair of large, dark-tinted sunglasses and placed them on her head. "No offense, Brennen, but I would rather not have my mind read any more today."

Brennen looked at the other two and gave Diana a smile. "That's totally understandable. I don't want to read it."

Without a better way to begin, Diana jumped right in. "The book deals with the possibility that science may be able to explain the unexplainable if it is allowed to do so. As it stands now, science will not allow for the studying of anything that can't be explained through physics and the like. To their credit, this is essential to keep society reverting to a superstitious mindset, willing to explain away nature's mysteries to angry dead things." She looked at the three visitors through her sunglasses.

So far, their eyes had not glazed over.

"And in my opinion, religion as a concept is outdated. It may have worked thousands of years ago, but today, the combativeness of the many world religions may have caused more deaths than saved lives. It may have worked in the past, but today, concepts such as slaughter, destruction, punishment, servitude, vengeful gods—it just seems a better, less violent approach is worth exploring." Diana looked at Beth before continuing. "Beth, I noticed you said the word 'Godtastic." Am I to assume you have a religious affiliation of some sort?"

Beth smiled. "Yeah. You could say that."

"Because I don't mean to offend your beliefs."

"No, ma'am. Don't worry about me. Go on ahead."

Diana smiled back. "On the other hand, rejecting anything spiritual or supernatural because it doesn't happen to follow the rules of science as we know it today is equally illogical. This thought process, to me, puts our values at risk. After all, if the universe is really just chemicals and physics, what is our motivation to remain good people? A pointless universe, in my opinion, is grotesque."

"But," Scott said, "what you're saying is that a world without spirituality is a stale world." He rubbed his hands together, as if nervous to say more. "But isn't spirituality, or consciousness, or whatever you want to call it, just more or less chemistry? Is it chemicals that are transferring between Brennen and people's thoughts?"

"Well, Scott," she said, "like I said, that's where science is at right now. My book suggests the possibility of an underlying consciousness that has been around since before the beginning. You see, it's very hard for me as an astrophysicist to accept without absolute proof that the universe arose out of nothing. Preexistence always exists." She motioned to Brennen. "You made a great analogy when you were explaining the difficulties when attempting to clear one's mind. You said it was like sand falling back into a hole. You are right, even the concept of 'nothing' still takes quite a bit of thought. The consciousness drones on in the background. Even when we sleep, our consciousness is expressed in dreams."

Brennen's ears perked at the thought of dreams.

"Okay," Scott said, "but where is your proof? I can't imagine Carl Sagan would accept something like this without it being put through the—what do you call it? The scientific method?"

Diana guffawed. "You are going to make a terrific lawyer, Scott. I will give you that."

Scott put on a proud smirk.

"It's called the vacuum state, or zero-point field. It's the measurable amount of energy left over when all energy has been taken away. You can Google it. The theory has been around for a long time and is very real. Though barely detectable in trace amounts, it's an energy source billions of times more powerful than you can imagine when applied to the universe." She cleared her throat and shifted her weight. "And I believe it could be the source of our consciousness, though my colleagues would certainly disagree." Her mouth smiled, but her eyes remained expressionless behind the shaded glass.

Beth watched Diana with the eyes of a school girl at her first rock concert. "So no one believes you?"

"It's not that they don't believe me," Diana said. "It's that consciousness is not open for debate. It has been deemed, for lack of a better word, an illusion—elementary brain processes."

Fearing to speak more, Beth did not further the conversation.

"That is pretty mind-blowing stuff," Scott said. "It kind of hurts my brain to try to just undo what Nova has taught me for years, but I guess until they can get quantum theory and relativity to agree, all bets are cosmically off."

"You sound like Manny," Diana said, "and that's just it. My theory doesn't disagree with any current scientific pedestals. It only adds to them."

"Who is Manny?" Scott asked.

"Her late husband," Brennen answered.

Diana shot him a look of disapproval.

"Sorry. I figured that out earlier—when I was reading your mind. My bad."

"You asked where my proof is, Scott." She pointed at Brennen. "For all I know, he's sitting right in front of me."

To Diana, Beth said, "So what does any of this have to do with Brennen?"

Diana waved a finger in the air. "Good point, Beth. Thank you for keeping me on track. Don't get me started, as they say."

Brennen ran his fingers through his hair.

"Brennen," Diana continued, "may I ask how long you've been using?"

Not being used to talking about his personal habits in front of respectable and sober people, Brennen squirmed. "Uh, about three years." He glanced at Scott, who was pretending to study the floor. "Yes, three years."

"And you mentioned you suffer headaches when your . . . *ability* kicks in?"

Brennen nodded.

Diana looked at her three guests from beneath her sunglasses with considerable concern. "Now first of all, let me say that I am no doctor and you should have Brennen's head looked into professionally. Please promise me you will do this when you leave. Secondly, what I'm about to suggest is my opinion only."

The three of them agreed.

"As far as *my* assessment of Brennen's hyper-natural

brain activity, I think perhaps the heavy amphetamine use has somehow granted him access to the background consciousness." She crossed her arms on the desk, attempting another angle of the explanation. "Picture the brain as a sponge that only allows a certain amount of liquid through."

"Like a filter," Brennen said. "I run my music through filters to focus on one set of frequencies while blocking out the others."

"Perfect," Diana said. "Now, instead of music, think of light. Better yet, think of the light off a slide projector before any images are put through it. Let's say this is the background consciousness.

She had their undivided attention.

"Now, to create an image of a blue sky, you must insert a slide that subtracts every other color but blue, right? In other words, that white light contains the potential to create every image you can imagine. It's only the filters that allow us to make sense of it." She looked at Dave, who had been staring at Brennen for some time. "Now imagine that our brains are simply filters making sense of this background consciousness, or 'Original Light' as I refer to it in the book. Without the filter, we would not know how to process the biological world. Perhaps Brennen is experiencing a partial tear in his filter, allowing him to see more than he is evolved to handle."

Scott stared at Diana droopy-eyed and loose-jawed. "So Glow put a rip in Brennen's filter, and now he can hear things that we just can't detect."

Diana released a brilliant smile. "I was wrong about the

lawyer thing. I think you would make an even better scientist."

"So," Brennen said, "I have substance-induced ESP?"

"I think your ESP could be caused by this rip, as Scott called it. It could be that you're tapping into untapped potential. I don't know how else to explain it logically. The implications are enormous to think about. Your dreams could be—"

"You mentioned dreams earlier," Brennen interrupted. "How does that relate?"

Diana threw up her hands. "Well, dreams could be just another level of the same large-scale consciousness. Awake or asleep are simply two states in the same projector light. Based on that logic, it could be possible to traverse dreams as well."

"What about seeing people in your dreams that are dead?"

Diana gave him another inquisitive look. She'd given thought to this several times since Manny died. It helped her through many down points to think about how Manny's consciousness might still be with her today. She could see her colleagues shaking their heads in dismay at the thought of it. "I really don't know, Brennen."

She despised uttering those awful words.

Brennen was distracted by the image of Triana waving to him, without words, as she sped away in the train. Perhaps the train was a stream of consciousness, filtered for his convenience by his subconscious mind.

"Hey," Scott said, "that was the name of your book, right? *Original Light*?"

Diana pointed a finger at him as though it were a gun and made a clicking noise as she fired. "You got it, Scott."

Beth broke her silence. "What about the animals? The dog, the birds, Dave?"

As if to reiterate her concern, Dave stood up and sniffed the air, never taking his eyes away from Brennen.

At last, Diana was stumped. She had researched her theory for months with Manny, covering every angle, dotting every *I,* crossing every *T,* but she had never considered the effect of the original light on species other than her own.

"You know, that is a better question than any of my students have ever asked me. I can honestly say I have never considered it until now. I feel like such an elitist *homo sapien.*" She rubbed her forehead lightly with her fingers while she pondered. Moments later she lifted her head in excitement. She had not had a Eureka Moment in what seemed to be decades. "It's a well-known fact that animals possess hypersensitivity to certain stimulus. Dogs are known to smell fear, bees can communicate over hundreds of miles, and Canadian geese rely on the earth's magnetic fields for navigation." She rubbed her chin. "It's just an idea, but maybe the animals are drawn to the underlying original light and want to become as close to it as possible."

"Become one with it," Beth said.

Just then, Diana's office telephone jolted everyone out of the deep thought to which they had been chained. The call sounded urgent and ended with Diana rising from her chair before she addressed her guests.

"I'm so sorry. I have an emergency department meeting I have to attend to." She quickly gathered a manila envelope and her mobile phone. “Listen, before you go, let me give you my contact information.” She produced a business card from her desk drawer. “This has my email address and phone number to this office. Oh, and just in case—” She turned the card over and jotted down a number. “This is my home phone and cell phone should you have any more questions.”

Scott accepted the card and secured it in his wallet. “No problem. Thank you so much, Professor Navarro. We have taken up too much of your time as it is.”

Diana gave Scott a business handshake while a special hug was reserved for Beth, explaining that it was indeed nice to meet her. Brennen had already absconded into the fluorescent-lit hallway.

Scott approached him soon after with Beth at his side. He put one arm around each of them. “I can’t believe it.”

“What?” Brennen asked.

“My best friend’s a freakin’ X-Man.”

16

October 30: Around Noon

A

Aside from the summer months when air conditioning was mandatory, Sergeant Pederson preferred the office windows open. However, the racket from the nearby helicopter made it impossible to conduct the meeting with his colleagues. It had already been a hectic morning. His washing machine at home had slipped a gear, forcing him to wear the same uniform for a second straight day. If that wasn't enough, the coffee machine in the break room quit working, making each task without his morning mug seem twice as complicated and take three times as long.

He arose from his swivel chair and slammed the window shut, reducing the din to a low rumble. "Jesus," he said, walking back to his desk, "what the hell are they *doing* out there?"

Sitting across from his cluttered desk were Detective Oakley, in business attire, positioned with one leg crossed over the other with clipboard in hand, and Officer Davis. He held a much more relaxed demeanor, holding a pencil and a Post-it notepad, bouncing his leg, without question annoying his partner.

He called them the Polar Pods—polar opposites, yet peas in a pod.

Detective Oakley spoke. "As part of Homeland Security

training for our SWAT team, the military loaned us a Blackhawk for a helicopter-repelling exercise taking place at our chopper hangar."

Sergeant Pederson muttered under his breath about the crappy timing of helicopter drills and reclaimed his swivel chair. The chair hissed as the weight of him was pushed from the padding. "Okay, what can either of you tell me about this Beth Perkins suspect?"

"Nothing, sir," Officer Davis said. "No public records, no social security number. Aside from the fact she is from Paiute Rock City, Arizona and is married to this Jacob Perkins guy." He peeked at his Post-it note pad to double-check his facts. "Who claims she killed someone named Betty Perkins."

"Perkins again," the sergeant said. "Was it Jacob's sister or something?"

"Not sure, sir," Officer Davis said. "The man's initial report was kind of vague. He just said she was related."

"Well, that's a bit weird, don't you think?" Sergeant Pederson asked.

"It gets weirder, sir," Detective Oakley said. "The morning shift surveillance team reported that the Reynolds suspect has not been back to his apartment since his interrogation. However, they did report a suspicious man in a security officer's uniform sniffing around the suspect's apartment."

Sergeant Pederson reached for his cup of coffee, only to remember there was none. He wasn't sure where she was going with this, but remained engaged.

"To make a long story short," Detective Oakley continued, "they ran the plates of the man's truck and it came back as being registered to Perkins Construction Company in Paiute

Rock City, Arizona."

After a short pause, the sergeant's eyes narrowed in comprehension. "Perkins *again*. Well, that is interesting, isn't it?"

The three exchanged glances until all eyes were on Officer Davis.

He looked less in sync than his colleagues. "What?"

Sergeant Pederson folded his hands flat on the desk. "Well what does that tell you, Davis?"

For a few moments he fidgeted and scratched his cleanly shaven head until the answer sparked to life through his eyes. "It means there is a probable connection between Beth Perkins and Brennen Reynolds."

The sergeant winked and nodded. "Details, Davis. It's always in the details."

"And here is another thing to think about," Detective Oakley said, ignoring her apprentice. "From what I can infer, Jacob Perkins is a respected man in his community. In fact, there are rumors of him being some type of preacher, or even a prophet."

The sergeant emitted a slight grimace. "Uh-oh. *That's* always tricky."

Detective Oakley adjusted her glasses and opened the clipboard, shuffling through papers until the correct one was located. "As you know, there have been several incidences of prophets disappearing across the country; one reported in Tennessee and two more in New Mexico. The Prophet John and the Prophet R.W."

"The Prophet Butcher case, sure," Sergeant Pederson answered.

"Well," Detective Oakley said, "based on the Reynolds interrogation, the guy is little off-kilter. I mean, let's be honest, he's a *lot* off-kilter."

The sergeant interjected, "So you think Reynolds could be the prophet butcher. Perhaps Jacob suspected something and had his man come down from Paiute Rock City to check him out?"

"I'm saying we shouldn't rule it out, sir," Detective Oakley said.

The boss chewed on the thought for a while. "Not bad, Oakley. Not great, but not bad." He began organizing the papers around his desk. "Let's keep on the Reynolds surveillance. I want both of you on evening surveillance tonight. Let's also try to get some more info on Jacob Perkins, as well. If he's a prophet, who is he 'propheteering' for, if that is a word. We need to double efforts to find the Perkins girl, too. I will notify Chandler, Gilbert, Mesa, and Phoenix police to be on the lookout for a female twenty-something with auburn hair with a mole on her upper lip. Some call it a beauty mark, I'm calling it a mole." He gave a no-nonsense look to both team members. "Do we copy?"

Detective Oakley looked at Officer Davis and back at her superior. "You want me go out with—"

"With *Davis*, yes. That is correct, Oakley. I told you, Johnson is out sick and it's gotta be you two tonight."

Officer Davis smiled and gave Detective Oakley a thumbs-up.

After the meeting, Sergeant Pederson sat with more on his mind than previously. Reynolds was suspicious, without a doubt, and would benefit from an earnest stint in rehab, but in his experience on the force, any case dealing with a prophet figure was both dangerous and complicated. In another world, one in which he could pick and chose the cases he worked, he would avoid any direct contact with contagious, cultic figureheads and their followers. However, he lived in *this* world, and in this world, he was sworn to protect the innocent, which is what he intended to do.

He again reached for his empty coffee cup. It was still empty.

"You've got to be shitting me," he said to himself. To anybody in the office who would listen, he said, "Does anybody have any effin *coffee?*"

B

Beth, Scott, and Brennen returned to Scott's apartment, all of them sporting new sunglasses.

Snippety greeted them at the door, furious. "Murowerr!"

"Hey, Snippety!" Beth said. "How *are* you?"

"Hhhh," she hissed.

"Oh my gosh, I think she's mad at us." To the cat, she said, "Are you mad that we left you alone?"

Snippety raised her paw in a high five, exposing her white belly. The undersides of her paws were pink. "Eer!"

Beth crouched down and picked up her feline girlfriend. "We're so sorry. We will take you with us next time."

Scott excused himself to his bedroom for a while, reminding the two of them that, as exciting as all of this was, he was still a law student with exams to prepare for. Brennen and Beth had been rather quiet on the drive back, leaving Scott with the burden of addressing many of the several elephants in the car. *What did they make of what Professor*

Navarro said? Is it safe to go back to Brennen's? What should they do now? Nothing had been decided, so Scott suggested they relax at his place to decompress and come up with a game plan.

Brennen found a comfortable area of the living room to lie down and stretch his back. Staring at the ceiling, he put his knees up and locked his hands behind his head, breathing audibly.

Beth sat on the couch with the weight of the day's occurrences, as well as past events, in her thoughts. She remembered the girl she used to be, eleven or twelve, new to the compound, playing Doomsday on the dirt hill with the other girls—always girls. Betty and Jane were among them. Many years her senior, she had always looked up to them. They were like aunts to her before they became sister-wives. Now, it was very possible that Betty was dead. Would Jane be next?

Doomsday was just a game, but was based in fact. There were community members and there were Othersiders. The members were righteous; the Othersiders were wrong-doers. The members were trustworthy and Othersiders were not. The Othersiders were to be feared. In the end, they would only cause harm. They would all be judged and destroyed, while the righteous would remain on the hill and be granted access to the celestial kingdom.

But there were facts about Othersiders she hadn't been taught. With every minute she remained in their world, she was forced to reassess them. Brennen was an Othersider, yet he helped her escape without asking anything in return. Dante was not only a very generous man, but put himself in danger to protect her from members of her own community. Scott was a gentle, kind, and thoughtful person (and excited her in more ways than she cared to admit). And it was hard to imagine that Professor Navarro, the smartest person she had ever been around, secretly wished her harm. These people were not evil. They didn't sacrifice barren women. They didn't murder people or implant devices into their hands. Mr. *Bratch* and *Jacob* did these things, and the people of the compound were either oblivious to it or they let it happen.

She looked down at her bandage and thought about her scar and her God. She had not had a chance to think of him over the last several hours, but now, in the silence, He once again entered her thoughts.

God.

She felt empty, as though abandoned from light and love. She grappled with the horror that her lover, her lord and savior, and her best friend had not only left her, but was never there to begin with. All the security in her recent life built from the kiss of God was taken away in an instant, leaving her to feel as though she were treading in freezing water that had been solid ice just moments before.

Her eyes welled with tears.

"Is everything all right?" Brennen asked.

Beth wiped the tears with the palm of her bandaged hand. "How about you? Can you still read thoughts?"

Brennen removed his sunglasses, still groggy from sleep, and met her with bloodshot eyes. "Uh, you are worried about Betty. . . . Something about Doomsday on a hill. You feel like you could talk to Professor Navarro for hours . . . and something about Scott—couldn't catch it—too many other thoughts going on."

Beth flipped down her sunglasses. "I'll take all that as a yes."

"It's never lasted this long before," Brennen said, letting his head succumb to gravity.

Beth watched as Snippety pranced around the corner and climbed onto Brennen, spun three times and set herself, sphinx-like, on his chest. She looked up at Beth, expecting a good petting.

"Eer," said the cat.

Beth noticed the living room ceiling fan in the reflection of Brennen's sunglasses. It was rotating, giving the illusion that Brennen bore pinwheel pupils spinning with crazed animation into space. Just beneath them was a scar on his cheek, about one inch in length that ran parallel to his cheekbone. Beth imagined Mr. Bratch or Jacob placing a tracking device in Brennen's cheek. She knew it was impossible, but the thought disturbed her nonetheless.

"How did you get that scar?" She waited an awkward amount of time while he ignored her. She tilted her head in curiosity. Two or three times she spoke his name while waving her hand in front of his eyes.

Still there was no answer.

She moved the cat aside and put her ear to Brennen's chest to make sure he was still breathing. He was. His heartbeat was soothing, but it was more than that. There was inexplicable pull that kept her head where it was. Like the pit bull, Snippety, and Dave, she felt a desire to stay. It wasn't a desire fueled by sensuality, but rather by vitality. While searching for the words to describe it, she realized she was tired, so tired.

She fell asleep.

C

What might have been discussed during the faculty meeting was lost on Diana. Any pressing departmental matters seemed trivial next to her earlier experience with Brennen. Now, late afternoon Friday, when most people were planning their weekend, she sat in her office with Dave, rehashing the events of the day.

She felt she had tried to explain too much to them. On the other hand, she had never witnessed abilities such as Brennen's. How could she do anything less but to explain, to the best of her ability, the phenomenon she had witnessed? She, of course, could have been wrong about everything. The mind, after all, is still quite an untapped processor of information.

She would have loved nothing more than to have the three of them walk back through her office door. Now that she had more time to prepare for them, she would sit Brennen down and ask him to elaborate on his experiences. She wanted to know him better. She, in a very real way, desired him. It was an odd desire—physical but not hormonal, tender but not loving. Perhaps it was what Dave was feeling as he hoisted himself on Brennen's shoulder. Perhaps they were both feeling the pull of the background consciousness. Perhaps it was her and Manny's theory come to life. Through Brennen, she may have had a personal brush with the original light.

Why the eyes? Why was he only able to read thoughts

when looking into someone's eyes? During the entire process of researching and writing her book, she failed to imagine how the original light might traverse between subjects. It was plausible that the eyes were the portal, yet it would be difficult to test the theory against measurable and repeatable means. It was already difficult for her colleagues to soberly accept, or even consider, the idea of a spiritual consciousness, let alone its means of travel. Furthermore, Brennen would have to be high for a *long* time in order to study his behavior, and she was reluctant to advocate the use of whatever substance he was using.

There could be other consequences as well.

At once, she was immersed in a disturbing thought. Lost in the wonderment of Brennen's extrasensory ability, she had failed to consider the potential danger he was facing. The drug itself. The catalyst of his abilities seemed to be a dangerous narcotic. If these symptoms started a few weeks ago it stood to reason they would continue to worsen from this point on. If, in fact, Brennen had somehow suffered a breach in his ability to filter out the original light due to continued drug use, what was the logical conclusion of the course?

She wished again she could speak to him and cursed herself for not obtaining any of their contact information. Haste had gotten the best of her when they parted ways: She'd handed Scott her card, but had not requested his in return.

To Dave, she said, "Wait a second. I can find him in the student directory. What was his last name?"

Dave had done little moving since Brennen's visit. He sat

hunched over with his eyes fixated on Diana. He seldom twitched his nose.

She sat upright, giving the university email directory her full attention. "Was it Barrington? Bartlett?. . . . Shit!"

Dave remained silent.

17
October 30: Dusk

A

The remnants of the dream scattered like roaches from a flashlight's beam. It had been dusk. The man had been in his early forties with blond hair, graying at the temples, and dirty-blue eyes. He was wearing a jogging outfit, although the man had not been jogging. He was approaching Brennen from the right, floating down a swift-moving river in an inflatable raft. In his right hand was a glass of red wine poured into a plastic wine glass, while his left hand supported the wine bottle in his lap.

Brennen had been standing on a decrepit wooden dock which looked to be on the verge of collapse. He remembered acting as the voyeur in the dream, observing the scene and the people within it. There were many—perhaps one hundred—indiscriminate people in separate rafts, passing him by. Their eyes all faced forward with blank expressions as the current carried them from the near-future into the present. Being the closest to Brennen, the man in the jogging suit had been no different. He remained blank-faced even as he took a sizable gulp from his glass, not bothering to wipe a small residual drizzle from his chin. As he drifted closer, the details of the jogger's face became clearer. His chin was weighted and sprouted gray-and-blond stubble. His eyes were motionless until they looked at Brennen.

Brennen felt a tinge of panic, as though he had been caught spying on the man. He was no longer watching the scene, but had become an active participant *in* it.

The dock began to creak under his feet. Brennen looked down to check his footing before he met the man's gaze once more. The jogger's lips peeled back into a wide smile, baring teeth stained with the wine, giving the appearance of bloody gums.

He raised his glass to Brennen as he passed.

A moment later, the dock collapsed and Brennen woke up on a couch with the sound of splintering wood in his ears and feeling of cold, dark water on his skin. He was sweating profusely while staring at an aging Marlon Brando in a framed Godfather poster fastened to the wall. It was coming back to him in gradual increments. He was safe, for the time being, at Scott's apartment.

He felt motion on his chest and was surprised to see Beth, who had been using him as a pillow, waking up with a puzzled look on her face. She scrambled for her sunglasses and brandished them with haste.

"Oh my God," she said, "I am so sorry." She jumped to her knees and rubbed her face. Her ponytail was crooked. "I saw Snippy sitting there, and it looked comfortable, so I guess I . . . I am so sorry."

"Don't worry about it. I totally understand."

Scott stopped in his tracks as he emerged from his room wearing a black Philadelphia Eagles tee-shirt and gray sports shorts. On his head were his Ray Ban sunglasses. "Whoa, I'm not interrupting anything, am I?" He let out a nervous laugh.

"No, not at all," Beth said, "I just . . . fell asleep."

Brennen teased her about her now disheveled ponytail as she attempted to tie it again to its original style. He threatened to take a picture of it, digging in his pocket to fish out his phone. Only when he was setting up the shot, did he realize it was dead. “Holy shite. What time is it?”

Scott consulted his phone. “It’s, uh, 5:36 p.m. . . . Friday.”

“I have to go. My phone is dead, my charger is at home, and I need to work tonight.” He began to scan the apartment for belongings, bumping an end table and nearly knocking a lamp over as he did. “If I don’t make some cash, I could be out of a place to live and I won’t have money to . . . well, to do anything.” This was not something he could risk—not now. “Scott, can Beth hang here for a while?” He grabbed his keys and shoved them into his pocket, his breathing now labored. “I’ll be back in a few hours, I swear.”

Scott shifted his bewildered gaze from Beth to Brennen. “Yeah, I guess so. I mean, if she *wants* to.” He again looked at Beth. “Would that be cool?”

She indicated that it would. To Brennen, she said, “You do whatcha gotta do and we’ll be just fine.” She smiled. “Just get back safe.”

Brennen lingered a moment on her words. It was the most casual, conversational thing he had ever heard her say.

Scott shot him a distrusting look. “Don’t think I don’t know you’re going to get your stash.” He crossed his arms. “Either way, you had better be back here. Don’t be a tweaker and disappear for days. You know the definition of insanity is doing the same thing over and over and expecting different results.” As if sensing the remark had been harsh, he shook his head and changed the subject. "Besides, I researched your situation with the Tempe PD. I need to talk to you about your options."

"Right," Brennen said, stung by Scott's comment. "Thanks, Dad." He opened the door and walked out, shutting the door with protest.

He made a fast descent down the two flights of stairs, using his hands to shield his eyes from the rays of sunset as best he could. As he neared the bottom, he saw a middle-aged woman floating on a tanning raft at the pool. She had taken an immediate interest in him as he descended the stairs. She began waving in his direction, but he hurried by her and made his way to the Escalade in the parking lot.

He approached the driver's side door and glanced again at the woman in the pool, who had since turned her attention elsewhere. The sight of her raft reminded him of the dream. He could only remember the greater details—the figures in the rafts, the river, the rickety dock, and the jogger with the red-stained grin—forgetting any events leading up to them. He thought of Professor Navarro and her theory of his condition. If his mind was somehow losing its ability to filter out this "original light" as she called it, and was now somehow connecting to thoughts of the minds of others and interacting with people who have passed on, would that mean that the people in his dreams were all dead? If not, who was the jogger? Had he also passed on?

Though he had just awoken, sleep had still evaded him. His energy had been steadily decreasing over the last few days and he was finding he needed more and more Glow just to stay awake for a few hours. He was sure the next batch of

Dante's finest would mesh and mold positive solutions from the negativity that now clouded his mind. He needed to get home, refuel, and make enough money to cover Dante's expenses and rent. After all, commerce had no exemptions for mind-readers. At the end of the day, a psychic without a home is just a homeless psychic. He would trade it all for some normalcy.

He revved up the engine and put the Escalade in gear when he heard a metallic crunching sound from the street. It was the unmistakable sound of a car wreck. Someone had failed to use their signal, Brennen assumed, running the other driver off the road and into a street sign near Scott's apartment. Airbags had been dispersed, but the driver seemed to be unharmed, though his car was taking up an entire lane. It was only a matter of time before traffic would begin to get congested.

Brennen squeezed by the flustered motorist, explaining with as much politeness as time would allow that he did not witness the accident and was in an unavoidable rush. He watched in the rearview mirror as the man paced the sidewalk while dialing a number on his mobile phone.

Brennen drove under duress on the way home, ignoring posted speed limits the entire drive. The exceptional Arizona sunset taken for granted as it had been for years.

B

After Brennen left, Scott tried to blank out his friend's incorrigible behavior by studying. He rocked back and forth on his La-Z-Boy, listening to an old song by the Irish songwriter, Enya, through headphones while brushing up on terminology for an upcoming exam in Constitutional Law. If his father walked through the door at that moment, Scott would never hear the end of how imprudent his study habits were. Fortunately for Scott, his father was not the type to make surprise visitations. In fact, ever since his overdose, there had been no "hanging out" with his father, no visits, only scheduled meetings where business was administered and allocated. He could hear the emotionless tone of the judge in his mind.

I'm telling you, young man, you need to decide on your area of concentration. No one will simply hand you a law degree because you took some classes for a couple years. Show some initiative. Or did the drugs soften your brain?

The thought of his father's condescending slights were enough to break his already weakened concentration. He removed the headphones and listened. Beth was still in the bathroom. Scott had suggested she might have a fresh perspective after a nice hot shower followed by some real dinner at one of his favorite restaurants. To his surprise, she had accepted the offer with practically no hesitation, leaving Scott thankful he'd cleaned the bathroom the previous day. There had been a time in his life when toothpaste globs and tub rings were acceptable, but those days were long gone.

He was unsure of what to do with Beth or where he could take her that didn't put her back into the hands of the prophet. He had found some interesting information about Jacob Perkins and his construction company, but would need more time figure out a way to prove Beth's innocence, or at least Jacob's guilt. He had established a trusting rapport with one of his professors in the degree program. Perhaps on Monday, he might offer some under-the-table consultation. In the meantime, Scott was aware that aiding and abetting her—and Brennen, for that matter—was dangerous, yet he was sure, in his gut, of her innocence.

Lawyers don't work on guts, Son. They work on facts.

He was also aware that the girl was burrowing into his heart at a rapid rate. She may have been an oddball with a jaded past, but from the moment she arrived at his door, something deep within him knew it would be difficult to see her leave. He had never been a believer in the concept of love at first sight, but he did consider love at *second* sight when he saw her that morning. If that wasn't enough to convince him, he was a firm believer of love at third sight when he saw her again waking from her nap that afternoon. Straight out of slumber, she was still angelic. To his regret, she had been napping next to Brennen.

Out of any other thoughts, this bothered him the most. Had she taken a liking to Brennen? What could she possibly see in an irresponsible Glow-head like him? As much as he liked his friend, his respect level for him had roller-coastered over the past twenty-four hours. Brennen, whom he hadn't heard from in two years, barges in his apartment, apologizes for past transgressions, and then has the nerve to not only bring drugs into his house, but use it in front of his face. Why would Beth find that a desirable quality? On the other hand, Brennen did introduce Beth into his life, and that was worth something.

You're a hopeless romantic, Son.

"Maybe so, Dad," Scott said to himself, "but at least I can still feel."

Though night had fallen and it was beyond normal

swimming hours, Mrs. Elhenicky was not normal. It was not much of a surprise, then, that she was still relaxing on a chaise lounge by the pool, Kindle in hand, when he and Beth descended the stairs with Snippety. She was all too prepared for conversation once they reached the stairwell, where she once again showered Beth with compliments and embarrassed her by asking if she and Scott were romantically involved. When she saw the cat, she insisted they take her out of the case for a closer look. It was several minutes before Scott was able to pull Beth and himself away by demonstrating a false sense of urgency. It was deceitful, but it allowed them a chance to get in his car and attempt to hurry out of the parking lot.

In his haste to leave, Scott failed to notice the commotion on the street. Before he knew it, he was behind a small traffic jam leading out of the apartment complex.

There was a loud rapping on Scott's window and the reflection of the interior lights made it difficult to ascertain the identity of the knocker. From Scott's vantage point, it was a person dressed in dark clothes, holding a flashlight. As the window rolled down, it took the shape of a Phoenix police officer.

"There has been an accident," she said. "I'm going to have to ask you to pull around and use the other exit."

Scott nodded. "No problem, Officer." He began to put the car in reverse.

The officer turned her flashlight to Beth and studied her face.

Beth managed to maintain a smile while squinting in the bright light.

"Thanks again, Officer," Scott said. "We have to get going." He pointed at Beth's bandaged arm. "We have to get her arm checked out. It's just a little burn, but you can't be too careful."

The officer did not answer Scott, but instead turned the flashlight on Snippety. "You are going with a cat?"

Snippety raised her paw at the officer, expecting a high-five.

"We take her everywhere," Scott said with a smile. "We have to. Otherwise she pees on my law books if we leave her behind." He thought his commitment to the law might in some way score points with the officer.

The officer was not amused. In fact, Scott was sure she was going to ask that he and Beth step out of the car for questioning. Only when the idea seemed inevitable did the officer step away and wave them on.

"That was not Godtastic at all," Scott said as he pulled out of the alternate exit.

Beth was holding a shaky hand to her forehead as if she was thinking of what to say. "Holy shit."

It was as good as anything.

C

Scott decided that a healthy option dinner would be just the thing to calm his nerves. They left Snippety in the car with the cat toy. She assured them she would be fine in the car (if the windows were cracked).

Scott took Beth to a restaurant specializing in falafel sandwiches served with custom salads and sauces. The patio overlooked the pedestrian-rich Mill Avenue district in downtown Tempe. With ASU in mid-semester, the surrounding nightlife was teaming with students eager for experience.

Beth continued to amaze him. It was true, he had not had much contact with people in his two years of sobriety, let alone someone of her beauty and mystique. In prior circumstances, he would have let his shyness silence him, yet, as out of practice with the female gender as he had become, she was able to make the words come with ease as they moved from one interesting topic to another. It helped that she was like a child in an ice cream parlor, experiencing this Othersider world with dreamy wonderment. For Scott, it was infectious. In many ways, her discoveries about pop culture were his re-discoveries, his re-born appreciation for the little things in life. With her, his worries, his studies, his father's pressure, all seemed epochs away, allowing him to enjoy *this* moment instead of one existing in the future or past.

She seemed different this evening, somehow *evolved.* Her smile was brighter, her laugh more genuine, and her eye contact became deep and engaging. Her shyness had given way to a bolder, more charming, yet humble Beth Perkins and Scott was overjoyed to be her guide through this special time. Not only was he a teacher to her, he was her most attentive student as well. He hung on every word as she spoke, sometimes through a mouth of falafel salad, about her community, Mr. Bratch, and Jacob.

"This may be the best salad I've ever had," Beth said, "Nothing like the thin lettuce we grow at the compound."

By now, she had enough trust in Scott to disclose the polygamy element of her life. He was able to process the information internally, hoping his discomfort was not sprouting from all over his face. The whole business with Jacob was, on many levels, profoundly wrong and he knew there was some form of legal recourse Beth could take given a little more time and an experienced lawyer.

Scott broke eye contact to take a bite of his sandwich. “Speaking of the compound, I found some interesting information regarding Jacob this afternoon.”

Beth’s interest was piqued. She sipped an iced tea and told him to continue.

“The use of GPS trackers, like the one you found in your hand, are not only illegal, but have been banned from production in the state of Arizona and are not being sold, at least to the public.”

Beth looked at her bandage. “So how did one end up in my hand?”

Scott cleared his throat. His water glass was empty and he was in desperate need of another. “Well,” Scott continued while scanning the restaurant for the waiter, “it turns out that, years ago, a Utah-based company, called The Aluluei Corporation, first manufactured an implantable microchip capable of locating an individual by mapping their direction of movement, latitude, longitude—basically GPS.” Scott took a moment to bring Beth up to speed on GPS in general. She had seen him use a maps program on his phone and was fascinated.

She comprehended with little difficulty.

“The Aluluei Corporation originally manufactured the chip as a means of not only storing medical records of patients suffering from Alzheimer’s and dementia, but tracking them should they become separated from their caretakers."

"Dementia is a kind of brain disease, I'm guessing?"

"Exactly. However, Aluluei overpromised their contracted hospitals on the number of units it could manufacture and could only produce one hundred of the one thousand agreed upon, which ended up in a lawsuit with the hospital. It wasn't long before activist and critics protested the use of the devices, citing they could be used for human repression, both domestic and political. For instance, if fallen into the wrong hands, kidnappers would have a way to track children and slaveholders would have a perfect tool to prevent their captives from escaping."

"Who in the world would do *that?*" Beth's face was dead pan.

Scott was caught off guard. There was a moment when Scott thought to answer her, as though she were serious. However, once he realized she was referring to Jacob (and at his expense, no less) he surrendered a laugh.

Beth joined him.

"You got me," Scott said, shaking a finger at her. "That was a good one. *Anyway*, don't make me laugh right now. I'm trying to tell you something."

Beth repressed a smile.

Scott scanned the room once again for the waiter. "So, five years ago, Aluluei halts all manufacturing of the chip and goes out of business. At the same time, three employees, rumored to have tested the implants on themselves unexplainably drop everything and move away. The unused chips disappear at the exact same time."

Beth looked confused.

"Keep in mind," Scott continued, "Aluluei was in southern Utah, only the next state up from here. So I did some digging into the lawsuit and was able to view the final expense report for Aluluei. One of the last entries was for a miscellaneous expense for one point one million dollars. And guess who the charge came from?"

Beth shrugged her shoulders, her smile receding into a blank stare.

"Perkins Construction Company."

Beth's expression flattened out, but there was no hint of humor this time. She looked at her bandage and rested her face in her hands. "Oh my God."

Scott could only look at her with empathy.

"Oh my God," Beth repeated. "That son of a bitch. That awful, horrible shithead of a man. Why is it always men? My whole life, they've shoved me in a corner and I stayed there. Like a little obedient dog, I did what they said. I feared everything they ever wanted me to fear. The apostles, who are probably all liars as well, were always threatening me with violence or with God—and then Jacob with his aggression. Always aggression."

Scott sat silent. Her venting, in his opinion, was justified.

"I'm sorry, Scott. You seem nice and all, but your species needs work. No offense, I'm just having a hard time coming to grips with the fact that I was basically a captive, along with a number of other girls." She took another sip of tea. "Betty had a scar, too, which means they probably tracked her movement and knew she took the key to the mail truck." Her expression saddened. "Oh my God, Betty."

"No offense taken, and you are right. You were a captive, an illegal captive in an illegal marriage. I think you may be able to make a case against Jacob. It will certainly be tricky with an entire community of fanatic cult members protecting him, no offense, corroborating Jacobs's allegations."

"None taken," Beth said.

Scott retrieved his phone from his pocket and began scrolling through his notes. "Now I'm going to read to you the three names of the people who disappeared from Aluluei. Let me know if any of them sound familiar."

Beth conceded.

"Bob Stanza, Kevin Jones, Larry Hitchcock."

"Larry Hitchcock! Yes, I *know* him. He's one of the guys who broke into Brennen's apartment; one of the guys Dante beat up. He is one of Jacob's apostles."

"I wouldn't be surprised if Jacob talked him into selling the chips for a piece of the celestial pie, so to speak. One point one million dollars for a black market technology and a man who knew how to boot it up. That's probably a drop in the bucket for Jacob. Such a deal."

Beth crossed her arms and looked out at the nightlife on Mill Avenue.

Scott searched for the waiter for the last time. Without warning he stood up, raising his empty water glass. "Hey, can I get some water over here or what!"

At once, the flustered waiter rushed to the table gushing exorbitant apologies.

"I've been sitting here for like five *minutes*, man," Scott said. "What do I gotta do to get some water?"

"You did more than enough, Scott," Beth said with one

eyebrow raised at him. Her arms were still crossed. To the waiter, she said, "*Thank* you for doing that. You are very nice."

The waiter accepted the compliment humbly.

"And," Beth continued, "Scott here apologizes for yelling at the whole restaurant." She gave Scott a smile. "Don't you, Scott?"

He was disarmed. There was no way he could counter this brilliantly played peace offering. He flashed a shamed smile. "I'm sorry, man." He looked at Beth. "I just got a little excited and I apologize unreservedly. We will take a check as well when convenient."

After the waiter parted, Scott adjusted his clothing, but could still feel Beth's eyes all over his face.

"You should relax a little, Scott." She reached out and patted his hand. "The waiter was busy. It looks like the restaurant is swamped tonight. They are doing the best they can."

Switching the subject, he offered to talk to his law professor on the following Monday if she didn't have an issue laying low with either him or Brennen over the weekend.

"Only if you promise not to stand up and shout at people."

Scott promised he would.

The waiter returned with the check and Scott filled it out, calculating the tip in his head. "And you know I can stay out of the way if you want to. You can hang out with Brennen."

"What are you *talking* about?"

"Well, I mean, you were sleeping on the floor with, or next to, him, and I just thought—"

"Scott," Beth interrupted, "I fell asleep next to him, that's all. What did we just say about calming down?"

Scott gave the universal sign for locking his lips shut and throwing away the key.

D

Sergeant Pederson tapped his pencil on his desk as he cradled the phone in his shoulder, listening to his boss, Lieutenant Sylvester Arroyo, as he bombarded him with questions he wasn't quite prepared to answer. To him, it was far better to keep his boss under-informed until the final details came in, than to give him half-cocked ideas with no tangible results. It was for his lieutenant's own good to selectively withhold information whenever possible, as anything less than rock-solid solutions to uncomplicated problems seemed to raise the man's blood pressure and send him into fits of cursing.

What he had selected *not* to tell him was the investigation of Beth Perkins was becoming complicated due to lack of cooperation from the Paiute Rock City police. He had been able to initiate contact with an officer on the main number, but after being given the run-around when he asked to speak to someone in authority, he hadn't received a returned phone call in five attempts. He had dealt with this before when dealing with them. Somebody was hiding something. All he knew was that Jacob Perkins had accused Beth Perkins of murder and wanted her brought back for justice. But how much justice can be conducted in a place so sheathed in secrecy?

He would be very curious to hear her side of the story. He wished the Perkins girl would come into the station; he wished it could be so simple. It was, after all, an entire community's word against hers. With any luck, he would be able to judge for himself who told the more palpable story.

He *did* disclose that Detective Oakley's due diligence regarding the community revealed that Jacob Perkins was indeed the spiritual leader of a polygamist religious order called the Fundamentalist Sect, or FS, known for unorthodox religious practices. The origin of the FS was unknown. The people who spoke about it chose their words carefully if they dared speak at all. From what she could deduce, The Prophet Jacob was either a self-proclaimed prophet (as was the case most of the time) or was given the title by birthright. Either way, there wasn't much known about him. Sergeant Pederson assured his boss they were following leads as fast as they were coming in. He didn't bother admitting that no leads were coming in, at all.

Lieutenant Arroyo's voice was shrill over the phone. "Polygamy? So they're *Mormons?*" It came off more of a statement.

"With all due respect, sir," Sergeant Pederson said, "*I'm* a Mormon. And to call these people anywhere *near* Mormons would be an insult."

"Touché, Pederson." His boss chuckled before changing the subject. "Now what about the Reynolds kid?"

"I've got my best two . . . well, I've got Detective Oakley on surveillance at the Reynolds residence right now. She has Officer Davis with her. Things are running as smooth as can be, I can assure you."

"Davis? The new guy?"

"Johnson is out sick."

"Whatever. Just get me some solid info soon; none of this half-assed cracker-barrel shit."

Though he had no idea what the lieutenant meant by the statement, he assured the man better information would be forthcoming and ended the call. He swung his swivel chair around, freeing the phone cord which had become tangled during the conversation. He muttered something about switching to wireless phones and reached for his coffee. This time, the mug was full.

Before he could take a sip, a cadet officer appeared in his doorway.

"Sir," she said, "a girl with red hair and a mole on her upper lip was spotted with a male driver near the Tempe/Scottsdale border. She has a bandage on her right hand and they are traveling with a cat. The Arizona Department of Transportation has the car registered under a Scott Barrett."

He set the mug on his desk. "Okay. This is good. Let's get on the phone with Phoenix PD and get some guys out there now."

18
October 30: Later that Evening

A

Being born and raised in Connecticut, Officer Davis considered himself an expert on East Coast culture. It was one of the few subjects he knew more about than Detective Oakley and he took advantage, explaining to her the architectural styles of New England.

She was not interested.

To Officer Davis, the Nantucket apartments looked as if a portion of the east coast had been displaced in the middle of the desert. It was painted blue, which appeared gray in the dark, and had several wooden posts bordering the walkway with knotted rope hanging between them, giving the appearance of a dock. They liked the charm of it. It had a little bit of everything: a nice laundry facility, a security gate, pool, and Jacuzzi. It even had a neighborhood brewery across the street with specialty hamburgers rumored to be quite good. The aroma had been stimulating their hunger since arriving hours ago.

Brennen Reynolds had not returned.

The hours had passed with the urgency of molasses, and the absence of their person of interest made the clock seem all the more malfunctioning. Though comfortable, the Tahoe provided very little in the way of entertainment. There was no MP3 player or satellite radio. Officer Davis fiddled with the radio until Detective Oakley slapped his hand away, preferring to listen to talk radio. Talk radio drove him nuts to the point where he would have to start conversations that, although interesting to him, were not met with the same jocularity by his colleague.

“No really,” he said, “would you rather be a cockatoo or a dolphin? Keep in mind, depending on the species, dolphins live around twenty to fifty years. You get to spend summers in the Caribbean and, since they have about the same size brain, you will probably be pretty smart, but you will have no thumbs.”

Detective Oakley sighed and adjusted her glasses, keeping the Reynolds apartment in her line of sight.

“But,” Officer Davis continued, “a cockatoo’s lifespan is forty to *sixty* years. So you get to live longer and you get to fly.”

Oakley made a motion to silence him, but changed her mind. “Wait, cockatoos live sixty years?”

Davis grinned and nodded. He was happy he was able to impart his knowledge to her. “So which is it?”

Oakley, realizing she had been sucked into one of his silly conversations again, shook her head. “I *told* you, I’m not answering these questions. They are stupid. I’m not ever going to be either one, so it doesn’t matter.” She began undoing her seatbelt and collecting her two-way radio.

“Where are you going?”

“I’m hungry. Plus, you’re driving me crazy.” She got out of the Tahoe. “I’m going to get one of those burgers from across the street. They smell too good and I can’t concentrate until I have one. Do you want one?”

He indicated that he did.

"Now," she said, "if you see anything suspicious, anything at all, you got your two-way. Buzz me on it. If Reynolds comes back, buzz me on it. You got it?"

"Copy that."

She shut the driver's side door and locked the truck with the remote control. He watched as she disappeared fast around the corner of the apartment complex, headed toward the tantalizing smell of the brewery.

He watched the Reynolds apartment for a few moments before he felt an urge to check his phone for any college football articles. Oakley would never allow him to play with his phone because she was worried the bright screen would attract too much attention to them at night. But a few seconds wouldn't hurt anybody. Besides, his team, the University of Connecticut Huskies, was without their starting quarterback as of this last week and he had been waiting for updates regarding his condition.

He looked around, making sure Oakley hadn't changed her mind about the burgers and was walking back toward him. Within moments his head was bowed into the light of his phone's screen and his thumbs were clicking and swiping their way to the news he was seeking.

A wrapping on the passenger side window startled him, causing him to fumble the phone, the brightness of which made it difficult to see anything outside but his reflection in the glass. He rolled the window down to see a sizable man wearing some kind of Halloween mask.

"Eh," Davis said, "Halloween isn't until tomorrow, bud."

In response, the man pulled out a taser gun and pointed

it at Davis' chest.

B

Not bothering to waste precious seconds fumbling with his keys, Brennen gave his front door a shove. It emitted a thudding sound as the faulty latch easily succumbed against the weight of his body. It felt like weeks since he was last here, speaking to Dante after the attack on Beth.

His focus was centered on getting his phone back and working, so he could start taking calls, so much so that he only partially acknowledged the eviction notice waiting for him fastened with Scotch tape to the front door. He found the charger on the desk, plugged it in and waited for it to come back to life.

The solution was clear. Tonight, he would make enough money to pay Dante and to cover rent. The business would be there, he was sure of it. If not tonight, tomorrow would be a big night, as people always needed rides on Halloween. He'd figure out how to pay his mobile phone, Internet, and electricity bills at another time. Perhaps they'd forget about him or let them slide. Perhaps they'd somehow disappear altogether.

Scott's words surged through his nerves. Expecting different results after the doing the same thing over and over was insane. Now, here he was after three years of Glow, without any forward progress. Here he was with nothing to show for the thousands of hours spent songwriting but a few songs that still needed proper mixing. Here he was alienated from his family. And here he was, averting people's eyes for fear of reading their thoughts. You couldn't get more insane than that.

What had he become?

He walked into the mixing room and stared at the lights of his big droid which had drained his bank account and maxed out his credit cards. They blinked at him in silent disapproval. He had not used them to their potential. Instead, he'd squandered their abilities while completing half-thought compositions. Though warned against it by real sound engineers, he smoked cigarettes around the equipment, filling the circuitry with tar. The same could be said about his *own* circuitry. How much damage had he done to himself in the three years since the Glow came crashing with wrecking-ball force into his life?

He imagined, for perhaps the first time, a life without Glow. It seemed a fantasy at this point—as realistic as a unicorn trotting through his door with a Marlboro cigarette hanging out of its mouth and asking for a light. On the other hand, going forward at this pace would lead him off the edge.

He thought of being lowered into the flames without the protection of Glow. How could he write music without it? He searched his memory, but could not remember a time when he wrote without it. To him, it was always imperative that he be *above* the flames when creating. Anything less was impossible.

He whipped around as he caught movement from the corner of his eye, only to feel like an idiot to see the familiar pulsating purple light of his Mesa Boogie guitar amplifier blinking away into the half lit room.

"Christ," he whispered, "I'm losing my mind."

If he were to break from The Glow, there would be very little chance of being able to write music. Not only would he be unable to swing the countless hours required to mix the music, but his creative crutch would be gone. All of this—the Eventide effects processor, the Focusrite preamps, the Powermac computer, the Pro Tools hardware, the expensive condenser microphones—every aspect of his planned future would be rendered useless, as it was all predicated on Glow.

At once, the most terrifying thought of all yanked on his spinal column like a child in need of attention:

What if he wasn't a songwriter at all?

He thought about it. He had taught himself all the instruments he ever played. He never took a lesson in the art of recording or soundproofing. Could it very well be that the songs he wrote were thousands of mish-mashed notes thrown together with a chintzy drum loop? What if they were just *noise*?

Another headache began.

He felt small. He thought of Professor Navarro's example of the slide projector—how the brain is a filter of sorts used to interpret an infinite consciousness that would be too complex to understand. If she was correct (and he had no better explanation), his "filter" had somehow torn, giving him a glimpse into an unexplained consciousness that allowed him insight into people's thoughts. As it was, he wanted no part of this extra perception. When he was young, he fantasized about having such a power. His Dungeons and Dragons characters and his gaming avatars were fortified with elixirs that enhanced human abilities—telekinesis, ESP, fire bolt—and he would feel a surge of exhilaration when he unleashed them. Now, he had such a power and all he felt was terrified, as if he'd flipped a switch that could not be unflipped; that he was permanently damaged. He wanted no part of it. He didn't want to know what people really thought underneath their smiles and he didn't want to be alienated by them for being able to take their deepest secrets from them. He wanted away from it. He wanted anonymousness. Perhaps if he stopped using, the tear would heal itself and bring him closer to that goal.

The thought gave him solace. Before the self-destruction began, before the personal and emotional wedges, he had once had a normal life. If he could just get back *to* zero instead of being divided *by* it, perhaps he could become someone again. Perhaps he could start tonight. The eviction notice, after all, was not going to go away on its own. The only solution to any of his problems at this point was common sense and money. He had squandered the former, but could make up the latter with a good night of driving.

His phone was back from the dead and was blinking at him as he rushed to the desk to check it. He had missed only one call, but it had nothing to do with driving. It was another call from his sister, Jen. Once again, she had opted not to leave a message. However, he saw that she left a text message this time. He knew she was going to lay into him for not answering his phone or returning her calls. There had not been a good time to speak to her. If there had been, the conversation would only serve to initiate the same argument that had lasted for three years.

As he read the text, the corners of his mouth looked as though weighted fish hooks had been pierced through them. He ran his fingers through his hair and did his best to reread the text as if the words would somehow change given enough time. They did not change. They remained locked to his pupils as he read them a third and fourth time. His eyebrows rose up while the eyeballs beneath them filled with moisture. His free hand covered his mouth as it uttered an almost inaudible whimper.

THANKS FOR RETURNING MY CALLS. WHATEVER. JUST THOUGHT YOU MIGHT LIKE TO KNOW THAT MOMS IN THE HOSPITAL WITH STAGE 4 CANCER IF YOU GIVE A SHIT.

The shock of the text made it difficult to process the movement coming from the vocal booth.

From behind him, a muffled voice spoke, “Don’t worry. I just need proof.”

Brennen turned to see a man dressed in jeans and a sweatshirt with the sleeves tucked under surgical gloves. His face was covered with a clear plastic mask that resembled a mannequin. The taser gun in the man’s hand was a clear indication that there would be no negotiating with him, nor would there be any chance of escaping.

With the best effort he could muster, Brennen ran as far as he could, which was about two feet before the taser's electrodes barreled through the air, striking him in the chest.

Like a blown circuit, Brennen was out.

C

On the way back to Scott’s apartment, Beth took in the Tempe night air while she and Scott talked. She pulled her hair up, rolled down the window and let the air fill her lungs. It felt crystalline, as though treated with extra oxygen, expanding her capillaries to a level never before achieved.

She heard rustling in the back seat and found Snippety.

After an entire afternoon of ignoring her store-bought toys, she was playing with a pen which Scott had inadvertently stolen from the restaurant. This somehow only further endeared her to the cat. As remarkable as she was, it was hard to imagine her as anything but a goofy cat.

As if woken from a daze, Snippety gave what could be construed as a look of embarrassment, and gave Beth a non-aggressive hiss.

Beth laughed, while Snippety raised her paw for a high-five.

Beth asked Scott for the use of his mobile phone again, with which she had become fascinated during dinner. She had observed Othersiders' mobile-phone behavior while sitting at the restaurant, their heads lowered, staring into their phones with their faces illuminated from the light, all in relentless pursuit of information. They researched whatever their hearts desired, the price of gasoline, of hotels, the weather in California, what the latest celebrity was doing with their bodies and with whom. It was all a torrent of new and fascinating knowledge, and she absorbed it like a sponge. Ever since she woke up on Brennen's chest, she felt somehow improved—"evolved" as Scott had put it.

She was able to pick up on social behavior like never before. During dinner, she eavesdropped on the couples surrounding her and Scott without missing the points he was so elegantly making. As he described his tumultuous relationship with his father, she understood the subtleties of sarcasm from the guy in the loose-fitting clothes and hat on backward sitting next to them. While the waiter was taking their order, she inferred how to show empathy from the girl playing acoustic guitar in the street behind them. During dessert, she learned how to flirt from a scantily clad woman at the bar next to them while Scott demonstrated a Google-search on his phone. It was a ritual to which she was now addicted.

Her attention soon shifted to the song playing through the car's speakers. Scott had also demonstrated to her how to advance to the next song on the MP3 player on his phone. She was amazed at not only how many songs Scott had stored, but his familiarity with them. He knew very detail—who wrote it, where it had been produced, what year it was recorded. His knowledge was intoxicating and she found herself entertained by his passion as he described each band, solo artist, or music genre. She would quiz him by giving him three seconds to name each song as well as the artist, while checking the answers on the MP3 player. He had not failed her once.

The most linear conversation they had had on the way home concerned Brennen. Though Beth owed Brennen unfathomable gratitude, she was uneasy with his abilities and felt horrible for it. If it weren't for him, she would never have come this far. He swooped her away from Jacob's men and gave her a place to stay. He introduced her to Scott, who introduced her to Professor Navarro, a woman with more intellect than Jacob could dream of possessing. Indeed, Brennen should be a hero to her, yet she was *scared* of him. Scott, as ecstatic as he was to be reunited with his friend, also confessed concerns for his privacy. He found it uncomfortable that Brennen had access to his thoughts.

"You know, Beth, there is a good chance that Brennen

will not be back later. In fact, he might not be back at all."

Beth lifted her head from the phone. "Why would he not come back?"

"I love him to death, but The Glow, as you know, has a way of making you do things you normally wouldn't do, including ditching your friends."

Beth looked at him with questions pending.

"Look, all I'm saying is if he has to get high, then getting high will take all priority. Everything else is secondary."

Beth stared at him. "He'll be back."

Scott adjusted to a more comfortable position while checking the rearview mirror. "And listen, with all the crazy shit that has gone on in the last couple days, I have no doubt that your life is in danger and I think we should start getting used to the fact that we will eventually have to go to the police."

Beth's face tensed with fear.

"Not yet," Scott clarified, "but soon. After we talk to somebody on Monday."

After some thought, Beth smiled at Scott and nodded. She turned again to face the breeze flowing from the car window. Her residual distrust concerning the Othersider government was difficult to shake. *Any* postponement concerning them was a relief. Likewise, the thought of spending extra time with Scott put her at ease. It was win-win situation for now. Soon they would be home where she would no doubt see Brennen's truck in the parking lot waiting for their return. If Scott didn't have faith in him, she certainly did.

She began researching the meaning of Aluluei and asked

Scott for the correct spelling. He gave his best guess from memory, which turned out to be correct. It seemed that Scott was always correct. She loved that about him, almost as much as the way his clothes fit his body. Of course, she loved his sense of humor and his intellect as well, and was humbled with how he was jealous of Brennen. Though he could be rude to people at times, he had a delicate side as well. She loved that, too.

"Ah, here it is: 'Aluluei: The Micronesian god of navigation.'" She smiled at Scott. "He shared his knowledge of the sea with his people, helping them find their way."

"That makes perfect sense." Scott rubbed his chin a moment before continuing. "What better name for a human navigation system. And like gods, they would always know where to find you." He put on a playful face. "See, Aluluei was a guy and he wasn't so bad."

Beth matched his humor. "Well, I suppose I can give him a pass." Her smile dropped to a frown as she turned from Scott to look out the window. "But you don't know Jacob, Scott. You have no idea what he is capable of." After a slight pause, Beth looked at Scott with concerned eyes. "Don't ever leave me with him."

Scott looked at her as long as traffic would allow before he nodded to her. "I won't."

She hoped he meant it.

She began to reiterate her frustration with men in her life, how she and her sister-wives had been under complete and total totalitarian rule by men since she could remember, how Jacob had squashed any opinion she had ever voiced, and how, even though there were only two or three boys in her childhood, they were all being bred to be apostles. It was this last complaint to which Scott took exception.

"Wait," Scott said, being sure to check his rearview mirror, "there were only two or three boys in your school? The rest were girls? That's, eh, those are some pretty lucky little dudes."

Beth's eyes widened with excitement. "Oh my God, I really love this song!" She leaned over the center console and increased the volume. The beat was driving and the bass was massaging her chest as it rolled along. The guitars were electric, like she had never heard before. She strained her voice to speak to Scott. "The guitar sounds so . . . . I know it's electric, but what makes it sound so, ah, liquidy?"

Scott looked overjoyed to be feeding off Beth's excitement. His voice went up a few semitones as he answered her through the power of the song. "It's called a *chorus* effect. It gives sounds that watery effect you're talking about. It was big in the 'eighties. So was this song."

She closed her eyes and let the music wash over her. "I love the *lyrics*, too." She opened her eyes and smiled at passengers in an adjacent cars as they passed.

The fire in her eyes, keeps me alive.

And the fire in her eyes, keeps me alive, keeps a' me alive.

. . .

"Here's your quiz," Beth said, covering the phone with her hand. "What's the name of the song?"

"That's *easy*," Scott yelled. "It's called 'She Sells Sanctuary.'"

"And what *band* is it, Mr. Law Student?"

"The—" Scott hesitated before answering, as though

contemplating how to respond. "Oh, you are going to love this."

Beth sat wide-eyed with a giggle in her throat.

Scott continued, "The band is called The *Cult*."

At once the car erupted with laughter as they thought about the irony. And for one long moment, Scott Barrett, Beth Perkins, Snippety, and The Cult sped down the street in the late October night with a good vibe and without a care. Perhaps it was the intensity of the positive energy that made the sudden absence of music seem so deafening and Scott's next words so foreign.

"Reer!" Snippety yelled.

"*Holy shit, get down*!" He turned the volume with too much force, breaking off the knob. It fell to the floor of the driver's side. His eyes were focused on the scene ahead. When she followed his gaze, the concern was clear.

The traffic accident at Scott's apartment had since cleared, yet three Phoenix police department squad cars were pulled up near the front pool of Scott's apartment. In the split second Beth was able to wrap her head around the situation, she could see Scott's neighbor, Mrs. Elhenicky, talking to two officers. One was looking about while speaking into her two-way radio while the other had his nose buried in his clipboard taking notes. Mrs. Elhenicky seemed to be making gestures, as if describing someone's height and hair length.

Beth ducked. Her hamstrings ached as she stretched herself as low to the floor as possible. She looked up at Scott. His eyes were perfect circles with dilated black holes for pupils. They were electrified while he scanned the rearview mirror.

"I'm just gonna keep on driving straight and go the speed limit—no quick moves." He sounded as if he were half addressing Beth and half talking to himself. "Wait." The black holes locked into the rearview mirror. "Oh, no. No, no, no, shit, shit, shiiit."

Unable to bear second-hand news for a moment longer, Beth raised her head far enough to look out of the passenger-side mirror. A squad car was creeping out of Scott's apartment behind them. It was dark, but she could make out the unmistakable rectangular shape of cop lights lying atop of the vehicle.

"*Scott?*" Beth said.

At once, the cop lights burst into life, shooting blue and red flashes into the night. Immediately following was the shrieking howl of the sirens.

Beth turned to Scott. "They are *coming. What are we going to do?*"

"I have *no* idea!" Scott's tone was an even match for Beth's. "We can't outrun a cop. No way. Completely stupid! We are just going to have to surrender! Hell, I'll just pull over right now!" Scott put on his blinker, moved to the side of the road and turned on his hazard lights. He put his elbows on the steering wheel and rubbed his temples, "We'll find you a lawyer, someone who will represent you pro bono."

"Scott?"

"I will do what I can, I swear." He continued his train of thought with his eyes shut, making small chopping gestures with his hand as he spoke. "You're the one of the most unique if not *the coolest* person I have met in a long time and I'll be *damned* if I'm going to—"

"Scott. Shut up for a second and look."

He opened his eyes and followed her gaze, where they both witnessed the squad car pull out of the apartment complex and accelerate down the street in the opposite direction.

Beth sat frozen, surrounded by untapped adrenaline and the sound of her heartbeat pounding through her throat. It was a full fifteen seconds before she could acknowledge what just occurred. All she could do was watch as the flashing lights became smaller and the siren faded away like a psychotic prankster running away with the last laugh. She turned to Scott, who was already looking at her.

They embraced without hesitation. And laughed.

With her chin rested on his shoulder, Beth exhaled. "Oh my god, that was *crazy*."

Scott pulled away so they sat face-to-face. "You okay?"

"I'm good. How are you?" Her breathing was still labored.

Scott looked away and faced the steering wheel once more. He checked the rearview mirror again and began preparing to drive. "I'm okay. I just. Eh. I'm not sure where to go at this point. Brennen's pad is out of the question. Now my place is locked down." He scoffed. "Sorry, I don't exactly have a high abundance of friends these days since I sobered up and became a study-monger."

She waved off his apology and changed the subject. "Professor Navarro left her card with her home number. It's in your wallet."

Scott looked unsure about contacting the professor.

"It makes sense," Beth continued. "She already knows the situation with Brennen. She knows he isn't full of shit. From what it sounds like, he's kind of like her life's work come to life. Come on, you saw the look on her face when Dave crawled up Brennen's arm. Besides, she works at ASU just like *your* professor. We could lay low until Monday, just like you said. If we ditch the car, there is no way they could track us to her place."

Scott said nothing, but began to raise an eyebrow.

"We already know she will listen to reason," Beth said. "What can it hurt? The worse thing she can do is hang up on you."

Nodding, Scott said, "All right, why the hell not. Good call." He began digging in his back pocket for his wallet. Within seconds, the hazards were off, blinkers were on, and they were headed to a safer place, farther away from the laughing siren.

D

Brennen awoke on his back, feeling groggy. He was bothered by a few things. The air around him felt stale and tight. The tiny room was dimly lit, causing him to strain his eyes in search of clues as to what was happening. His stomach was empty and his bladder was full. These were meager agitations compared to the fact he was strapped to a hospital gurney with a large syringe full of air sticking out of his arm.

His first instinct was to scream and kick his feet. While he couldn't yell due to the gag in his mouth, he was able to kick quite well. In doing so, he struck a knobby object with his ankle, sending shooting pain up his leg. He could only lift his head a small amount, but it was enough to see the object he kicked was a metal wheelchair.

Where the hell was he? And was the room vibrating?

"Ah," said a muffled voice in close proximity, "the YouTube Prophet awakens."

Brennen tried to speak through the gag.

"Oh, I'm sorry," the muffled voice said, "I have gagged you. Let me help you with that. I should mention that if you scream, I'm going to pump this air into your heart." The man removed the gag with one hand. Though the light was poor, it was clear the man was wearing the same mask as earlier.

Brennen obeyed. He was frightened out of his mind. Not only because he knew this man was dead serious, but because he had no idea what he had done to get on his radar. His gag reflex kicked in as what appeared to be a baseball-sized sponge was pulled out of his mouth. He smacked his lips to kill the taste.

"Okay, what—?" Brennen paused to rethink his wording. The last thing he wanted to do was upset this person. "Okay. I realize that I am in trouble . . . that I have . . . *offended* you in some way. And I apologize for doing so . . . but—and I hope I am not pissing you off when I tell you I don't know what you're talking about—I don't know what you mean by YouTube prophet. . . . I'm sorry."

As if expecting such an answer, the man woke his laptop, illuminating his face. The mask stared him down. Brennen remembered his mother wore a similar mask on Halloween many years ago with the intent to make herself look like a gypsy, but it looked more like a mannequin with a dead-pan expression. The only visible trait of the man was his murky-aqua eyes transpiercing the space between them.

"You know exactly what I'm talking about," the mannequin said. He pressed play on the laptop and turned it around to face Brennen.

Brennen watched the entire video. It was the footage of Brennen taken by the magazine salesman. He watched with embarrassment as he saw himself waving the birds away. At one point, it appeared he was giving the sign of the cross to the camera. Could this guy think that was a religious gesture? His eyes scanned to the title of the video.

JESUS: ALIVE AND WELL AND LIVING IN TEMPE, AZ!!!

Brennen shook his head in protest, but remained silent. He was mesmerized, not so much by being abducted by a man in a mask, but by how horrible he looked in the video. His cheeks were gaunt, his hair looked oily, and his clothes were ill-fitting. He had not recently seen himself anywhere but in the mirror, which had, to his dismay, found ways to lie to him for years, selectively presenting only what he could glimpse at one angle. It failed to show him the grotesque manner in which his collar bone jetted out of his neck when he turned his head away. His movements were as jerky and unpredictable as his breathing was labored. He felt like he was witnessing someone posing as a mutated version of Brennen Reynolds—and he despised him.

"That was a neat trick with the birds," the mannequin said.

Having forgotten about the man for a moment, Brennen looked at him as if for the first time. "The video was filmed by some guy selling magazines. I told him to stop filming and he must have posted it on YouTube. Apparently, it's gone viral."

"Ah," said the man, "but he also said that you were reading his mind. I would very much like to be witness to that."

"Well, yes, I was reading it at the time," Brennen said. He looked into the man's eyes, but he was not able to read his thoughts. "But I can't *actually* read minds. At least not at the moment."

"That's more or less what the last prophet said." The mannequin turned to pick up a glass jar that held what appeared to be a human finger with a ring on it. "I kept his 'holy ghost power' ring as a souvenir before I buried him."

Brennen would never have considered himself one to vomit over the sight of a human finger, but seeing the intricacies of it just inches from his face made his cheeks tingle with threatening nausea. He wanted to shift to a more comfortable position, but there was none.

"Are you saying you are a *less-than-genuine* prophet?" the man asked. "If you are saying that, then I should push this air into your bloodstream right now." With a steady hand, the man set the jar down and placed a thumb on the plunger of the syringe.

Nothing, to Brennen, had ever looked as deadly as the empty air within it.

"If you *are*, in fact, a prophet, then, I will of course need some proof." He moved his hand off the syringe to scratch what appeared to be a stubble-laden chin. "I have no tolerance for those who lie and feed off the fear of others, and profit from it."

Though time was something he could not afford, Brennen paused for the right words. It didn't seem like the man was going to accept anything but a full demonstration of his power. If it was a prophet the man needed, a prophet he shall get. As much as the thought of pretending to be a prophet was uncomfortable, the sight of the needle was horrible and the thought of air being pumped in his heart was worse. Would death be instantaneous or would it take time? Would it make a sound? He imagined how it might feel when the air bubble reached his heart.

He began to panic. "*Fine*," Brennen spouted. "Sure, I am a prophet. Not a very good one, mind you. I'm, uh, a *little* new at it. But I *can* read minds . . . normally."

The mannequin's stare was ominous. "Then all you have to do is read mine."

"And I *will*, man. I will."

The man sighed. "Why do I feel a 'but' coming on? There is always a 'but' with you people."

"The *only* problem is I need to be awake when I do it—*really* awake." Brennen bobbed his head up as he spoke, causing his neck muscles to strain as they met the resistance from the straps. "I'm feeling groggy as hell right now. I'm assuming you drugged me with something after you tased me. Some kind of downer?"

The muffled-voice man threw up his hands. The frustration could be heard through the mask's breathing hole. "So what do you want me to do about it?"

"What I'm saying is that I need . . . I need to get high. I need to get high. Not in a marijuana kind of way, either. I need some Glow, that's what I need. And there is some in my pocket." Brennen rolled to the side to expose the correct pocket to the man. He gestured to the pocket with his eyes.

Again, the man stared dumbfounded. "Are you *serious*, dude?"

Now it was Brennen who addressed his companion with

seriousness. "Look, man. You zapped me, choked me out with chloroform, put me in this vibrating room and shoved a loaded needle in my arm because you want proof that I'm a prophet. I am offering you that proof. Now I told you what I need to make that happen." They locked eyes for several moments.

The man gave in.

Brennen's assailant, not risking loosening the restraints on his prisoner, assisted in removing the paraphernalia from Brennen's pocket and proceeded, under careful instruction, to help Brennen read minds. Not wanting smoke in the room, he opted to smash The Glow onto an old DVD case and chopped it into a thick line using a credit card. He then placed the case by Brennen's nose and allowed him to inhale it through a rolled dollar bill.

For the first time in Brennen's tenure with Glow, he did it reluctantly. The video, the nightmarish image of his emaciated face and body haunted his mind. As much as reality has been a burden to him, it was nevertheless inescapable. It was grim. At best, he was ripping the filter in his brain. Worst case scenario, he was dying.

Amid the revelation, Brennen felt he was being rude. "Do you want any?" Brennen asked as large amounts of the powder burned through his sinuses and into his brain. His eyes were watering. The mannequin had done a shoddy job cutting it, resulting in a bigger rip than he was expecting. It was fierce, but better Glow racing through his veins than an air bubble.

"I don't touch the stuff," the mannequin said. "It's bad for you."

Brennen scoffed at the irony as he did the second half of the line. His breathing was shallow. "I think I've had enough." As he spoke, his own voice sounded as if it were being run, like modular synthesizer in one of his songs, through a high-pass filter back through a low-pass one. It was soaring through the air, then deep under water, back above water and deep below it. He experienced what felt like an electric ball drop from the base of his brain, split at his groin, and shoot down to his toes and begin to crawl back up his legs.

"Are you okay, dude?" the man asked. He sounded far away.

"Yes, I'm fine," Brennen answered. He realized his eyes were shut, when he could have sworn they were open. He was watching an increasing amount of light move toward him. "I *think* I'm fine."

The electric ball moved to his stomach.

Above water, below water.

The electric ball moved to his chest.

"What's wrong with your eyes?" a distant voice asked. He thought he recognized it as a man he encountered long ago—a man with the face of a mannequin.

It reached the brain.

19
October 30: Evening Travels

A

Brennen Reynolds, or what once was Brennen Reynolds, at least in part, was traveling. At first, objects in his field of vision rushed past him. He could not identify them, as they went by faster than he cared to calculate. It was difficult to judge which direction he was going, if any direction at all. Soon after, distortions to his vision began to drastically change his view of the world. The visuals before him became tubular in nature, carving a tunnel with every turn of his mind's eye. Every color he witnessed became dyed in warped blue. Sooner still, his same field of vision became compressed into what he could only describe as a fish-eye lens shrinking in size. There were voices, though he could not gage how many. Hundreds of them, perhaps thousands, even *millions* of murmuring voices tickled the middle of his mind as he moved forward. When blended together, they became the sound of white noise, but he could tune into any one of them if he wished. He heard a woman's laughter and stopped to laugh along. He heard a baby's sobbing and stopped to dry the tears and lull it to sleep. And he heard the desperate voice of a man asking if someone was okay. Soon it became a predominant voice as loud as a jackhammer. It was enough to break his concentration, if in fact he *was* concentrating.

In a moment, the blue-tinted tunnel began to sputter out

of control. This fish-eye view expanded and everything flashed red.

He opened his eyes.

B

"Hey, man. Are you okay?"

Brennen blinked several times before the mannequin came into focus. He had been shaking him with a good amount of force. His eyes looked maniacal beneath the mask.

"How long was I out?" Brennen asked.

"About ten seconds. Your jaw dropped open and your eyes rolled back in your head. It was freaking creepy."

With his system flooded in Glow and desperate to be free from the straps, Brennen had no time to waste. "It doesn't matter." His tone was serious. "Here's what you need to do. Clear your mind, and whatever you do, do not think of your real name or where you are from."

"What? *(Harvey Bellinger, North Carolina, Raleigh).*"

"Your name is Harvey Bellinger. You are from Raleigh, North Carolina."

Harvey stared at Brennen for a few moments. "What *(what the hell is going on*)?"

"What's going on, Harvey is that I am reading your mind. I am reading your mind because you asked me to. You wanted proof, remember? Now, I don't have all day."

"Yes. But *(I kill false prophets).*"

"I know you do, Harvey. You showed me the finger in the jar. Hey, man, I'm not here to judge. Everybody has a hobby. I'm not going to tell anybody. If I'm being honest, I'm scared, and I just want to provide you with your proof so I can be on my way."

"Okay, so I will say that you are clever, but you could have somehow known this ahead of time and you have been playing me for a fool *(I miss my dog, Freddy. Why did I just think that?)*."

Brennen sighed. "I'm sorry you miss Freddy. I'm sorry he got hung up in your hammock last week and choked to death at ten years old. It *sucks*." At this last thought, Brennen became quite empathetic. He imagined how hard it would be to lose Snippety and he had only known her a short time. "I hope you understand now, Harvey. I really need this needle out of my arm, man. I really hate needles." He nodded at the empty syringe inserted into this vein. "Look, I know about Freddy, I know about your prophet hobby and I even know why you do it." Brennen had read his mind in an instant. He frowned at the information collected. "But I'm not sure you want me to say it. It's kind of personal."

Harvey through his arms up again. "Go ahead, dude. See if you—"

"You were molested. At the age of five by your—"

"*All right, fine!*" Harvey waved off the rest of the sentence like an umpire calling a player safe at home. "I *get* it! You can read my mind. You are definitely reading my mind." He sat back in his chair and crossed his arms like a concerned parent about to scold a child. Just as fast, he uncrossed them and rested his hand on his hips. In a final gesture, he ripped his mask off and rubbed his face in his hands. He was in his thirties with shaggy brown hair with a narrow face dusted with a light goatee. He tried to stand up but hit his head on the ceiling and slumped back in his chair with his elbows on his knees. "This is . . . this is totally wrong, man."

After an awkward silence, Brennen interrupted. "Eh, Harvey?" He gestured towards his restraints. "The straps? The needle?"

Harvey jumped up like a host trying to accommodate an unexpected guest. "Oh, yeah. Shit. Sorry, dude." He removed the needle with some skill and went to work on the straps. "You know, the other so-called prophets all said the same thing to try to get out of it." He scoffed. There were nerves in his laugh. "I guess I never really thought about what would happen if one of you guys was real."

Brennen had never felt so relieved to be sitting up. He rubbed the tender area where the needle had been and flexed his fingers. The Glow was crashing into his central nervous system like angry waves. He was resisting it at all costs.

Harvey handed him cotton ball drenched in rubbing alcohol. "Don't worry, that needle wound should be fine. I do this for a living. I'm a nurse in my day job. I'm on a two-week vacation. But I guess you knew that already, huh?"

Brennen nodded though he had not. "Well, listen, Harvey, are we good to go here? Like I said, your secret is safe with me." He rubbed his hands together. "If it's good with you, I'd like to just get out of this little room here and get back home."

"It's a van," Harvey said. "Speaking of which, I should probably turn off the engine. I need it running to keep the equipment on, otherwise it drains the battery. Trust me. Don't be surprised if it dies on us." He nudged Brennen's shoulder like a familiar friend.

A van, Brennen thought. Now that he had a stress-free look around, he could see the features, though they were disguised. It was a long utility van with a gutted interior. The front and back were divided by a makeshift barrier. The walls and ceiling were covered in soundproof tiles, similar to what he used in his own apartment. This, no doubt, kept the noises to a minimum.

As much as he was terrified by Harvey, Brennen couldn't help but feel for him. He had learned a lot about him by reading his mind and felt horrible for doing so. These were private thoughts that should remain so. They shouldn't be caged and dissected like a lab animal. Harvey was an oddball—something to which Brennen could relate—who had without doubt suffered some sort of breakdown. He had made some poor decisions, to be sure, but there was still hope for him. It would seem logical, with the right professional guidance, he could be corrected. Like an old washing machine, perhaps he just needed a good jolt to start working properly again. After all, people can change. They can *heal.*

Brennen hoped, for his own sake, that they could.

"And," Harvey added, "I wouldn't go near your apartment for a while because the cops are watching it for some reason. They must have put surveillance on you after the SWAT team showed up." He threw up his hands. "I'm not even going to ask what you did. I don't care."

"Terrific," Brennen replied. Why there would be a stakeout at his apartment, he could only guess. Perhaps Sergeant Pederson was keeping a watchful eye over him. After the interrogation, looking and acting the way he did, why *wouldn't* there be a tail on him?

He ran his fingers through his hair and rubbed his face.

His movements were smooth and calculated, or at least they appeared to be. The YouTube video had made him suspicious that the space between his perception of himself and how he appeared to others was larger than he had previously recognized. Much larger. It was a new insight, and if it weren't for Harvey's unorthodox manner of unearthing it, Brennen might never have known about it. In a very real way, he owed Harvey his thanks.

Harvey spoke while digging through a box of what appeared to be electronic gadgets. "I had to take a couple cops out to get in your apartment. I wheeled you out in that wheelchair, so the surveillance camera probably caught it all on tape. It's okay, though, they can't identify me, and they couldn't see the van from their vantage point. We're good."

"You killed two *cops?*" Brennen asked.

"Dude, *no*. What do you think I am? A dick? I just knocked them out with a taser and some chloroform. I only kill false prophets."

"Terrific."

On the other hand, Harvey could very well be certifiable.

C

The fluorescent lights at the Motel 6 were unflattering as he stared at his reflection. Every pock mark, zit, blemish, cut, scrape, scar, or blackhead Mr. Bratch had ever accrued seemed to stand out like phosphorus to a black light. Still, he continued practicing his laugh as much as he was disappointed with the results. Age was pulling his chin off his face. The crow's feet he noticed years ago were now turning into pterodactyl claws and his cheeks bore deep grooves when he grimaced. He accentuated this by making a face, as if he were saying "eeee," over and over.

He readied himself once more and burst into laughter.

But it wasn't quite right. He stared at his own smile with frustration, mining it for possible improvements. He turned to the side as an attempt to catch his profile as best he could. While doing so he belted out another laugh. To his disappointment, he still could not match the look or tone of Richard Gere. Mr. Gere knew how to laugh—*really* laugh—without sounding foolish or effeminate. He could handle himself in any situation with grace and just the right amount of style and manly charisma. Mr. Bratch had none of those attributes. He had a face that naturally reverted to a scowl no matter how he contorted his face.

He tried another tactic. "*Ha* ha ha ha ha!"

Nothing.

He chose another vowel to accentuate. "*He* he he he he." He tried switching the vowel as well as the cadence. "Ho *ho* ho ho ho." Deciding that sounded too close to Santa Clause, he tried a mix of all three varieties. "He he ho *ha* he he ha."

Richard Gere was nowhere to be found. Instead, in front of him was the same uniformed Mr. Bratch that always accompanied him to the bathroom. He wished he looked as though he *belonged* in a uniform. Mr. Gere was able to pull it off as a navy officer in *An Officer and a Gentleman.* He was just as believable as bad cop in *Internal Affairs.* Why couldn't *he?*

Giving up on the effort for the time being, he turned from the mirror and walked into his tiny room. He cleared the packaging of a newly-bought mobile phone charger from the bed and sat at the edge of it with his back straight. The charger had been plugged into Dan Tenner's phone and placed on the nightstand.

He picked up a chocolate bar purchased earlier and devoured it, relishing in the disobedience. The Prophet Jacob had outlawed such candy, claiming it contaminated the soul. It was home-cooked meals or nothing at the compound. In fact, many times Jacob would announce a barbeque over the PA system in which attendance was mandatory. *Everybody to Home Base in an hour for a barbecue. Everyone to Home Base in an hour.* Home Base had been a place of discipline, but it could also be used for prayer and barbecue. If Mr. Bratch had it his way, it would be a place of shameless eating of chocolate bars as well.

He sat upright to brood about his escaped water buffalo. How dare she jeopardize his security in the compound by trying to run off? Where was she going to go? By now, all the police departments of the Greater Phoenix area were aware of her alleged murder up in Paiute Rock City. However, he would just as soon find her himself. In his opinion, Jacob was wrong to include the police on her search. It was best if Othersider law was kept out. Should they find her, however, he would hope they'd return her with no questions asked. In past encounters, they would grow annoyed by the lack of cooperation of the Paiute Rock City Police Department and stay away. This was best for everybody. Should they come snooping around too close, Jacob, and that fat, crazy, awful alpha-wife of his, Lou Ellen, would do whatever it took to protect the integrity of the compound.

Lou Ellen used intimidation in the compound. That's how she commanded respect. She would threaten people. Odd threats. She'd once threatened she'd turn him, Mr. Bratch himself, into a letterbox should he speak to her in an insubordinate tone again.

Whatever the hell that meant.

Regardless, he had to take it because she was Jacob's wife, his first wife, his most powerful wife. If he were Jacob, he'd just kill her. Deep down, really deep, he suspected the man was afraid of her. In any case, by themselves they were unpredictable. Together, they were as unstable as unchecked plutonium.

For now, he would have to remain stoical and wait for Beth, or the Brennen kid, to slip up and come to him. He was, after all, patient like the Komodo dragon. Richard Gere had nothing on him there.

On the bright side, killing Dan Tenner had awoken in him an appetite that had long lay dormant. He enjoyed taking the man's life, in much the same way he enjoyed the candy bar. He yearned for another chance to do it. If he could catch Beth Perkins, perhaps he could yet have such a chance.

Should the girl slip away from him, he fretted as to how he would deal with his life. Being excommunicated would prove difficult. Without a social security number, or the connections to obtain a false identification, he would be hard-pressed to find meaningful employment. He considered a job in landscaping or other under-the-table vocations that wouldn't make him a sitting duck for the FBI. Perhaps he could take up drug dealing like his friend Dan Tenner. As he saw many times in Philadelphia, he could coordinate a drug operation somewhere—hire eleven-year-olds to be lookouts, pay the dealers a percentage of every bag of cocaine sold—

but it would require startup capital, of which he had none. All he had, Jacob owned.

It was useless thinking about it. The best he could do for himself was to find Beth.

He reached to the night stand and checked Dan Tenner's phone. Aside from some frantic texts from his wife (to which he replied that he was to be home soon and not to worry), there were no messages from user Brennen to dealer Dan . . . yet.

The Komodo Dragon sat, scowling.

And waited.

20

October 30: Shortly After

A

Diana Navarro scampered to straighten up the house before her guests arrived. She had agreed to the visit before she had considered the messy condition of her house. It was of small consequence, and chances of either Scott or Beth noticing were slim, but it mattered nonetheless. She had every opportunity to call him back and cancel yet she did not. Instead, she washed out a dozen mugs in haste, attempting to hide her caffeine addiction before the doorbell rang.

As a rational human being, she knew harboring a murder suspect was unwise and could lead to negative social consequences. However, it was Manny's voice in her mind that drove her.

Come on, Kitty Cat, she imagined him saying as though he were alive, *these kids need your help. Besides, this Brennen guy could be proof of your theory, our theory, and I think we owe it to ourselves to warn them of the danger Brennen could be in.*

She supposed she could have spoken with Scott over the phone regarding their situation, but their conversation had been hurried by urgency and a bad connection. She understood Beth was an escapee from some sort of cult up north and was being falsely accused of murder, and there was something about an illegal tracking device found in the girl's hand. Scott's apartment was unsafe and they needed a place to regroup and meet with Brennen. It was this last part that moved her to invite them. Brennen was the key. Just as they needed to contact Brennen, Diana was also desperate to speak with him. She needed to warn him of the harm with which he was inevitably flirting.

The doorbell rang just as she finished setting the last coffee cup in the cupboard. She greeted them like long-lost friends returning from world travels. Scott possessed all the same charm and politeness of his previous visit. He offered several apologies as to their intrusion into her life for a third time. He wore a red whistle around his neck. Though she thought it odd, she didn't inquire about it. She waved off the gestures and assured him that the intrusion was not a problem. Whether she meant it or not, she wasn't sure. She was too distracted by what the two were carrying. Scott held what could be nothing else but a box of kitty litter with a scoop wedged in the center and Beth, somehow cheerier, held in her hand an animal carrying case containing an orange cat.

"Eer," said the cat.

Diana put her hands on her hips and cleared her throat. "Oh my, uh, what do we have here?" Though she was not thrilled with the thought of stepping on kitty litter, she heard Manny's voice once more.

Come on, Di, give them a chance.

Beth approached Diana and gave her a hug with her free arm. "Thanks so much for seeing us, Professor Navarro. We are so sorry that we forgot to mention that we had Snippety with us." She lifted the case to place the cat in a better light.

"We mentioned her earlier. She's had some contact with Brennen, and she's, well, not exactly a normal cat now."

This was not the same Beth that Diana had met earlier that day. She was still looked the same, yet *this* Beth was much more graceful and confident. There was no question about it.

As to the cat, she needed only to think of Dave sitting atop Brennen's shoulder to understand the potential remarkable quirks it might possess. Dave was near Brennen for just a short while before demonstrating some pretty phenomenal behavior. She could imagine how a cat might react given broader exposure.

Her hesitation regarding the cat faded fast. Before she knew, she was not only welcoming the cat, but was helping her out of her case in order to hold her in her arms. The cat's eyes were mustard yellow with intense, far reaching pupils. Her nose was pink with a black dot on the tip. Her expression was kind. In fact, if Diana didn't know any better, it looked as though Snippety was smiling.

"We brought the litter just in case, but I don't think we'll need it."

"Why is that?" Diana asked.

Without answering, Scott turned to Snippety. "Snippy, do you need to use the bathroom?"

"Eer!" She put her paw up.

"Well, go find it and come right back, okay?"

Without further exchange, Snippety trotted down a long dark hallway that led to a bathroom. She closed the door behind her, being sure it did not latch.

Diana stared with a blank expression for a few beats. She

should not have been surprised considering the day she'd had, but her brain was not wired to accept this sort of behavior from a cat, or any other animal, for that matter. She struggled for a retort, but could not find one before Beth changed the subject.

"How is Dave?"

Diana's smile faded. "He's pretty good, thank you, but I must say, he was awfully depressed after Brennen left. I think he—" She was distracted by the sound of the toilet flushing. She looked to see Snippety emerge from the darkness of the hallway and rejoin the group. She sat and looked at each of them, as though addressing them in a meeting. Diana was beside herself with delight. A laugh erupted out of her that neither Beth nor Scott seemed to expect. As a further surprise, the laugh was followed by a snort. Diana put her hand to her mouth in embarrassment. "Excuse me, but that is the cutest thing I have ever seen. What else can she do? You're not going to tell me she talks, are you?"

Snippety made some attempts, without success, at what seemed to be a hard "g" and a "y." She shook her head and said, "Mow." The sound was baritone.

To Diana, Scott said, "That's Snippy's way of saying 'no.'" He rubbed his chin. "Oh, she can communicate. I'm just not sure it's physically possible for her to formulate words."

Diana subconsciously mimicked Scott's gesture. "So she can understand English, but she can't speak it." She spoke it as a statement. "Sounds like my mother while I was growing up, rest her soul."

They all laughed.

As much has Diana could have studied the cat all night, she did intend to speak with her guests about a number of issues. Instead, she found herself playing hostess for much of the time. Not having a lot of company in the few months since Manny's passing, she felt out of practice. She poured them each a glass of water and sat them around a couch, often over-asking them if they needed anything to eat. They did not.

Diana listened without judgment as she was debriefed on Jacob and the compound, Beth's escape, Larry Hitchcock's intrusion, and Dante's rescue. Her interest was piqued at the mention of the illegal use of Aluluei's tracking devices on the women of the community. She was a scientist, and conducted herself as such. She asked well-thought-out questions at the right time, keeping the conversation coherent.

Beth's story was horrific. Beth's husband, this Prophet Jacob, was a monster the likes of which Diana had only heard on the evening news. He was beyond forgiving. Even the coke-head who killed Manny had some redeeming qualities. At least he expressed his regret in court. Jacob, on the other hand, was a patent sociopath with no such capability.

Diana examined the scar on Beth's now un-bandaged hand. "You need a lawyer for sure, honey." She motioned to Scott. "And your professor is probably a better bet than any court appointed lawyer she was liable to end up being assigned to."

"Yes," Scott said, "*that* is what we are thinking."

"You could also go to the cops," Diana said. "They might

take a look at this hand and believe your story, or at least investigate it."

Beth looked down, taking her hand back. "I'd really rather not, Professor Navarro. Jacob will find a way to win a lawsuit. Besides, I don't trust the police."

Diana raised her eyebrows and nodded.

Scott set his water down and leaned back on the couch. "I think my law professor can help her on Monday. I have to see if he'll help with Brennen as well, if he ever gets a hold of me. Even though he's probably out getting high."

Diana shot a look to Beth.

"Scott doesn't think Brennen's coming back. He thinks he's too far gone." She gave Scott a disapproving glare.

Diana put a finger in the air. "That's what I need to talk to both of you about." She leaned forward to pet Snippety who had found a resting spot on her knee. "We need to talk about Brennen."

Diana had some talking of her own to do. She explained her concern regarding prolonged drug use as it pertained to his mind-reading. It was within reason that Brennen's condition would worsen with the continued use of the drug and the consequences would be unpredictable. He could suffer internal hemorrhaging or perhaps experience lost time. If he were to be swept away into the original light, he could slip away indefinitely. In his mind, he would be lost while outwardly, he'd be in a coma.

Her guests looked wary.

"What I'm saying is if the amphetamine is the catalyst for his condition, then any further use could cause a complete tear; a full breach."

"Holy shit," Beth said.

Scott understood at once. "He would be blindsided with too much information." He turned to Diana. "What would happen if someone's filter were to be totally removed?"

"I wish I knew, and that is precisely what I am afraid of. I don't think our bodies are equipped to handle it at this point. It would be my guess that information of that magnitude would be too great for any one person to handle without the proper amount of evolution to pad the change. I don't think anybody could survive."

Snippety climbed from Diana's lap to her chest until they were nose to nose. "Mow!"

"No shit, Snippy." Scott sat hunched over on his seat, leaning his elbows on his knees. "Well, let's all just hope we hear from him soon."

B

WHAT HOSPITAL IS SHE AT??

Brennen tried for the third time to text his sister, but he had not heard anything back. He felt no ill will toward Jen and her current vindictiveness. She was hurt by his three-year avoidance of the world, and giving him a taste of his own medicine was her way of expressing it.

Because of the police surveillance team at Brennen's apartment, Harvey insisted he drive Brennen to Scott's. In fact, he insisted he go everywhere with Brennen. Brennen was his prophet and Harvey his loyal follower. As much as Brennen was uncomfortable playing along with the prophet scenario, it was eerie to attempt an argument with Harvey. There was something behind his eyes that gave the impression that the slightest deviation from the Harvey

Bellinger Code of How Things Are could disturb his tranquil mood like a rock thrown into still water. So he let Harvey not only believe he was a prophet, but described both Beth and Scott as fellow followers. As crazy at it sounded, Brennen thought of a way he could make it work for everyone involved.

He had a plan.

"So what are you a prophet of?" Harvey asked while adjusting the driver's side mirror. "What's your message?"

Brennen was busy musing over the many gadgets tucked away in the center console of the van. They were small wonders—miniature plastic bricks with attached magnets, wires with connections he didn't recognize, batteries of some sort—and they were everywhere he looked. His pupils scanned each of them with electric veracity.

Zing

Zang

Zing

Perhaps one more text to Dante was needed before quitting for good. Perhaps his previous idea of quitting Glow cold was premature. The thought was terrifying now that he was under its influence. Maybe he could just put in a half order this time before saying good-bye to Glow. Maybe he'd have to wean himself off the Glow. He had heard, at least he told himself he had, that quitting cold turkey was dangerous to the nervous system. It could very well be that just one more visit from Dante wouldn't be a bad idea, at *least* to say good-bye. He didn't have the immediate funds, but could pay Dante back with interest. He had done it before.

It was a thought.

Before long, Brennen realized he had not addressed Harvey's question. It seemed like ten minutes had gone by since he asked it. His mouth was dry and his eyes were big. They looked like black opals in the passenger vanity mirror.

"Eh," Brennen said, "I'm a prophet of . . . *free will*, I guess. Yes, free will." He changed the subject. "What is this?" He held up one of the plastic bricks.

"Oh, that's a tracker for cars. You put them on the undercarriage and you can track where they go." Harvey produced a proud face and looked at Brennen. "I use them to follow the false prophets. Works like charm *(I miss Freddy. It's been three weeks and I still can't believe he's gone. He was all I had. He was the best dog).*"

Brennen looked away, feeling guilty about his accidental intrusion into Harvey's mind. "Trackers? What is the deal with everybody having trackers these days?"

Harvey looked confused. "What do you mean?"

"Nothing." He had been distracted by Harvey's dog and felt a need to console his odd companion. On one hand, it might be best to leave the subject well alone. On the other, maybe talking to someone about it would be cathartic to Harvey. Perhaps if he could just talk about it, let some CO_2 out of the keg, so to speak, he wouldn't be so prone to murdering people.

This latter way of thinking prevailed. "Hey, Harvey, I just want to say that I'm sorry about Freddy. From the way you describe him, he seemed like a good dog."

Over a minute of chilling silence overcame the van as they were nearing Scott's apartment. Brennen scolded himself for bringing up the subject. Harvey would not look at him so there was no way to read his mind. He was sure, at any moment, Harvey was going to pull down a side road and finish the needle job he'd started earlier.

Harvey broke the silence. "He was a good dog, indeed. Thank you for acknowledging." After a few moments, he continued, "I prefer dogs. They're much more loyal than cats. Do you know what I mean?"

Brennen studied the tracker in his hands and contemplated. "I used to. My opinion is about fifty-fifty these days."

Harvey changed his demeanor as though a circuit had been re-engaged. "Hey, is there a reason your buddy's place would be swarming with cops?"

It was true. Scott's apartment looked like a hornet's nest full of blue wasps busily padding around the nest. Without a word being spoken, Harvey made it through the intersection without attracting suspicion. Brennen could only guess what had happened with Beth, but he knew it wasn't good. He cursed himself for not getting there earlier as he fumbled for his phone. He shouldn't have left to begin with. Yes, he needed the tip money to pay rent this month, but, as it turns out, he didn't end up driving anyway. To add insult, his friends were now in danger.

To Scott, he texted:

WENT BY YOUR PLACE. COP CITY. WHERE YOU AT?

Brennen stared at his phone in anticipation of Scott's reply while Harvey pulled into a nearby shopping plaza and awaited further instructions. It was difficult to sit still while his mind was in so many other places. He hoped beyond hope that Scott and Beth were in a safe place. He knew they were out there somewhere. He also new Beth's extremists were out there hanging on every word of their leader.

It was time Harvey was introduced to the plan.

"Okay, Harvey. What if I were to tell you I knew where to find a false prophet."

Harvey looked at Brennen and answered without hesitation. "I'd say I would be very interested in that information *(I am very interested in that information).*"

"Good," Brennen said. His phone vibrated. Scott had replied.

1026 E LODGE DR, TEMPE. ASAP.

Brennen's thumbs moved with fervor as he replied. He purposely shielded his answer from Harvey.

ON MY WAY. HAVE A FRIEND. THINKS I'M A PROPHET. LONG STORY. PLEASE PLAY ALONG.

"Now, Harvey," Brennen said, "let's go find you some sunglasses."

C

HOWDY! NOT AT HOME. MEET AT 1026 E LODGE DR, TEMPE. THIS WILL BE THE LAST TIME, MY FRIEND. BR.

*****

GOT IT. BE THERE IN 15 MIN.

D

Scott scraped the leftover shredded chicken into a bowl and placed it on the kitchen island. Snippety soon appeared, jumping on a contemporary-style bar stool. With her front paws on the island, she began to devour it.

"Remember, Snippety, if we ever get separated, you listen for this whistle."

Snippety stopped chewing and raised her head, as if annoyed by the repetitive nature of the instructions.

"Okay, fine," Scott surrendered, "didn't mean to insult your intelligence. We just worry about you, that's all."

"Eer!" Snippety said before resuming her meal.

Besides the bizarre and dangerous circumstances, Scott couldn't help feeling he was somehow more content that he had felt in years. After receiving the strange text from Brennen, he was glad his old friend was on his way back, as promised. At least they could keep tabs on him from this point on. After hearing Professor Navarro's hypothesis, they'd decided via unanimous decision that leaving him alone was unwise. Scott was unsure as to the stranger Brennen was bringing, but at least there was someone around should Brennen drop into convulsions. Whoever it was, if they had half a brain they would see that Brennen had a problem. On the other hand, if they believed Brennen was a prophet, their sanity was questionable. They would find out soon either way.

His gaze turned to the living room where Beth and Professor Navarro sat engaged in deep conversation with moments of laughter. The way they were situated on the chairs with their sunglasses on, they looked like a couple of girls shooting the breeze on Miami Beach, exchanging advice over some cold Coronas.

Beth Perkins, Beth Perkins, Beth Perkins. Like moistened fingertips across the edge of crystal wine glass, it resonated with him. If he wasn't sure if he was a believer in "Love at third site," he wholeheartedly subscribed to "Love within the first forty-eight hours." Though unsure of how his law professor would react to her story, he was nevertheless honored to participate in her attempted emancipation from Jacob. The prophet was calculating and cruel, which weighed heavy in Scott's stomach. As much as he was enjoying his time with her, he had to remind himself that she was in danger, being pursued by dangerous people. He wanted nothing more than to protect her from it as he said he would. He might have failed his father by becoming an addict, but he had a chance now at new beginnings. He might not ever have his father's respect again, but he had hers. She was his chance to solidify his change as a person—his return to *being* a person. He could once again be the man he was before his fall, and *this* Scott Barrett kept his promises.

Don't ever leave me with him, her voice repeated in his head.

He would not fail her.

The doorbell rang, prompting Scott to don his Ray Bans.

Brennen was wide-eyed and wired, as expected, with the newcomer at his side. He was overweight to an extent, a lanky man in his thirties wearing a light-green windbreaker with a white tee-shirt underneath, blue jeans, and Birkenstock sandals. He had a scruffy goatee and was sporting a pair of sunglasses of his own.

Beth and Diana congregated around the two of them to give greetings. Brennen's friend waved at them with schoolboy shyness. From his awkwardness, it was clear the guy had never perfected the art of smiling.

To Brennen, Scott said, "Are you good, man?"

"I'm good. It's all party bus."

When Scott heard their familiar high school vernacular

spoken by his old friend, he couldn't help but laugh.

Snippety pranced around the corner and sprang into Brennen's arms, who, overjoyed to be reunited with his cat, addressed her in falsetto baby-talk while she purred.

In the meantime, Diana looked out the window and asked them where they parked.

Brennen's guest didn't hesitate to answer. "Oh, I parked a few houses down." He put his hands in his pockets and rocked from his heels to his toes. "I make it a habit never to park in front of a house I'm visiting." He remained for a moment with a close-mouthed grin before he lunged at Diana with this hand extended. "My god, where are my manners. My name is Ha—"

Brennen cut his guest short and introduced him as Henry, the newest addition to "the group."

"It is my pleasure and honor to serve the Prophet of Free Will," the guest said. His expression teetered between bashful and proud. "If any of you need anything, I'm here for you." He tapped his hand to his chest in earnest.

They all welcomed their new friend into the group, filling the room with awkward energy.

To Brennen, Diana said, "Oh, by the way, Brennen. I know someone who would like to say hello." She made a beeline to her bedroom, located down same darkened hallway as the bathroom. "I'll be right back."

While setting Snippety down, Brennen bounced his gaze between Scott and Beth. "I had no idea the address you texted belonged to Professor Navarro. How the hell did *that* happen?"

"Well," Scott said, "we ran into a bit of a snag." He took a seat on the living room couch.

Harvey, with Frankenstein swagger, sat down and crossed his legs while listening intensely to Scott. Beth, uncomfortable with him, opted to take the long way around the coffee table to join Scott on the couch.

"Well, Brennen," Beth said, "I'd say you're not going to believe this, but from the last couple days we've had, I guess nothing will faze you at this point."

"Brennen?" Diana said.

The three of them turned to see her emerging from the hallway looking pale, as if she had received some awful news. Her eyes, though veiled by the sunglasses, were sullen.

Sensing urgency, Brennen excused himself from the conversation, leaving the others in painful silence.

Scott turned to the newcomer. "So, *Henry*, where are you from?"

E

Brennen was pulled into Diana's bedroom without warning. The master bedroom was sizable with a modern contemporary décor. The carpets were plush with a walking rug running from the bathroom to a sliding glass door leading to the outside. His foot caught the corner, causing him to stumble as he crossed the room.

As exciting as being pulled into a woman's bedroom might have been in different circumstances, it was obvious to him Diana's gesture was not one of desire. He knew better. Although she carried it well, she had to be nearing twice his age. Besides, he couldn't imagine his condition made him the least bit desirable.

"What's going on, Professor Navarro?"

"This is hard to say," she said, "and I can't believe I'm even considering saying it." She dropped her head and exhaled. "It's Dave." She picked up a shoebox from her dresser and opened it. "He's dead."

Inside the shoebox, lying on a bed of tissue paper, was the lifeless body of Dave. His position was fetal and he was at peace.

"I just found him in his house. He was alive just a few hours ago."

A look of horror overcame Brennen. "Oh, my god. Did I somehow . . . *do* this?" He felt his pupils pinging back and forth. "You mentioned animals may be somehow hypersensitive to my . . . filter rip, or whatever you call it. Do you think it overloaded him?"

"I really don't know, Brennen," she said while taking a seat on the edge of the bed. "It very well could have. Or it could be that he died of old age. He was over twenty years old, after all." She stroked Dave's cheek with the pad of her forefinger while choking back a tear. "I just know he was my friend and I want him back. And, um, I was wondering. . . ." Her voice faltered.

"Professor Navarro, I am so sorry. I had no idea. This is insane." He ran is fingers through his hair. "Sergeant Pederson already thinks I'm a murderer. Do you think I may have inadvertently killed—"

"I'm not concerned about whether your abilities attributed to his death. What I am wondering if you can bring him back."

Brennen stood tongue-tied, leaning to one side.

"Look," Diana said, gesturing with her hand, prepared to

defend her suggestion, "it's just that there is all this talk about you being a prophet. And I've seen some you do some amazing things, and . . . well, what if you *can* do Christ-like things? You can read minds when you're high, what if you can bring things back to life? Have you ever tried?"

"Well, no."

"Are you high now?"

"Ashamedly, yes. Very much so." He thought of Dante due to arrive at any minute.

"Well, what can it hurt?" She held out the shoebox to Brennen. "Can you try? *Will* you try?"

Without further discussion, Brennen accepted the box and sat next to Diana on the bed. He lifted Dave off the tissue with care and cupped him in both hands. The chinchilla was still warm on his fingers. Feeling rather silly, he glanced at Diana who was watching the process with curiosity. He put his thumbs on both sides of Dave's cheeks and began to concentrate. He let his mind go, hoping he might get back to the place he was inside Harvey's van. He closed his eyes and did his best to probe the rodent's recently emptied mind for any residual signs of life—any moto-neural switch that may bring Diana's dear friend back to her. He felt nothing, but continued to try, knowing Diana's hopes were rooted in his success.

He heard a light tapping on the sliding glass door. Prepared to see a member of Beth's group smiling maniacally at him from the outside, his eyes sprang open and focused on the noise. To his relief, it was a queen palm just outside the sliding glass door. It had been caught in a slight breeze causing it to thwack itself against the glass.

Dejected, Brennen shook his head and placed Dave back in his resting place. "I'm sorry, Professor Navarro, I can't do it. Something is missing. I can't explain it." He ran his fingers through his hair and cleared his throat. "I don't know the first thing about resurrection."

Diana understood. She replaced the lid to the shoebox and walked it to the dresser where she paused. "Okay, Brennen. You're clear." She turned and smiled. "Manny always believed the savior was coming. So out of respect for him, please forgive me," She put a hand in the air and breathed a sigh of relief. "I was just checking for his sake."

She set the box down, kissed her finger, and placed it on the box. "Good-bye, Dave."

F

Diana again joined Brennen on the edge of the bed.

Even after crossing every milestone on her path to intellectual nirvana, she was still learning about herself, particularly when it came to grief. She noticed it made her behave out of character. With Manny's passing, she lost the strength to defend herself. Had he been alive, she would have been able to fire back with witty rebuttals at all her peers and colleagues who criticized her book. Now, she felt as though she couldn't fight her own battles. She let her publisher field all the negative press of the book in *their* words, *not* hers. She *let* the negativity fester.

Now, with Dave's passing, grief again maneuvered her like a crazed puppeteer, in an unfamiliar direction. It allowed her to encourage a person with a chemical dependency to get high in the hopes he might be able resurrect her dead friend. She was beside herself with embarrassment. A world in grieving was indeed a world in chaos.

It was from this humbled mindset that Diana explained to Brennen about the dangers of the full breach.

He listened closely to her. And when he explained to her about the blue tunnel and the murmuring voices, she listened back. She was fascinated beyond words.

G

Mr. Bratch pulled up next to a large inflatable ghost, put forth by a festive neighbor, two houses past the address provided in Reynold's text. He never parked in front of a house he was planning to visit.

He had been dressed and ready to go when the text arrived and had made good time getting to the house. Ironically, it came just minutes after he finished a phone call with the Prophet Jacob himself.

If you find her, the prophet warned, *you let her know I've got Jane here with her three daughters. You tell Bethie that all of their current lives and afterlives are dependent on her return, if you know what I mean.* This no doubt meant their lives were in danger. *You also tell that blasphemous little apostate that if she comes back, I will drop the murder charges and call it all a big misunderstanding. Everything goes back to how it was.* This was a complete falsehood, Mr. Bratch knew. *And remember, Bratch. If you don't find her, don't bother coming back. You're one anonymous phone call to the FBI away from a . . . less than ideal life, do you understand?*

He did.

With the interior lights of the F150 off, he went to work on the combination lock and placed it in the center console. The toolbox lid, half obstructed by the tarp under which Dan

Tenner's body lay, gave way enough for Mr. Bratch to remove a pair of rubber-tipped gloves, the shotgun microphone, headphones, portable battery pack, and brass knuckles from it. It was a familiar routine, one that he had perfected years ago.

He removed his Maglite from his tactical belt and pointed it at the floor of the backseat. The bloodstains were minimal—nothing that couldn't be cleaned spotless after the cadaver's appropriate burial back at the compound.

From outside the house, there appeared to be a minimal amount of people inside it. There was a two-car garage with no cars parked outside of it. The interior lights of the house perforated into the night, exposing some unidentifiable shrubberies in the front yard.

He liked the house. It had a rather bland stucco exterior, but it was comfortable. Though his purpose tonight was to invade it, it didn't stop him from house-hunting in his mind whenever possible. He imagined owning a house like this with old friends coming to visit him often. He saw himself greeting them with a Richard Gere smile as they presented him with a bottle of Chianti Classico Reserva as a house-warming gift. He would have them take off their shoes to avoid staining the carpet. Or perhaps, hardwood floors would be a better choice. Red oak.

In another life, he thought.

He would have no such house and had no such friends.

He kept in the cover of adjacent oleander trees as he approached the house, pointing his microphone as he went. He heard murmuring of what appeared to be both female and male voices, but he could not guess how many. He thought he might have heard someone mentioning something about a breach of some sort.

After a few moments, a sudden absence of light caught his eye. Someone had turned off a light, either from the backyard or within the back of the house, signifying a dark and unused area of the house was now available.

He quickened his pace toward the darkness.

21
October 30: Night

A

Brennen took immediate note that Beth was all smiles when he and Diana emerged from the hallway.

"Henry is going to help us with Jacob," she said. She glanced at Scott and back to Brennen.

Brennen stopped in the middle of the living room to look at Harvey, who was busy peering out the window to the front yard. "*Did* he?"

Harvey answered without taking his eyes from the window. "Yessss, I did." His voice trailed off. "Hey what kind of truck did you say the guys from the compound drove?"

They all exchanged glances.

"Ford F150 extended cab," Scott said. "Why?"

Harvey turned from the window to look at Brennen before turning to Beth and Scott. "Oh, no reason. I just, uh, want to make sure. I want to be on the lookout for them, just in case." He looked guilty of something. "Excuse me a sec, people. I forgot something in the van and shall return momentarily." His heavy frame stressed the hardwood floors as he made his way to the foyer.

"Hey, did you see a red Dodge Neon out there?" Brennen asked.

"I did not," Harvey said. He then nodded to everyone before shutting the door behind him.

To Brennen, Scott asked, "Did you tell Dante to meet you here?"

Brennen managed the beginnings of a rebuttal, but his voice trailed off.

"You *did,*" Scott continued. "I remember Dante drove an old red Neon. You told him to meet you here." He turned to Diana. "Dante is his dealer."

Brennen felt the distrust fill the space between him and Diana like a gas leak. "I'm sorry, Professor Navarro. I texted him before I knew."

"Knew what?" Scott asked.

"I told him about the full breach hypothesis." She was walking to the couch from the hallway. "Let's just say he has been warned."

Beth excused herself to the restroom and gave Brennen a hug and kissed his cheek on her way. As she walked down the hallway, she said, "You need to quit that stuff, Brennen."

He felt self-conscious with all eyes on him. It was as if a video camera was recording his every move, from every possible angle, and broadcasting across a major network. "I know. I know." It was a moment that lasted an eon. He felt low as he slumped into the living room chair, and sank deeper into the flames.

"Okay," Diana said, taking the attention away from Brennen, "that is settled. Brennen is now aware of the potential danger. Should this Dante person arrive, we just send him away, right, Brennen?"

Brennen nodded.

"Now," Diana continued, "what I think we should focus on is calling the police."

Scott began shaking his head.

Diana gestured down the hallway. "I know, Scott, she doesn't trust the police. Now I know you talked about waiting it out until Monday to see what your law professor thinks, but that was before this Henry guy shows up and starts talking about going to deal with Jacob *personally*? That is starting to sound somewhat combative to me."

"Well," Brennen said, "how else is anyone supposed to deal with someone like Jacob? He holds influence over an entire community up there—like one or two hundred people from what I understand."

"*He's* not playing by any rules," Scott said. "He's above the law and abusing his power. If we have any shot of enforceable litigation against him, I think it's best to talk to an experienced attorney before turning the whole thing over to the law."

Several moments passed in silence while Brennen, Scott, and Diana let the pros and cons of the various scenarios marinate. All three of them seemed timid to lay any more weight to either side of the argument.

Brennen leaped from his slouchy posture. "Where is Snippety?"

Before the others could answer, Harvey returned from the outside explaining that there was a Ford F150 parked two doors down.

B

Mr. Bratch surveyed the backyard as he skulked soundlessly across it. Surrounded by eight-foot masonry walls, as was the style in most of the Tempe area, it was small, no more than twenty feet deep, with a grassy clearing leading to a small patio area, complete with a Jacuzzi topped with a heavy vinyl covering that folded back on itself for easy removal. There were plenty of tall landscaping fixtures to provide cover while he figured out a way into the house. He was an expert burglar given his experience working both below and above the law. In his opinion, most yard features designed with privacy in mind also accommodated foul play. To be sure, not all houses were created equal; some had easier access points than others. None, however, were as easy as a sliding glass door without a reinforcement brace. As it happened, this house had such a combination.

He stared through the glass into a very dark master bedroom as he listened through his headphones to the sounds coming within the house. He heard a female voice, but he could not confirm whether or not it belonged to Beth. She heard Jacob's name mentioned by more than one male voice. He was at the right house.

He hitched the microphone to his tool belt and placed both hands on the sliding glass door, fingers outstretched, and pushed up. The rubber tips of his gloves made easy work of lifting the door over the security latch and down the track until warm air from the house poured onto his face.

"Hhhh!"

Following the sound, he looked down to find a cat hissing at him. In the darkness, it was all eyes and teeth. Without hesitating, he scooped up the cat and clamped its mouth shut with his fingers. It made creepy guttural noises as it clawed the space in front of it, catching Mr. Bratch's face once or twice.

In a panic, he lifted the Jacuzzi cover with his foot and

threw the irate feline in the water, closing the lid and locking it into place with a nearby bolder with impressive efficiency. He wanted to smash its skull, but its protests were nicely muted under the thick vinyl as it was. It wasn't going anywhere and would not last long in the water with little air to breathe.

Let it drown, he thought.

He was in the house now, passing a dresser, atop of which was a shoebox, as he slipped the brass knuckles over his gloved hands. He was unsure how to proceed. He had the knuckles and a pocketknife—more than enough to take out the whole house. From the sound of it, there were two men and two women. He could, if desired, go in guns a-blazing. In fact, his killer instinct preferred this. He would be gone and under the protection of the compound within hours. If he took only Beth, the others could act as witnesses who'd seen his face, now bleeding with identifiable cat scratches. This would not do at all. He had a decision to make, and the sooner the better.

He froze, Komodo-like, as he heard someone coming down the hall.

"You need to quit that stuff, Brennen," a girl's voice said.

It was her: Beth Perkins, loud and crystalline in his headset. He hadn't heard her voice since before the dance at Jacob's warehouse on the night of her escape. She had squeaked out a mousy "Hello" while blowing up balloons for the guests. He hated that voice. He hated it because it belonged to the person who had caused him so much personal anguish, bad blood with his boss, and exposure to the Othersider world. It was the voice of prey, and it was now walking straight toward him.

It appeared he wouldn't have to make a decision after all.

C

Brennen followed Harvey to the driveway with Scott and Diana close behind. Like a White House tour guide, Harvey was walking backward while explaining to his small crowd that, after hearing Beth's story of the false prophet, his followers, and the tracking devices, he became alarmed. Having had some experience with the lengths people will go to find a person of interest, he was unconvinced they had shaken Mr. Bratch's pursuit. He concluded by drawing their attention to a white F150 parked about one hundred feet down the road.

In an instant, the truck revved to life and sped away, sending the Halloween decorations in the neighbor's yard swaying eerily in its wake.

A dreadful feeling began to overtake Brennen as he stared at the truck disappearing around a corner. How did Mr. Bratch find them this time? There had to be some kind of rationale attached to it. They weren't, after all, dealing with The Terminator here; there was no chip in his brain allowing him to scan for coordinates in infrared.

No. It was more probable that Larry Hitchcock had taken down Dante's plates after getting his ass kicked. Mr. Bratch, having a fair amount of resources, was able to run the plates. The thought was hard to process; still, the evidence continued to compile in his head. He had texted Dante well over fifteen minutes ago and he was nowhere to be found. In his stead appears an F150, in all likelihood belonging to Mr. Bratch.

"Can Beth confirm that it was them?" Diana asked.

"It was," Brennen said. "It was Bratch."

"Well," Diana said, "just for my piece of mind, let's ask her. Where is she?"

"I thought she'd be right behind you," Scott said. He looked to Diana and back to Harvey. The three bounced terrified looks off each other for several seconds while her absence became heavy.

Scott took flight toward the house, followed by Diana and Harvey.

"I'll check the back!" Brennen called out. In an instant he was at the side gate and noticed it was unlatched. Not taking Diana to be one to leave a gate open, his suspicions were gaining credibility. His brain moved quicker than his feet, which tumbled him on the dark sidewalk, smacking his head as he went down. He saw blue sparks on impact, but recovered. "Beth!" he shouted. He could hear similar calls from within the house. He jumped to his feet and sprinted through the backyard just as Diana was turning on the outside light. She was addressing him in alarm while pointing at the sliding glass door.

"The back door was open!" she cried out.

Scott was busy in the house yelling Beth's name.

Brennen sucked in a second wave of anxious thoughts, marinating deep within his guts. "Snippety!" he howled. "Scott! Do you have eyes on Snippy?"

At once there was the sound of a whistle being blasted throughout the house. Brennen joined the others scrambling through the interior of the house, until they all ended up by the patio, panting with emotion.

"I don't believe it," Scott said, "why would they take the cat?"

"Or kill it," Harvey added.

"It wasn't *they*," Brennen said. He feared, at any second, his eyes would spot a lifeless lump of fur on the ground, yet he scoured for it regardless. He had to know, either way. "It was him. It was Mr. Bratch."

"Wait," Diana interrupted, "what is that noise?"

They all listened as strange infant-like noises seemed to be coming from the ground. They all turned to Diana who, having heard it first, seemed to have the best idea as to its origin. Her attention turned to the Jacuzzi. "There! That rock is not supposed to be on the cover."

Brennen was the first to reach the lid. He threw the rock to the side, cursing as it landed with a thud. His heart was overworked with Glow and anxiety as he threw open the cover. There, clinging to the underside of it, was Snippety.

She was alive . . . and she was wet.

D

Infuriated, Scott said. "I say we get in the van and go after her."

"We can do that," Henry said.

"He's got a huge head start on us," Brennen said.

Scott shook his head. "Yeah, but we know where he's going. Paiute Rock City. The compound is in Paiute Rock City. If we leave now, we can try to beat them there and stop him from taking her to Jacob."

"We can do that," Henry repeated.

Scott looked at Brennen. "If he takes her back there, it's all over."

"Scott," Brennen said, "I want to get her back as much as you, but I'm not sure you're thinking clearly."

Scott stepped up to Brennen with a warrior soul. "*I'm* not thinking clearly? *Me?* And you've been *Confucius* this whole time?" He was growing more livid with each rebuttal. "*You've* been out of your mind this whole time, man. You show up at my house after I haven't seen you in two years, you're wired out of your mind, you bring Glow into my house, smoke it in my car, in front of me, when you *know damn well* that I can't be around that shit. Because why, Brennen?"

Brennen bowed his head and started waving his hand.

"No. Don't *dismiss* me, man. I asked you a question. Because *why?* Because *I* got my freaking life together. *I* had the *guts* to sober up. And it's hard, man. That's right; if you think I don't want a hit of that shit when you do it, think again. But I don't—and you're still living in that same smoky-ass place about to be evicted."

Brennen crossed his arms and made a motion to speak, but failed to get the words out before Scott seized the silence once again.

"And not only do you show up high, but you show up with Beth, and then you *leave* her with me. 'Okay, Scott, nice to see you, here's a girl, see ya, Scott.' No, don't worry about it, Brennen, it's not like I have to *study* or anything." He was borderline hysterical, if not lunatical. "But it turns out all right because she's a cool girl. She's beyond cool, she's *awesome*. Yeah, I have a thing for her . . . and no, she's not a 'redhead rescue' like freakin' *Draya* used to say. She's different. And she's in some serious trouble because *you* just texted Mr. Bratch her address! Now listen, man, I made her a promise. I told her I wouldn't leave her with Jacob, so I'm not going to leave her with him. I will at least *try* to track her down by myself if I have to, but I am *asking* you, as a friend, to go *with* me because I need your *help*. I would *hope*, after all the *shit* I've done for you that you would have the *decency* to *return the respect!*"

For the first time since Scott set eyes on him, Brennen's fiery pupils seemed to mellow. His face softened and, if only for a moment, resembled his goofball associate, his good friend, Brennen Reynolds.

"Okay, man," Brennen said, "you are right. I'll go."

"We can do that, by the way," Henry said. He seemed to be stuck on the sentence. "Track her down, I mean."

Diana ignored the comment and stood with her arms crossed, scuffing the ground with her foot. "I'm sorry, guys, but I think it's crazy. I don't have any better answers, but I certainly can't go with you."

"We wouldn't want you to," Scott said, "you've done enough already."

"So you're saying you think we can chase them down?" Brennen asked Harvey.

"No. I'm saying we can *track* them down."

"Henry, what the hell are you talking about?" Scott asked.

"Well, when I went out to check the truck, I had a feeling the coincidence of another F150 parked near the house was a little much. And after hearing Beth's story about being bugged, I thought why not, eh, bug them back?" He stood, meeting each of their gazes, not comprehending what the big deal was. "I put a magnetic tracking device under his car. I do it all the time."

"Henry," Scott said, "I'm beginning to believe you're a genius."

Snippety concurred. She sat on the patio table with her pride intact. With her wet fur sucked to her tiny frame, her head looked enormous. She looked like an alien Muppet.

"That's right, Snippety," Brennen said, "you're coming with us, right?"

She held up a paw and nodded her head.

"Okay, girl," Brennen answered, "but you are staying in the van."

"Let's get moving, then," Scott said, addressing the other two, "grab what you need."

Harvey stood blinking. "Wait . . . did the cat just *answer* you?"

"Long story," Brennen said.

Five minutes later, after being fortified with protein bars and water, courtesy of Diana, the four of them were off to follow the tracker's signal, or *would* have been had the van started.

Part Two: Offense

22
October 30: Night

A

The prophet sat in his swivel chair, looking out the office window with his back to Lou Ellen. She had come to his office door several times in the last few hours, but he had refused to see her. After Mr. Bratch's phone call several hours prior, he was secure in the knowledge that Beth would soon be back and would be sacrificed to God. Lou Ellen, ever the doubter, would only serve to undermine his confidence.

She'd bullied her way through the apostle guarding the office. She often got her way in the long run. She was the only person who wielded that kind of authority over him. She was his first wife out of seven, and had since given him eight children, the most children out of any of them. As the midwife of the entire community, she was an indispensable part of daily operations—and she knew it. At times, she would leverage her position to test her limits as she was testing them now.

He could feel her glaring at the back of his neck.

"Mr. Bratch has reclaimed Beth," he said as he swiveled around to meet her glare. "He will be here within an hour or two."

She looked larger and older tonight than he could remember. Her hair, pulled back with a single wave sweeping across the brow, was disheveled, with roots that looked as though they had been dipped in gray paint. She was ever-expanding, with so many un-burnt calories that her prayer dress had become ill-fitting at her midsection which now heaved with impatience as she breathed.

"Just what the hell were you thinking, Jacob," Lou Ellen asked, "calling the Othersider police?" Without allowing for an answer, she added, "How could you bring them here and jeopardize our way of life?"

The prophet sighed, putting his elbows on his desk. "Lou Ellen, I told you. With Beth's name all over the city, it makes it hard for her to go anywhere. With nowhere to go, it makes Mr. Bratch's job a lot easier to find her." He made calming gestures with his hands. Lou Ellen never truly understood that his words were that of God's and they were final. "Ya gotta scare the fox out of the hole. Besides, if they had found her, they would just bring her back here and let us take it from there. As it happens, Mr. Bratch is on the way back with her and you don't need to worry."

This made Lou Ellen jump out of her seat to approach him, her chair squeaking with volume into the room as the force of her body caused it to scrape across the floor.

Years of lifting children had broadened her shoulders, giving her a hulking frame that loomed above Jacob. It unnerved him enough to force him to stand up, if only to gain sufficient footing. He rested his hand on her shoulder in a calming manner.

Without warning, she slapped him hard across the face, snapping his jowls to the side and back into place. "Don't you fuckin' tell me not to worry."

Stunned, Jacob could only hold his cheek and glare at her with malice.

"You know damn well what's coming. God does not wait for his sacrifices. Without the sacrifice, the Othersiders will come and they will come in droves. They're probably on their way, for all the hell we know." Her eyes were wide as she bared teeth while she spoke. "It has been too long already. The end of the world means the end of evil and the triumph of righteousness. And we must triumph."

"Get the hell out of my office, Lou Ellen." Jacob pointed to the door with a shaky finger.

She lingered for a few moments longer. "You know what we have to do."

The prophet scanned her face. "If it comes to that, we will. But you should trust in what God says." He once again pointed to the door. "Speaking of which, He told me to tell you to take Betty's remains to The Trees for disposal. While you're there, prepare the area for sacrifice. If you're still interested in an afterlife, I suggest you get a move on."

At first, Jacob thought she might assault him again or spew some nonsensical forebodings of letter boxes, but she glared at him before stomping out and letting the door slam behind her.

B

Beth awoke, much like she had days prior, to the humming of a truck engine and desert shrubs whizzing by at eighty miles per hour as the headlights jetted out into swarthy highway. This was her second time waking. The first time, she'd made the mistake of lifting the tarp in the back seat to find Dante's lifeless body of beneath it. The image of his vacant eyes staring into nothing haunted her. As she awakened this time, she opened her eyes as to not draw attention. She could see the center console between the front seats. There were two rolls of masking tape, a Sharpie and a combination lock.

Though it felt like months ago, she remembered the fear of leaving the compound—an exciting fear, a fear of an unknown, yet limitless, future. Now she was again afraid, but the fear was dreadful in nature as she traveled down the same highway back to the known and the familiar.

She reflected how Mr. Bratch was able to get her out of Professor Navarro's house without a sound. She remembered the sad look on Brennen's face as she walked down the hallway to splash water on her face. The next thing she knew her arms were without leverage and her lungs were without power and she was getting dragged outside. There was a skill to the maneuver that rendered her helpless like never before. He had overpowered her and she hated him for it, almost as much as she hated herself for not being able to let out at least a whimper to alarm the others.

She remembered being thrown to the grass and tasting dirt, but her memory provided nothing else in the way of clues. The throbbing at the back of her head explained she must have been knocked unconscious, but did not explain how long she was out. Her guess was an hour, maybe two.

She was bullied by the biggest bully of them all.

Her God, she decided, was female.

She closed her eyes and focused her thoughts on the combination lock.

C

Moving on with her evening proved difficult for Diana. As much as she tried, she couldn't help thinking that she'd sent the boys to meddle in a situation that was leaps and bounds over their heads. She was not as studied in extremist religious groups as she was in quantum mechanics, but various headlines on the nightly news over the years had painted them in a dark light. Cults did not take well to strangers and applied rather violent tactics when dealing with them.

She'd known better. Though she never went to private schools, and therefore forewent any IQ testing, she felt herself an intelligent human being. To this point in her life, she could rationalize her behavior in most cases. Now, however, she found herself asking how she was allowing herself to let this happen.

Sure, if she got involved, there would be write-ups in local papers. Her position at the university, already in a precarious position due to her book, would be compromised. Her colleagues, supercilious assholes they could sometimes be, would no doubt resort to ostracizing her. It would be a life-changing decision and she wasn't sure she was ready to change her life, at least not yet and not in this way.

On the other hand, if she were to remove her own need for self-preservation, these people were in trouble. If she applied the scientific method, forcing herself to extreme lengths to minimize bias while examining the situation, it would be clear what needed to be done.

She recalled Brennen giving her the name of the sergeant in charge of the investigation. She did not forget his name: Sergeant Pederson. "Damnit," she said while picking up the cordless phone off its cradle. She got as far as to dial a few numbers before hanging up.

"Damnit."

D

"Ah, the princess awakens," Mr. Bratch said. He had been waiting for the girl to wake up. He didn't think he'd hit her hard enough to cause her to sleep away their entire trip together, but perhaps he may have laid into her head pretty good with the brass knuckles.

He laughed to himself. She was going to be sacrificed soon, anyway. So what if the God-bait returned to the compound with some bumps and bruises? As long as he could resume his life, free from complexities, he was as giddy as a kindergartener on recess.

He scarcely recognized her in her Othersider garb. She looked no different than any other girl he witnessed frolicking about Tempe and Phoenix. He wondered if he would have found Beth had the prophet not made the gutsy call to involve the police. It was a risk, yes; however, had she been able to find appropriate shelter, or even go to the police herself, perhaps she would've been lost forever. As it turned out, she'd fallen into the incapable hands of addicts and dealers. Sometimes Jacob's methods and the madness meshed with surprising cohesiveness.

During their three-hour trip together, Mr. Bratch had spent a good deal of time thinking of the upcoming sacrifice. He thought of Beth on the altar, neck tendons grotesquely disfigured, the gag muting her screams. He only wished he could be the one to wield the dagger.

She sat with her arms crossed, keeping her eyes away

from his. "You proud of yourself, Mr. Bratch?" She raised her hand and stroked the back of her head. "Congratulations. You beat up a girl half your size."

Mr. Bratch stared forward. He had not heard sarcasm out of her mouth before and was taken aback.

"So," she said, "you're taking me back to the compound of the great and mighty prophet." She used her hands with expression as she spoke. "To sacrifice me to a God who doesn't like that I can't have kids. Because that makes so much sense, right?"

He wasn't sure if it was a question or a statement.

"No. I totally get it." She held up her bandaged hand. "Maybe you guys can put another tracking device in my hand to make sure I stay in the grounds."

Mr. Bratch was again speechless. He liked it better when she was sleeping.

"*Really*, Mr. Bratch? A *tracking* device? Do you know how *crazy* that is? And to call it a kiss from God? I mean, do you *really* believe the shit that comes out of Jacob's mouth?" She waited for any type of response, but none were forthcoming. "You were an Othersider once. You have to know on some fundamental level that it's all crap." She looked at him. "Are you scared of the prophet, Mr. Bratch? Maybe he has something on you? Are you hiding out? Running from the law?" She narrowed her eyes. "Are you a child molester, Mr. Bratch?"

He was infuriated by the comment. This was not the same girl who'd left the compound. He wanted to set the record straight with this new Beth and explain the world of difference between a prostitute killer and a child molester. He wanted to justify his transgressions in Philadelphia, but he refrained. He owed her no explanation.

"Shut up, Beth. You watch that insubordinate tone with me, or I'll clock you in the head again." He shot her intense glances, jerking his eyes between Beth and the road. "I don't know who you think you are now, but it won't matter anyway. They're at The Trees, setting up the altar as we speak. You'll be dead and gone within a couple hours, with a dagger in your heart. What do I care what you think? Just sit back and shut up."

He was expecting his words to cause her to cower and pout. Instead, she laughed. She tried to hold it back, as if she were concerned she might hurt his feelings, but soon she buried her face in her hand, trying not to giggle.

"Is something funny, Beth?"

She waved him off. "You know, Mr. Bratch, someday this is all going to change. The world is going to wake up and realize aggression doesn't work anymore. It's over. Thanks but no thanks." Her face relaxed as the giggle spasm subsided. "But until then, *eat shit, Bratch!*"

He had never seen sparks like he experienced at that moment. At once, he heard a crack in his orbital bone next to his eye. He knew Beth had punched him, but he had no idea how she managed the force behind it. He was almost resigned to believing she had somehow been infused with super-human strength until he realized she'd taken the combination lock from the center console and looped it around her middle finger, giving her a steel knuckle. Even after the realization, he was unable to respond until the knuckle come at him twice more, once across his nose and again into his teeth, knocking half of his right incisor back into his mouth.

On pure survival instinct, he was able to fend off any subsequent blows and bring the truck to a halt on the side of the road. The pain in his eye was matched only by the dangling nerve endings of his tooth against his tongue.

Before he was able to release himself from the seatbelt, Beth was slamming the door behind her and running for what appeared to be a patch of pine trees looming ominously in the northern Arizona night.

He threw open the door and gave chase, spitting the remains of his tooth as he ran. She was a dead woman. Not even the threat of the old man could stop that now. Seeing red, he was unable to reason a why he shouldn't kill her. He knew Jacob may have some problem with it—something about kicking him out of the compound—but he didn't care anymore. He would like nothing more than to feel her life flee from his hands. The killing urge was as unavoidable as it was inevitable. All he needed to do was catch her.

And when he caught her, he would kill her.

E

The tree branches scratched her arms and face as she ran past. She could hear the sound of Mr. Bratch's labored breathing no more than fifteen feet behind her.

Her own breathing was beginning to worry her. She had never run so far at such a sustained pace. Her lungs suffered as a result, both cooling and burning simultaneously. She could not hold air long enough before expelling it all, only to gasp for it again. She knew her chances of losing him were slim, but her odds were better if she were to circle back to the highway, where, at the very least, she could flag down a vehicle, just as she had done with Brennen. With any luck, the driver would not be up-to-date on wanted murderer suspects.

There was also a chance, although slight, that a hasty Mr. Bratch might have left the keys in the truck before taking pursuit. She could drive the truck a comfortable distance from him, being sure not to leave fingerprints on the steering wheel, and ditch it, along with the dead body, before she was seen in it. Dante, bless his soul, would understand.

F

Diana paced the dining room. She knew, in her heart, that Brennen Reynolds was the proof she and Manny were looking for—proof that her theory was correct, or at least on the right path to being correct. Life was not explained by all things being the sum of their parts. She believed there was more going on underneath—deep underneath—what she currently knew. There is a type of consciousness running with and through us. There were signs of it in places medicine ignores. Autism patients experience it when they play an entire piano concerto after a one-time listen, or crunch sizable numbers, at calculator-like speed, while performing other tasks. These are additive abilities, yet they are explained away as destructive brain damage. Dave was aware of something as he crawled up Brennen's arm. Snippety, after prolonged contact with him, demonstrated a higher level of intelligence than a chimpanzee.

And she let him go battle a dangerous extremist group.

She was reminded of her brief leisure times in Harvard yard while at school. There, she'd lie down to clear her mind of the concepts of the day and contemplate her place in the world. There was an inscription written in Latin above the arches leading into the yard from Mass Avenue. Though she looked at it countless times before finding shade beneath her favorite Horse Chestnut tree, she only inquired as to its meaning on her last semester when one of her classmates not only knew the meaning, but pointed out that it was, in fact, a double-inscription, with the second half covered by ivy. The meaning stuck with her more than any subject studied in a classroom.

She spoke it out loud into her empty kitchen. "Thrice happy and more are they whom an unbroken bond unites, and by no sundering of love by wretched quarrels shall separate before life's dying day."

Life was too short for quarreling, especially with herself. If she didn't act, she knew she would forever regret it. Beth was as pure of a soul as she had met since Manny. And Brennen. Brennen was unique. An anomaly, tapped into a world of which she only had theoretical knowledge . . . until now. She felt, all of them, bonded, and allowing them to drive to this dangerous place without help would be breaking that bond entirely.

She was not serving her kind by allowing it.

Once again, she picked up the phone, this time letting it ring. "Hello. May I speak to Sergeant Pederson?"

G

Well into his fifties, Mr. Bratch was feeling his age upon him. The years had slipped away from him much like Beth was slipping away from him now. His feet stomped zombie-like on the ground as he crashed through the pine forest. His right eye was swollen shut and his entire upper jaw was a constant source of pain that pulsated through his mouth with each step. It was age versus youth, injury versus health, and he needed to change his tactics soon if he had any hope of ending her life.

"*You've got nowhere to go, Beth!*" he shouted through uneasy breathing while his ever-swelling lip affected his speech. "*Every cop in the state is looking for you!*" He paused for an answer, but none came. "*There is no one coming to save you. Your friends are long gone! We will find you!*"

His hate drove him forward, listening for Beth's footsteps in the darkness. She was about twenty yards ahead and seemed to be turning back toward the highway.

He was desperate to bring fear back into his victim.

"*What about Jane, Beth? What about her daughters? Your nieces? Jacob has them all. Their afterlives are riding on your return . . . . If you don't care about your afterlife anymore, what about theirs?*" He paused to take breath, putting his hands on his knees. "*He's going to kill them all if you don't show up! Can you live with that? Can you live with that, Beth?*"

23
October 30: In the Meantime

A

Sergeant Pederson slammed down the phone and looked at Officer Davis, still sulking, embarrassed from being tased by a civilian earlier in the evening.

"Get over it, son," Sergeant Pederson said. "Where is Detective Oakley?"

Davis explained that she'd left the station to follow a lead on the Reynolds case and would be back later.

The sergeant looked around with concern as if trying to devise a plan without Davis taking notice. "We need to get to Paiute Rock City with a small SWAT team. Now. How long to get there via squad car?"

"About five hours, sir."

"Too long. What about the chopper?"

"Our chopper's speed is about one hundred twenty miles per hour, but we have several pieces of departmental gear, permanently attached, that will create quite a bit of drag. Besides, you'll never fit a SWAT team in there."

"Shit. We need to get there faster."

Now it was Davis who looked around, until it looked as though a doorbell rang in his head. "What about the Blackhawk? A Blackhawk's speed tops off at about one hundred eighty-three, depending on air speed and drag, of course. That would get us there in just under two hours. It will also hold a small team." He rubbed his bald head. "I think it's still in the department's helicopter storage hangar for the night."

"You're absolutely right, Davis. Maybe that taser gun actually *cleared* your head." He pointed at him. "See? You *check* the details and you take some *initiative* and good things happen. I'll clear it with the military and ask for a pilot. Since Paiute Rock City won't cooperate with the case, you call Arizona Highway Patrol and have some officers meet us off the compound somewhere. We don't want the extremists getting spooked and pulling a Waco, Texas incident on us. Got it?"

"Yes, Sarge. Can I ask what's going on?"

"Get my gear; I'll explain on the way."

"Get your gear?" Davis asked with confusion. "*You're* going up there, too?"

"That's right, Davis. And so are you."

B

Beth's leg muscles cramped mutinously against her will as she pushed herself to reach the highway. She felt her feet anchored, as if by wet tar, to the forest floor, causing an undesired sluggishness to retard her ability to outrun her nemesis.

She glanced back into the darkness where she could see no sign of Mr. Bratch, but could hear his footsteps moving forward.

Jane

She pictured Jane and her nieces bound and gagged somewhere in Jacob's office, awaiting word of their fate—a fate resting on Beth.

As much as he didn't want him there, Mr. Bratch was in her head. He asked her a direct question and she needed to reply, at least to herself. Could she live with herself knowing that her sister-wife and three nieces were killed because she refused the Prophet Jacob? She knew, after all, this was no bluff. Jacob was a man of his word when it came to death threats.

She limped onward, wishing she had not heard Bratch's words. Through the dense cover of the pine trees, she could see the freeway clearing. Mr. Bratch's truck, the size of a toy car from her vantage point, became backlit as a vehicle drew closer. She leaned against the rough bark of one of the trees to catch her breath, keeping well out of sight.

Instead of speeding by, the vehicle slowed to a crawl just beyond the abandoned truck, twenty yards from her. It pulled over and parked.

She was sure Larry Hitchcock had returned.

C

Mr. Bratch could see out of his one good eye when the headlights on the vehicle turned off as he approached the clearing. He thought he could hear the murmurings of people in distress, yet the sound of his winded breath interfered with his ability to hear clearly. He stood, doubled over, as he tried to control his breathing long enough to hear the voices. It was Beth. He was sure of it. No other sound other than hers could bring his blood to a boil and splash his vision with red. She would be his prized kill—more valuable than all the Philadelphia prostitutes combined.

He spit out another mouthful of blood and set out, with renewed fervor, to get his hands on her.

He was tackled when he reached the clearing. Too exhausted to defend himself, he was lifted off the ground with ease, arms constricted to his sides, and thrown hard to the ground, grinding the right side of his face deep into the gravel.

Rolling onto his back, Mr. Bratch pulled the Maglite from his belt and illuminated it in the direction of the voice. It appeared as though he'd been attacked by a hulking mannequin holding a taser gun. "And just who the hell are—"

At once, he went from being out of breath to being hit with nine-hundred-thousand volts of electricity.

D

Scott rubbed Snippety's white chin. She lay lethargic in a box of wires while Brennen and Beth hoisted Mr. Bratch's unconscious body into the van and onto a gurney in the back. He strapped the man's limbs down with rubber tubes.

They pulled the van among trees to veil it from the curious eyes of the nighttime passersby on Highway Eighty-nine. Beth, near hysterical and winded from running, had disappeared into the back of the van while Scott hid Mr. Bratch's F150 truck deeper in the cove of trees, being careful not to leave fingerprints on the steering wheel or center console. The truck had a strong odor from which Scott was more than happy to escape. The entire back seat was covered with a tarp concealing something he was happy to leave well enough alone.

Brennen, badgered by bats eager to use him as a roost, opted to stay in the van as the tasks were executed. Scott was surprised the entire operation of binding Mr. Bratch and hiding the vehicles had taken less time than expected. They were finished by the time Beth began to breathe easy again.

During their excursion from Professor Navarro's house, Scott had learned Harvey's real name, but part of him wished he hadn't. There was something about the efficient way the man tied Mr. Bratch to the gurney—not to mention the presence of a gurney at all—that implied this was not Harvey's first experience restraining someone. In many ways, it was best if Scott knew the bare minimum concerning his enigmatic accomplice. It was true, with his mannequin mask, Harvey came off as rather creepy. Yet, without him, Beth's reacquisition would not have been possible. For this, Harvey was as endeared to Scott as any friend of old. Were his methods questionable? Yes. Was he mentally unsound? Of course. But as Scott watched Harvey bind Mr. Bratch, there was no one in the world he trusted more.

"Hey, Eagle's fan," Mr. Bratch said.

It took Scott a moment to realize the voice was addressing him. He glanced down at his Philadelphia Eagles shirt and back at Mr. Bratch.

"Where am I?" Mr. Bratch demanded. His lips smacked with thirst and a slight wheeze emitted from his lungs.

Beth reached behind her and grabbed a bottle of drinking water and poured water into Mr. Bratch's mouth. He lifted his head to greet it, wincing while he gulped it down.

"You're expecting a thank you, Beth?" He looked at her with hatred and doled it out in equal amounts to the others. "What's with the sunglasses? You look like a bunch of loser Blues Brothers."

Harvey grabbed Mr. Bratch's face, digging his fingers in

the scratches, and slammed his head hard back on the gurney. "In the interest of time, I'm going to let the Prophet of Free Will answer your question for you. Before I do, let me give you a word of caution. When he addresses you, *don't*, under *any* circumstances think about your name or where you are from." He kept Mr. Bratch's mouth shut with his hand, forcing Mr. Bratch's nostrils to flare as they bore the brunt of the breathing. "Now listen close. This is important. Do *not* think about any dark secrets you might be hiding." He pointed a meaty finger in Mr. Bratch's face as he spoke. "Now, without further *adieu,* I present to you the prophet."

Brennen waved off the introduction and walked on his knees to the gurney, crouched over the nose-breather, and scanned his eyes for several seconds. He raised his eyebrows. "Holy shit. *Really?*"

"What is it?" Scott asked.

"Okay. Well, his name is Jerry Bratchlek, an ex-Philadelphia cop wanted by the FBI for the murders of several prostitutes."

Mr. Bratch arched his back and screamed into Harvey's hand as though a knife had pierced his spine. He writhed about, but the rubber straps held him to the gurney.

Scott looked at Mr. Bratch, dismayed. "*I remember* you, man!" I was a kid in Fishtown when the prostitutes were murdered. They never found you. There was a *manhunt* for you, for God's sake! My dad wouldn't let me leave the house after dark for *days.* That was *you?*"

"Well *well,* Mr. Bratch," Beth said. "Now *that* is fascinating information." She shook a finger at him.

While locking eyes with Mr. Bratch again, Brennen said,

"And someone named Dan Tenner is rotting in the back seat of his truck. Who the hell is Dan Tenner?"

Scott was reminded of the odd smell coming from underneath the tarp in Mr. Bratch's F150. Whoever it was, the name was equally unfamiliar to him.

"It's Dante," Beth said, shaking her head. "He killed Dante."

Brennen dropped his head and palmed his forehead. "I knew it. He killed Dante for his mobile phone, knowing I'd contact him." His voice was stressed and sullen, changing to angry and powerful. *"Didn't you, you piece of shit? You murdered Dante for a phone!"* Without warning, he struck Mr. Bratch, close-fisted, across his face while Harvey continued to hold the man's mouth shut. Mr. Bratch looked with hate-filled eyes at Brennen as his muffled scream filled the soundproofed van.

Beth moved to restrain her friend. "Brennen. *Brennen.* Calm *down.* Hitting him isn't going to help the situation at all. There has been enough beating the shit out of each other for one day. Just concentrate on mining him for as much information as you can."

Brennen looked at her and complied.

To the others, Scott said, "Let's just get out of here, back to Tempe."

Beth sighed. "I can't."

The comment dropped the entire van into silence.

"It's my sister-wife, Jane," Beth explained. "Jacob has her and my three nieces. He's going to kill her if I don't come back." She paused to adjust her sunglasses. "He'll do it. There is no doubt about it. If I . . . if I can at least *talk* to him

. . . *try* to reason with him . . . . She trailed off and shook her head. "I have to go. I have to try."

"Beth," Scott said, not believing what he was hearing, "That sounds crazy. You have to know that."

"I understand, Scott. You don't have to go along." She addressed the others while giving Snippety a head scratch. "And that goes to all of you. You have been nothing but kind to me. Even though I was a total stranger to you, you have believed in me when you could have just left me on the street. I really appreciate it. Thank you so much." She sighed. "If you don't want to go, it's okay. I can either walk, or Mr. Bratch can take me."

Brennen glanced at Mr. Bratch to read his thoughts. "He's going to kill you."

"No way," Scott said. "It is total suicide to go alone. No. I told you I wouldn't leave you with Jacob and I'm going to follow through. If you want to go, I'm coming with."

Scott glanced at Brennen, who nodded with his friend.

"You don't have to," Beth said.

"Forget about it," Harvey said. He slid his mask off and tossed it aside. "We're in. Besides, I'd like to talk to Prophet Jacob myself." He exited the van and walked around to the driver's seat, slamming the back doors shut as he went.

"What do we do with him?" Scott asked, gesturing to Mr. Bratch.

"He's staying right there," Beth said. She began tapping her skull. "He's got info up here concerning Jacob that we could use."

Snippety placed a paw on Beth's knee. She didn't say anything.

Scott was humored. He gave a quick glance at his surroundings—the van, the girl, the friend, the bad guy, and the intelligent animal—and let out small laugh that caught the attention of the others. "I don't know about looking like the Blues Brothers," he said, shaking his head, "but I definitely feel like I'm in a Scooby-Doo episode."

E

As she worked, Lou Ellen sang a customized rendition of the Alphabet Song softly to herself, "ABCDEFG, you are going to H-H-Hell. . . ." Lou Ellen hadn't taken Betty's body to the trees as the prophet ordered, at least not right away. She made the executive decision to drive her maroon F150 to the storage shed near home base, just down the street from the prophet's office.

She was livid. If the prophet wasn't willing to take the necessary steps to protect the community from Othersider infiltration, she would do it. The old man, Jesus Christ incarnate or not, was losing his grip on reality. He was an arrogant bastard and this was the stupidest thing he had ever done. He had no idea what he had started by involving Othersider cops. All she knew was that someone had to finish it. Someone had to prepare. She appointed herself, Lou Ellen Perkins, first wife of the prophet.

Her prayer dress was caked with dust from wrist to ankle and her feet itched within her black boots. The giant wave of hair across her brow had become even more disheveled, leaving heavy sweat-laden strands clinging tight to her plump face.

Cursing the situation, she undid the locks to the storage

shed, murmuring biblical passages to herself in between loud outbursts. Double doors swung open on their own accord, exposing a work bench complete with a rack of tools, a lawnmower, an expandable aluminum ladder, and, under a black towel, several wires and five bricks of plastic explosives.

She made several trips from the shed to the interior of home base, being careful to place the C4 in inconspicuous places throughout. With the walls standing at eight-feet high and reinforced with coiled razor wire, there was no escape from the room. It was like a small racquetball court with one entrance so narrow it hardly allowed her wide frame to cross.

One way in, one way out.

Of course the members were clueless as to the true purpose of home base. Other activities were practiced there that evoked a communal spirit. Barbecues were hosted, dodgeball games for the girls were played, and the entire community joined here together in large mandatory prayer circles. Tonight would be their last visit, barring any more stupid moves by Jacob. There was no chance she would allow the Othersiders to spoil her way of life. Tonight, whether Jacob knew it or not, the entire community would all be returned to God.

Except, of course, for her and Jacob. They would survive. They would move on and start another community—one farther away and with a lower profile. She could deliver her own baby. She had done it before. In fact, for the last ten years, she had delivered all the babies in the community. She was, in many ways, more important than Jacob. She could create life where as Jacob only took it away.

The song suddenly changed tone. The notes remained the

same, but the words became squeezed biblical passages as she mashed them together to fit the alphabet cadence. "God calls forth desperate times, and I shall respond ten-ten-ten-fold," Her breath was labored as she attached wires to one of the putty bricks. "For you have girded me with strength for battle; you have subdued under me those who rise up against me."

She considered the deadly effects the explosives would have on the members of the community, yet she continued her duties without throttling down her efforts. The apostle husbands, their many wives, and the children—many of whom she'd delivered into the world—would not only understand her actions, but thank her for them in the afterlife. Praises would be spouted to her in heaven when she joined them later down the line. She only needed a few more years in this life to secure her own afterlife which would no doubt be enriched after tonight. With any luck, her actions tonight would expand her afterlife options to include more freedom, a stronger influence on former sister-wives, and the ability to be exonerated from second death—the final death of her spirit. If God was truly just; if there was intent behind Him kissing her hand, He might even allow her a new husband to serve, or even rule.

Just the thought of it made her tingle with anticipation. In heaven, she would be a star.

In the meantime, she grabbed another brick of explosives from the shed and waddled back to home base to secure it under a teeter-totter.

"Now you're going to H-H-Hell. Next time won't you sing with me. . . ."

24
October 30: Devil's Night

A

With its headlights out, the white van crept over the lengthy ridge that concealed the Perkins' compound, illuminating a menacing light into the otherwise blackened night. Coming to a final halt, Brennen looked straight ahead from the passenger seat and noted the landscape. He had never been to the northernmost parts of Arizona and was surprised to see that the pine trees were gone, replaced again by sparse desert with stubble patches of brush that swayed in the cool breeze.

Harvey had removed the barrier separating the front seat from the rest of the van, easing communication with the group. Brennen looked in the back to see that Beth and Scott were crouched close between the two seats, studying the same view of the compound; Snippety was sleeping in a cardboard box behind them. Mr. Bratch remained gagged on the gurney.

Beth pointed out the Paiute Rock City squad cars patrolling the perimeter. She scrambled to her knees, opened the double doors and hopped out to stretch her legs in the fresh air. The interior lights were switched off, keeping the darkness as their cover.

The others soon followed suit. It had been a long ride. Except for Beth's voice giving an occasional driving instruction or warning the others about what to expect from the compound, it had been over an hour of cramped silence and they were all feeling it.

"So," Beth said, "we're going to have to sneak in by foot. There is just no way we will be able to surprise him if we drive up in a large white van."

Mr. Bratch laughed from under his gag, causing the group to gather around the van's open doors and peer in at him.

"What are *you* laughing at?" Scott asked.

Beth answered for him. "He's laughing because he doesn't think I know about the traps set in the ground: trip wires, explosives, and whatnot. Jacob is big on blowing things up. What Mr. Bratch doesn't know is that I've been aware of them for some time." She stared at Mr. Bratch as she spoke. "And just because he *thinks* I'm an idiot, doesn't mean I *am* one."

Mr. Bratch rolled his eyes and breathed through his nose. There was no more laughter after that.

Brennen still felt an enormous amount of grief over Dante's loss and an equal deal of animosity toward his killer. Here was a mindless murderer—a cold and cruel example of his own species—sitting strapped to a gurney. Would he not be doing the world a favor if he snuffed him out of existence? As much as the thought remained bullet-pointed in his mind, he knew Beth was right. There had been too many cruel acts executed in the past forty-eight hours. Had Beth not been there to stop him, he may have added to that murky pool of deeds and regretted it for the rest of his life. He had thrown enough wedges between himself and others to last several lifetimes. Becoming a killer would only serve as another one, permanent and irreparable. He needed the opposite of hurting people. He needed to help them, starting with his own friends and family.

He checked his phone for any texts from Jen concerning his mother, but there was no signal.

"Wait," Beth said. Her attention was drawn to the compound.

Soon Brennen, Scott, and Harvey moved around the front of the van to join her. A dark pickup truck sped away from the center of the compound that was doused in outdoor lighting, and to the left of the main complex.

Beth looked through a pair Harvey's surveillance binoculars. "That's Lou Ellen, my sister-wife. She's also the community midwife. She gets all the extra privileges because she's been around the longest and has given Jacob the most kids." She turned to Scott. "He gave her that truck as a birthday present last year. She's the only female allowed to drive."

"Where's she going?" Harvey asked.

"She's probably headed to The Trees. It's a place about a half mile west of the complex. It where the sacrifices are made . . . where Jacob speaks to God. If he sent her alone out to the trees, she must be doing something for him." She handed the binoculars to Scott. "You know, it wouldn't be a bad idea for one of us to follow her and see what she's up to. In many ways, she's just as dangerous as Jacob."

She glanced at Mr. Bratch. His eyes were shut. Somewhere during the trip he had noticed a connection between Brennen looking into his eyes and extracting information from his head. His lids had been squeezed shut ever since.

Scott lowered the binoculars from his eyes and looked at Beth. "I'm not leaving your side again 'til this is done, one way or another. Maybe Brennen can do it."

"No," Beth said, "Brennen's abilities will probably be of more use at the compound."

"Whatever you need me to do," Brennen said, "I'm here to help." He glanced at Scott and gave a reassuring nod.

"Well," Harvey said, "I came here to meet the False Prophet Jacob and have a chat with him in my van. That is what I intend to do."

"You don't have to, Harvey," Brennen said. "As a matter of fact, you've done enough. You don't have to do anymore if you don't want to."

"Hey, man. You are the Prophet of Free Will. I'm not going to just bail out."

Brennen had become weary of maintaining this façade with Harvey. It was obvious Harvey had some issues, particularly the death of his dog, and had crossed a few legal lines along the way on his bizarre vacation, but he could be fixed—at least that's what Brennen needed to believe. In a way, Brennen equated Harvey's salvation to his own. If there was hope for Harvey, there was hope for him. How then could he continue to extract services from him using dishonest pretenses as leverage? He wanted nothing more than to clear the air with his loyal companion, yet he remained silent, frightened of the aftermath such a confession might cause.

There was a rustling from the van. A moment later, Snippety appeared and sat on the foyer of the van. "Eer!"

"She's volunteering to go," Brennen said.

Snippety raised her paw in affirmation.

"No way," Scott said, "it's too dangerous." He looked at Snippety and said, "You'll never make it back—"

Before any of them could make a move, Snippety's superior agility overwhelmed them. Within a few seconds she had jumped from the van, through a patch of desert brush, and onto a treaded footpath leading toward the western road on which Lou Ellen was traveling. She looked back at them before continuing.

"It's okay," Harvey assured him, "She's got natural night vision and can avoid people. No one will suspect a thing."

"In a way, she's the best one for the job," Brennen said. Although what he said made sense while leaving his mouth, he was nevertheless terrified for his cat. He wanted to lunge after her and hold her tight, but he knew in the short amount of time he was able to spend with her, that she was strong-willed. And there was no catching a strong-willed cat that didn't want to be caught.

Beth's voice trembled as she spoke. "You come back when you're done, Snippy. We'll figure out what you saw. Okay? And stay away from rattlesnakes."

Snippety raised a paw.

Scott grabbed the whistle from around his neck and raised it. "The *whistle*, Snip. If you get lost, follow the *whistle! We will come find you!"*

Beth spun around and put her finger to her lips, signaling to Scott to lower his voice.

And then Brennen felt it. It happened. It couldn't come at a worse time. Was it the curve from her hip to her thigh? Was it the way she carried herself with confidence? Her kind soul?

Perhaps it was a combination of all three and more. It was Beth, but it was Beth on a new, intense level and Brennen was either newly enamored by it, or had been from their beginning just a couple short days earlier. As much as he resisted it, it was nonetheless true. Brennen was attracted to her.

Worse, he had feelings for her.

“Shit,” Brennen said to himself.

“What is it?” Scott asked.

Brennen was taken aback, not realizing he had everyone’s attention. “Nothing,” he said shifting his weight from side to side, crossing and re-crossing his arms. “Just worried about Snippy.”

When their attention returned to the cat, Snippety was gone.

B

The blades of the Blackhawk helicopter chopped through the night air with the persistence of a hyperactive second hand of a sonic stopwatch. Despite his protective radio headset, Sergeant Pederson’s ears pounded in rhythm. His vocal chords were raw from yelling above the din.

He was addressing Officer Davis and a small team of SWAT officers as to the landing plan and ensuing raid on the Prophet Jacob’s property. In his hand was a midsized electronic tablet-illuminating-map of the area. With their under-lit faces, the team inherited a sinister look, like an elite military squad, charged with hunting aliens in a blockbuster sci-fi film.

“Okay, listen up,” he said, holding the tablet in view of the rest of the squad. His voice cracked from the strain. “We are approximately *here*." He circled the corresponding area with his finger. "And we have an insertion point set up with Arizona highway patrol *here*, approximately a half mile west of the compound. We will exit and start setting up a perimeter moving east bound. AZ highway patrol will do the same coming from the south and the east. The compound is backed up against a northern mountain range, so we don't need a northern point—"

Davis interrupted him by tapping his arm and holding out a two-way radio.

Looking as if he'd been punched rather than prodded, Pederson said, "What the hell do you want, Davis?"

"Sarge, it's Detective Oakley at the station, sir. She said it's urgent she speaks to you. You should probably take the call."

Sergeant Pederson glanced at the rest of the team before accepting the radio from his colleague. He raised his index finger, signaling the team to hold tight as he ordered Davis to patch him into the headset. "Oakley, this is Pederson, what do you got for me?"

Sergeant Pederson's face displayed a gamut of emotions while he listened to the new information. "*What?*" The question was asked more out of disbelief than for a need for clarification. He adjusted his position and depressed the two-way talk button. "*You have got to be shitting me.*"

C

Jacob sat in his office chair flipping his butterfly knife while staring at the computer monitors displaying various angles of the compound's perimeter. There was no sign of Mr. Bratch.

He had successfully captured Beth and had been calling every hour or so with updates. The last time he'd called was a few hours ago now, reporting all was running smooth and on schedule. He should have been here by now.

Mr. Bratch was never late.

Larry Hitchcock stood, as he always did, guarding the doorway, ready to adhere to the prophet's every whim. Looking more like an Ozark mountain man than the chief protector of an important prophet, he kept his weathered eyes occupied as he adjusted the sling that suspended his broken arm. In a holster nestled on his left side was a Sig Saur 9mm pistol. It was fortunate for the community that he was an ambidextrous shot.

"Where the hell is Mr. Bratch?" the prophet asked the computer screen.

"I don't know, sir," Larry responded. "Maybe Lou Ellen has seen him pull up. Where is she now?"

Without taking his eyes off the screen, the prophet said, "I was talkin' out loud, Larry. I didn't need an answer. The good Lord only knows how many times I have to tell you that I like to talk out loud."

The clanking of the knife continued.

"Sorry, sir," Larry said.

"Don't be sorry now, just . . . be quiet." Jacob glanced at his handheld GPS screen and noted the red dot representing Lou Ellen. "And to answer your question, Lou Ellen is at The Trees taking care of Betty and setting things up for the sacrifice. She spent some time dilly-dallying around home base for Lord knows why. *Now* she's running behind. Everybody's running *behind* today. What in the devil's nation has gotten into you people? I organize for you all, I pray for you all, I speak to *God* for you all, and you would *think* I could get things done with just a little more *efficiency* than this."

He turned to address the corner of the office which was occupied by Jane and her three nieces, all gagged, bound and chained to industrial-sized eye screws fastened through thin carpet and into the concrete floor. They all looked to the ground when Jacob fixed his dead-fished eyes on them. Two of the girls had been crying.

"Y'all had better hope, for your afterlife's sake, that she shows," Jacob warned. He ordered them to look at him, letting his threat soak in before returning his attention to the screen.

The clanking stopped.

Jacob stared in disbelief at the south-facing surveillance monitor. There, bathed in high-quality night vision imagery, making her way to the compound accompanied by two Othersiders, was Beth Perkins.

"Speak of the devil."

Jacob reached for the two-way radio with the intention of raising Lou Ellen when the phone rang. It was the LAN line, which rarely made a sound. He turned his gaze over to Jane and the girls, and back to Larry Hitchcock as if they could magically make the phone stop ringing. "Now who the hell would be calling at this hour?"

He answered on the fourth ring.

D

The mystery of The Trees had always been fascinating to Lou Ellen, even as a child. Nobody knew how they got there.

Some said God himself planted them in this place in the middle of the desert to show the original members of the community where to build their temples. Sometime before she was born, the original community was raided by the police. Many children were separated from their families—too many, in fact—so much that the state had nowhere to place them. It was argued in court that the children were not allowed to be taken from their homes, by anybody, without the consent of the parents. Because of this loophole, the case was thrown out and all the children were returned to their rightful families.

The Othersiders had failed to take them.

The remaining Prophets, namely Jacob's father, Paul Perkins and his cousin, Raymond (of a different name), had a moral dispute. The practice of sacrifice had been banned by Raymond's sect. "Unquestionable authority" had been granted to Raymond, forcing Paul, and the original members of his community farther south, never to have contact with Raymond's sect again. It was said that this group of trees, "God's Forest" as they called it, was a vindication to the community of The Prophet Paul Perkins that their beliefs and practices were the sacred and the righteous, chosen by God.

Now, many decades later, The Trees still stood as a reminder to Lou Ellen of her righteous path. Sixteen of them in total, many now dead, towered twenty and thirty feet high. To the extent of her knowledge, they were some type of pine with wide trunks and rough bark. They were her salvation in times of doubt; they were her own form of self-healing, and she felt blessed to be one of the few in the community allowed access to them.

She hopped out of the truck and began fumbling with her keys, looking for the correct match for the Caterpillar bulldozer she was approaching. It was as large as they made them. Jacob spared no expense when it came to the tools and machinery used to demolish, flatten, and build again the houses and commercial spaces that had helped expand his business sevenfold over the years.

Without a lack of grunting, she was able hoist herself over the crawler section of the vehicle and squeeze through the door of the cab. She admired the various gears and controls as her meaty fingers pushed the key in the ignition and brought the beast to life. The diesel motor growled, the exhaust pipe stack blew out its first drag of smoke, and the super-duty headlights struck the incoming trees with a blinding fluorescence.

She maneuvered a lever controlling the bulldozer blade with an experienced hand, raising it five feet in the air, making the hydraulics whine. Within moments, the tracks were moving toward one of the trees. It was not the first time she had maneuvered the vehicle in this fashion. She had made many runs on several of the sacred trees.

The push frame leveled as metal made contact with bark as it continued to push forward without protest. The tree, already deadened by similar rituals, tilted thirty-five degrees until the bulldozer stopped its advance, leaving a deep pocket of earth underneath the massive root ball.

With the Caterpillar running, Lou Ellen slipped out of the bulldozer cab and returned to her pickup truck. She moved a pipe wrench aside in the bed, and grabbed one of two lumpy canvas bags which she dragged from the bed of the truck and let hit the ground with a heavy thud.

"Sorry, Betty, "she said, amid heavy panting.

The bag scraped over the ground as Lou Ellen used her quadriceps muscles to pull it backward toward the suspended tree. From there, she rolled the bag into the gaping crevasse, where it landed lifeless next to several small wooden boxes she had dumped here on previous occasions. On each of them, stenciled in black paint, was a single letter of the alphabet.

She murmured a small prayer and repeated the process with the second bag.

With both halves of Betty dumped under the tree, she walked several yards to the sacrificial circle positioned at a natural clearing within the trees. There, two bloodstained aluminum benches were illuminated by the bulldozer's headlights. They were intersected just off center to form, in essence, a cross.

With the tip of a soil shovel retrieved from the truck, she carved a circle in the gravel around the benches. Without rest, she removed several necklaces of rosary beads from the inside of her boot and laid them in a pre-ordained fashion up and down the cross. Her heart pounded as she murmured more prayers and kissed the scar on her hand.

"Those who cannot provide shall be given back," Lou Ellen whispered to herself while the bulldozer purred in the background. "Just in case you *do* come back, Beth. We'll be waiting."

She threw the shovel aside in haste, made her way back to the bulldozer and threw it into reverse, returning the tree to its original resting place. It nestled in the ground, as if Lou

Ellen was never here and Betty had never existed.

She turned off the ignition.

At once, her ears were filled with a faint noise, soft at first, yet increasing in decibels with each moment she sat. It was the definitive sound of Othersider technology, of threat into action, of the ultimate end of times.

Panicked, she jumped out of the bulldozer cab, returned again to her F150 and sped away, dust spewing from the back tires as they spun forward toward the compound.

E

Had Lou Ellen had the inclination, the wherewithal or the instinct, she might have realized that every move she made was being observed, processed, and reflected in the yellow eyes of a furry orange cat.

25
October 31: Past Midnight

A

Jacob was discombobulated when he hung up the phone. He wasn't sure what he was more concerned about: the line of questioning he'd just endured during the telephone conversation with the police or the images he was witnessing on the computer monitor. His mind raced from one to the other, paralyzing him from making a decision either way.

How could they know? Why the cops would be asking questions about The Aluluei Corporation was beyond him. Somewhere, someone had made a connection.

On the monitor, Beth was standing a hundred yards from his office, not scared for her life, not begging for forgiveness, but waving into the camera, yelling at him—antagonizing him. Who did she think she was? He was her husband, her *prophet,* for Christ's sake.

"What was the telephone call about, sir?" Larry asked.

Before Jacob could berate Larry about asking stupid questions again, Lou Ellen's voice crackled in garbled fashion into the office over the two-way radio.

"Jacob, git your . . . ether. They are on . . . ai! Are you . . . ere? Over."

Jacob picked up the two-way radio. "Calm down, Lou. What did you say? Over."

"I said the . . . ed Othersi . . . here!"

"Now, listen, Lou Ellen. I don't know what *your* problem is, but we have a real problem. I just got off the phone with a Detective Oakley of the Tempe Police Department. They were asking about a company I did business with a few years back. They may be in our hair in the next couple of days. Not to worry. God has told me we will prevail. Over."

Lou Ellen's voice fired back with virulence. "Listen, Jacob, you *idiot!* The Othersiders are *here! Do you understand? They are already . . . ing here!"*

Jacob stared at the radio as if trying to extract answers from it. Like elongating sunset shadows, comprehension cast itself across his face.

The sound of Lou Ellen's voice shrieked again over the radio. "I just heard the *fucking helicopters, for the love of Jesus! Letterboxes for all of you!"*

He looked again at Beth flagging him down, mocking him, daring him to come out for a showdown. His interloping, intervening, *inconvenient, infertile* little apostate seventh wife, Beth, was calling him outside to play. Oh, he would *play* with her all right—her *and* her little friends.

He scanned Jane and her daughters' faces and realized that Lou Ellen had been right all along. The end of days was upon them.

"Lou Ellen, you need to prepare home base *now.* Over."

"I already *did,* you piece of shit! The detonator is in the top drawer of the desk in your *office! Over!"*

Jacob paused, letting the insult pass. "Copy that." To the room, he said, "It's time."

Without further contemplation, Jacob flipped the switch engaging the compound-wide intercom, and depressed the button. "Attention, all members of the community. This is your prophet. I am happy to inform you that I have just received word from God that tonight is the night. It's the night we've always talked about; it's *your* night; the night you all meet God. All of you to home base in three minutes." He paused to look again at Beth in the monitor. He stared at her as he opened his desk drawer and removed from it a military-style detonator. "And remember, now," he continued, glancing at the many red dots on the GPS screen, "God knows where you are at all times. I can't guarantee a long afterlife to those who are tardy to home base. Please look good for God, folks."

Inhaling, Jacob Perkins closed his eyes. When he opened them again, he was The Prophet Jacob. His voice lowered an octave as he addressed his people. "Behold," he said, "the days of thy deliverance are come . . . inasmuch as my people shall assemble themselves to the celestial kingdom, I have kept in store a blessing such as is not known among the children of men. The kingdom of heaven is at hand . . . prepare the way before my face, for the time of my coming; for the time is at hand. Behold, I come quickly."

He released the talk button and turned to Larry Hitchcock. "You know the code to the gate at home base, my friend. Once every one of them is in there, you lock the door from the inside. Let no one out. You will be meeting him, too."

The two of them could see members of the community already beginning to make their way to home base.

The prophet fixed his gaze on Larry and motioned to the door. "Now go."

B

“Oh, my God,” Beth said.

She realized the effectiveness of her strategy as she witnessed the community members flocking to home base. It had worked *too* well. She antagonized him and he responded by sending everyone to home base. She knew waltzing into his office would be futile. One of the apostles guarding the door would have her chained to the floor in no time. The intent was to coax him outside to have a conversation. She knew, of course, Jacob would be in his office, watching her from his desk. She knew he would be shocked to know that she was aware of the location of the camera, that she was able to maneuver around all the traps, and that she had brought Otherside friends with her. But she needed his attention, to *talk* to him. To go to these extremes, however, was irrational, even for Jacob’s standards.

Scott watched as people began filing out of their bungalows into what looked like a barricaded racquetball court. “What the hell was that announcement all about? Where are they going?”

“They are going to home base. He’s promising them an opportunity to meet God and secure their afterlives. This isn’t good.” She looked at Brennen with an empty expression. “He’s going to kill them all.”

Brennen tried to let what Beth said sink in, but was distracted by the noise in the sky. “Does anybody else think that helicopter sounds like it’s getting closer?”

“Sounds like that thing is landing out there,” Scott said.

"The blades are slowing down."

"Well, why the hell would a helicopter be landing out *here*?"

"Professor Navarro, bless her soul," Beth said, "she must have called the cops. She was really scared for all of us. She must have panicked." She looked at her friends. "That's why Jacob is freaking out. He's being raided. And now the cops are here for me as well as him."

"Or me," Brennen said.

Without another word, Beth began screaming into the camera to Jacob, begging the prophet to stop the order.

C

The members of the Prophet Jacobs' community filed into home base in droves. Having been awoken from their slumber, many of them were still rubbing sleep from their eyes as they looked around. The numerous women were excited. Clad in prayer dresses, some hand-in-hand, others reassuring their infant daughters that everything would be all right, they entered home base with wonder in their eyes and love in their hearts. Some had eyes moistened with joyful tears and hugged one another in anticipation of the event. In the corner of home base, a group of girls took advantage of the unexpected playtime and engaged in an extemporaneous game of hopscotch using faded chalk markings from a previous gathering. Whispers of God could be heard amid bright, uninhibited laughter that bounced off the eight-foot walls and echoed throughout the complex.

The apostles were scattered among the crowd, tucking their white button-down shirts into their church pants and doing their best to correct the bed hair that had accumulated in the wee hours of the night. It wasn't every day, after all, that God announces a visit. They needed to be ready when asked to Come Home.

Larry Hitchcock stood at the gate, greeting all the members and taking account of all who had passed through it and those who had not yet had the honor.

D

The silence returned to the desert night after the Blackhawk's engine relented and the inertia of the spinning blades succumbed to gravity. They landed just outside a curious group of ancient trees standing alone among the brush. Moving among them now was Officer Davis doing his best to keep up with the squad. He had never been on any busts in his short time on the force, much less a raid on a fortified compound occupied by an extremist group. The stakes were high and he was doing his best to convince the others that he knew what he was doing. At last check, his gear was in order, his revolver was securely in place and his mind was clear. He was proud to be an officer of the Tempe Police force and was ready for anything, until his boss came out of nowhere and slapped him on the shoulder, causing him to flinch.

"Whoa there, son," Sergeant Pederson said. His voice was loud and direct. "I didn't mean to scare you."

"You didn't, sir."

"Listen, we've got a bit of a problem. There was a pickup truck sighted speeding away from this area just moments ago. As luck would have it, one of the members must have been out this way when we arrived. Chances are they saw us coming and are warning the others right now."

Davis nodded. "Copy that, Sarge."

"We are going to have to speed things up a little quicker than expected. Arizona Highway Patrol just pulled up two squad cars with more coming. We are going to catch a ride with them and sneak up to the complex with the lights off. The rest of highway patrol will be completing the perimeter from the east side of the compound. Long story short, I need you in one of those squad cars now. Oh, and Officer Davis? Your boot lace is untied."

Davis looked down to see that his bootlace had indeed come undone and was hanging on the desert ground. "Ah, shit," he said, and bent down to remedy it. He heard Sergeant Pederson continue to move ahead.

While crouched, an object caught the corner of his eye. In the darkness, it appeared to have a metallic quality to it—man-made. He was told to use his flashlight sparingly as the beam could be seen from far away and could compromise their position. However, he was also instructed to follow his instincts, and his instincts told him it would be worth his while to investigate.

He placed the flashlight parallel to the ground and illuminated what appeared to be a shovel several feet in front of him. Though the shovel was the initial object of interest, the light illuminated something much more intriguing.

He turned the flashlight off and stepped closer to the object before splashing it with light once more. It appeared to be a cross made out of aluminum benches. It was dressed with ceremonious beads of some sort and stained with what could have been black paint (or something else). Davis guessed it was something else—something that dripped from human beings when flesh was cut. It was eerie, and it was suspect.

"Uh, Sarge?" he asked. He wasn't sure if he spoke loud enough for his boss to hear.

Sergeant Pederson's voice cut through the darkness after him. "Officer Davis, are you on the double or *what?*"

"Yes, *sir,*" replied Davis, "I'll be right there! I'm just—"

He was interrupted by a hissing sound. At first, he was certain the sound came from a rattlesnake. Logic deflected the thought when he remembered that rattlesnakes don't hiss, they rattled. Cobras hissed, but there were no cobra species in Arizona that Davis knew of.

The noise came again, just five feet away from him in front of one of the trees. "Hhhhh."

Not wanting to get bit by a rabid raccoon or possum at this juncture, he risked his position once more and turned on the flashlight toward the sound.

It was an orange cat.

It was patting the ground with one paw. "Hhhhh."

"Jesus," Davis said to the cat and he turned off the light, "you scared the crap out of me." Talking to it somehow alleviated the threat of the animal. "You should get your ass out of here."

"Eer," said the cat.

Through the darkness he could scarcely see the cat continuing to pat the ground and hissing. He heard it begin to scratch at the ground.

"Eer!" it said, "Hhhh."

"Yeah, you said that before." He looked over to the area where he knew his boss was becoming livid with him. "I get it, cat. You're crazy. Good luck with that."

He turned and quickened his pace, intending to report the suspicious cross to Sergeant Pederson.

"Here!"

The sound froze Davis in his tracks as though the ground had frozen over, trapping his feet in ice. He turned back to the cat. "What did you say?"

"Here!" the cat said.

Astounded, he shone the light once more on the cat. It began running in circles, patting one paw on the ground. He followed it like a stage light on a theater actor in a maniacal monologue. It ran to the nearby shovel and patted it, looking at him the entire time with desperate yellow eyes, before returning again to the ground in front of the tree.

"Here! Here! Here!"

Before the cat could call him an idiot, he turned out the flashlight and made for the shovel.

Out of the darkness, his boss yelled, "Officer Davis, are you dense? Get your ass up here now!"

"Actually, Sarge, I'm going to need an officer to assist me. We've got suspicious activity; possible bloodstains on what looks to be benches used as some type of sacrificial alter. A shovel nearby suggests recent digging. I'm going to check it out."

"Are you sure, Davis?"

"Positive, sir," Davis shouted. He looked toward the cat. If he didn't know better, it was listening to, and comprehending, the conversation. "You told me to study details and make decisions. Well, the devil's in the details, and it happens to be Devil's Night. This one is on me. You go ahead."

"Copy that, kid," the boss said after a short pause. "I'm sending Officer Coppa. You be sure to report those details to me. Good luck."

"Copy that, Sarge," Davis said. "You, too!"

Together, officer and cat began to dig.

26
October 31: In the Meantime

A

Jacob kept an eye on Beth via the computer monitor while he stripped to his long johns and, from the bottom drawer of his office desk, produced a white, button-down shirt, a pair of white pants, and a clip-on tie of the same color. His pot belly jiggled over his tiny wrinkled legs as he bent over it to step into his pants. He was paraphrasing conflicting scripture under his breath. "And again, if your enemy shall smite you a second time, bear it patiently, and your reward shall be a hundred-fold."

He tucked in his shirt and clipped his tie into place. He picked up a black apron from the drawer and donned it around his waist. It was an apron of ritual, stained in black to represent the color of blood once it has dried. It was a symbol of the sacrifice, the gift to God.

Lastly, he flipped his butterfly knife closed and slipped it into his pocket.

Cling.

Clank.

Cling.

"On the other hand, Beth," Jacob continued, "since indeed God considers it just to repay with affliction those who afflict you, you and your Godless friends shall suffer for an eternity."

From the westward camera, he could see that Beth and her accomplices were cutting across the yard, about fifty yards from his office. He radioed ahead to his third-hand man, Chris Hanner, and gave him their position.

He looked at his reflection in the office window. The Prophet Jacob Perkins returned the gaze.

He addressed his three prisoners, now staring at the floor with fear pouring from their eyes and gags stifling their words. "I'll be back for you soon enough."

With the two-way radio in one hand and the detonator in the other, the prophet exited the office and went to confront his enemies.

B

Beth had succeeded in steering her friends away from any areas that might contain explosive traps set for Othersiders. As they zigzagged their way across the outer grounds toward the complex, they could see both Jacobs' office and home base no more than fifty yards away.

"We have to hurry," Beth said as they made a northeastern cut to the complex. "We have to warn them that something horrible is going to happen."

From what she could tell, most of the community members had taken their place within home base. She recalled all the disciplinary reforms she'd witnessed within its walls, all the punishments given by Jacob, or any of the other apostles, all in the name of God. It was no wonder, then, that Jacob would set up a mass suicide within the same concrete walls. She had no idea what tortuous plans he had in store for them. Would it be gas? Fire? She could imagine what would happen, and her imagination had improved a great amount over the past few days.

She was reminded of a dream she'd had at Scott's apartment while resting on Brennen's chest. It was a dream of water—a river. There were people in rafts floating down the river to an unforeseen darkness they were helpless to steer themselves from. All she could do was sit from the bank and watch them go by one-by-one. It was the same feeling she had now. Again, she felt helpless to stave off the dark future that lay in front of the people of her community, many of whom were dear to her heart.

She should have been trying to help these people ever since she escaped. She should have taken her chances with the Othersider law. How much worse could it be than adhering to Jacob and his idea of right and wrong?

She thought back to a time she would have loved to join them. Even recently, this event would have been an answer to her prayers: a dream come to light. She envisioned herself among her sister-wives and their children, shaking with anticipation of God's Coming. Now, however, it was a nightmare come true, and all she could do was watch from afar.

The feeling of guilt quickened her pace.

As promised, Scott stayed by her side, stride for stride, but Brennen had fallen behind. He was panting as though he had not run in years.

"Come *on*, Brennen," she said. She stopped and looked back to see Brennen struggling for breath, but acknowledging that he understood. He had become strangely silent, as though he were slowly fading into obscurity.

"That's far enough, Beth," an unfamiliar voice said. "I've

got orders to bring you in."

She turned to see the apostle, Chris Hanner, garbed in Paiute Rock City police attire, pointing a gun at her.

C

According to Larry Hitchcock's calculations, all but eight members were accounted for at home base. He had ordered everyone to form a giant prayer circle. Each family would hold hands with the next. The youngest member of the family would then hold the hand of the oldest member of the next family, and on and on, until together they formed a community-wide circle around the edge of home base. Together, they would pray to God. Together they would meet Him. Together, they would be sent back to Him. As an apostle of the community and closest to the prophet, he was honored to be in charge of the ritual. As a father, he felt fortunate for the love of his seven daughters, one son, and four wives, and watched them with pride from the gate as they took their place in the circle. They would need him by their side soon.

He spoke to the prophet from his two-way radio. "It looks like I've just about got everybody here, Prophet Jacob. Everybody but Jane, her daughters, Chris Hanner, Lou Ellen, and Beth. Still no sign of Mr. Bratch. "

The prophet's voice came in clean. His voice was deeper than Larry had ever heard it. "Forget Bratch . . . and I can handle Jane, Lou Ellen, and Beth myself. Shut the door and lock it."

"Taking care of it now."

After a short pause, the prophet added, "You've done well, Larry. Over and out."

Without further discussion, Larry Hitchcock set the radio aside and used all the strength in his good arm to swing the steel door shut. It latched with a thunderous boom.

He entered the lock code, 0-1-2-5, and joined his family in the prayer circle, tears of humility swelling in his eyes.

D

Brennen saw the Paiute Rock City police officer's face go from pure cocky to abject confusion as his legs were taken out. It seemed the only thing he could do was pull the trigger, which he did, and hope it hit one of his targets. Soon after, the gun was swiped from his hand and thrown to a dark patch of bushes out of anybody's reach. The wind had been knocked from him and as he held his ribs, he writhed on the ground, moaning while attempting to see who was responsible for the hit.

"Harvey!" Beth shouted. "Thank God. You're pretty good at tackling." The moon was just bright enough to catch her smile in the dark.

"Just glad I can help the prophet," Harvey said, wincing. He shook out his hand. Droplets of liquid could be heard hitting the ground. "And I played a little football in school."

"You okay, man?" Brennen asked. He hated being called a prophet.

"Yeah, I'm good."

"I think you were shot," Beth said. "Let me see." She pulled up Harvey's sleeve and turned his hand over. "You've been shot in the forearm. There is a hole on each side." She demonstrated each hole, turning over his hand twice. "You're bleeding pretty badly."

Harvey opened and closed his hand a few times. "It

should be all right, dude."

"That does not look good," Scott said. "You need a doctor, Harvey."

Harvey began shaking his head.

"Harvey," Brennen said, "this is serious shit." He motioned to the rest of them. "We all appreciate what you've done here. You've gone above and beyond what you needed to do." He put a hand up to signal him to stop. "But it's not too late for you to get out of here, man. The cops are obviously here and it's dangerous for you to stay, you know?" Brennen crossed his arms and tried another approach. "I think you had a *really* bad breakdown in reaction to losing your dog. Like . . . *really* bad. And, you know, you've done some pretty bad things, but it's not too late. You could wipe your hands of all of this and . . . turn it around and get back to normal."

Harvey, having become concerned by the blood sliding off his arm, nodded in agreement "I *have* been feeling a little better about Freddy." He looked at Beth and Scott. "It feels good to talk about it."

Scott threw up his hands. "Hey, man, you miss your dog. Nothing wrong with that."

"You should really go, Harvey," Beth said. "You need a doctor. And there is nothing more you can *do* here."

Chris Hanner moaned again from the ground and Harvey kicked him unconscious.

"Ah, dudes," Harvey said, "are you sure you wouldn't be mad?"

They all assured him there would be no ill will. After a few moments of debate, Harvey bid them farewell.

"And *Harvey,*" Brennen called out, "I'm not a prophet."

"I know you're not, man," Harvey said, smiling. "I've known for a while. But you guys are like the best friends I've ever had, so I let it go." In a moment, he was running toward the van. Only his footsteps could be heard until they, too, disappeared.

"Hello, Beth," a voice said.

Backlit from the lights of the compound, a figure approached. From the shadows, Brennen saw a dangerous-looking old man wearing all white with a black apron tied around his waist. He held both hands above his head. One held what looked like a walkie-talkie while the other held some type of device. The man needed no introduction.

"Jacob," Beth said.

Scott stepped between the two of them.

"*Run, you guys!*" Beth screamed. "*Warn the others! He's got a detonator! He's going to blow them all up!*"

"You can go ahead and run, boys," Jacob said, shaking the detonator. "There ain't much you can do now. The only way they are getting out of there is through God, through me, and my trigger finger."

"I'm not going anywhere," Scott said, focusing on Jacob.

Brennen turned to go, but remained a few moments longer and looked back at Beth. His eyes went from wolf to puppy-dog. Could he leave her with this monster? Would he see her again? What about Scott?

Beth screamed, "*Run!*"

E

Brennen ran.

Straight toward home base. He told himself that Beth would be able to handle herself. God knows she had shown she was capable. Further, Scott had more than convinced him that he would not leave the girl's side, regardless of the consequences. If Brennen didn't warn the others, no one would. As for Jacob, Brennen had a moment to match the face to the man Beth had spent two days describing, and it took less than that to know he was psychotic enough to blow up home base with all his followers inside. The man was eerie. He scared Brennen in ways he had not experienced since vivid childhood nightmares.

His lungs contracted with force, still cold from the air he had put through them, but he managed enough power from them to yell with force as he approached home base. "*Hey! Listen to me! You are all in danger! You have to get out of home base now!*"

There was some sort of singing or chanting from within that dissipated as he began to yell. He could only see concrete walls topped with coiled razor wire. What the hell were they doing in there?

He stopped about fifty feet from the walls, not daring to step closer. "*The place is going to blow! You are all in danger! Please!*

From his vantage point, he could see heads pop up over the wall to peek at him. He imagined the people were standing on each other's shoulders for a chance to see the lunatic yelling at them.

It was a woman's shrill voice that answered him. "*Go away, Othersider! Leave us alone!*" There were several affirmations of the sentiment that followed.

Another voice, this time a young girl's, shouted, "*Vengeance on those who do not know God and those who do not obey the gospel of our Lord Jesus!"*

Again, more affirmations.

He was not going to reach them, at least not by any conventional means.

F

Harvey was back at the van before he knew it. His toes itched with whatever spiky desert plant had been rubbing up against them as he trampled through the landscape in his Birkenstocks. His forearm was now beginning to throb and sharp pain surged up the length of his arm as he released the back door latch and threw the doors open.

Mr. Bratch was gone.

Sensing movement out of the corner of his eye, he ducked just in time to miss a right hook swinging at him.

Grabbing Mr. Bratch's wrist as it went by, Harvey was able to use the momentum of his adversary and slammed him head-first into the side of the van. The clash of skull and steel created a dull thud that reverberated down the ridge and across the compound grounds.

Mr. Bratch collapsed to one knee, his hands placed on the dirt for balance.

Harvey held his head down, making leverage to stand hard to come by. He spoke with a calm demeanor. "I know you were a tough guy in Philly. I understand you a dangerous criminal wanted by the FBI. I get it. Hell, I can even *relate* a little bit." He pushed Mr. Bratch's face toward the ground. "But I have to say, I'm . . . just not impressed. Now, I am in a massive hurry right now. I really can't be bothered with you. I think you just picked the wrong person to tangle with and on the wrong night."

Mr. Bratch was nose-to-nose with the dirt and breathing out loud. He turned his head to the side in an attempt to make eye contact with Harvey. “Everybody . . . has a bridge of the nose.”

“What?”

Before Harvey could further contemplate the meaning of the sentence, Mr. Bratch reached over his head and grabbed Harvey’s suppressive hand and yanked downward. Like a skilled prize fighter, Mr. Bratch sprang to life from his crouch and threw a wicked-looking uppercut.

The punch was blocked, brass knuckles and all, and buried deep into Harvey’s hand with a smack.

Mr. Bratch stood face-to-face with Harvey with a look of enormous confusion.

“You’re a douche-bag, dude,” Harvey said.

He cracked Mr. Bratch’s nose with a head butt.

G

Brennen dug the paraphernalia out of his pocket and stared at it for only a few moments. The decision was easy. Should he never come back to the world this time, at least he went out trying to be of some help. It was rational, and possibly the only time he had ever felt good about his choice to use it. This time—this last time—his intent was pure and his reason sound. Though it had left a wake of fractured demolition in all facets of his life over the last several years, perhaps tonight he could find some good in The Glow, some positive nugget he could take away from the many years being possessed by it. Maybe he could redeem himself, if only for a short while, from a wasted life.

“Better than nothing,” Brennen said.

He sparked the lighter and took an enormous rip.

No sooner than the substance reached the base of his brain, he fell backward under his feet as though he'd been shut off from a remote source. His back arched grotesquely as if a rope was anchored to his sternum and he was being pulled to the sky. His eyes fluttered and rolled up into his skull into unconsciousness—or hyper-consciousness.

27
October 31: Travels in the Witching Hours

A

Brennen Reynolds, or what once was Brennen Reynolds, at least in part, was traveling again. Speed could not be identified nor gauged as he moved forward into, down, and across the blue-tinted tube with the fisheye-lens view. It was the same tunnel he'd been in earlier in Harvey's van. Yet this time, he was ready for it. Just like visiting amusement parks as a child, the second time on the roller coaster was always the more exploratory. Without succumbing to fear around every curve, the second time was for the raising of the hands around the loops and for screaming in triumph rather than terror. For Brennen, the second time was all the time he needed.

He willed the white noise, the millions of murmuring voices, to bend in the direction of what he needed to hear. Like locking into radio frequencies, he filtered out the multitude to focus only on the voices that mattered. Of those, he focused on those who mentioned a prophet, and of those, he focused on only those mentioning the Prophet Jacob Perkins. He found hundreds in one area. He had reached home base.

"*Hello, Donna Brenner of Saginaw, Michigan,*" hyper-conscious Brennen said.

"How do you know my real name?" Donna's conscious

answered. "I haven't used it—"

"Since you ran away from home at the age of twelve. Your parents angered you, so you hitchhiked out west. You have always regretted it."

"Who are you?"

"Who do you want me to be, Donna?"

"I want you to be God . . . and my dear departed mother."

"Well, then I am both, Donna, and we need to tell you that your life is in danger. The prophet is not a decent man. Everything he told you is a lie. He means to explode the room."

"But—"

"I have spoken with many others already, Donna, and they mean to leave as soon as the door is open. Would you happen to know the code to the door?"

"My husband, Larry, knows the code. He is the only one."

"Thank you, Donna."

B

Scott had heard enough.

Jacob was as dense as he was crazy. As effective as any lawyer he had heard, Beth had stated her case with enough elegance and solid reasoning to make even the most corrupt judges pause for consideration. But Jacob did nothing but spout nonsensical scripture and berate her with insults while threatening to blow up his community. His terms were simple, if Beth returned to him, all would be forgiven and the members would be able to go back to their lives on the compound. Scott, of course, didn't believe a word of it.

He held Beth back as she tried to approach the madman.

Scott knew that Jacob had nothing left to lose. His kingdom was about to be raided by the cops any minute, and whether Beth came with him or not, there was nothing stopping him from killing her and setting off the detonator. Jacob wanted to get his hands on her to kill her himself. She was, after all, the reason for the demise of his reign. Had she not escaped, she would have never met Othersiders. She would have never befriended Professor Navarro, who called the cops on the entire operation

Where the hell were the cops already?

"Come on now, Beth," Jacob said, "come back to your loving husband."

Screaming noises could be heard from home base. It sounded through the din almost as if people were afraid, though no explosion had occurred yet.

Jacob looked over in the direction of the noise. "What the hell?"

Scott capitalized on the diversion. He leapt forward and bear-tackled Jacob, causing the two-way radio and the detonator to fly in opposite directions onto the ground.

Jacob went down on his back like a sack of gravel.

Scott knew, as a young lawyer, it would be difficult to find gainful employment with an assault and battery charge following him everywhere he went, but his adrenaline controlled his actions now, and his emotions manipulated him like an amped-up puppet-master with a taste for violence. He punched the old man in the face once. Twice.

"Scott!" Beth screamed. "That's enough. You've got him. He's an old man. He's not worth it!"

As if to prove her wrong, Jacob cracked a closed fist on Scott's jaw.

The old man could hit.

"You crazy son of a *bitch*," Scott spat through grinding teeth. He grabbed Jacob by the front of his shirt and threw his head back to the earth. With both hands, then, he found the prophet's throat and began to strangle him.

Assault and battery was upped to attempted murder.

Beth ran up to the brawling men and attempted to break it up.

Jacob fended her off with swift kicks to her knees and shins. She was surprised at the strength Jacob possessed for someone his age. She grabbed his foot as he attempted a third kick and twisted outward. She saw him cry out in pain as he grabbed for Scott's neck, breaking off Snippety's whistle as he grasped air.

Jacob reached deep into his pocket.

"Scott! Look out! He's *got something in his pocket!"*

Clink.

Clank.

Clink.

Before Scott had a chance to assess the significance of the sound, the butterfly knife was at his throat.

Slit.

All focus Scott had on Jacobs's throat had now turned to his own as he grabbed at it, blood running between his fingers as he did. He fell away on his own back and struggled to his knees. He looked at Beth with puppy-dog eyes as he attempted to swallow several times.

He heard her screaming, but the more intensity she put into it, the softer her voice seemed to come. He saw darkness fogging his peripheral vision as he felt an incessant itching in his vocal chords, leaving him with a burning need to cough.

He succumbed first to the cough and then to the blackness.

C

"*Thank you, Larry,*" the voice said. It was as calm and soothing as a tranquil childhood memory.

"Will I ever hear from you again?" Larry asked.

"*I don't know, Larry.*"

"What do you mean you don't know?"

"*Nothing can be certain, Larry. But it can be dreamed.*"

"I understand," Larry said.

"*You have my love, Larry, and the love of these people you will save. Always.*"

"Thank you for coming into my life."

"*You are welcome, Larry. Now, you know the code. Please open the door.*"

0-1-2-5 *click.*

D

Beth watched in terror as Jacob rolled onto his hands and knees, coughing from a bruised esophagus. In the dim light, Beth could see that the man was bleeding from his nose and a cut on his upper left cheek. She had never seen him bleed. In fact, for many years, she didn't think him capable. Now, he was mortal to her, just a man who has taken a beating from another man.

She was torn between leaving Scott's side and finishing the job Scott had started. Scott lay with his head in her lap while she tried her best to stop the bleeding from his neck. While distracted by Jacob, it was difficult to tell if Scott was still breathing. Maybe a little. Maybe not at all. He had lost blood, to be sure, but she was unskilled in nursing and had no way to know if he was bleeding out.

Jacob was still armed with his knife which he now held up defensively, staring at her with his dead-fish eyes while he felt around on the ground around him.

"You," he said, "you just stay right where you are."

He was after the detonator. She could not allow him to recapture possession of it, even if she died trying. She placed Scott's head on the ground beside her with has much care as time would allow. "I'm so sorry, Scott. I'll be right back."

But no sooner than she made it to her feet, she saw Jacob rising to his feet, five feet away with detonator in hand. He cocked his head sideways, his brow furrowed, his eyes narrowed with hate, and his jaw protruded outward, causing his frown lines to crease as blood dripped through them. It was the most stringent look of disapproval Beth had ever seen.

"Don't do it, Jacob," Beth pleaded.

Jacob bowed his head and locked eye contact with Beth like a salivating wolf. "Never you mind, Beth." He wiped blood away with his sleeve. "We are *way* beyond that now."

He stared at her.

"God*damnit*, Jacob. Why do you have to be such a psycho? What do you *want* out of all of this?"

Jacob continued to stare at her. Or was it *through* her?

After several seconds, Beth lost her patience. Somehow his silence was the scariest tactic he had ever used on her. "*Jacob, what do you want?*"

Beth watched as the prophet's face began a metamorphosis. His head straightened out, his jaw became relaxed and his eyes widened. Soon he stood, mouth agape, looking over and above Beth with an expression teetering between puzzlement and wonderment.

"It's . . . *Him*," Jacob said. His voice was quivering. "Oh, Bethie. It's Him . . . I can hear him. Talkin' to me." His tear ducts began to fill with liquid as he kept his gaze fixed away from Beth.

"Who?" Beth asked.

"It's . . . it's *God.*" Laughter escaped his lungs. "I *mean* it this time, Beth. For the first time in my life, I *really* mean it. It's *God.* I'm full of God!"

Now it was Beth who stared with a blank expression back at Jacob. As far as she was concerned, Jacob had finally gone insane—even more insane than he was.

"He's talking about *you*, Beth. He wants me to . . . He wants me to—" For the first time he looked at Beth, not with the eyes of a prophet, not with the face of an over-bearing husband, but with the expression of an old man who had long since lost his way; a man whom she could forgive. "He says he knows you. And he wants me to give you this."

He offered her the detonator.

E

Winded, Davis crouched above the hole while Officer Coppa shoveled out heaping mounds of dirt and set them in a pile next to the hole. They had made substantial progress in a small amount of time, working in thirty-second shifts or until each felt their arm and back muscles surrendering to lactic acid. The cat, on the other hand, worked full time.

The shovel hit the ground with a hollow thud.

"What was that?" Davis asked.

"Feels like wood," Officer Coppa said. "I think it's a box of some kind."

Indeed, it was. As Officer Coppa dug around it, Davis crawled down in the hole and, using his fingers, was able to free the object from its burial place and set it on the ground. He brushed it off and shined his light on the top.

It was a small wooden box, no bigger than a milk crate, with the letter A stenciled in black ink across the top.

It looked to be nailed shut with plenty of gaps between the lid and main compartment. While keeping his light fixated on the box, Davis motioned at Officer Coppa to pry the box open using the shovel.

With the nails caked with rust, three attempts were needed to un-pry the lid. The first was a weak attempt, while the second was fierce—an overcompensation for the previous. When the lid refused to budge Officer Coppa jumped on the handle, causing the box to relinquish its grasp on the lid. Dust floated through the beam of the flashlight as it exposed the contents of the crate to the men.

Davis turned his eyes away from the sight. "Jesus *Christ!* Is that what I *think* it is?"

Officer Coppa illuminated the hole in the ground and spoke in a flat voice. "I think I see another one."

F

It all happened instantly.

Jacob's head snapped forward with the sound of cracking bone. He had, moments prior, been walking toward Beth with the intention of handing her the detonator. Now he had fallen with rag doll limpness onto his belly with the detonator a few inches from his head on the ground.

It was her sense of hearing that offered the first clue as to what happened. It was heavy breathing—a woman's heavy breathing.

Her eyes caught up to speed as she saw Lou Ellen standing over Jacob, wild-eyed and ragged, wielding a pipe wrench.

Lou Ellen hit Jacob in the head two more times with the wrench, cursing at him as she went. "You *stupid* son of *a bitch!"* If she hadn't ended Jacob's life with the first hit, she finished the job with the last two.

With her free hand, she moved Jacob's head to the side and grabbed the detonator.

"*Lou Ellen*," Beth screeched, "what are you *doing?*

"What do you *think* I'm doing, Elizabeth? I'm finishing what *you started!"* She picked up the detonator from the ground and stood up. "You are the ultimate apostate, sister, *and you have destroyed us all!"*

From the darkness, a stressed voice shouted: "This is the Tempe Police Department! Drop the weapon and get down on the ground with your arms out where I can see them."

There was a moment when Lou Ellen looked into Beth's eyes. Beth saw no trace of a soul at all.

"*She's got a detonator!"* Beth screamed.

Lou Ellen only managed to get her finger near the trigger of the detonator before the SWAT team opened fire.

Technically, she was dead before she hit the ground, but the muscles in her body tensed as she went down.

Her trigger finger twitched.

In a flash, home base was gone.

G

"*Brennen!*" Beth screamed.

She pointed at Scott and said to the police officer who'd gunned down Lou Ellen, "His throat has been cut, please help him!" Without thinking, she ran in the direction of home base, parts of it now burning in the aftermath of the explosion. The air was still warm from the blast as she cut through the grounds of the compound toward ground zero. Here she was, between two of the most unselfish people she had met. These were *good* men. Behind her lay Scott. Both elegant and feisty, she'd be sacrificed a hundred times over for the chance to let him know how she felt about him. Ahead of her, somewhere was Brennen, who in a very real way, had made her transformation possible.

She heard the police call to her several times by name, warning her of the danger ahead, but she ran toward the wreckage regardless. Though she had no qualms about conversing with the law at this point, she would not go another second without knowing whether or not Brennen was alive.

She had made it fifty yards in what seemed like only a few seconds. As she approached the walls of home base, she saw the destruction the explosion had caused. The razor wire was missing on several parts of the structure and the south-facing wall had a hole in the cement wall through which she could see the rebar supporting it. Heat poured from the center. From her vantage point, there was small fire burning inside. She felt her blood chill as she imagined members of her community burning in disfigured positions—poses dictated by the blast.

But there were no burning people that she could see as she entered the room. The object on fire was, in fact, a wooden teeter-totter which she'd often set her nieces on during mandatory barbecues. There were other objects: various toys, several books, perhaps bibles, which all sizzled and popped like embers in a camp fire, but no sign of human remains.

"Brennen! Brennen let me know if you are okay!" She stood in the center of home base and gave it another three-hundred-sixty-degree view.

"Beth?" a voice called. "Is that *you*, Beth?"

It was Larry Hitchcock's wife, Donna. She stood on a ridge some thirty yards away, accompanied by several people around her. They were all approaching her with curiosity.

"Did you hear him, Beth?" Donna asked. "He spoke to all of us. It was *glorious.*"

Beth didn't want to know what Donna was talking about. Truth be told, the members of her community now made her nervous and even a bit ashamed that she had called this place her home and these people her neighbors. Now, they were foreign to her. *They* were on the other side. "No, I didn't. Sorry."

"Oh, Beth. It was glorious . . . so, so very glorious."

"Listen, Donna, or any of you," Beth said. "I am looking for a friend of mine. Did you happen to see him or hear him before home base blew up?"

"There was somebody," Larry said, "an Othersider. He tried to warn us just before the voice warned us. It sounded like he was just outside the south wall."

"A voice warned you?" Beth asked.

"In our minds," Donna said. "All of us . . . in our minds."

Without carrying the conversation further, Beth ran through the hole in the wall and began scanning the south grounds, in the dark, for a sign. She called Brennen's name several times as she zigzagged across the dirt fields in front of the burning building. It seemed hopeless. Where was he?

How was Scott? Was he being tended to? She looked out to the spot where Lou Ellen had been gunned down. There were dozens of flashing police lights now. She never thought she'd be glad to see them, but she was.

In the distance, she heard the helicopter start up again.

She took one last look back at the grounds. The sinking feeling in her gut was doing its best to convince her that her friend was gone, blown up in an attempt to help a community of strangers taught to despise him.

Something caught her eye as she looked away—a tiny flash of something glowing in her direction. As she approached she saw there were two of them glaring at her like iridescent marbles. As she came closer still, she saw the object was dark, rather large, and alive. Were those feathers?

She was taken aback.

Near the ground, staring at her with police lights and fire reflected in its eyes was a spotted owl. Underneath it, as though being guarded by it, was the body of Brennen Reynolds.

H

Though he could not respond to her voice, Brennen could hear it. He knew she was helping him to his feet from place he had been lying for what seemed like weeks. He could smell burnt hair, most likely his eyebrows that had been singed away in the flash.

More than any sensation, however, was the painful tingling in his hands. It felt as though the funny bones of each elbow were being pelted with a ball-peen hammer. Surges of electric-like pain rampaged into his fingertips.

He could assess that the helicopter he'd heard earlier was now moving away from him. He could even walk with Beth's help. He could do all of these things, but he could not see.

He was blind.

He could have cursed the explosion for leaving him a shell of a man, but he wasn't sure if he didn't owe the event a debt of gratitude. The explosion snapped him from the blue warp, that much was certain. Had it not happened when it did, it was debatable whether he would have ever woken from it. In fact, after all he had been through tonight, or put himself through in the last three years, he found himself feeling more grateful than he could ever recall. He was a train wreck, but he was alive.

He heard footsteps approaching.

"Reynolds," an assertive male voice said. "You look like shit. Let's get you checked out."

He recognized it as the man who interrogated him at the police station. "Sergeant Pederson," he said, raising one hand while supporting his weight on Beth's shoulders. "Listen. I told you. I don't know what is going on or how I had the dream, but I didn't kill Triana Linden."

"I know you didn't, son," Sergeant Pederson said.

"What?" Brennen was dumbfounded.

"On the way here, my detective informed me that Triana's

killer was found in Gilbert. It was some boyfriend from first grade who buried her. He gave a full confession."

Brennen dropped his head in relief and shook his arm, as if trying to flick the tingling sensation out of his hand onto the ground below.

"Now," Sergeant Pederson continued, "I'm not psychiatrist, but you should probably lay off whatever substance is causing those crazy dreams."

Brennen nodded.

"Where is Scott?" Beth asked the sergeant.

"Scott's taking a ride in the Blackhawk to a nearby hospital. His lacerations were deep and he's lost a lot of blood. Time will tell."

A squad car pulled up near him, grinding its wheels in the gravel.

Brennen asked Pederson, "I'm guessing you spoke to Professor Navarro?"

"She told us everything: Jacob, his extremist group, Aluluei and the human tracking devices, the sacrificing . . . everything." He shined a flashlight in the back seat of the squad car and illuminated a familiar face. "Except she didn't explain who *this* guy is. We found him trying to run from us aways down the road. Any ideas?"

Beth noticed that Mr. Bratch had a face that now looked unrecognizable, like a bruised melon with a pair of eyes with a ripened plumb for a nose. The man was unrecognizable. "That's Jerry Bratchlek, ex-Philly cop wanted by the FBI. Google him."

"I will certainly do that," the sergeant answered. He put his hands on his hips and changed his demeanor. "Listen,

Beth. I know you've been through a rough couple days. We should, however, sit down and have a little conversation, just so I can have something to report back to my lieutenant. You've been accused of some things. Yes, it is true that your accuser ended up to be a crazy person who inserted microchips in your hand . . . and who is also now dead. This works in your favor. All the same, though, I will have to ask you a few questions after you've had some water and a chance to calm your nerves. Some statements from your fellow community members probably wouldn't hurt, either."

"I understand," Beth said. "I'll do whatever I can do to help."

Two officers approached Brennen from the left. It took him a moment to realize they were not here to slap handcuffs on him, but rather to administer first aid to the burns on his face. He realized he had not yet told anyone that he had lost his sight.

"Now, son," Sergeant Pederson said, "I have to say, I've worked a few cases with some extremist organizations before, and some of them did not end nearly as good as this. More times than not, the mass suicide is successful. When you get a chance, maybe someday you can tell me how a . . . an Othersider, as they call us, was able to convince a group of one hundred brainwashed followers to disobey their prophet and run away."

Brennen shook his head and smiled. "Not much to tell, sir. I can be pretty persuasive, I guess."

Sergeant Pederson responded with a shrug and began motioning to his men to round up as many members of the Fundamentalist Sect for questioning as he could. As he began to walk away, he stopped and addressed them again. “Oh, and since you two seem to have the answer to everything tonight, there was a white van parked on the premises earlier and seems to have disappeared just prior or just following the explosion.”

Brennen laughed. “You got us, Sergeant. We hitchhiked here. Guilty as charged.” He attempted to put up both hands. “The driver said he was in the mood for adventure when he picked us up, but I think he got more than he bargained for when everything went down. He freaked out.”

Brennen again shook his hands with vigor.

“I think he said his name was Henry,” Beth said.

“Hmm,” the Sergeant said, “he got out just in time. Lucky son of a bitch.” He turned and walked away from them, finishing his sentence to nobody in particular. “A lot of lucky people tonight.”

EPILOGUE

Brennen sat at the edge of the hiking trail just before sunrise, holding the newly deceased quail in his tingling hands while trying to subdue the many thoughts and memories arresting his mind.

Zing.

Zang.

Zing.

It had been six months since the events at Jacob's compound, three of which were spent healing his third-degree burns, waiting for his singed eyebrows to grow back and listening to the news on his phone, waiting for the police to sort out exactly what happened.

They concluded, as best they could, that a religious extremist group known as the Fundamentalist Sect, headed by the Prophet Jacob Perkins, attempted a mass suicide in Paiute City, Arizona in the early morning of October 31. And, thanks to Brennen Reynolds, Scott Barrett, and one-time sect member, Beth Perkins, they failed.

Many fates were set in motion as a result of that night.

Though his rescue attempt had been successful, saving all but two members from the blast, the true depths of the madness into which the cult had sunk was discovered in the following days. A half mile outside the compound was a sacrificial burial ground enclosed in a cluster of trees. In addition to a bloodstained aluminum altar, several small crates had been found buried beneath the trees. All of them contained human infant remains, all of them male.

Forty-two lettered crates were uncovered, each labeled with a single letter—A, B, C, D, like an alphabetical filing system or the skeletal outline to a novel. For reasons unknown, the alphabetic system never reached beyond the letter "H".

It had been reported that the community's mid-wife, Lou Ellen Perkins, claimed the deaths throughout the years as still births to the grieving parents. However, law enforcement doubted the validity of the claim. It was deduced by Tempe Police during the investigation that the infanticides were Lou Ellen's attempt to control the group's population. Having enjoyed secrecy for decades, a larger polygamist population was not sustainable. There was an estimated one man per every seven women in the community. More males, it was assumed, would upset the family balance, leaving several displaced males who were not apostles, and held no power. In a few decades, this would equate to an overabundance of angry, over-sexed young men.

In short, the male children were perceived as threats and were dealt with as such.

The Tempe Police Department received praise for the handling of the situation and was given credit for saving the members. This was Brennan's idea, as he didn't want the media attention. The headlines in the *Arizona Republic* read: POLICE FORCE PERSUADES 100 TO EVACUATE. AVOIDS CATASTROPHE. It was a strategic morale-booster for the police force, which was catching slack for their failure to apprehend an infamous serial killer, aptly named The Prophet Butcher.

As far as the media knew, the Prophet Butcher remained at large, but inactive since around the time of the explosion.

When Brennen explained this to Harvey, the man felt neither vindicated nor proud. He was, in fact, deeply remorseful for how he handled things and was riddled with shame, something to which Brennan could relate. He was currently seeing a psychiatrist and in the process of moving to Arizona to start a new life, vowing to help Brennen find a way to use his powers in a positive way.

As they had every day since the incident, Brennan's hands tingled as though they had fallen asleep during the night and never awakened. As he held the lifeless fledgling within them, they burned as though his funny bones had been tickled with the harsh peckings of a ball-peen hammer.

Examining it at every angle, it was clear the quail had only recently passed, either by starvation or lack of water. The desert, after all, was an unforgiving place and provided little leeway for error. In all likelihood, it had become separated from its mother and siblings and never recovered.

The skyscape, uniquely Arizonian, began to swell in huge masses of peach and purple hues as the sun began to peek over the Mazatzal Mountains, several miles east of Scottsdale. Hiking was his new escape. He often found himself awake in the wee hours and would be compelled to walk this trail, to take to nature, walking stick in hand, and think.

For the first time in years, it was good to be alive.

At the same time, he missed his old friend, The Glow.

Oh, did he miss it. But he hated it as much as he loved it. And with any destructive relationship, he knew it would kill him to mix with it again. This, of course, didn't mean he was without temptation. He felt safe in the knowledge that he would surely drop into a coma, bouncing eternally in the blue warp, should he cross paths with it again. He wished he had never met it. He still remembered the scraping sound as Draya pushed the first taste of it toward him across the glass table. It forever echoed within him, reminding him of the changes it brought about.

Since being blown up, animals ceased to be drawn to him, yet his thought-reading continued long after he sobered up and continued to this day. Whether his filter had been torn just slightly more that night as to allow the continued curse of hearing minds, he didn't know, but the power remained, permanently.

His sister, Jen, considered it a blessing, but it was a burden and a curse to him. Because of it, human contact was awkward and social situations made him nervous. He shied from them when opportunity presented itself, which made others around him uncomfortable. Secretly, everyone avoids a mind-reader. Privacy in the cerebral cortex, in his opinion, was imperative for the civility of thinking people and he felt like a living contradiction to that order.

He was an intruder.

Opaque aviator-style sunglasses, much like the pair he was wearing, were much more than a fashion statement for him. They were a shield.

His phone vibrated and recited an incoming text in a robotic voice, breaking his current line of thought. "HOW IS THE BLIND PROPHET TODAY?"

It was Scott, of course, texting him from Quebec, three

hours ahead of him. He must have been in a shit-giving mood because he was certainly giving Brennen shit. He knew Brennen hated being called the Blind Prophet, alluding to his injury, but he did so anyway. That's what friends do.

In any case, Brennen laughed. Scott had sustained his own injuries that night and continued to heal well. One of his vocal cords had been damaged from Jacob's blade, leaving him with a raspy voice, akin to Marlon Brando's Vito Corleone. As a result, Brennen affectionately called Scott the Godfather.

As it happened, the Godfather's dad was able to pull strings at McGill University in Montreal where Scott was able to transfer and enroll early, specializing in human rights law.

He and Beth were seeing each other, long distance, until Scott completed his studies.

Beth Perkins.

Damn.

As much as he tried to avoid thinking of her, she would return with a vengeance in his mind, stinging him like the recoil of a rubber band, punishing the user for the resistance put upon it. She was rapidly excelling in core classes at Scottsdale Community College and spending her free time helping former members of the Fundamentalist Sect re-program their lives. She also helped convince the state of Arizona to order, and fund, the surgical removal of illegal human microchips from a majority of the women of Jacob's compound.

Professor Navarro, now Beth's mentor, was finding social and financial success with her book, *Original Light*, now on its way to being a national bestseller. She was more than happy to provide Beth with room and board while she continued her studies. Having both suffered the recent loss of a loved one, the bond between them was natural and symbiotic. The three of them, Diana, Beth and Dave, made a nice family unit.

Brennen was able to see both of them frequently, as he gave Professor Navarro carte blanche to study his powers and try to develop a better understanding of their origin, their implication, and their future effects on not only him, but the general public.

Brennen, though a bumbling idiot in front of Beth, at least was able to speak to her with some normalcy in his dreams. He dreamt of her often. Within them, he was able to make her laugh, which he loved. Sometimes, she would even let him flirt. Of course, this would change when he awoke. Realizing immediately he had been ogling his best friend's dream girl, he felt horrible. However, he couldn't control his dreams any more than he could control how he felt. After all, Beth *was* in his dreams, increasingly, which by definition, made her his dream girl, too.

He would have to suffice with that. Scott was back in his life. It was a friendship that he would not jeopardize again.

"Okay, go," the Blind Prophet said to the bird.

As the quail sprang to life and fluttered away from his tingling hands and across the Creamsicle sky, he couldn't help but smile.

It made him smile every time.

His condition had left him with one last mysterious talent—a healing power in his fingertips which he spent most days pondering ways to wield constructively, without drawing unwanted attention his way. God knows there was enough attention at the Mayo Clinic after his mother walked out of her hospital room, symptom-free of cancer, with jogging shoes on her feet. "A miracle" they called it, and had patients lining up around the door ever since.

He didn't know what he was, but he knew what he was not. He was not a songwriter, at least not anymore. After that night, he was evicted from his apartment and was forced to sell his equipment to settle his rental agreement. He now resided at Jen's house on the condition he "stay sane." She now served as his biggest advocate and fiercest defense against the Jacobs, the Bratches, and the Drayas of the world.

His choices over the last years had been poor, he knew, and his judgment nonexistent, but bad people and bad influences would nonetheless be avoided going forward.

He was done with them.

A new occupation was imperative, but he had no idea what line of work three years in a hole would qualify him to do. It was Professor Navarro who suggested he become an animal behaviorist. He liked the sound of that.

He remained sitting on the side of the trail with his forearms resting on his knees, rubbing his tingling hands together. It was peaceful moments like these that allowed him the reflection needed to appropriately analyze, compartmentalize, and reconcile the past. The flames he avoided for years had come and gone, yet he was still alive enough to hear the sounds of the canyon in the morning. He was on the other side.

"Eer," said the cat. She emerged from behind a large

barrel cactus, careful not to step on any spiny desert brush as she did. She found a comfortable space near his pant leg and sat next to him to watch the sunrise.

He could feel her presence and reached out to give her a pet. She was a dusty mess. "Did you have a good walk?"

She nodded and put a paw in the air.

His phone vibrated spoke again, "YO. GOING TO WORK. WHERE R U? WILL U BE BACK SOON?"

It was Jen.

He smiled in spite of himself. Of course he would be back soon.

He removed his sunglasses and rubbed his eyes for better focus. Together, man and cat watched as the quail joined several others in flight and disappeared into the mountain side.

"I'll be there soon."

Thank you:

To Anna, for your kindness, understanding and belief. To my first editor and dad, William Mantle. A lifetime of gratitude to you, too deep for words. To my daughter, Lynsee: I will always be proud. To Mrs. And Mr. Kwan for providing me the support and time needed to succeed. To Tim Kiger: My friend, thank you for being there through the good and the more challenging times. Thanks to Kim for being my sister. To Samanwill Stokes and Mike Lockard for providing positive influence. To Theodora Bryant and Jeff Karon for keeping the ship sailing in the right direction. To LeShawn Smith for being LeShawn Smith. To Lt. Mike Pooley of the Tempe Police Department for keeping things real. A Special thanks to Carolyn Jessop for inspiration, Bernard Haisch and Peter Russell (the original Professor Navarro), and Neil DeGrass Tyson for not only giving me an affinity for deciphering Latin inscriptions, but keeping me curious, informed and always for want of knowledge. You have helped thy kind. Thanks to Matt Serano (for putting creativity first, no matter what an ass I was making of myself), Chris Blades, and lifetime friends (in alphabetical order), Andrew D'Ippolito, Matt Molitor and Chris Williams. It's been a while since we were three. And last but not least, thanks to Snappity (Snappy), the cat. You are missed.

Made in the USA
Middletown, DE
11 July 2018